Knowing
Joe

Roger Lightup

First published in Great Britain in 2021 by Roger Lightup
310 Liverpool Road Cadishead Salford M44 5UG

Also by Roger Lightup

My Magnificent Year
Accidental Damage

For Sue my soulmate, best friend and my inspiration

We're all islands shouting lies to each other across seas
of misunderstanding
Rudyard Kipling

Acknowledgement

As Covid-19 began to spread the Government decided to lockdown the entire country to control the spread of this evil virus and protect our NHS. Along with millions of others across the UK I dusted down a couple of long forgotten projects to keep myself occupied until things 'got back to normal.' By April 2020 with no end in sight and seeing an unexpected opportunity amidst all the bland sameness I began writing **Knowing Joe** which takes as its inspiration an enigmatic friend who passed away some years ago.

Whilst I have written this book it would not be as it is now without the amazing input from Rod Watson, Sue Atkinson and my sister Valerie Brame who not only offered advice and counselling but offered considerable help getting this manuscript over the line. I will be forever indebted to them for their wisdom.

Dedication

All proceeds from this book will go towards the Motor Neurone Disease Association in honour of a great friend who was battling this incredibly evil disease throughout the creative process of this book. We need a cure and all the money raised by sales of this book will help this exceptionally worthwhile cause.

Contents

Chapter One : Thunder   12

Chapter Two: Woodwork   42

Chapter Three : Conversations   63

Chapter Four : George   85

Chapter Five: Viewing   106

Chapter Six : Variations   134

Chapter Seven : Seaside   164

Chapter Eight : Impressions   199

Chapter Nine : Approaching   214

Chapter Ten : Funeral   226

Chapter Eleven : Letter   260

Chapter Twelve : Afterwards   263

Chapter One : Thunder

Charlotte Summersby was the embodiment of helplessness - star crossed in love and ill-fated in work. In short she was where she was because of a number of factors which were out of her control. Experience had shown, from her perspective, that whatever she tried to do made no difference at all. She was a victim of circumstance, a small rudderless boat in the ocean of life buffeted by storms and tides. There had been some, minor, successes along the way but during one of her rhubarb gin-soaked analyses of the pros and cons of her life these were forgotten in a tsunami of memories of the immense concomitant failures. She had seen her relationship with Joe as a way out of her previous issues with men. Joe was strong and kind and, most importantly, he also needed Charlotte to anchor his life. One issue was that Joe was Joe and that was, in itself, complicated. After all it was Joe being Joe that led to Henry entering her life and, to be blunt, her empty bed when Joe was away on one of his far too frequent trips.

Notwithstanding past failures and fiascos Charlotte had decided that today was decision day. The day when she decided, no one else, the course she was going to set for the immediate future. After two years of juggling men and emotions, Joe and Henry, love in various degrees of dependency, she had unearthed her pink pukka pad from beneath a pile of half read or abandoned books at the bottom of her shared space in the Brunt/Summersby wardrobe. This particular pad held a special place in Charlotte's life – she used it for lists of things: holiday clothes, to do lists, bucket list etc. as well as important recipes which she had, in most cases, never used; and other stuff. It seemed to be the ideal receptacle for her deliberation on the good and bad points that would inevitably lead to her casting aside one of the two men who were not only occupying her thinking but also causing her not inconsiderable angst.

She had found a fresh clean page, brewed herself a cup of her favourite Peruvian blend of coffee and with her legs curled underneath her on the settee she was primed to begin her task. She had already Googled a list of the key aspects of a successful relationship and she began to draw her matrix:

	Joe		Henry	
	Pro	Con	Pro	Con
Conversation	Yes	X	Yes	X
Reliability	x	Yes	Yes	X
Financial stability	Yes	Yes	Yes	X
Kindness	Yes	X	Yes	X
Physical attractiveness	Yes	X	Yes	X
Personality	Yes	X	Yes	X
Loyalty	x	Yes	Yes	Yes
Understanding	x	Yes	Yes	X
Emotional stability	Yes	X	Yes	X
Sexual compatibility	x	Yes	Yes	X

Looking at her chart the decision seemed perfectly clear – dump Joe, full-steam ahead with Henry. Yet as she started to re-evaluate all her answers for Henry she felt less convinced of their veracity and more pulled towards Joe as the person who could, only could, be everything she wanted. The fact that, over the past two years, he had not actually managed to convince her that he was meant for her weighed heavily on her mind. She sat doodling on her pad for several hours reallocating ticks and crosses as she sifted through her collection of favourite memories of each of her lovers. These were accompanied by a fair number of incidents which also made her wonder why she was even considering that either of them should have any right to a place in her heart.

After lengthy consideration she came back to where she had started – Jack the lad vs dependable; whirlwind vs unhurried; controlling vs gentle; and distant vs close – and decided as clearly as she could with so many unknowns to factor in that, all things being equal, Joe would have to possibly go with Henry being the replacement. As she had never spoken to Henry about his becoming the sole focus of her attention, although she was reasonably sure he would be enthusiastic if not ecstatic, a lot of work remained to be done. First, she had to make absolutely sure she was, indeed, making the right decision and second, she had to clarify Henry's long-term aims and objectives. The next two weeks were going to be all-important in determining Charlotte's medium to long-term happiness.

"Charlotte, you ready yet?"
"Joe hang on a bit. I'm still getting dressed. It's much easier for you, but I need to have a shower – not that you'd think of that – do my hair, make-up and stuff. Want to look nice for you if we're going out."
"OK but it's getting on!"
Joe's driving was never the best. One hand on the wheel while the other was constantly adjusting the radio, using the hands-free or, more than likely, stroking Charlotte's legs. Being in a car with Joe always seemed to mean that he took advantage, to some extent or other. Not that Charlotte always objected but, and it was a big but, she wished he would take a little more care as he hurtled along. Turning, at speed, using only the palm of his hand to turn the wheel, was a technique which she felt he must have seen used in TV cop shows, but whereas it looked very flash in that context, it wasn't so impressive, as far as Charlotte was concerned, especially when his other hand was otherwise occupied! Charlotte's squeals of horror at such eventualities only caused Joe to laugh and renew his efforts four-fold or even fifth-fold.
After one or two near misses and a relatively restrained discussion about issues relating to Brexit, which was a perennial topic of discussion and disagreement, they arrived at the Istanbul Grill. Charlotte was a typical remoaner as far as Joe was concerned whereas he was a deluded leaver from Charlotte's perspective. For them to have an 'evidence based' discussion without either of them losing their temper was very unusual but it was an issue that echoed through households throughout the UK in 2017. The Brunt/Summersby household was no different and it had become a subject to avoid, if possible, as neither side was ever going to change their minds.
"Think I'll have the steak. What d'you fancy remoaner pants?"
Joe had lost the most recent skirmish relating to the five things he thought the UK would benefit from as a result of leaving the EU. At a push he could cite two without really being able to back them up: immigration and fisheries, but he still felt confident enough to tease Charlotte, albeit gently.

"I'm going for the fish pie — had enough meat this week. Yeah fish pie, seasonal veg and garlic mushrooms to start."

"Yes, I'll have some of that as well as long as the fish hasn't been imported from Europe," teased Joe.

"Oh, come on," Charlotte sighed, "You know we disagree on this. We voted differently on this, we'll always disagree, so why not just give it a rest?"

"OK, sorry. Probably shouldn't tease so much. You're entitled to your views, aren't you?"

"Thanks. Don't want to spend the whole meal sniping at each other do we?" Charlotte's first task of the weekend was to try and agree to some time together — a holiday. She felt this would be a good opportunity to test out her theory regarding Henry. She was still scared of doing the wrong thing. She had to be sure.

"No of course not."

"I was wondering what you wanted to do for our anniversary. D'you realise we've been together for two years in a couple of weeks time? D'you fancy going away somewhere special for a few days to celebrate?"

"Well obvs we're not talking Europe here."

Charlotte looked away as Joe mentioned Europe again and she started drumming her fingers on the table to show her irritation.

"Where do you fancy?"

"Well I've always fancied Turkey in one of those 5* all-inclusive hotels. I've heard so much about it and it seems to be **the** place to go at the moment so what about there?"

"Like the idea of Turkey. Not so keen on the all-inclusive bit......"

Charlotte was one of those people who, unlike Joe, liked to experience a country or city from the inside — the little things: family run cafes and bars, street food, anything that was away from big chain restaurants and glitzy hotels. Airbnb in a village, self-contained cottage/villa on the shoreline. As close to nature as she could get and as far away from Joe's ideal, a massive pool, all-inclusive bar and huge buffet meals, as she could get. They had only been on holiday together once before. Competing schedules had meant that only a snatched week in Paris had been possible squeezed in between essential sporting commitments, Joe, and an important reunion, Charlotte. She really wished they had not started this conversation with Joe setting out his stall so clearly and she knew she would have to respond sensitively so that they could reach a compromise which didn't trample all over her principles.

"...you know they are a bit over the top, some of those all-inclusives. Don't you think?" Charlotte looked at Joe for some support. After all, Charlotte thought, the location might play a crucial role in the final outcome. "Why don't we get some brochures or check online to see if we can find something that best meets both our needs."

Charlotte's softer tone of voice had served to calm Joe down and he had stopped looking irritated and was waiting patiently to make his contribution.

"Well," he started but before he could go any further a waiter arrived to take their order. Dealing with ordering drinks and food and navigating some additional choices as some of the dishes were unavailable rather changed the mood and after the waiter had left holidays were temporarily forgotten. There were other even more important things to discuss.

"I hate that, when restaurants run out of food – really popular stuff - and it's only early. You'd have thought they would be better prepared." Joe was back in irritable mode. Charlotte dreaded the onset of IM because she didn't like what might develop: one possibility, worst case scenario, was a ruined evening – quite often, she remembered this as the most usual direction of travel – and then the others were scaled back versions of grumpy, inconsolable or both. Charlotte knew from past experience she had to move seamlessly into using her most sympathetic tone otherwise it would be like pouring petrol on to an already blazing fire – not only wouldn't she get to eat the meal they had ordered she probably wouldn't be going on holiday anytime soon.

"So annoying that I agree, but," she reached her hand over the table to cover Joe's before she continued, "your second choice sounds just as good and I think he'll make sure you get some extras, especially as you seemed to take it so well. It works wonders sometimes, rather than going loopy."

"Yes, he dealt with that well, to be fair. It's not his fault anyway so we just need to make the best of it." He held on to Charlotte's hand and pulled her gently towards him for a kiss. Crisis over. Turkey here we come, thought Charlotte.

"We could go to the travel agents tomorrow see what deals they've got, couldn't we? It's not long before we would need to go. Might get a late booking special. Be a lot cheaper if we can." Charlotte was moving into over-drive so that the menu incident was properly forgotten and they could move on.

"Yeah, let's do that. We could go in the morning before I go off to London. Be nice to get it fixed."

Charlotte was pleased she had managed to steer Joe away from an all-inclusive extravaganza. The holiday was her idea so there was no way she was going to let Joe control what type of holiday they were going on. She was only too aware of the importance Joe attached to his trips away but at least she had managed, in theory, to pin her elusive pimpernel down to spending some time exclusively with her somewhere nice and warm. Turkey had been on her bucket list for ages and now it was moving a step closer. Getting away from all the distractions at home as well as from the pressures of her work, at a time when her relationship with her boss was at an all-time low, was another distinct attraction. Working in the debt collection sector had never really interested Charlotte. She was constantly being set new attainment targets which inevitably meant putting the squeeze on more people who had found themselves unable to keep up the repayments on their mortgage, car finance or credit card. Charlotte did not want to be in the business of making other people miserable, nor did it fit with her moral values. She was not a capitalist. She really and truly did not support the pursuit of wealth above all else as a worthwhile ambition.

She had been sucked into this particularly unappetising area of work as a penniless mature student who needed to make some money in the summer vacation in order to fund a holiday. At that time Charlotte worried less about where money came from than she did now. She would have drawn the line at human slavery or drugs but pretty much everything else she would have regarded as being OK.

At first she had found the work easy as she was just a junior call-handler, answering queries and using her powers of persuasion, honed by participation in several intense training workshops, to get people to, at the very least, reschedule their payments over a longer period of time in order not to get into more debt. Her success at the lower levels of intervention did not go unnoticed and in a very short time she made it first to the rank of Shift Leader and then to the dizzying heights of Assistant Manager (Early Intervention). In fact, so highly was she thought of that for the whole of her degree course she was able to pop in to do shifts evenings and weekends and holidays as she chose.

When her less than dazzling university career ended in an all too predictable 3rd class honours, slotting into, what was, back then, a reasonably well paid and convenient work pattern seemed logical; and much better than joining the interminable and ultimately rarely successful milk round process. In the years since she had become well-established in her managerial role and had also managed a move to Manchester without it affecting her position. Even so she had not become any more comfortable with the ethics of the job as her moral scruples started to play a more and more important role in her life. Even though that had become more of an issue for her, during the Brunt years, she had never taken the opportunity to look elsewhere for a permanent, though in all probability less well paid, replacement as she was never absolutely certain the bills were going to continue to be paid due to Joe's lack of transparency on the matter of his income.

Another factor in the morality vs workplace ethics argument was the role played by Henry in her 'in and out of work activities' because he really fitted in for Charlotte who, as far as work and love were concerned, had been more or less happy to make do with what came her way. However, she was now trying to gain complete control by drawing up a strategic plan for her future. Morals and ethics actually, despite Charlotte's virtuous outbursts, had previously come second to an easy life, but now she was determined things were going to change.

She really, really wanted to love Joe Brunt. After all she shared a bed with him, shared common interests, not least concerning environmental matters, and had cooked most of his meals on a regular basis since they had been 'together'. They got on well, mostly, so she often pondered, was it more convenience than emotional closeness that kept them going? However, with his mind and body frequently being elsewhere she had had lots of time on her hands. Good old very straightforward Henry fitted exactly what she required to complement what she had with Joe, but she wasn't sure she really loved him either.

She knew it was not love that had often added a delicious frisson to Charlotte's working day especially after a particularly successful coupling in Joe's absence. It was the fact that she and Henry worked together, albeit in different sub-divisions, so that on such occasions she could extend her perambulations around the corridors of Hazelcroft Recovery to include Henry's preserve in the hope of a chance encounter, a brief touch of hands near the watercooler or a warm smile as she passed his work-station. Just enough to not only bring memories of their lovemaking flooding back but also to enable her to attack her latest unwelcome task with renewed gusto after returning to her hot-desk. Henry made Charlotte feel special, really special in his own idiosyncratic way. Just a look. Just a touch. Charlotte did not want to know how or why, she just wanted to bathe in that feeling. Although she did have to be careful during these periods of reverie not to bump into abandoned post trolleys or other unattended objects.

Whilst having Henry in her life was in many respects very convenient, and frequently exhilarating, it did involve quite a few buts and for that matter, ifs. One of the principal ifs was Barbara, his ex. Quite a big if judging by some of the photos Charlotte had seen. Barbara was large and was also someone Henry talked about quite a lot. Over drinks, over dinner, after sex and, indeed once very recently, with disastrous consequences, during sex. On that occasion as they were moving towards a joint and joyous crescendo, he screamed out her name in the most unfortunate context. 'Barbara, Barbara I love you!' In amongst the ardour and passion he must have realised his heinous error because, after thrusting Charlotte unceremoniously to one side, he got out of bed and started putting on his clothes all the while muttering apologies to the traumatised Charlotte. Without waiting for a post-match debrief he hurriedly left the bedroom and the last Charlotte heard of him was the front door slamming.

Rebuilding their relationship after such a monumental faux pas had been quite problematic. Charlotte was much keener for the liaison to continue because it suited her purpose given her doubts about Joe, whereas for Henry he had to make considerable efforts to free up time from his other involvements to meet Charlotte's demands. Charlotte felt that Henry would welcome the jettisoning of Joe as he would no longer see himself competing for her affections which would have the added benefit of him wanting to spend more time with her. Eventually, at an office leaving do, Charlotte managed to have a few words with a still visibly chastened Henry assuring him that she fully understood his slip-up.

"It's OK Henry really it is. I get that you really loved Barbara. I absolutely get that and if you still want to see me then that's really great. I love our time together and don't want to lose you over a... misunderstanding."

Charlotte knew that keeping busy with work or making the most of Joe's time at home or fitting in a session with Henry had been good for her mental stability – being alone with a bottle of gin did not appeal. Love appealed but, without that, she realised she just had to make the best of what was on offer.

After the holiday in Turkey had been booked, two weeks at the Club Turan Prince World in Antalya, they had to hurry back home so Joe could sort out his last minute, or, more truthfully, all of his packing for his boys' trip to watch England at the Oval. While he was creating mayhem in their bedroom trying to find some of his favourite clothes, she was downstairs responding to his occasional demands for help.

"Have you seen my Ralph Lauren top?"

"Which one?"

"The blue one. Should be in my drawer."

"Is it still in the wash basket? Didn't you wear it last week?"

"No not that one."

Charlotte did most of the laundry related tasks in the Brunt/Summersby household – washing, ironing, folding etc. All she expected Joe to do was to make sure things were put away in such a fashion that they could be easily found in situations like the one in which they now found themselves.

Shouting upstairs and downstairs was usually fairly unsuccessful. A lot got lost in translation and with Joe getting more exasperated and Charlotte getting more involved in a simultaneous texting exchange with Henry, fixing up their extra-curricular activities for the next few days, meant that progress was slow.

She had been feeling particularly tired recently and this debacle was making her more irritable than usual whilst playing another round of hunt for Joe's stuff.

"It's my blue one," shouted an ever more desperate Joe, "with white piping round the collar and on the sleeves!"

Through her irritation Charlotte noted with surprise a rare example of Joe appreciating the finer aspects of fashion detail as a way of differentiating his clothes.

"It should be in your drawer." Henry had just texted that he was up for 'S on Sunday at yours' which had distracted her more than somewhat from the distance learning session she was having with her partner.

"Are you fucking listening?" roared an incandescent Joe. "I asked you if there was anywhere else it could be. What are you doing down there? You're obviously not really trying!" Joe's raging voice had changed to more of a whiny, pleading little boy voice. Charlotte carefully switched her phone off and slipped it into her jeans pocket. She was always very careful with her phone – she had seen far too many TV dramas where careless people were caught out by being slipshod in concealing their duplicity. Phone secured, she set off on her rescue mission.

"OK, I'm coming up now. You'll never find this bloody top unless I help you, will you?" she bellowed as she stomped her way up the stairs. She was not going to be sad to see Joe's car speeding off down the hill because it meant she could forget about him for a while and get everything ready for Henry's arrival. She wanted it to be just right as this was the first time they had been able to get together since Barbarargate which had caused such a rift between them.

"OK, where have you looked, Joe?"

"I've been through all my shirt drawers and I've looked at the pile on the dresser."

"Have you looked in the wash basket. Just in case?"

After a brief disappearance Charlotte returned with a blue Ralph Lauren tee with white piping. She held it aloft so that there could be no mistake.

"Voila!" she announced. "Voila c'est sale! So, you'll have to choose something else now."

Joe snatched the errant garment from her hands and sniffed the armpits. He shrugged, "That'll do, just have to up the deodorant levels for that one! Thanks for tracking it down."

"Trouble with you JB is that you give up too easily. Don't really know what you'd do without me to find stuff, organise you."

"C'mon you!" Joe lunged at Charlotte trying to push her back on the bed all the time laughing. His anger had been quickly forgotten. It was an old ploy for Joe - if you love me, you'll let me have a quickie.

Charlotte's mind was elsewhere and missing the cue entirely pushed Joe off forcefully with a grunt. "Don't you just think you can pleasure yourself whenever you want to, you bugger. You were screaming blue murder a few minutes ago. You're going to be late if you don't get a move on you know."

"Sorry love just thought you'd be OK. It's usually OK isn't it?"

"Joe you're going away, again. You've just lost your temper, again, and now you want me to block all that out and join in a bit of rumpy-pumpy. You shouldn't have left it so late to get yourself ready, shouldn't have lost your temper and, last of all, you shouldn't have taken me for granted."

"OK fair do's, I went too far there. Sorry," he blew Charlotte a kiss and attempted to pat her bottom as she walked past.

"I just get a little bit fed up with your tantrums. You need to be a bit more thoughtful."

"Sorry."

"OK, now get a move on or it won't be worth going at all!"

Charlotte liked Joe, sometimes she even convinced herself that she loved him, but at other times she found that the sheer effort of organising things for him far outweighed the enjoyable parts, if she thought about them too much. So, as with so much in her life, she didn't. and the rollercoaster ride continued unabated. He was very good for flowers, after an argument; cooking when he discovered a new recipe which he liked; treats – cinema tickets, unexpected trips; and sex when he wanted it and how he wanted it. Joe was good on Joe's terms and for making up to Charlotte when he had upset her. However, the overwhelming plus point for Joe was he always, well almost always, came through with the money they needed to keep going. How he did it, Charlotte was not really sure; talk about logistics and other work related topics generally went over her head. Laura's frequent entreaties to find out what on earth he did fell on deaf ears. It was never the right time to explore the complexities of the Brunt finances. Their relationship was after all, ultimately, based on mutual convenience as her earlier assessment had confirmed. Charlotte was a beautiful, quiet woman who always made an impression in pubs, restaurants, parties. She invariably attracted admiring glances from both sexes which would have helped more than somewhat with her lack of self-esteem if only she had taken any notice. Joe, on the other hand, was always the life and soul of the party when they were out with friends. He was the one for jokes and repartee whereas Charlotte preferred to let him be the centre of attention so that she could catch up with the gossip, and not take too much notice of the banter/insults being tossed around. She remembered when they had first met.

"You look really fed up. Would you like a drink?"

Joe Brunt had been sitting in the bar of the Fallowfield for about 20 minutes waiting for Jane. They had been seeing each other for a couple of weeks without making any real progress. She was a friend of a friend and Joe felt they had been set up as two people who, unknown to themselves, would be likely to get on. The fact that they had not gelled very well was seen by Joe as a reflection on the judgement of their mutual friend rather than on any lack of effort on behalf of Jane or himself.

Joe had had a bad feeling about tonight from the start. Hitherto Jane had always been early, always texted to keep him up to date with her proximity and had always exuded enthusiasm which had never been quite matched by the reality of their time together. On this occasion radio silence had been maintained all day which was unheard of and less than encouraging in relation to the progress of their fledgling relationship.

In the absence of Jane, Joe had been enjoying his pint and indulging in one of his favourite pastimes, people-watching. One person, in particular, had attracted his attention. She was sitting in a corner booth in the pub nursing what looked like a gin or a vodka from the balloon shape of the glass she was sipping from. She looked as if she was flicking through content on her phone. Occasionally she would also be two-thumb typing as if she were having a two-way live dialogue with someone. However, mixed in with these periods of activity, she also spent long periods staring into the middle-distance frowning and, to Joe's mind, looking wistful. During this period Joe had tried not to stare too closely as he conducted a series of scans around the bar as if looking for someone during which he would pause so he could observe, unobtrusively, what his potential damsel in distress was up to.

Eventually, having decided that Jane was a no-show, Joe decided to approach the apparently friendless woman. His reasoning was that he needed a refill anyway so if he offered a drink to the lonely woman on his way through, he had nothing to lose and, judging from his considered opinion, plenty to gain.

As Joe spoke the solitary lady looked up and smiled, "Thanks that would be really nice. Rhubarb gin and tonic please. Saw you looking at me surreptitiously. Wondered if you would come over. Had such a shitty week it would be nice to have a chat."

The next two hours were spent with Charlotte telling Joe all her troubles, explaining the reasons why she had recently left Scarborough, and with him being an ultra-sympathetic listener as he warmed more and more to somebody who he had initially felt sorry for but gradually realised he had lots in common with.

In the weeks following this chance encounter Charlotte and Joe spent every possible spare moment doing things together and finding out more and more about each other. This was what Charlotte came to refer to as their halcyon phase. Everything had been perfect almost, as she came to realise, too perfect and so it was inevitable that when Joe asked Charlotte to move in with him, she was absolutely thrilled to accept. After so many disappointments Charlotte really felt that Joe might be the one. He was so attentive and caring that even Laura had been in favour of the move. Subsequently Charlotte looked back on that period of their relationship and wished that life could go back to how it had been then, uncomplicated and fulfilling, and not so problematic and so much like hard work.

Charlotte only risked entertaining Henry at Chez Brunt when she knew Joe would be away for at least two/three nights so there was no possibility of being interrupted. He always phoned to let her know when he was on his way back so there would always, she reasoned, be time for an emergency evacuation in the unlikely event he was to return early. The reasoning behind her extra-curricular dalliances was, after all, to supplement her life with Joe but she had absolutely no intention to put that relationship at risk if at all possible. After all Chez Brunt was a very pleasant 3 bed semi in a very desirable district with handy restaurants, pubs and a very well kept park area. Living there, at very little extra cost, in comparison to her previous very pokey little flat, in a not very desirable part of Scarborough, meant it was not to be given up lightly. They had tried an outlying Premier Inn once or twice but Charlotte felt quite exposed in that setting and far preferred taking the chance of Henry being spotted arriving at 42 Lediard Avenue. In addition, being in the rather sterile atmosphere of a hotel chain bedroom Charlotte missed her creature comforts and also as a precursor hated having to pack everything she required into an overnight bag. Another overriding consideration was that Henry got a definite thrill out of being 'in Joe's house', as an interloper.

One principle benefit of being responsible for sorting out all the domestic arrangements in the house meant that in reality entertaining weekend guests without anyone else, ie Joe, finding out was surprisingly uncomplicated. All Charlotte needed to do was to make sure the bedding was changed and washed and dried before the wanderer returned. Sheets and duvet covers were never ironed and, to be fair, Joe probably would not have noticed if the bedding wasn't changed for weeks or maybe months! In the ordinary course of events it was Charlotte's sense of pride that kept things clean and tidy. There was little pressure on that front from Joe. Henry was due to arrive on Sunday after lunch which meant a nice leisurely afternoon of Prosecco and sex carefully distributed around watching a box set.

Charlotte had decided to leave any discussion of the future until breakfast just before Henry was due to depart. She felt that would give plenty of time to assess how likely Henry would be to want to take matters to another level. Charlotte had literally no idea what Henry would be choosing for their entertainment. He had a penchant for violent, macho films which often left Charlotte hiding under the duvet as bits of body and armoured equipment were blitzed across the screen as the result of a series of ever more devastating explosions. Henry knew Charlotte didn't really enjoy that particular genre but he enjoyed 'looking after' her when she was frightened and snuggled up to him for reassurance. DVD box set watching had become a ritual for Henry and Charlotte involving ensuring maximum comfort, plenty of what Charlotte referred to as 'finger food', in the nicest possible way, and an ample supply of drink – Prosecco and red wine - so no one was inconvenienced during the 2 to 3 hours devoted to the process

Fortunately, every room in the Brunt household, except the bathroom, was equipped with a TV, even the kitchen was included so there was the opportunity of watching their film anywhere they fancied. Of course, the master bedroom had the biggest screen, a 55 inch top-of-the-range, as Joe and Charlotte watched most of their TV in their big double bed. However, the TV in the guest bedroom was more than adequate for Charlotte's purposes as she had little use for surround-sound and a subwoofer, she only really wanted an excuse to be in bed with Henry. Gentle hairy sensitive Henry.

"Hi. What y'doing this weekend?" It was Laura, who was bored, wanting to lure Charlotte out for a night of Prosecco and cavorting at one of her favourite nightclubs. Laura liked nothing more than a party night with some of her friends.

"You've not been out for ages. You're getting really boring you know. We're only going to have a few drinks and have a dance."

The problem with Laura's idea of a 'few drinks' was that she often managed to blag them into clubs where they were having special two for one offers or better still free drinks, especially if she managed to gate crash a party or a business function. Of course, on these occasions it was very difficult, if not impossible, to keep a check on what they were drinking. If it was free, as soon as they finished one drink then it was time for another and so on until somebody, usually Charlotte, realised through their drunken stupor that they should probably/definitely be heading home. Charlotte knew of old that there was a heavy price to pay for a night out with Laura, usually a banging headache which never seemed to dissipate until she had had a very late and very light lunch. If Charlotte was going to be able to fully enjoy her time with Henry then she needed to avoid one of Laura's nights out at all costs, but she also had to be careful not to appear too hostile otherwise she might occasion a big fallout with Laura which, from previous experience, could have an adverse effect on their relationship which would require another Prosecco soaked evening to sort out.

"Well," she began, knowing even as she spoke how unconvincing she sounded, "you see I was planning on staying in..."

"Nah you don't want to do that. It'll be more fun if you come out."

Charlotte knew she had started badly so she tried another tack: "Been really busy lately, birthdays, a couple of works do's and that. I'm not really in the mood for a girl's night out and..." Charlotte left this comment hanging in the air. She knew the last thing Laura would want would be someone who wasn't up for it. She never knowingly let anyone piss on her chips. Charlotte's best way out was to make Laura decide that actually literally she didn't want her along anyway. The last thing she would want would be someone who wouldn't drink enough, wouldn't stay up late enough and, worst of all, someone who wouldn't get up and dance every time one of 'their songs' was played.

"What do you mean - been out a lot. You sound like an old woman. It's the weekend. Time to go out and socialise!" Laura's sentence ended in a shout to try and engender some excitement in her friend who was clearly not being very co-operative.

"I'd love to come out with all you lot. You know I would but I just need a night at home. I need to wake up on Sunday with a clear head. We'll do it another time, I promise we will. I really don't want to let you down, I really don't. I'm tired Laura. Really tired and pretty broke too." Charlotte had given it 100% on the excuse scale, she just didn't want to go out and just had to hope and pray Laura would see it from her point of view.

There was a long pause. Laura was obviously thinking, weighing up what she had been told.

"OK Ms Grumpy," she said finally, "Just this once have a night in and miss out on all the fun if you really think you need to. You owe me though - next time you need to remember this no-show, because you'll have to make it up to me. OK?"

"Yes OK. Thanks for that Laura. I'll get a couple of early nights and then I'll be good. There's no point going out if all I'm thinking about is when I can go home. I'm glad you realise that. Thanks."

With Laura safely dispatched, although, she fully appreciated she would only discover at what cost at a later date, Charlotte was certain that she would at least be able to welcome Henry bright eyed and bushy tailed when he arrived. She felt they had not only got some ground to make up after their recent contretemps but she wanted to get crystal clear in her own mind whether Henry was able to live up to his checklist status. Charlotte spent the rest of the day shopping, drinking coffee and tidying the house. It was something she always did when Joe was away, otherwise he was always in the way and particularly for Henry time she wanted everything to be just so. Joe didn't get being tidy, generally, neither did he, as another general rule, respond very well to Charlotte's entreaties about the 'jobs' that needed to be done around the house. As Charlotte worked her way round on this occasion she noticed a number of changes: the shelving in the bathroom had mysteriously appeared on the wall; the mirror in the spare bedroom was now firmly fixed to the wall; and, to her absolute amazement, the toilet which had been waiting for a fresh coat of paint for about 12 months was resplendent in a fresh coat of magnolia. Joe had been busy, unusually so. She made a mental note to thank him when he got back. Maybe, just maybe, the worm was turning.

The only exception to Joe's aforementioned tardiness about tidiness was when members of his family were due and he didn't want to be embarrassed, particularly if it was his Mum, who was more than likely not only to spot the untidiness but also comment on it and lay the blame firmly on her son's shoulders. He hated being the object of someone else's jokes and so, on such occasions, he instituted an allegedly forensic cleaning programme. Although supposed to be very thorough Charlotte was always amazed that the whole process only took around 10 – 15 minutes but nevertheless seemed to achieve the desired effect, at least for Joe. Tidy for Joe meant that things couldn't be seen. After one of his 'forensic sessions' books and magazines could be found pushed under chairs and sofas; clothes would be stuffed behind cushions; and all the stray plates and cutlery would be rushed into the kitchen ready to go in the dishwasher.

Of course, that was as far as they got because as far as Joe was concerned the dishwasher, along with all other domestic tasks, was Charlotte's sole responsibility. Even so it caused many arguments, especially late at night, either because it needed loading or unloading, or there was a lack of cups, or plates so they could not have a brew or serve up a takeaway etc.

Having got all the essentials together she settled down to watch a film. A good romcom, which would have had Joe running to his PlayStation. The Last Summer was about halfway through when her mobile started vibrating. It was Joe. It was so unusual for him to ring when he was on one of his jaunts that she was unable to keep the surprise out of her voice as she answered: "Joe what a lovely surprise!"

"Hi Charlotte, how y'doing?" Joe never really wanted to know how she was. She needed to be absolutely full of cold or crying uncontrollably to elicit a caring response. Charlotte was immediately on her guard.

"I'm good thanks. Just got a nice film on. Why, what do you want?"

"Well, I was just wondering if you'd mind if I didn't get back until Tuesday. "Got some things that need to be sorted out and I won't be finished to get back on Monday. Is that OK?"

"Joe love, you're hardly ever here anyway so what difference is another day going to make. Honestly!" Charlotte was not trying very hard to hide her exasperation.

"You sure?" Joe was using his pleading voice now which was something Charlotte could easily exploit.

"Look I said it's OK if you need to stay on but..."

"Of course, I'll make it up to you when I get back. Goes without saying!"

"OK love so what time on Tuesday?"

"Round teatime. I'll bring a takeaway if you want. Text me on the day and let me know what you want."

"It'll be Chinese, I can tell you that now."

"OK." Joe reluctantly agreed – it was his least favourite takeaway but in order to placate Charlotte he thought it would be best to go along with her idea. "What you doing tonight?"

"I'm in the middle of a film. I told you! Really enjoying it actually and then I'm going to catch an early night."

"Thought you might be off out with Laura on one of her wild nights."

"She did phone, but I managed to get away with it. She was very persuasive, but I really didn't fancy it. If I'm honest I'd sooner go out with you than get a hangover with the girls."

"You sure? Never stopped you in the past!"

"Yes, but the last few weeks have been great – I've noticed that you've even managed to do a couple of the jobs that have been waiting to be done for ages. I really appreciate it when you help and contribute, after all, this is your house. When you take more notice of what I say makes me feel more part of it like it's really me and you. Not me versus you or you in spite of me."

"Not sure what you're trying to say here, Charlotte. We've talked before about marriage we decided..."

"I know. No, that's not what I'm talking about. I think we've been more of a partnership lately and I wanted to let you know how that makes me feel." Charlotte was starting to feel rather guilty with the imminent arrival of Henry for their liaison à deux and her probably final decision about the future of their relationship. In any event she didn't want to get involved in any discussions about marriage just prior to entering into another chapter of unfaithfulness with Henry. This had happened before – deeper feelings for Joe surfacing just before Henry was due to arrive. She couldn't help wondering whether she could only deal with messy relationships, would anything else be too straightforward, too normal, not exciting enough for her. After all, she reasoned, if Joe would only be around more, in his useful persona, Henry would have been surplus to requirements. In fact, the more she thought about it the more unsure she was about her previous decision. "You see even though you try not to show it you can be a soft bugger sometimes and that's the Joe Brunt I like. Soft and cuddly."

"Oh, give over Charlotte don't go lovey-dovey on me. Especially when I'm not there. Not a great idea with me on my own miles away."

"All right I'll keep it for Tuesday. I assume you'll go to the Great Wok for our takeaway. I'll look at the menu and let you know what I want."

"OK look forward to that. See you on Tuesday, love."

"Keep safe and drive carefully! See you then."

Charlotte put her mobile phone back on the coffee table very slowly. She started thinking about the good things about Joe and started wondering whether she had been fair to him when weighing up her pro's and con's. They often seemed to communicate better on the phone than in person – he tended to take her more seriously at a distance. If they were together he was very often looking for a cuddle or something overtly sexual rather than having a proper conversation. In fact, they'd often sorted out differences of opinion by phone, especially when they needed to clear the air over a pressing issue. Pushing these thoughts to the back of her mind Charlotte returned to her romcom, whilst trying to rekindle thoughts of a mutually satisfying Sunday afternoon with Henry.

"If you were a real friend Charlotte. A real friend, you wouldn't argue with me."

It was 3:15am if Charlotte's bedside alarm clock was to be believed. Her beauty sleep had been rudely interrupted by a phone call from Laura. Missed her last bus, no taxis for at least an hour, so who else could she possibly turn to.

"Charlotte, why you not speaking. It won't take you long. Quick nip into town and back and you'd help your best friend who's in serious trouble. I mean..."

Charlotte decided to cut into Laura's rambling monologue: "Why didn't you think about getting home an hour ago instead of waiting till now? " She could feel herself getting angrier as she spoke. "You're a real nuisance, you do know that don't you?"

"Wouldn't have bothered you if there'd been anyone else. I knew you'd be cross with me," Laura's slurred words only just made sense. Charlotte put her on speakerphone so she could keep talking to her while she did a minimal amount of dressing prior to setting off.

"You're a real mate. A real mate you know that don't you Charlotte..."

"I'm a fool coming out at God knows what o'clock to rescue you because you're too pissed to get yourself home. You are in a right state. Did you fall over?"

After having rescued Laura from her safe hiding place behind a refuse bin full of rotting food outside a Chinese restaurant, she realised she was soaking wet and as it was a dry night this raised her curiosity levels considerably.

"Nah don't think so. I did spill some drinks in the club, I think. Things got a bit out of hand." Charlotte later discovered that Laura had in fact been responsible for knocking over a whole round of drinks carefully balanced on a tray being carried far too near where she had been dancing. In fact, the subsequent altercation had led to her being thrown out of said club as the door staff had identified her as a troublemaker.

"Thanks Charlotte, sorry to disturb you, did he mind? You know, your lover."

"You mean Joe? No, he's gone away for the weekend. One of his cricketing jaunts."

"No, your lover. You know the guy who flits round when Joe's playing away."

Charlotte had never mentioned anything to Laura about her doubts about what Joe was actually doing when he was away. Neither had she mentioned Henry or, at least, she thought she hadn't. For a moment she worried that the Prosecco had been doing the talking but then she realised it was nothing she said but all in Laura's fervent imagination. All she had to do was ignore her and then they would be home and it would all be forgotten.

"Dunno what you're talking about, you daft mare! Haven't got time for anything on the side. You're too pissed to even know what you're saying." As Charlotte stopped talking, she realised that the slumped figure of Laura indicated that she had fallen asleep so any further conversation on this awkward subject, or for that matter anything else, was completely unnecessary.

"Come on, time to get out." Charlotte had been nudging Laura gently for a minute or so without any result, so she resorted to more vigorous shaking coupled with shouting. Eventually she managed to steer her very unsteady friend to her door where she propped her up while she searched for her keys in her capacious handbag.

Job done she returned to the car and spent the journey home pondering the awful possibility that somehow Laura had found out about the existence of Henry. She was sure she had never mentioned him to her, why should she? She wasn't likely to boast about such a thing. She knew that Laura would be the worst person to find out because she would, inevitably, spread the news with their mutual girlfriends who would be delighted to know that, quiet as a mouse, Charlotte had a bit on the side. Charlotte had always managed, at least she thought she had managed, to keep her rather active sex life to herself. What she did in her private life was strictly her business. She had had too many disappointments in life by taking people into her confidence only to find that, as a result, her activities had become public knowledge. Up until now Joe and Henry had worked out fine for her, although she realised that her meeting later on was going to be crucial to see if they could still recreate the closeness which they had previously enjoyed and whether, moving forward, it was going to be just Henry and Charlotte in line with her previous decision.

Things got off to rather a bad start with Charlotte's afternoon of unremitting pleasure and assessment. Henry had arrived late. He had brought as his choice of boxset the Ultimate Rambo Collection and right from the off he had been extremely contrite, apologising for the slightest thing and saying 'excuse me' all the time. Charlotte had spent almost the entire weekend relaxing, preparing herself for a romantic afternoon followed by being pleasured by Henry at his best. Not demanding and assuming, but taking his signals from her and making her the focus of attention. Being awoken by a drunken Laura had been a very unwelcome interruption to her preparations and now, having taken a break from the dreadfully violent DVD, Charlotte was locked in the toilet weighing up her options. Carry on with the date as planned, even though it had been rather less than overwhelmingly successful so far, in the interests of her broader evaluation, or, very worst case scenario, call a halt, and risk losing Henry if she feigned either a headache or a bad stomach- ache. This would consign her to a future relationship with Joe which she had, until this moment, been ready, or more or less ready, to terminate.
"I'm really not enjoying this film," Charlotte began on her return from the toilet. "I was really surprised when you brought another one of your blood and gore films. You know I don't like that sort of 'entertainment'. I was rather looking forward to something a bit more romantic and funnier especially as we had a bit of a falling out last time we met."

"I'm sorry, I ran out of time. I was late setting off, I just grabbed a box from my stash. I didn't really look at it very carefully. Stupid really because I remember what you said about Rambo before."

Still apologising, still playing the naughty boy, Charlotte had never been very impressed by role-play. A previous very short-term boyfriend had wanted her to act out a situation where she had to put him in a nappy and suckle him. This particular vignette never made it from the planning stage as Charlotte had, very abruptly, curtailed her after-work drink with someone she had previously regarded as very hot.

Charlotte needed to lift the mood, change direction or else she was not going to achieve what she wanted from Joe's absence. She was fairly certain, fairly certain, Joe was up to no good. She wasn't going to submit him to a lie detector test because, in any event, his absences suited her purpose – sex and fun with Henry on a just-in-time basis. She leaned across to Henry, carelessly spilling the last of his generous portion of popcorn, kissed him firmly on the lips, grabbed his hand and started pulling him towards the stairs and the carefully prepared spare bedroom.

The doorbell of the Brunt household chiming followed by a loud banging on the door itself woke Charlotte with a start. Entwined as she was after making passionate love for some while past involving a very innovative Thor's Hammer she unceremoniously pushed Henry away from her, grabbed a towel from the foot of the bed and hastily wrapped it round her as she rushed down the stairs.

2:15 am according to the hall clock.

"Mrs Brunt? Are you Mrs C Brunt? I am PC William Dove; this is my colleague PC Sophia Wyatt. Can we come in?"

Quickly glancing at the two uniformed officers standing on the doorstep brandishing their warrant cards Charlotte could tell from their extra serious look that they were bearers of bad news. She felt distinctly underdressed for entertaining members of Her Majesty's Constabulary who had wrongly assumed, as so many people did, that she was Joe's wife. It was too late for any debate about who she was. She had opened the door and her guests were now in the hallway waiting for instructions. Deciding against the popcorn strewn lounge Charlotte opted for the only other possibility, and she ushered the policeman into the dining room which she had cleaned quite thoroughly only a few hours before.

"Look, we're sorry for disturbing you so late at night. Mrs Brunt?" PC Dove sounded very nervous and uncertain, his voice trembled as he spoke, and he kept looking at his companion for moral support.

"I'm sorry, it's Bill's first you know, his first fatality," PC Wyatt butted in rather spoiling PC Dove's more sensitive approach by mentioning death without either a) any preamble or b) naming who had died.

"Someone's died? Who? Is it my sister?"

"No it isn't ma'am. I'm sorry but before we go any further can I just clarify ...."

Charlotte was rapidly descending into hysterics as PC Dove tried to go through his strict protocol. First of all, establish who you are talking to and then break the news gently. She was sobbing uncontrollably. As PC Wyatt moved to console her the dining room door opened.

"Charlotte is anything wrong? What's going on? Why are the police here?"

Ignoring the intrusion, apart from motioning Henry to sit down, PC Dove made an attempt to establish some order and to get through the business at hand.

"Now Mrs Brunt, I'm sorry ..."

"You might be sorry," Charlotte exploded, "but I'm not Mrs Brunt so I don't know what this has got to do with me. If it's one of Joe's family you need to contact him, he's away. Back on Tuesday ..."

"We know that Mrs...?"

"It's not Mrs anybody. I'm Charlotte Summersby, Joe's partner. You mentioned a fatality." Charlotte managed to speak through the sobs which were racking her body. "Can we clarify for the avoidance of doubt whose fatality?"

At this she buried her face in PC Wyatt's chest barely noticing that her loosely tied towel had slipped from her shoulders during the interview and as she had become more distressed.

"So, I'm sorry this really hasn't gone as planned, Charlotte. PC Dove and I have come to inform you that Mr Brunt, Mr Joe Brunt has been involved in a car accident and has been pronounced dead at the scene. We..."

Charlotte's hysterical sobs moved to another level on hearing this news. In her grief she pushed PC Wyatt away from her and threw her now completely naked body onto the floor where she proceeded to beat her fists onto the recently installed deep pile carpet shouting, "Joe Brunt! I fucking told you not to drive so fast you stupid, stupid man..."

As she ranted Henry made an executive decision and managed to drape the discarded towel as best he could to cover most of Charlotte's body.

"How did it happen? Do you know what happened? Probably driving too fast, not paying attention, fiddling with his phone I expect."

"There's no clear indication of how the accident occurred at this stage," PC Dove was using his most soothing voice to try and calm the situation whilst at the same time making every effort not to let his gaze stray to the now mercifully semi-naked woman lying on the floor. "As far as we know there was no other car involved. That's really all we know at the moment."

As Charlotte's sobs subsided, she realised her predicament lying, virtually naked, on the floor in front of two policemen, barely shielded by one of her towels, and realised she needed to act.

"Henry, you need to help me here," she barked. Obviously, her naked state had clearly become considerably more important, in the short term, than the apparent death of her partner/lover. "Henry can you go and get my dressing gown please and if I could ask you both," indicating the policemen who were sitting very awkwardly staring at the floor immediately in front of them, "to look the other way. I need to get myself dressed so we can progress this matter."

Henry returned to the fray shortly afterwards with Charlotte's gaudiest and most inappropriate dressing gown. Charlotte effected a quick change from badly draped towel to the complete cover of a fluffy pink knee-length dressing gown which, thankfully from Charlotte's perspective, covered all her private parts whilst at the same time looking particularly girly. Acceptably clad she did her best to leave the room serenely and for some inexplicable reason shouted casually over her shoulder as she went, "You can both look now I've gone!"

The PCs were hugely relieved that the rather well-endowed or unfortunate, depending on your gender based view of the debacle that had ensued for the last few minutes, partner of the prematurely deceased male had left the room, admittedly, in a rather peculiar manner.

Dove turned to Wyatt: "WTF are we going to put in our report? Do we need to put in the bit about where she was lying naked on the floor screaming? How do we describe her? How much..."

Wyatt, ever the mistress of brevity and the *mot juste* interrupted, "Distraught, we just say Mrs or Ms or whatever was distraught at hearing the news that her partner had died in an RTA. No point in going into too much detail, we can save that for when we get back to the station!"

PC Dove looked rather shocked at his colleague's lack of empathy with the bereaved woman. "Not very supportive there, Sophia. Can't really share that sort of information with the others, can you?"

"You must admit, I know I shouldn't, but that was hilarious. The sight of her...."

Upstairs the situation had deteriorated considerably since Charlotte had flounced out of the dining room. Henry was not being very helpful or supportive, nor was he making a particularly positive contribution to Charlotte's evaluation of his medium and long-term future prospects.

"Look, Henry, I don't know. I have no fucking idea. You were there, you heard what they said. Although for the life of me I cannot imagine why you joined in. Anyway why do you keep asking such stupid questions?"

As she ranted she was hastily pulling on her knickers, fumbling to find where her bra had been thrown during the prelude to their lovemaking as well as trying to unravel her dress and brush it down so it did not look too crumpled.

"But where was he? Why was he driving so..."

"Shut up, Henry, I don't know. Joe is dead. Stupid bastard drove into a tree by the sounds of it. No one else was involved. Thank Christ he didn't kill anyone else while he was doing it. Don't suppose you give a flying fuck about me. I'm in bits. My head's spinning here. I've got to go downstairs to talk to the police again and answer their questions so the last thing I need from you is more stupid questions."

As her voice reached a crescendo at the end of the sentence she turned away from the crestfallen Henry and flung herself on the bed, so recently the scene of a particularly successful sexual encounter.

She lost control again as she pounded the medium hard Vi-Sprung mattress with both clenched fists.

"Stupid stupid stupid bastard. What am I going to do now?" She started sobbing again clutching onto the pillow for support.

Henry bravely, some would say foolhardily, approached the bed reaching out to give Charlotte a supportive cuddle. Without any ceremony his approach was firmly rebuffed.

"Get off. What d'you want now? You..."

"I wanted to hold you. To..."
"Well, I don't need any holding now or anything else for that matter. We'd better go downstairs."

"So, you're Mr Day?"
"Yes."
"And you're a friend of Ms Summersby. That right?"
"Yes, that's right, a friend."
"Who was staying the night while Mr Brunt was away?"
"Yes, that's right."
Henry had decided that the monosyllabic approach would serve him best in the rather awkward situation he found himself in. Foolishly Charlotte and he had spent their few minutes away from the police squabbling rather than planning. In that short break it hadn't struck either of them to think how they were going to explain the incongruity of the situation which the police constables would have to address. Henry found himself as a centre of attention in the unpicking of this situation. PCs Dove and Wyatt were having great difficulty keeping straight faces as they delicately probed the present circumstances. To them, using common sense, rather than any carefully honed skills as would-be detectives, it was plain as a pikestaff that Ms Summersby had been caught in flagrante delicto. Mr Day had been caught with his trousers down or, as in this case, carelessly draped over the 43 inch TV screen in the Brunt spare bedroom where Charlotte had, rather recklessly, thrown them. As Henry fielded the evermore incisive questions he kept having flashbacks to the earlier sexual congress. Charlotte's naked body, her sighs and moans interrupted his train of thought.
"Mr Day, sorry. Did you catch my last question?"
"Sorry no, no, what was it again?"
Charlotte, surrounded by discarded tissues and cradled in PC Wyatt's arms, was seeing Henry in a different light as he struggled to offer a convincing story to the inquisitors or even to, inevitably, tell the truth. After all there is no law against infidelity providing it had not had any material influence on the matter in hand. As far as Charlotte knew Joe had no idea what she got up to while he was away. As Henry dithered and hesitated Charlotte wondered what she'd ever seen in him. His previous prowess in bed had been eclipsed by his total inability to rise to the challenge here. Rather regrettably, in light of her earlier decision, Henry was very clearly and comprehensively ruling himself

out of the contest to become Charlotte's longish-term lover. She mused that if Joe had ever found out about him he would have had no trouble at all in sorting him out.

Unable to bear any more equivocation Charlotte interrupted the questioning: "Sorry, sorry can I just interrupt. Not sure who Henry is trying to protect here but I don't want to keep any secrets or make you think something odd is going on here. Henry is my lover, that's all there is to it! My partner, the late Joe Brunt, travels – travelled a lot with his work as well as going on frequent sporting jaunts and while he's been away Henry has moved in to, as it were, keep me company. Our relationship hasn't done anyone any harm and more importantly Joe knew nothing about what was going on. So as far as your enquiries are concerned I can't imagine what relevance our relationship, or Henry's presence here at," she glanced briefly at her watch, "3:30am has on the passing of Joe which you are, presumably, investigating."

PC Wyatt was unable to hide her shock and embarrassment at what she had just heard – an unambiguous, full frontal confession of Charlotte's unfaithfulness, something that they might have had to use the thumbscrews to extract in different circumstances. She also couldn't help noticing that Henry, the errant lover, was looking exceedingly nervous as the real, and blatantly obvious, reason for his presence was being revealed in all its glory.

PC Dove, far from being able to hide his shock, was having great difficulty controlling his laughter. What had been a fairly routine trip to break sad news, offer condolences and make preparations for Charlotte to identify the body had by turns changed, from being a farce involving nudity and bad language, to flagrant dishonesty concerning illicit sexual congress. As he tried to suppress his laughter he was also trying to work out a way to get back to the subject at hand. However, as he tried to process this, matters took an even more lurid turn.

Charlotte's state of mind, in the aftermath of receiving news about Joe's passing, had deteriorated to such an extent that rather like a demented person she had lost all inhibition. She continued her revelations with more unnecessary details about her relationship with Henry and Joe in the preceding month.

"You see Henry is a good man. Good in bed, in fact so good I would give him an excellent on Trip Advisor." Everyone in the room was dumbstruck as Charlotte rambled on. Henry, who was most intimately involved, stared into the distance open-mouthed and the PCs did not know where to put themselves as they continued to write every word in their notebooks. They knew, from a police point of view, they should intervene but a perverse sense of devilment made them want to hear more.

"You see, Joe was never very adventurous in bed. Just wanted his conjugals, twice sometimes, and he was OK. No foreplay or after-play, just bomp and that was that. When I met Henry I just couldn't believe my luck. I think he had a PhD in Karma Sutra studies and he liked, or to be more correct loved, seeing how many..."

The PCs had heard enough and PC Wyatt particularly could not bear to hear any more: "Now, Charlotte, I think your....well to be honest I think you've lost the plot a bit here. Can we just get back to some practicalities please, because I think we need to be getting back to the station and I'm sure you need to get back to bed." As soon as she said these words she regretted it but decided to plough on regardless. "You see we just need to know when you last saw Mr Brunt, if you knew where he was going when he left here on Saturday and what he was doing while he was away. So, we need to get those points down and we also need to arrange for you, Ms Summersby, to identify the body as soon as it is convenient, either tomorrow or Tuesday, if that is possible."

Not for the first time in his short career the rather ineffectual PC Dove was very grateful for his colleague's intervention. He was far too engrossed in listening to Charlotte's graphic revelations to be bothered with police work, which was a major factor in his lack of progress in the force so far. Focus and attention to detail were frequently a problem. PC Wyatt had saved the day.

"Sorry, I didn't mean to go on so much. I think it must be the grief," blathered Charlotte as soon as PC Wyatt finished. "I last saw Joe on Saturday morning; he was going to London to watch a game of cricket at the Oval with some friends and I didn't know any more detail than that. He did phone to say he was delayed and wouldn't be back till Tuesday though. So as usual I was going to clear up after Henry and me had finished and then I was going to wait for his return. Only now he won't be coming back."

Charlotte started sobbing again and PC Wyatt moved towards her to console her, again, as her crying became more uncontrolled.

"Look, I hope you've got everything you need now," Henry suddenly sprang to life, somewhat unnecessarily, as if he was trying to bring matters to a conclusion even though it was hardly his place to do so.

"Yes, Mr Day I think we've more or less finished here now thanks. If we could fix a time for you, Ms Summersby, to come and identify the body, please."

After PC's Dove and Wyatt had left Charlotte wasted no more time with niceties and after a brief instruction to Henry: "I think you'd better go as soon as you can." She walked slowly up the stairs and went into her bedroom, shut the door firmly behind her and collapsed onto the bed fully clothed. As she tried to come to terms with Joe's death she remembered one of his favourite quotations: "Life is like a picnic and then in the middle you hear a distant thunder." Engulfed by that same thunder she sobbed herself to sleep.

Chapter 2 : Woodwork

It was 9.30 in the morning. Since being woken two hours previously by a phone call from the local newspaper Charlotte had barely managed to make herself a cup of coffee and some toast as she tried to keep up with the deluge of texts, WhatsApps and actual phone calls. Obviously, the news about Joe's death had been featured on a newspaper feed somewhere and had been picked up by close and, not so close, acquaintances of Joe's such that it seemed the whole world knew about the tragic event. Exactly how everyone knew who she was and how she could be contacted was of very little concern.

Charlotte's head was in a mess, still trying to come to terms with Joe's death as well as both the chaotic and embarrassing incident the previous evening involving two well-meaning PC's and the total disintegration of her project to sort out her somewhat complicated love-life. One contender had written himself out of the reckoning by way of a countryside tree and the other by way of messing up big style when under pressure. Putting these thoughts to one side a wry smile came to her face as she recalled the younger of the two policemen, a trainee as she recalled, who didn't know where to look when she experienced a rather awkward towel malfunction. Unfortunately, this memory also highlighted Henry's wholly unnecessary, and utterly unsatisfactory, involvement. It would have been so much simpler if he had just kept out of it completely and remained hidden away. Although, she was quite certain, after a peremptory banishing of him from the premises, after the PCs left, that she wouldn't see or hear anything from Henry again.

Time for reflection was extremely limited as text messages kept pinging in: Sorry to hear the news hun. RIP Joe xx

Can't believe he's gone. You OK? Xx

Very best wishes at this difficult time X

The general themes were sorrow and not really knowing what to say, although having said that everyone was painfully aware it was a difficult time for her. Offers of help from people Charlotte knew nothing about seemed oddest. Yes of course she wanted help, a cuddle or a hug would not have gone amiss. Charlotte realised she had very few people she could reach out to especially in view of her recent decision to delete Henry from her life. Wary that a reporter from the local newspaper was due shortly she scrolled through some more messages on her phone.

"Charlotte you OK babe? Just read the news. Can't believe it. You OK?" It was Laura wittering on. Thank God, thought Charlotte, at least she was spared breaking the news. However, she wasn't going to get the chance to get a word in any time soon. "What happened babe? Can't believe it. Just cannot believe it. Where was he? How are you? Do you want me to pop round? Charlotte?"

Charlotte felt obliged to interject as her friend sounded in no mood to stop firing off questions and she had no time to talk. "Look, Laura, thanks for phoning. Appreciate it. Can't believe it myself. Stupid sod smashed into a tree in the countryside. He was away for a couple of days on one of his cricketing jaunts. He was coming home tomorrow and now I've got to go to the morgue this afternoon to identify him. Can't believe it. So lonely. Really miss him." With that Charlotte began to sob.

"Hey look, don't get distressed. I'll come round OK. It'll be oneish, is that all right, I won't be able to get away before then?"

Charlotte only managed to say OK through her sobs before a robust knocking at the door announced the arrival of what Charlotte hoped was the reporter. "Got to go," she announced and put the phone down abruptly. As she got up, she caught sight of her tearstained, puffy face in the full-length mirror which had in the past featured so prominently in her sexual adventures with the deceased, JB. In amongst the grief, she allowed herself a moment, heartlessly interrupted by a further banging on the door, to remember just how Joe's warm hands caressing her naked body in front of the mirror had made her feel. She blushed at the thought and rushed towards the door which was still being viciously attacked by someone who sounded as if they were attempting to wake the dead.

"Sorry to keep you waiting," Charlotte yelled as she threw the door open.

"I was a bit worried you couldn't hear me. In the circumstances I thought you might still be asleep."

"Fat chance of that. What with phone calls and messages? Feel a bit overwhelmed, to be honest."

Standing on the doorstep, looking very sheepish was a young fresh faced male, short, rather overweight, wearing a badly fitting suit and looking for all the world as if he wanted to be anywhere else but waiting to interview a very attractive, recently bereaved woman.

Charlotte, still wiping away her tears with the backs of her hands, immediately took to him. The last thing she wanted was someone who was going to make things worse, put words in her mouth or make Joe out to be at fault. Her first impression was that she felt Jake, as he subsequently introduced himself, would be just the right person to tell her story to.

"Come in young man. You look a bit scared," Charlotte was trying to put the reporter at ease but in so doing she seemed to be entering patronising mode.

Jake tried to gain control of the situation: "Hi Mrs Brunt I'm Jake Strand from the Advertiser. I won't take up too much of your time, but I need to get a bit of background detail on Mr Brunt..."

"It's not Mrs Brunt it's Charlotte Summersby actually," Charlotte interrupted. "Mr Brunt's partner."

"Sorry Charlotte, is it OK to call you Charlotte?"

Charlotte nodded vigorously.

"OK. Well, I just wanted to find out what Mr Brunt did, whether you had any children, any involvement in the local community. All that sort of thing if possible."

Charlotte immediately felt foolish and completely out of her depth. She knew so little about Joe's life she suddenly realised that inadvertently she was wasting this young man's time.

"Well, don't really know where to start, Jake. This is all off the record of course..."

"Yes of course."

"But I didn't know Joe all that well at all. As I'm starting to realise. Now you might think I'm stupid..."

"I'd never say that Charlotte. It's not for me to judge." Jake was quick to reassure Charlotte of his professional credentials.

"I didn't even know where he worked, nor who his mates were or anything. He worked very hard, he was away for two or three days most months and apart from that we enjoyed evenings at home and trips out for meals, the cinema, that sort of thing," Charlotte had run out of things to say. She had told Jake pretty much all she could.

"Well, OK, I see. So, you don't want me to use any of that in my article? Charlotte don't you know anything else? Help me out here. I've got a couple of thousand words to write on this story. It's on our front-page this week. I need to know some more detail. Did he like any sport?"

"Football and cricket but he wasn't really fanatical."

"Did he like a drink? Did he go to the pub? I mean, Charlotte exactly how long had you known Joe?" Jake was beginning to lose his cool. He was interviewing the person whom his editor had told him would be the big feature in the next edition. Sad photo possibly paired with a photograph of the wreckage and lots of details about her relationship with the deceased. Instead, what he had got, so far, was a lot of stuff off the record which didn't help anyway. Front page lead to a little box on page 10 in an instant.

"So, if you've only known him such a short while is there anyone else who I could contact who knew him from before you two met? They might be quite useful. If you knew anyone." An air of desperation was beginning to creep into Jake Strand's voice.

"Well not really. As I say we kept ourselves pretty much to ourselves really. I've got lots of names of people, but I don't know anything about them at all either really. I suppose you could try his local the Crown & Anchor. He spent enough time down there."

Charlotte was at a loss to know what else to say. However, she knew one thing for certain: the more she blabbed on the less sense she was making. It shouldn't really have been a surprise that one day her lack of knowledge about Joe would cause her problems. Laura had tried to make her see sense, but to no avail.

"Don't you know what he does? Where the money comes from?"

"No, he always says not to worry. He'll sort it out."

"But he could be a drug dealer or something. Why would you not want to know?"

"Because he never encourages me. The washer/dryer broke down last week. I always do all the washing and everything."

"All of it? Everything? That's a bit unfair? You're not even married, not that you should necessarily do everything even then. What even washing his kecks and stuff?"

"The point I was making, Laura," Charlotte realised she was using her teacher voice, "was that when the washer/dryer broke he had a new one delivered and the old one taken away within 24 hours. That's always what happens so I don't ask any questions."

"But, well I can see when it's like that it sort of works, but..."

"Laura, I really don't care you know. Some people wouldn't like it, but it works for me. It really does."

Looking at Jake trying to get a story and failing on every level she wished she had taken Laura's advice and probed a bit more. She had never really given a second thought as to whether Joe was involved in anything illegal never needed to, but now he was dead that was one bombshell she could do without.

After a few more minutes with Jake struggling hard to come up with any questions he may have been able to ask to try and glean any useable nuggets of information from Charlotte he closed his notebook with a forlorn, "If you remember anything of interest Charlotte please let me know," and headed for the door.

Charlotte had barely had time to pick up her phone to catch up on who had been in contact when Laura breezed in.

"Babe, you OK? Big hug," and with that she launched herself at Charlotte so forcefully that they both ended up on the hall floor in a scrum of arms and legs. Charlotte's instinct was to cry, but the stupidity of the situation made her giggle.

"Hey, look I've not got long. Need to get to the morgue to identify Joe."

"Don't they know who he is already? They came and told you he's dead?"

"I "I know, but I've still got to do it. Suppose they can't just assume. Anyway, I've got 10 minutes."

As Charlotte drove to the hospital, she felt nervous, she was sweating and quite unready to put on a brave face. She'd seen plenty of episodes of Silent Witness, so she knew what a morgue was like, what happened there, but it was a bit different if the corpse on the slab was your ex-partner. She was trying to think through everything that was going to happen when she eventually found the morgue which, she anticipated, would be a nightmare of its own. She didn't want to let herself down by crying or, much worse, fainting. Maybe she should have let Laura come with her, but she really didn't think it was fair, even though she had virtually insisted that she should come. It was going to be traumatic enough for her without possibly having to support Laura as well. Laura was much worse at crying and getting emotional, so initially Charlotte had felt she would be better off on her own. Now as she walked through the corridors of her local NHS Foundation Trust Hospital she was much less sure. Signage to Gynaecology, Podiatry and other familiar disciplines had long since dropped off and she was following an incredibly quiet corridor at the end of which she could see what looked like a firmly locked door, covered with signs. To the left of the door there was a sanitizer station, for the living, Charlotte presumed, as she obediently squirted some gel on her hands and made sure she distributed it evenly.

She pressed the button on the right-hand side of the door and after a brief pause it opened. A short way down the corridor there was large desk behind which was sitting a middle aged bespectacled lady who was typing busily. Charlotte coughed as softly as she could and the lady looked up.

"You alright there?"

Charlotte's inappropriateness filter was fortunately disabled during this exchange otherwise she may not have responded as she did. "OK thanks. I've come to see Joe Brunt. I mean I've been told I need to identify the body prior to the post-mortem."

"OK thanks. What name was it?"

"My name is Charlotte Summersby."

"No, The deceased's name love. I need to know their full name."

"Josiah Thomas Brunt."

"Thanks." She proceeded to tap into her computer, rummaged, apparently aimlessly, for what seemed like a lifetime and then looked up again with a triumphant look on her face.

"Found him! OK follow me to the viewing room please. We're not allowed to call it the chapel of rest now. Something to do with Data Protection or Health and Safety Executive or equal rights, I think."

Before she knew it, the nurse had closed the door and she was alone in a small room tastefully decorated with several vases of fresh flowers. The hospital smell had gone, fortunately, and there on a trolley was Joe looking peaceful, almost beautiful. During all the time Charlotte had known him she had rarely seen him still, like this. He never napped, he was always doing something even when he was watching TV, especially sport or the news, he was always shouting for his team or ranting at some twat of a politician. She had probably seen him asleep a couple of times no more. He was always up first, doing things.

As he lay on the slab she realised just how tall he was. A big man. She looked down at his face and stroked his skin, pressed her fingers to his lips and whispered, "I love you." Immediately afterwards she turned away quickly as she remembered what she'd probably been doing either at the moment, or at the very least shortly after, he died in their spare bedroom with her ex-lover. As she prepared to leave the room, she was pleased to see he was at peace now, no more rushing around trying to keep on top of what he had to keep on top of to earn a living. She closed the door behind her, spoke briefly to the morgue attendant, signed the relevant papers and after a brief stop at the sanitising station she opened the door to go back into the hospital leaving death behind her ready to face any new challenges that awaited. One of the main ones, which she kept trying to push to the back of her mind, was the issue of money or, to put it plainly, how was she going to be able to keep going and pay all the bills without Joe's magic money tree being around.

As Charlotte entered 42 Lediard Avenue she closed the door carefully behind her and, for the first time since she moved in, fastened the chain that had always hung loose serving only to rattle annoyingly as people brushed past. She also switched the answerphone on so that she would not be interrupted and opened the package which had been presented to her by the visiting policemen the previous evening. It contained Joe's phone and his wallet and some money, £154.63p, which had been in Joe's pocket. She hesitated for what seemed like ages before she tried to switch Joe's phone on. Of course, it was dead. Hardly surprising given the length of time it had been since it would last have been charged. A brief search around the various plugs in the kitchen located Joe's unique charger and even though Charlotte didn't want to pry she knew she had to examine his phone – at least his contacts – so that she could start the job of officially advising people of his demise.

In the time it took for her to make a brew Joe's phone had sufficient charge to be available for interrogation. As she looked for his contacts Charlotte felt guilty for spying or intruding into his private space. She had never seen herself as one of those women, those women who could not wait to delve into their boyfriend's phones to prove that they were cheating on them. In fact, she was anxious not to pry – she did not want to know anything that would cause her any more grief. All sorts of scenarios were flashing through her mind. All she wanted was contact details of friends and work colleagues that she had no knowledge of, so she could make them aware of the situation even though she was clear that quite a few had indeed already contacted her. She decided that using Joe's phone to break the news would be rather spooky so she began making a list of names and numbers so she could work through them and send them each a message. She decided against doing a group message in case it might cause confusion, or indeed disharmony, as she didn't know anything about any of the names and their potential inter–relationships.

After laboriously transcribing the details she needed she started sending the message which she had carefully drafted:

> Hi X, I am Joe Brunt's partner and I am messaging you to let you know that, very sadly, he passed away yesterday after a car accident. I found your name in his phone and thought you would like to be informed. No details have been decided yet about the funeral. As soon as I know what's happening, I'll let you know. Charlotte.

After having omitted any contacts obviously referring to takeaways (11) or taxi companies (5) or tradespeople (4) and sundry others that didn't look like people who would want to know Charlotte had sent 23 texts and although she had no intention of setting up a spreadsheet to analyse replies she was intrigued to see what sort of responses she got.

In the few minutes she had spent with Laura earlier on they had started to work on a checklist of things that needed to be done to move things along. Laura was very good at strategic planning or Googling, Charlotte could never be sure which, but in their brainstorm they'd come up with a number of issues which needed to be resolved: post-mortem; funeral; wake - Laura was particularly focused on this aspect of the proceedings with her events background; Will, if any; probate; and as an afterthought what would happen to Joe's pension, if he had one. All of which left Charlotte with quite a lot to do. With the messaging situation having quietened down considerably Charlotte started working through the list to try and establish some sort of order. From a cursory glance at some of the leaflets she had been given at the hospital she realised the post-mortem situation would resolve itself, so she concentrated on her next priority: funeral directors.

Using an extremely helpful website, localfuneral.co.uk, Charlotte soon had a list of four or five funeral firms reasonably close by so, knowing very little about what was involved, she started making phone calls. "Hello, Piggott and Co. Funeral Directors. We offer unbeatable value at this most distressing of times. My name is Robert Piggott. How may I help you?"

Charlotte had become distracted during the rather lengthy preamble and there was a noticeable pause after Robert had finished speaking such that he started speaking again as Charlotte came back to her senses.

"Hello, is everything OK there?"

"Yes sorry, sorry. Robert is it?"

"Yes that's right. Piggott & Co..."

Charlotte was acutely aware that she might be subjected to another outpouring of introductions, so she cut in: "OK well, my partner has died..."

"I'm sorry to hear that Mrs?"

"No, it's Ms. Ms Charlotte Summersby actually. We weren't married. Yes, well Joe's died and I'm not sure where to go from here?"

"I do understand Ms Summersby. May I call you Charlotte?"

"Yes of course."

"Thank you. Yes, well I am sure Piggott & Co with our personalised approach to the funeral process can help you through what, at first appears, to be a minefield. We like to get involved pretty early on, and it sounds to me as if you're at that stage, so we can help you get your priorities sorted out so that you will know exactly what you need to do. This firm is a great believer in the personal touch so rather than talk now how would it be if I came round to see you – say tomorrow?"

"I don't know, thing is I've got quite a few places to phone and I was really just looking for prices at the moment. I'm working on a very tight budget so I'm looking just for general information really."

"Well, yes," Robert paused before continuing in what, Charlotte would later describe, as an overenthusiastic yet sympathetic tone. It was apparent that this was the way he spoke to all casual callers – 'another death another payday' had always been the less than charming unofficial motto of Piggott & Co. "You see overall costs are very difficult to predict because there are so many unknowns at this stage. If I can just run through a couple you will see what I mean," pause "there's the coffin; church or crematorium; church and crematorium; car or cars; flowers or no flowers; donations in lieu etc and that's before you come to the bunfight/wake. There's a wide range of prices for coffins for a start. Depends on what sort of wood you are looking..."

"Oh no, I don't want to waste wood." Charlotte broke in rather abruptly. "I was looking at wicker or cardboard for the box, something that will biodegrade over time. See what I am really looking for is a woodland burial..." A sudden cacophony of coughing emanated from the phone followed by snorting and an abject apology for interrupting.

"...I'm sorry Mr..."

"Piggott."

"Yes, Mr Piggott I'm sorry. You OK?"

"Yes, I'm fine now. Please carry on, Mrs Brunt."

"No, sorry, I told you it's not Mrs Brunt, Joe and I never married. We were going to, but Joe's untimely death meant that he was taken too early. Anyway, as I was saying – perhaps I should have said this at the outset - we had, somewhat fortuitously, decided that a woodland burial would be the kindest for the planet."

It was during the halcyon days, Joe and Charlotte had just finished making love in a corn field no more than a couple of hundred yards from the Fox & Pheasant, where they had previously enjoyed a delicious lunch. They were still enjoying the afterglow of a blissful simultaneous orgasm, Charlotte's third of the session, if truth be told, and she was picking stray pieces of grass out of Joe's hair and stroking his face newly bedecked with a sprinkling of beard hair as he had yet to shave after declaring, some days before, he wanted to see what he looked like with a beard. Charlotte was not convinced this would be a good idea – itchy to kiss, smelly if not kept clean and, fundamentally, not a look she liked.

Joe sat up brushing grass and earth from his shirt and then tried to pull his pants and trousers up without breaking the idyllic moment. However his wriggling broke Charlotte's reverie and she stretched and started to pull her dress down which had earlier in the throes of passion, been pushed unceremoniously up to her waist. During the individual and collective upheaval, the two lovers glanced at each other, smiled coyly and then looked away.

Charlotte broke the silence, "You know I love being in the country. Not just like this but the sights and the sounds and smells, getting away from the city always makes me feel more relaxed. I think there are more endorphins in the country. I read that somewhere, I think. Anyway, a short break always makes me more able to cope with everyday life. It's just so good to get away. I'm so glad you brought me closer to the natural world and got me over all my hang ups."

Joe finished adjusting himself and reached over to draw Charlotte towards him. They kissed warmly as they fell back into the cornfield once more.

"I just love being with you wherever we are. Absolutely agree about the endorphins though."

As they both got themselves organised/decent in their cosy alcove beneath a much neglected and overgrown dry stone wall they started a grass fight, pulling out tufts of grass and throwing them at each other whilst giggling the whole time and, ironically, reviewing their environmental credentials.

"I could not believe how little recycling you did when I moved in especially when, in every other sense, you are so much into the green agenda," Charlotte said whilst dodging a massive handful of grass aimed playfully at her head. "I mean you just used to put everything in your purple bin. "Scruff. You just didn't give a toss. Did you?"

"Well, there was only me there, couldn't be bothered sorting stuff out, rinsing takeaway containers, plastic milk bottles etc. Boring. So, I just put it all in the old pedal bin and tipped it into the purple one just before it was going to be emptied. It was my routine..."

"Left to your routine the world would soon have run out of resources though – wouldn't it? Good job you saw sense pretty quickly though, otherwise I would have left you in your midden!"

Having just narrowly avoided another mass of grass Joe adopted a hurt expression as he replied: "Yeah, I admit I missed a trick there but don't forget it just hasn't stopped there – look at all the litter picking we do now and don't forget this, I've even agreed to use my body to nourish a tree after I die. Now come on you've got to admit I'm well into the green agenda now, aren't I?"

"You're doing a lot better Joe Brunt. A lot better. Let's hope the trees can manage for a lot longer before they're getting sustenance from your gradually decaying corpse."

As she remembered this rural frolic, that had sealed their woodland alliance, Charlotte was pleased to relive those moments of casual sexual pleasure in amongst the current maelstrom, particularly as she was having to deal with Mr Piggott the archetypal old-fashioned purveyor of funerals.

"So, are you able to accommodate these requirements, Mr Piggott, or do you think I would be better off looking elsewhere?"

"Well yes, now I think we..." Mr Piggott's voice tailed off. He was clearly out of his comfort zone which had been pretty obvious ever since his very hesitant reaction to Charlotte's initial sortie into the world of alternative undertaking. Piggott & Co would not be asking for a listing, any time soon, in the natural burial section of the endless funeral director's websites that were available on the Internet. However, it soon became clear Mr Piggott was not going to give up without a fight: "Yes now, just let me recap – so you are thinking of a woodland burial? Well, you know I can see where you're coming from in these environmentally sensitive days but they're not without their pitfalls you know. That's not to say it's impossible, but it would be, counterintuitively perhaps, more expensive than the more conventional route. You would have to bear that in mind I think when coming to make your final decision. I'm sure we'd be able to accommodate you, but I think we would need to sit down together and go through all the details and look at some comparisons before I could be happy you were making the right decisions for the interment of your partner. Now I know you must be busy but," at this Mr Piggott adopted a slightly more authoritarian tone, "I wonder if you could spare some time tomorrow to, as it were, bottom this out. I could email you some details and maybe we could have a chat over coffee. You're of course very welcome to come here by all means or I would be happy to call on you. Really whichever is the most convenient for you."

At this the ever more egregious sounding Mr Piggott stuttered to a halt after briefly going into hyperdrive in his attempts to stop Charlotte interposing any possible alternative to his proposed meeting. Charlotte sighed deeply rather more inwardly than outwardly, but nevertheless audibly, as she accepted the inevitability of her acquiescence to Mr Piggott's request.

"Yes, on balance I think we ought to meet tomorrow, so maybe lunchtime?" Charlotte was thinking that would at least give her time to have a decent lie-in before tackling a funeral planning conversation. "Would that be convenient? You can come here, I'm not going to bother to get all dressed up to go to an undertakers, do you still call them that? You've probably got a more 21st century term now? You can see I've had no experience of this sort of thing before. Sorry, come here for oneish if you can. If there are any problems, late running that sort of thing, then I'll let you know so you can adjust your ETA." A rather prolonged silence followed such that

Charlotte somewhat brusquely added: "Mr Piggott are you still there? Is that timing OK for you?"

"Erm, yes sorry Mrs Brunt, no sorry, sorry Charlotte I know you said you are not the deceased's wife. Sorry for that. No, yes, that'll be fine. Looking forward to meeting you."

With telephone numbers and addresses duly recorded, their conversation came to an end, with considerable relief for at least one of the parties. Mr Piggott realised he was going to have to put in a considerable amount of research into natural burials if he was going to seal the deal on Ms Summersby's funeral requirements. Only then would he earn his 15% bonus from his grandfather who was the titular head of the Piggott's funeral empire, such as it was, since both his father and his four sons had all long since decided that funerals were not for them in light of all the digital enterprise solutions that were available for them to utilise their not inconsiderable talents. Turning on his Acer laptop he began Googling in order to find the solution to the dilemma of how to realign the Piggott's business model to encompass what would inevitably involve unavoidably muddy woodland scenarios. He fully appreciated such challenges would have to be seamlessly endured/circumnavigated in order to deliver a funeral experience which would lead to satisfactory commendations on the mortician's equivalent of Trip Advisor such that Piggott and Co could benefit from more profitable, even though possibly rather wet, forays in the future.

Charlotte was feeling reasonably pleased with herself as she finally managed to wrap things up with Mr Funeral Director. As another first experience associated with Joe's death, she felt she had held her own, not been cowed and had made clear her baseline, woodland funeral or bust. For Charlotte, this sense of achievement was a new thing coming from such an unlikely source – she was in control of Joe's farewell and was making sure their shared objective was going to become a reality. Even though she had no better idea regarding prices she really couldn't face a compulsory competitive tendering situation between lots of Robert Piggott soundalikes. Life, as JB had so recently discovered, is too short, so she resolved to get things done rather than get terribly anxious about getting a bit of a cheaper deal. She would just have to use her charms on Mr Piggott in order to get his lowest price.

Next on her list was where to hold the wake. Charlotte had never been to a funeral before so knew nothing about the choices available or how much notice venues required. She thought that would be something she needed advice on so put it on a list of things to discuss with Laura when they next met which she had a feeling wouldn't be too long. As she started to make a list of what you would want from the wake there was a rather tentative knock on the door. It was her local Yodel delivery woman.

"Parcel for The Occupier. Is that you?"

"Yes thanks."

"OK make your mark here love." The Yodel driver proffered a handheld device and indicated where she needed to make her aformentioned mark.

"Thanks for that. Have a nice day!" Charlotte was well aware of the depressing working conditions endured by delivery people. She continued to be amazed at just how cheerful they managed to be in their minimum wage, zero hours bubbles. She wished she had had her purse with her but instead she just mouthed, "Thanks," to the retreating figure who was already near the front gate speeding on to her next parcel drop.

Charlotte closed the door and started weighing the parcel in an attempt to find out what it contained. An oblong box, plain packaging, quite light, unexpected and mysterious.

After slicing through endless lengths of brown parcel tape she reached two very inviting flaps which she pulled open quite forcefully thereby ensuring that the box's contents, two dozen carnations, spilled onto the floor in some considerable disarray. As she scrambled to pick them up without doing any more damage, she discovered a black edged card: In Sympathy – really sorry, speak soon Hxx

Beautiful flowers and a sophisticated card, handwritten in an elegant script. The card was scented with what Charlotte deduced – she had a very fertile imagination – was an expensive perfume perhaps Chanel, Yves St Laurent or Givenchy: these were the names that came immediately to mind. So, an image of H as a refined woman started forming in her febrile mind although she was puzzled as to how she could, in any way, be connected to the Brunt/Summersby relationship. Charlotte clumsily arranged the latest bunch of flowers in one of her least used vases and tried to ignore the chaos as she racked her brains to remember anyone she may have met, or Joe had talked about. H – Helen, Holly, Heidi she could not remember a single H.

Her memory search was brought to an abrupt halt by the sonorous Wagnerian music she had chosen for the landline ringtone. She nervously reached for the handset. Could this be the mysterious and possibly wealthy, H?"

"Hello."

"Charlotte?"

"Speaking."

"It's Hannah. Did you get the flowers?"

"Yes thanks. They're beautiful. Carnations are my favourites."

"Oh, thank goodness. Only I got a text to say they'd arrived. New technology it's marvellous isn't it. When it works."

Charlotte decided not to launch into a rant about the gig economy at this juncture and replied: "Yes, it is. Look I'm sorry...."

"Yes of course that's why I phoned. Look I know you must still be in shock but I wanted to talk to you. Not sure phoning is best. It's difficult...."

"Sorry you said you were Hannah. Should I know you? I'm Charlotte Summersby. Joe's partner. Is that who you wanted to speak to?"

"Yes, yes – sorry. Look lets meet up for a coffee or a prosecco only..."

The thought of a Prosecco fuelled afternoon with someone she did not know did not sound at all attractive to a rather fragile Charlotte. "Look I'm sorry Hannah as you can imagine my Joe only died early hours of this morning and I've got rather a lot on at the moment. Not sure when I can get out."

"Well look I don't want to say too much now, but Joe and I used to be married so it's really important – can I pop round? It won't take long to put you in the picture, but I reckon it would be better face-to-face. Could you make it tomorrow just for half an hour? Honestly won't take any longer.

"Charlotte took a deep breath all the while trying to gather her thoughts. Hannah, the newly revealed ex-wife of her partner, was being very persistent, but it did seem that whatever she had to say was particularly important to her, and Charlotte had to admit finding out more of her backstory might be of passing interest to her as well. Without a trace of enthusiasm in her voice Charlotte replied: "OK let's make it tomorrow. 10.30 if that's alright with you?"

"Yes, that's fine. See you then."

Although meeting up with Hannah meant Charlotte would have to forgo her lie-in it sounded as if it would be worth it. Less than ten minutes after the redoubtable Hannah had, against all the odds, achieved her purpose Wagner was at it again. Charlotte's shaking hand almost conspired to throw the handset onto the floor as she lifted it from its cradle:

"Hello."

"Hi!"

"Hi."

"Is that ...erm...is that Joe Brunt's house? Er...sorry to bother you but...I got this number from..."

"Well yes, no," pause "you see" pause "I was Joe's partner. Well. You see he died last night."

"That's why I'm ringing. I'm George, George Brunt. Joe's brother..."

"Joe's what? Joe's brother? I had no idea he had a brother," pause "You're his brother you say? How can that be? We've been together for two years. He never mentioned you. In fact, as far as I can remember, I have to say my brain is not working very well at the moment, he only ever told me about his mother to be honest." Charlotte paused for breath she was aware she was burbling. Random groups of words were cascading from her mouth as she tried to digest what he had just said.

"Well, to be fair to Joe maybe I'm his little secret. Definitely the only secret brother anyway." George's feeble attempt to make a joke missed the mark so he tried another tack. "Joe and I had said ages ago that you ought to know about me but...what with everything we never got round to it you know how things are – families, always problems.

Charlotte was by turns incensed, intrigued and frustrated. Knee deep in funeral plans, now she had to adapt herself to the fact that Joe, her soulmate, her bedrock had been hiding at least two momentous secrets from her. The lies, the sheer barefaced cheek of it. Yet on balance Joe had been a nice bloke so maybe there was a good reason for keeping George and indeed Hannah hidden from her view – she needed to find out more about him, but this was not, definitely not, the best time to do so.

"Well George, I don't want to be rude," Charlotte was still trying to gather her thoughts and she realised her words were coming out rather slowly almost Dalek-like although she had no wish to exterminate anyone – at least not yet, "but I'm really busy at the moment. I'm sure you'll understand I'm trying to sort out everything – funeral, bank accounts let alone mystery brothers."

George's laughter stopped her in her tracks. "That's why I phoned, I want to help, and I thought it might be useful for me to get involved. I know all the family dynamics and I'm at a bit of a loose end. Between jobs actually. So, I could help out – extra pair of hands. I know he could be a right bugger when he wanted to be. Don't suppose he's sorted out his last divorce yet knowing him..."

"Look George I'm in a bit of a mess, mentally. Joe's death came as a great shock to me. I'm only just getting my head round it and I just need to catch my breath really."

"Well, I phoned to offer to help you. I cannot imagine what you're going through, honestly. I just thought that there must be things I could do to help and as his only close relative I don't want to meet you for the first time on the day of the funeral – that would be crazy. How about we do dinner one night? Be good for you – no meal to cook, get out of the house, nice relaxing evening?"

Charlotte was extremely unsure as to how she should proceed with a rather pushy George Brunt. Dinner for two, or no dinner and leave discovering exactly who George was and how he fitted into the increasingly complex Brunt dynasty until later. Curiosity, what Laura would later refer to as nosiness, was beginning to get the better of her. However, somewhere in her frazzled thought processes a note of caution sounded as she reasoned it might be better to seek some sororal advice before committing herself.

"Oh, George, as I've said things are so chaotic here at present, I going to have to pass on dinner for now. Just let me get my head round things a bit more before we get together. Can you leave your number and I promise I'll get back to you? I really do appreciate you getting in touch even though it has come as quite a bit of a shock, well, on top of everything else, quite a big bloody shock actually."

"OK, fine, Charlotte." George sounded quite relaxed about being rebuffed. "I realise my phone call has come right out of the blue, but I didn't want to waste any time getting in touch. Joe had a real problem dealing with me...I'll leave it there for now. We can meet up whenever you want . Just make sure it's before the funeral!"

"OK. Thanks George. I'll do my best."

So, Joe Brunt, allegedly, had a brother. As if Charlotte had not had enough to deal with in the short time since his death, now she had to come to terms with George being on the scene. Processing the short conversation Charlotte realised that she had not really given George much of a chance to say anything about himself. After all, it wasn't his fault Joe had kept his existence a secret. With of all things an ex-wife and a brother on side she was hopeful that before the funeral she would have got a pretty good picture of the previously unknown life of J Brunt. The last thing she wanted was to find out any more secrets at the funeral/wake which would be emotional enough without having to deal with any more pressure. Charlotte felt she'd been steamrolled for the second time in a matter of a few hours such that she turned her mobile phone off and after locating the socket on the wall disconnected what she still referred to as the landline with a highly satisfactory click.

Peace descended. Turmoil ceased. Tumult desisted but the mess persisted all around her. Time was passing at an increasingly/ominously fast pace as her list of jobs, meetings etc got longer and the time allowed got shorter and shorter. However, it was 5:15pm and the world would have to pause whether it wanted to or not. Alexander Armstrong and his pointless friend Richard beckoned from Joe's 55-inch wall mounted LG TV. Nothing, but nothing was going to get in the way of that.

As Pointless came to an end Charlotte foolishly decided to reconnect with the outside world. Her decision resulted in yet another phone call only minutes later.

"Mrs Brunt?"

"No, it's Charlotte Summersby."

"I mean is this Joe's wife?"

"No, I'm Joe's partner. We never got married, fortunately."

"Sorry, what did you say? Not his wife fortunately, his partner? Don't get this modern lingo. Does your status really matter? As far as I understand it, you're just the latest in Joe's long line of conquests eh! Never quite fulfilled his promise to you, eh, dear." Not waiting for a response, the caller ploughed on. "I was just phoning about, you know, the arrangements, you know for the funeral. You see I want to be involved. I think I ought to be involved. Yes, in fact, I'm certain I should be involved. Married to Joe for longer than I care to remember. I think that makes me entitled, don't you?" Charlotte was flabbergasted. If she could believe her ears this was the second woman within a matter of hours claiming to have been married to Joe, her Joe, the late Mr Brunt. Two wives and one brother – how much more could she take ? "I'm sorry, who is this? You see Joe and I had only been together for two years before he passed away and

I'm taking a while to get up to speed. What with everything! I've had to identify Joe's body earlier on and the phone never stops ringing..." Charlotte stopped short of revealing any other details to her latest unknown caller.

"Sorry love can I just butt in there. You see I can help you there..."

Alarm bells began ringing for Charlotte with the words, 'I can help'. She claimed to have been married to Joe for eight years but Charlotte had no idea whether the relationship with Joe had ended harmoniously or not and, more importantly, she had no idea what she meant by 'help'. Actual help, take over everything help, or something in between. As with the two previous telephone conversations with hitherto unknown relatives Charlotte felt certain a face-to-face meeting would be required, somehow or other, to establish exactly what Mrs Bossy Boots actually wanted.

"...because I know all about Joe, his family, such as they are with the poor health, they've all suffered- but you'll know all about that I expect and his friends. Yes, love, I can help you with all of that."

"Thanks, thanks for that," spluttered Charlotte as she tried to simultaneously process what Mrs Bossy Boots was saying and work out the consequences for her of allowing a previously unknown wife to 'help'. "Look I don't know whether you remember but you never introduced yourself..."

"Sorry my name is..."

"No, no, not yet, I've not finished yet. Sorry, but this really isn't a good time. You have absolutely no idea what I'm going through here. No idea." Charlotte paused long enough to catch a breath but not long enough to let BB start off again. "Look you said you were married to Joe for eight years. You're the second person that's been in contact today saying they used to be married to Joe. Don't get me wrong, I never thought he was a virgin but managing to fit all this stuff in when he was only 42..."

Charlotte stopped as she could hear Mrs Bossy Boots was apparently choking and gasping for breath at the other end of the phone. "...You OK? Sounds as if you're struggling to breathe. Is there something the matter?"

For a few seconds all Charlotte could hear were rather muffled sounds of choking, nose blowing and gasping. A loud clunk followed by a silence was broken by Mrs Bossy Boots whose voice seemed to have gone several octaves higher than earlier in the conversation, but was still sounding as if she might be the victim of an attempted strangulation.

"What did you say? Did I hear right? 42. That dirty old blackguard 62 if he was a day. I'm sorry to break the news to you deary. 42. I've heard a few of Joe's stories but that must be the best yet if you actually believed him. Oh, my Lords what a cheater." Gradually as Mrs Bossy Boots was speaking her voice became less high-pitched, more controlled and more modulated.

Charlotte was absolutely stunned. Her world had been turned upside down, again. She was beginning to wonder just how many more of Joe's secrets she was going to uncover before she was able to lay him to rest. Having already discovered that the real Joe was nothing like the Joe she thought she had known the sooner he was safely installed in his woodland burial ground, ash tree planted firmly to benefit from his putrefying body in its wicker casket, the better. Then perhaps she would be able to expunge all the memories she had of the times spent with someone she could only now consider as a complete charlatan.

"Look Mrs/Miss..."

"OK. So, Joe, you tell me, was 62 – nearly pensionable and I thought he was in the prime of his life. We had so many plans when work permitted to travel perhaps, buy a bigger house – in the country..."

"Look love we really do need to meet. I can help you I'm absolutely sure. Clearly you really didn't know Joe and I think you deserve to find out more about him. I'll keep it short for now just suffice to say that he was a born liar, opportunist, womaniser and much worse a fantasist especially where money was concerned. He had so many moneymaking schemes that were going to make his fortune. Eight years full of hope which ultimately put me in a rehab ward after I had a breakdown because my world fell apart. Anyway, I've said enough for now. Just let's fix a date so I can give you some more background about Josiah Thomas Brunt and his many peccadilloes!"

After Charlotte put down the phone having made arrangements for, what purported to be, a highly revelatory meeting with her new besty Alice, she rocked backwards and forwards in her chair for a few moments before she began to sob her heart out with a series of prolonged gasps for good measure as she tried to control her grief. Charlotte had always managed on an 'it is what it is basis' but now that had led to her being suddenly enmeshed in commitments to a man who died so unexpectedly, that she knew none of the passwords to his online accounts or even, heaven forbid, the address of his employer. As she sobbed she vowed never to let anything like this happen again. She vowed to herself that she would in future be in control of her destiny, if at all possible.

Chapter 3 : Conversations

Charlotte woke up with a start, looked at her watch, 6:45am, and prepared to resume her night's sleep. Didn't really need to wake up until at least 8am, she thought. However, as she closed her eyes again a horrible realisation began to surface in the deep recesses of her mind – it was Tuesday and Tuesday was the day she had foolishly agreed to three meetings, no, including one with the egregious Mr Funeral Director, it was actually four! As these thoughts began to race around her brain Charlotte realised that this was no time to sleep. Much better to use the available time to prepare herself: firstly for coffee with Hannah, who in a previous telephone conversation had claimed to be married to Joe at some stage; Alice, which thankfully was going to mean a trip out away from phones, memories and mess; the aforementioned Mr Piggott; and then, the cherry on the cake, George Brunt who from his phone manner could be the most useful person to contact her so far although, given his more distant relationship with Joe, she was rather unclear as to whether he was going to be very helpful in unlocking much of the back story of her late partner.

Unable to face a massive clear up operation in the sitting room Charlotte decided to set herself up in the little used dining room in Joe's rather spacious semi-detached home. She felt it was best to put on a show of pained forbearance rather than absolute disorientation in order to make the most of her upcoming conversations. The last thing she wanted was to spend her time sobbing her heart out to people she had never previously met and may not want to meet again. As she finished her breakfast she paused to wonder just why she hadn't got Laura, irreplaceable Laura, involved to offer support initially but also for after the event corroboration as they tried to piece together what knowledge they had gleaned. One thing she was aware of was that, at this late stage, Laura would have a full day planned around experiences for her wealthy clients or relaxing at a health club which she was 'road testing'.

"Hello Charlotte? Charlotte? It's Hannah, we spoke on the phone."
"Yes, that's right, good to meet you."

Something in Charlotte's manner or appearance must have alarmed Hannah as she stepped back from the doorstep. "Is it still OK to meet up? I should've checked. We could always do this another day."

Now she tells me, Charlotte thought, having more or less forced herself on me over the phone. Now she wants to postpone the whole thing. Realising that in contrast to an immaculately coiffured Hannah she had barely dragged a comb through her hair for days and forgotten her make up such that she probably looked a complete mess. Charlotte rushed to reassure her visibly shocked visitor, "No, no it's quite OK. Sorry not felt like applying the warpaint since ... but no, I'm fine. Really interested to know what you have to tell me." Charlotte added the last sentence in order to encourage Hannah to overcome her obvious initial reticence caused, she surmised, by her dishevelment and to continue the meeting as scheduled.

"Oh, OK then, sorry but I really don't want to burden you. I've no idea what it must be like to be in your position so seeing you...not looking...well, I just thought perhaps I wasn't being very considerate."

"No, no come on in Hannah." Charlotte ushered Hannah into the house in the direction of the dining room. "Let me take your coat. Tea, coffee or whatever? I've got fruit juice – orange or apple – or just plain water? Just what you want really."

Hannah slipped off her coat to reveal her approach to make up exemplified her whole approach to her wardrobe. She was wearing, a rather too short for her age, Charlotte thought, figure hugging dress which probably revealed rather too much of her cleavage for a death-related chat over a morning coffee. Actually, Charlotte reflected, she looked very good for her age and made her casual T shirt and leggings outfit look quite out of place.

"I'll have a coffee thanks Charlotte. If it's not too much trouble?"

"No trouble at all. I'll make proper, so it'll take a few minutes. OK?" Charlotte backed out of the door as if she was trying to conceal a dress malfunction, pleased that she had bought herself some time to rush upstairs while the coffee was bubbling to "fix" her make up and present a rather more composed look to Hannah on her return.

"Here we are. I've brought a few biscuits as well. Do you take sugar?"

"You needn't have bothered you know."

"It's OK it's only a few chocolate hobnobs and custard creams."

"No, I mean your make-up. I know, if you're not in the mood, just how difficult it is to be motivated. So, thanks for that."

Charlotte was less than thrilled by Ms Patronising's opening remarks. She had wasted precious time to try and impress her only to receive a grade A put down. An icy chill descended on the room already quite cold enough in the complete absence of any heating. Charlotte proceeded to spend the next five minutes trying to encourage a recalcitrant gas fire into action all the while apologising to Hannah for not having made sure the room was warm prior to her arrival.

Having eventually managed to get the fire going Charlotte slumped in her seat and took a sip of her unpleasantly tepid coffee.

"So, Hannah," she began and failed to get any further.

"Yes, well I heard about Joe's passing and I wanted to find out how he died, after all, we were married for eight years."

Charlotte regretted trying to swallow a mouthful of coffee at exactly the same time as Hannah uttered those unforgettable words. Coughing uncontrollably, she distributed the contents of her mouth over the neatly displayed biscuits on the plate between them.

"What did you say?" she spluttered.

"Eight years love. Eight bloody years, although God only knows how I managed. It was OK for a while – he'd walk out, I'd walk out – and then we separated, I never managed to get the divorce sorted out. There was still something there you see even after all the affairs, drunken molestations, weekends away with I knew not whom. It was proper edge of the seat stuff with Joe."

"Look, Hannah, you see up until yesterday I had no idea Joe had been married – I thought he was 42 not 62 and that he'd never been married. Call me naïve but we'd only been together for two years, we had a pretty free and easy relationship – suited us both really – no great commitment..."

"Well at least you got that figured out. I trusted him for years, forgave him for years. I mean when he was lovely, don't get me wrong, charm the hind legs off a donkey he could, but when the light finally dawned, I realised what a fool I'd been. Through it all he was a very private person – never talked about himself except in riddles although he could be the life and soul of the party when he wanted to be."

"OK who's ready for a dance?"

Charlotte, Joe, Laura, Les and a few others had gathered at the Sun Inn for their Disco Daze night. It was a Friday, and the bar was packed with couples out enjoying the end of the working week alcohol fix. As Sweet Dreams Are Made Of This started pounding out from the speakers, positioned rather uncomfortably near Charlotte's right ear, Joe had leapt up and proceeded to grab Laura by the hand and escort her to the small sticky square of carpet which served as the dancefloor. They were soon gyrating in response rather than in time with the music leaving the rest of the group fiddling with their drinks and looking at their phones.

Joe always made a beeline for Laura on nights out. Although she was Charlotte's best friend and confidante, she liked Joe and thoroughly enjoyed his company. A little too thoroughly for Charlotte. Not to be outdone, on this occasion at least, Charlotte smiled at Les and jerked her head towards the dancefloor.

"OK then," he shouted following her across the room.

Les couldn't dance, he had quite a lot of problems walking, so Charlotte found his shambolic dancing rather attractive after the John Travolta promenading of Joe. Charlotte's dancing style was discreet and amounted to little more than shifting her weight from one foot to another at a speed that, generally speaking, reflected that of the music. As Les and Charlotte jigged Laura was being thrown around the tiny space a little over enthusiastically by Joe.

Yes, reflected Charlotte – quite the party animal – especially if other women were involved.

"All my girlfriends thought he was great. Always polite to them; attentive to them; and complimentary to them. He always seemed so charming, but what I learnt over the years was the number of times he went just that little bit too far – a quick drunken smooch, a misplaced hand here or there. Apparently, they had all endured his overness – over attentive, over complimentary et cetera. It was a real shock when I found out I can tell you."

Charlotte was lost in thought for a couple minutes as she recalled how a couple of women she had been friendly with had suddenly dropped her and wanted nothing more to do with dinner dates or party invites. Could that have been anything to do with Joe's overness? Even Laura who always took Joe in good part had mentioned, without wanting to rock the boat or be disloyal, that Joe had been, a bit too flirty, is what she had called it. She always blamed the drink, and, in any event, it was a bit of excitement for her in the absence of a long-term partner.

"Sorry," Charlotte broke the awkward silence. "What you said explains a lot to me. I've lost a couple of friends over the years – just wondering if that was due to Joe's unwanted attentions – would make a lot of sense."

"Yeah I can see. I mean really I didn't want to meet up just to moan about how much hard work Joe was. What I wanted to deal with, and that's why I thought it would be better in person, was what really finished things for me was the thousands and thousands of pounds he owed on credit cards. What I wanted to check, and remember this was 5/6 years ago now, is whether he had dealt with all that stuff, whether you need to be prepared to sort the mess out. He used to juggle credit cards – you know, changing from one to another when the interest free period ended – but he couldn't help adding to the debt – gambling, horses that was the root of the problem."

"... You won't be surprised..." Charlotte was struggling to put together a coherent sentence "... in view of what we said before I had no idea. We lived reasonably comfortably – I contributed very little and Joe was always generous especially when he had been away on a business trip or football..."

"Business trips? Where did he go? Can't imagine why he would be going on business trips. When we split up, he was working as an archivist."

"What? What did you say? An archivist? What the hell do you mean?"

"As far as I know he was a senior manager in an international logistics firm. Are you going to tell me...things might have changed since you knew him."

"Well, they might but I think he's been putting one over you. He's proper been leading a double life. Well at least you can now look for evidence – I mean you look very organised here. Have you started looking through his paperwork yet?"

Charlotte started laughing as she stood up and asked Hannah to follow her as she set off in the direction of Joe's study.

"This," she waved her arm airily in front of her, "is what I was trying to keep from you. This, as far as I can tell, is all of Joe's stuff."

Hannah started a forensic examination of her hands only looking up to say: "Christ all fucking mighty, you really have been left in the shit."

A 'quick chat' had become a full-on three-hour psychotherapy session by the time Charlotte was finally able to usher Hannah out of the front door not wanting her 9.30am appointment to overlap with her 1.00pm. She needed a clear head to deal with Mr Piggott in order to make sure she: a) kept to a very tight budget; b) got the funeral she and Joe decided upon during their extremely fortuitous conversation; and c) she adhered to her tight schedule because, as she relaxed with a cup of tea, stretching into the evening she had two further meetings, two further odysseys into the unknown before she could draw down the curtain on the day.

As she sat musing, she remembered that her carefully planned idea of making detailed notes had come to nothing, as she realised she was in fact sitting on the very notebook that she should have been writing in.

A very firm rat a tat a tat followed by the cacophony of noise which indicated the Brunt's wireless doorbell had been activated found Charlotte fast asleep, teacup in hand and a large damp patch expanding across her lap. A second rather more desperate attempt to gain attention woke Charlotte at last. Immediately aware of her parlous state – her legs were strangely wet – she leapt into action which served only to jettison the cup which immediately collided with a bookcase and being bone china shattered into a million pieces. As a further pounding noise echoed from the hallway she glanced at her watch, 1:20pm, so at least Mr Piggott would have to start by apologising for his late arrival before any other matters could be discussed which, she felt, put her in the driving seat.

In her desperate attempt to get to the door quickly and save Mr Piggott the need to pummel the door further with his bare hands, Charlotte tripped over a hole in the carpet she had been meaning to attend to for longer than she could remember. Hauling herself up she lunged for the front door. She seized the handle and flung it open so forcefully that it ricocheted off the wall, leaving a large dent in the plaster, and straight into a rather startled Mr Piggott who was knocked off his feet by the impact.

Charlotte started laughing hysterically – maybe it was a result of the tension building up in the past few days, pent-up emotion, coursing through her veins and exploding in a sudden crescendo. In fact, she laughed so much that she fell over again, this time knocking her head on an inconveniently placed table thereby rendering herself unconscious. As Mr Piggott retrieved himself from his horizontal position, he gingerly approached the front door only to catch sight of the prone body of Charlotte in a maelstrom of plaster dust and broken table. Ascertaining that she had now regained consciousness he pulled her to her feet.

After a very pregnant pause Mr Piggott began dusting himself down and, ever the professional, proffered his hand: "Mrs Brunt. Oh no, sorry, I've done it again, sorry it's Charlotte isn't it, sorry. Well, are you OK?" Hardly waiting for a response Mr Piggott continued, "Look I must apologise for being late before we start. My last visit overran the lady was..."

"Yes, very well, never mind that," Charlotte was not in a good mood, she was tired, wet, in quite a lot of pain and completely unprepared. "I think you'd better go in there," indicating the dining room, "while I just go and sort myself out a bit. Is that OK?"

"Of course, Charlotte you take as long as you need. I can just get my paperwork sorted out."

It was only then that Charlotte realised that a briefcase malfunction must have occurred in the front garden after Mr Piggott had been attacked by the Brunt mahogany-panelled front door. Pieces of paper interspersed with grass and leaves were overflowing from the top of Mr Piggott's bag, papers which had obviously been very hastily stuffed back after a brief spell of freedom amongst the weeds and leaves which usually occupied this far from hallowed space.

"OK great only take a few minutes and then I need to find my notes before we start. Do you want a brew? Tea or coffee?"

"Tea, three sugars please."

"OK, just give me a minute."

Robert Piggott had been waiting patiently - very patiently for a man who just suffered a pole axing as a result of an unyielding door flying into his face; very patiently for a man who had a further three potential funeral customers to see before he could return to the welcoming arms of Mrs Piggott and a Tuesday night regular: cheese and onion pie, chips and peas; very very very patiently for someone who, according to his watch, had been waiting 35 minutes for a cup of tea.

At last, the door opened and a newly attired Charlotte entered: "Here we are, tea, not sure how many sugars you said so I brought the bowl, biscuits and I've got some cake if you want me to bring it through?"

"Thank you, Charlotte. No, I'll be fine with biscuits. Really need a cup of tea though. OK Charlotte, I think we need to get on with things if you are feeling OK. Do you want to start and tell me what you want from your dignified farewell to Joe so I know best how we can ensure we meet your every need."

Charlotte bristled at the idea of a dignified farewell. From what she'd already heard from Hannah at her 9.30am briefing the Joe she was going to bury was not the man she thought she knew. She was dreading meeting up with Alice and George later on because she could hardly imagine that they would be bearers of anything other than more bad news. She had even begun to think about keeping the whole thing very simple and, using knowledge gained from watching far too many TV detective dramas, wrap the body up in a weighted tarpaulin and put Joe in the boot of her car and tip him in the nearest bit of deep water hoping that nature would do the rest.

"Well Mr Piggott, Robert?"

"Yes, that's fine. No need to stand on ceremony..."

"Well Robert what we had decided, when Joe and I spoke about this a few months ago was to keep it simple. Woodland burial, wicker casket, no flowers, close family and friends, humanist celebrant to head things up and a couple of eulogies, to be fair not sure who will be doing those, we even discussed the music but at the moment I can't find the list in amongst all the stuff I'm sorting through. Anyway, we'll need somewhere indoors just in case it starts pissing down, which would be just my luck. Can't help thinking Joe is enjoying putting me through all this though. Definitely don't feel as warmly about him as I did."

"Sorry to hear that Charlotte. Why do you feel like that?" Robert had moved away from his practical matter of fact approach to the obsequious manner he had used during their initial phone conversation. Charlotte noted the shift, resented him prying into her affairs but in the absence of anyone else she decided to burden Robert with what she had learnt so far about the 'real' Joe Brunt.

After Charlotte had finished her monologue Robert offered some words of sympathy that sounded very much like they came from one of his many pre-owned scripts before he returned to the real topic in hand: how much money could he realistically charge Charlotte for a 'simple' funeral.

"Yes, well as far as I can see, at the moment, I think you've covered most things although I have to say it might be a bit tricky to find a woodland burial site that's not quite a drive away. Anyway, how about cars? Do you know how many you'll want? Have you thought about pallbearers – do you want relatives or friends, or we can provide that service. You've said no flowers what about donations in lieu? Have you given any thought to a charity that might be appropriate? These are all things we need to consider moving forward." Surprisingly, Robert was being economical with the truth here, very economical, as he knew, from his research that there were quite a few woodland burial sites to choose from within 10 miles. When he had Googled 'woodland burial sites' Robert had been absolutely amazed to find any possibilities – being truthful before Charlotte mentioned it, he had absolutely no idea what a woodland funeral was. He had never been asked to facilitate one in fact the very concept of a natural burial went against the grain of the unofficial Piggott motto: 'death makes money, charge them what they can afford'. The dead don't count! This had been their byword for many years. The Piggott's didn't really like getting involved in what they saw as the lower end of the business – natural or simple were not their favourite words: they preferred elaborate and lavish. "I've brought a couple of brochures along which I printed off from the Internet. As long as you know roughly what you want, we can sort everything else out. It's looking like a ballpark figure around £8K although that's going to go up if you decide to go for any embellishments."

In the mood Charlotte was in embellishments were the very last thing on her mind. What she did want to sort out, though, was the list of music if she could find it, but that would have to wait.

"OK well, I'll look at the brochures then. Only really want two cars, everyone else can follow on as far as I'm concerned. Don't want a lot of palaver. I've not been to many funerals, but have you got one of those trolleys you could put the casket on? Save all that awkwardness and shuffling about plus he was quite a heavy bloke. Hate to see anyone struggling. Was there anything else you need to know now?"

"Donations, that was the only other thing and I've just remembered, do you want us to produce an Order of Service? We'll need a good quality photo for that. You won't want a blurry image will you, and do you want a photo to rest against the casket? Most people do that these days, I must say."

"No problem yeah I'll sort out the content and find a good photo. That sounds good. Is there anything else?" Charlotte was conscious that the time was fast approaching for her meeting with Alice in town. Given Robert's lateness, the front door altercation, her need to retreat from the field of combat to change her clothes and the pressing need to bring Robert up to date on some aspects of the newly discovered truths about Joe Brunt, time had literally flown by necessitating a quick change of gear.

For Robert almost clinching a deal made the time spent with Charlotte well worthwhile even though his carefully ordered afternoon had been thoroughly wrecked as a result. 'A funeral in hand was always worth two as yet unquantified possibilities,' was another of his favourite sayings at any gathering of funeral directors. There was always tomorrow, a discount no more than 5% as a way of apology, and large dollops of his graveside manner to clinch a sale!

For Charlotte Tuesday had, so far, hardly been the best of days. She was at a loss to recall just why she had arranged to meet up with quite so many people on one day. Especially so soon after her partner had died, unexpectedly, and she feeling totally shitty trying to come to terms with everything. Even when she was at work, she liked to limit her public-facing contacts to no more than two a day, before and after lunch, and with an ample sufficiency of watercooler breaks in between. Even without the traumatic circumstances surrounding her meeting with Robert her three-hour session with Hannah would have been enough to send her scampering to a darkened room in an attempt to avoid the onset of on earth shattering migraine. As she tried to reassemble the unfortunate hall table from the scattered fragments she shuddered with embarrassment and began to realise just how professional Robert had been managing to continue the meeting in spite of everything that had happened. Just as she remembered the look on his face as he lay poleaxed on the garden path the phone rang. Fearing the worst, she picked it up.

"Hello."

"Hi gorgeous. How are you?"

"Oh Laura, thank goodness it's you!"

"What d'you mean?"

"Lousy day so far. This funeral business is really becoming a pain. It's taken over my life."

"Thought you were doing OK lovely when we last spoke."

"So did I, but that was before Joe's past started catching up with him..."

"What d'you mean? Catching up with him..."

"We...how long have you got? Actually, I've not got long myself, I'm meeting Joe's first wife..."

"Meeting Joe's what?"

"His first wife."

"I didn't know he'd been married."

"Nor did I and that's the point. I've already spent three hours this morning getting acquainted with his second wife, would you believe?"

"Let me get this straight, nice Joe, life and soul of the party Joe," who couldn't always be relied upon to control himself. "Thoroughly besotted with you Joe." Laura thought this was the time to lay it on thick, Charlotte was obviously under a lot of pressure. No time for a post-mortem!

News to me thought Charlotte. Have to pursue that idea another time.

"All I ever heard about was Charlotte this and Charlotte that," even when he wasn't controlling himself too well. "Dark horse so he'd been married before had he?"

"Yes and not only that, the bastard was 62. Can you believe that?"

By the time Charlotte got to the doorway of Daphne's tearooms she was not only very late, but she was flustered and in need of some quiet convivial conversation. Looking through the window she could see marooned in amongst a dozen or so empty tables the very epitome of someone who the Joe she thought she knew would never have had anything to do with even if she had been the last woman in the world. She looked rather plump, fussily dressed with a swathe of scarves draped around her capacious neck and her hair cut in a very severe bob. Her Joe had always, always, loved her long blonde hair. He was always paying her hair-related compliments. Alice, or at least the woman most likely to be Alice, given that there was no one else in the tearooms and she was over three quarters of an hour late, looked like she had had a bob since the time before last when they were all the rage. Before she had spoken a word, Alice had a mountain to climb to establish a good relationship with Charlotte.

Pushing the door open and fearing the worst Charlotte was greeted somewhat over enthusiastically by the sole occupant: "Charlotte, Charlotte over here – it is Charlotte isn't it?"

"Sorry I'm late Alice. I've had quite a day so far, to say the least."

"Well then you make yourself comfortable. I've waited for you to arrive before ordering anything. They're very good here. Now do you want afternoon tea or just a drink? I am easy either way."

"You know an afternoon tea would be really nice. I didn't so much skip lunch as completely forget what time it was. Usually very set in my ways but today..."

"OK I'll get a waitress to come over so we can get things started."

Mrs Bossy Boots from yesterday had now become much more like a best friend. She clearly recognised Charlotte's fragile state of mind and was organising things without being overbearing about it. Maybe thought Charlotte, Alice, notwithstanding first impressions and her bossy nature yesterday, could be just the person Charlotte needed to keep her head on the straight and narrow. She started to relax and reappraise her afternoon tea companion – maybe her hair was OK, it didn't look quite so severe as at first glance; maybe she wasn't as plump as she had first thought, something to do with the light in the corner had made her look rounder than she actually was; and the scarves were actually really nice close-up, the sort she might have bought herself. After a brief silence following an ambitious arm-waving, cooing, smiling display from Alice, who looked for all the world as if she was looking for a mating partner rather than a waitress, a young lady wearing an inappropriately short skirt, Charlotte just could not help noticing this, worn over a pair of thick dark tights arrived at the table tablet at the ready to take their order: "Are you alright there?"

"Well Charlotte," said Alice in a very inclusive voice, "I think we agreed...."

Alice was looking at Charlotte as she spoke, encouraging her involvement.

"....to have afternoon tea for two. That's right isn't it?"

Charlotte nodded enthusiastically.

"With tea or coffee, ladies," interjected the waitress whose name badge identified her as Samantha.

"Tea for me."

"And for me, thank you."

"OK I'll bring those right over for you. The food will be 10 to 15 minutes if that's OK."

As soon as Samantha had retreated to the kitchen Alice moved her chair close to the table and leant forward before, she spoke:

"Now about Joe." In an instant Alice's tone of voice had changed. No more inclusivity here, it sounded as if she was on a mission – revenge thought Charlotte. "When I phoned you, I think I opened your eyes a bit. I sensed a bit of rose-tinted spectacles regarding Josiah but now he's gone, thank goodness, I don't have to stay quiet any longer."

"Well, yes, your call shocked me a bit. Felt a bit of a fool for having been taken in to be honest. I mean Joe was always a bit larger than life so maybe I shouldn't have been so surprised. It's just that we were..."

"Happy, yes I know, that's the way he worked. He just seemed to float through life never took anything seriously..."

"That's true. Whenever I tried to sort something out with him...he would never argue. Just charm and bribes."

Charlotte remembered the charm, but the bribes....?

"Look Joe, this is taking things too far. You told me that you were going on a stag do with a workmate. OK that's fine but then I saw him, Ronnie I think you said his name was, in Waitrose doing some shopping. I don't get how he can be in Magaluf and Waitrose at one and the same time. That does not make any kind of sense to me."

"Look babes, you've no need to get so irate, must have got our wires crossed. It was Donnie's do – don't think you've ever met him, works in Swindon but I've known him for a few years. Think he asked me to make up the numbers to be honest. There were only 10 there. I just went to keep in his good books – there might be a promotion coming up and he could be one of the key players going forwards."

Donnie not Ronnie – simple slip of the tongue – and Charlotte had swallowed the story without question. She seemed to remember during his explanation Joe started massaging her shoulders gently but powerfully only moving onto her breasts when he could feel her responding to the long slow strokes of his muscular hands. After that things were a bit blurred, but she was fairly certain what had the potential to be a full-scale row had ended up in passionate lovemaking somewhere between the first and second landings of their newly installed Neville Johnson staircase.

In any event Charlotte had evidently been satisfied, if not so much by the explanation as the tender massage and the ensuing sex, such that the Magaluf affair was not so much of an issue when she awoke from her snooze nuzzled into Joe's chest. An excellent Chinese had finally banished any possibility of a rift between them.

Charlotte was convinced that that wasn't the only time he had used such blandishments to deflect any criticism or mistrust either in her relationship with him or indeed in his relationships with others.

"We were married for six years and during that time we lived mainly on my wages. He was always working on something that was going to make a fortune – he designed some early computer games, tried to get funding for all sorts of wonderful gizmos but they never came to anything. He was always tapping me up for money to make a prototype or visit another computer nerd who he thought would be able to help. Turned out most of the stories were just flannel and cover for dalliances with very attractive young ladies – there was some truth – just enough to string me along – distract me, keep me off the scent. You know what I mean. When I found out about the extent of his unfaithfulness – to be honest I always suspected something was up, sex was always his way round something, not for its own sake – anyway when I found out what was going on I just cracked. I must have told you I went into rehab. I'd really hit the drink big style and needed a lot of help to get myself sorted out. I found a load of telephone numbers in a notebook he kept hidden in his sock drawer. He also had loads of letters from the women who he met up with. I was wrecked when I found out. All the help and support I'd given him only to discover he was nothing more nor less than a charlatan."

"It was always a rollercoaster with Joe though. He'd be off on one of his trips which suited me and gave me space – then he'd be full on for 2 to 3 weeks and then be off again. Other women being on the scene had crossed my mind fleetingly but never that he'd been married not once but twice! I really can't understand how he managed to keep that from me. I thought I was cuter than that. OK, so here's the thing – why? Why did he need access to so many women – two wives, maybe more casual flirtations and then me. Why was he so needy, what pleasure did he get from all those relationships?"

"Well, there you have it – I gave up worrying about this ages ago. Probably around when I heard he'd got married again. We fought and fought over the terms of the divorce, over money, over the car, over everything. Nothing was easy with Joe. He had to have things his way. My way or the highway he kept on saying in conciliation meetings and the like. Wore me down in the end."

After several cups of tea and numerous monologues from Alice the more memorable and relevant to Charlotte concerning: Joe's inveterate untidiness; and his inability: to cook, dress fashionably, or keep to time. For Charlotte, the most poignant part of the conversation concerned Joe not wanting to have children. After all she and Joe had had numerous conversations about children, the pros and the cons, all to no avail as he would not be shifted although, through Charlotte's rose-tinted spectacles, she felt he had the makings of a great dad. She bade Alice farewell, turning down her offer of help in getting the funeral over the line, just in time for her to grab a taxi for the final appointment of the day.

The bar of the Red Lion was unhelpfully empty for 5pm and Charlotte felt very conspicuous sitting endlessly checking her phone whilst sipping her raspberry gin and slimline tonic. Fixing a time and place to meet George had been awkward but completely necessary bearing in mind his newly established status as brother of the deceased. In fact, reflecting on her two earlier uncomfortable conversations, for Charlotte at least, being uncomfortable had seamlessly become the new normal! Hearing so much new information about Joe in one day was proving very difficult for Charlotte to process. Their apparently open and honest relationship, albeit with some minor issues, had been totally ruined by what Hannah and Alice had told her earlier. No secrets, they had agreed when Charlotte had confessed that she had, in her youth, managed to string along quite a number of young men simultaneously.

"So rough guess, how many partners have you had? Round figures like. I'm not going to ask you to name them all." Joe had challenged her.
They had been in the pub for a couple of hours – the beer and gin had been flowing and Joe was in cheeky mode which over the time they had been together Charlotte had got quite used to. She had had to do a striptease in the bedroom; have sex in unusual places; dress up, dress down; BDSM sessions – all when Joe was feeling 'cheeky' which was usually when he was under the influence.
"Bit of a challenge that y'know. What d'you mean by partners? People I've been out with, sexual partners – there's not been so many of them – or what. You need to be more precise."

"Precise is it now. All I want to know is how many guys you've been out with on a couple of dates. Don't want a complete breakdown by age, religious inclinations etc."

"Well, it's probably 25," Charlotte laughed sheepishly. "In my 20's I must have been doing something right because I seemed to be out on a date with a different lad several nights a week – none of them were serious it was the 00's after all. I was just out for a good time and where I worked and socially, I seemed to keep striking it lucky. My hedonistic phase that's what I call it."

"Hedonistic eh," Joe mocked. "So, what did this hedonism consist of – free lunches, drinks, knee tremblers. Sounds all rather debauched!"

"No, come on Joe, you said you didn't want chapter and verse on all of this. I'm just giving you an insight on how things used to be for me. Young, blonde, footloose and fancy free. It was a whirlwind. Nothing like that now."

Subsequently Joe had often referred to this phase in Charlotte's life and tried to get what he referred to as the gory details of some of her relationships. Sitting waiting for the brother Joe had never talked about Charlotte became acutely aware that she had never once managed to get any information on any of Joe's fidelities let alone his infidelities! He had always managed to avoid making any contributions to this discussion by plying Charlotte either with more drinks or kisses so that the subject of the conversation could be changed almost without her noticing. She kicked herself virtually for being so easily distracted!

In George's continued absence Charlotte tried to focus on what she had learned earlier and what aspect she specifically wanted to pursue. Joe's age was a key issue. She had had it confirmed that he was in fact 62 years old even though he only actually looked 45ish but what wasn't clear was when his subterfuge started. Why was abundantly clear – how was another matter. The other issue was work. Although Charlotte had never seen any evidence of his income or savings, money had never been an issue and their lifestyle was in keeping with his role as a senior manager in an international logistics company. A role that involved him spending regular periods of time away from home.

Charlotte looked anxiously at the pub clock only to realise that George was actually 40 minutes late. She was just about to finish the last of her drink and abandon the meeting when the street door flew open and a very flustered and sweaty ginger haired, bespectacled man virtually fell into the pub and started staring wildly around the room. He matched the brief description that he had volunteered on the phone, so Charlotte pushed her chair back and stood up.

"George! Over here!" She called out. "It's Charlotte!"

George's arrival and demeanour did not immediately appeal to Charlotte, however she was hoping that he would be able to shed some light on the situation from his point of view which meant she was not going to be deterred by first impressions.

"Oh hello, hello. I'm sorry I'm late. Trains. Wrong pub. Sorry, sorry," George spluttered as he approached Charlotte's table brandishing a number of plastic bags in addition to a man bag slung casually over his left shoulder. "Look. Hi. Charlotte? Great. Look let me get rid of this clutter. After making you wait for so long, I must owe you a drink. Now you sit down, and I'll sort it out. Please, what can I get you?"

"Gin and slimline tonic please – make it a rhubarb one."

"Oh, you go for the fruity ones. Not a gin man myself prefer real ale - single or a double my treat, to apologise."

"OK I'll go for a double then. Thank you."

After a flurry of activity George retreated to the bar leaving the table and the surrounding area strewn with bags: H & M, M & S, Home Bargains and Aldi. A very inclusive mix, mused Charlotte, as she prepared herself for a further wave of words from George who seemed much given to talking in staccato sentences. She felt that rather like an over-active clockwork toy she would only need to feed in a few simple questions before George would be sufficiently wound up to keep talking for the rest of the evening.

George even managed to make the task of buying two drinks into as much of a Herculean effort as delivering his purchases to the table, not only involving his utmost concentration but also that of a young lady who foolishly got sufficiently involved at the bar to be carrying over a random variety of snacks as well as a further drink which George had apparently bought.

With the departure of Sarah back to her bar stool George sat down and raised his glass: "Cheers. Good to see you. Thought I'd get some nibbles. Not sure what sort you like but I've tried to cover all bases: crisps – Salt and vinegar and cheese and onion; nuts oh God I hope you're not allergic, scratchings and I got a lemonade..."

"Well done George, that's a proper feast. No, you're OK I'm good with nuts in fact I like all of these." Charlotte waved a hand towards the snack mountain while trying not to emulate her drinking companion in talking so fast that all his words seemed to be in some strange way combined. "Yes, I was beginning to wonder whether you were going to turn up. You know, once you got over 30 minutes."

"Yes, I'm sorry about that, seems that there must be two Red Lions round here and I chose the wrong one!" After a few sips of his beer George seemed to have managed to control his breathing and the previous torrent of words had slowed almost to a trickle. "Y'see I'm not very familiar with this area at all. Anyway, it's really good to see you. How are you?"

"Well, I'm a bit stressed if I'm honest. This whole business, you know, Joe dying so suddenly, me having to arrange his funeral because, as far as I knew, there was no other family and now you appearing from nowhere..."

"This is a really tricky situation because I don't suppose I've had any contact with Joe for 4/5 years now. I don't do Facebook, Twitter and that sort of stuff and we'd not actually met up for that period of time. I only found out because John one of his cricket buddies, messaged me and suggested I get in touch. Last time I met Joe he was married to Hannah."

"Yes, I know about Hannah now, in fact I met her earlier on today. Sounds like she had a pretty rough deal with Joe," Charlotte wanted to try and keep some control of the conversation as George seemed to be rather too concerned with his own story rather than filling in some of the blanks for her. After all she only had limited time to spare. "It's been rather a busy day actually because I met Alice as well, I assume you know about her?" George nodded, "So leaving the bevy of ex-wives aside can I pin you down because what I'm interested in, to start off with, is why did you have so little contact with Joe, and any info really about his Mum and Dad because Hannah didn't seem to know if they were around and whether there were any other siblings around either."

"No, no Mum and Dad died quite a few years ago now. Surprised Hannah didn't know that. You see the Brunt's were a pretty dysfunctional family. Mum and Dad got divorced about 15 years ago, they'd been separated for ages. Me and Joe left home as soon as we could when we were teenagers. Oh, he was a bastard our father. Loved his drink. When we were younger it was OK because he would just come home late from work, pissed, have his tea and then fall asleep in front of the telly. He wasn't any trouble. Mum just used to do everything, I mean everything for us and him and he gave her just about enough to survive on. When money got a bit short, they did have rows, he never hit her or anything. Anyway, as time went on things got worse. Mum had to work, she spent the rest of her time looking after us and keeping the house together. When he started hitting her and keeping money back she decided to leave him and that's what caused trouble between me and Joe. He's older than me, five years older, so when the split occurred he was old enough to do his own thing which left me to look after Mum which meant sleeping at Auntie Winnie's part time and in grotty private lets while Joe had a good job and lived in a flat of his own. He never really did anything to help so I stuck with Mum, and him and I met up at family occasions when he could be bothered to show up. I don't know, but I think Dad drank himself to death, he could never come to terms with Mum having left him and Mum just wore herself out. I think she became a bit of a recluse in her later years. Joe came to the funeral and all that – helped pay for it, which was a bit of a surprise actually."

The once almost deserted Red Lion had now filled up to the stage where having a private conversation was becoming rather difficult. As George had been talking so his voice was becoming quieter and quieter and Charlotte had had to move her chair closer rather than asking George to speak up so as to avoid the whole of the saloon bar hearing intimate details of the fragmentation of the Brunt household. Needless to say, during their somewhat short-lived relationship, Joe had mentioned none of the details of his family life to Charlotte.

"It's complicated."

"What's complicated Joe? I was just asking about your Mum and Dad. You've never mentioned them, and I've never met them. Seems weird. You're obviously not very close to them and we are having a heart-to-heart and I just want to get to know you better. That's all."

The Brunt king size bed was often the place for intimate discussions either pre- or post-lovemaking. They had discussed previous relationships, previous favourite positions as well as personal redlines – involving other people either for sex or a relationship and any kind of bondage were the only areas that, so far, had been ruled to be out of bounds – as well as how much they loved each other. Good food; good drink; an early night; fairly abandoned sex – Charlotte had never managed to emulate the abandonment that she enjoyed with her first lover, a student teacher at her sixth form whose memory still made her shudder with delight – and a postcoital discussion before sleep. In fact, the discussion sometimes led to a return match as Joe was wont to call it.

"Yes, so we weren't close and when I heard the news I really thought I ought to get in touch to see if I could help financially, and in any other way I can, to sort everything out. Look it's getting a bit crowded in here – I mean does that bother you? If not it's OK I was just wondering whether you want another here or maybe we could get a bite to eat. You must know somewhere decent nearby I should think."

Once again Charlotte was left feeling defensive with a barrage of questions to answer. Yes she wanted help any help, financial help yippee; yes she fancied something to eat – three gin and tonics were taking their toll; and yes it was getting too noisy, but where to start to not appear too greedy – food or money or to stay?

"Sounds like a good idea there's a lovely Italian round the corner I'm sure we could get a table there. Do great calzone and pasta dishes to die for."

There, she'd sorted everything out and left the issue of money and help for further discussion. After initially being rather put off by Mr Brunt Jnr Charlotte was warming to the rather overweight, balding gentleman who seemed to know quite a lot about her departed partner's life. In order to move things along she pushed back her chair and helped to round up George's liberally distributed bags and get them in some sort of order for the short walk to Bella Roma

A brief chat, find out a bit more about her increasingly more mysterious partner, get to know his brother and then move on to the next stage of funeral organisation. That was Charlotte's hastily mapped out plan for the evening but that was before George showed his true colours. At 2am after a six-hour drinking session, sandwiched around a lovely meal, Charlotte not so much fell out of the taxi as embraced the pavement outside her house. Clearly the taxi driver had had enough of his passenger, as he rushed round to shut the door neatly picking his way through Charlotte's spreadeagled limbs in order to do so, and then left the scene at speed without even a glance back to see if Charlotte had managed to raise herself from her undignified position. His later discovery of a number of plastic bags full of takeaway food boxes, clothes and books on the rear seats served as a brief reminder of his pathetic fare and although he felt a momentary sense of guilt he decided to take no further action in relation to restoring the items to their rightful owner. He put the food into his recycling bin and shoved the other bags into the 'lost property' cupboard at All the 6's Taxicabs' depot not thinking he would hear anything more.

Charlotte meanwhile was still trying to work out exactly where she was and what had happened. She had a very vague memory of getting into the taxi. She had begun to feel rather unwell and George had phoned for a cab. After that things were less clear. She could remember being rather happy in the pub. Might have done a bit of singing...as she tried to get a picture of what had happened she realised her more immediate problem was that she was soaking wet, lying face down on the pavement, hopefully, near her home. Although, from her current position, it was rather difficult to tell where anything was. She could see car wheels, kerbs, rain running down the gutter one way and then turning the other way she could see a rather blurry red brick wall that looked strangely familiar.

"Hi Charlotte! It is Charlotte isn't it? Are you OK? My God you're in a bit of a mess aren't you. Look, are you OK to get up? Is anything broken? How long have you been here? I think I'd better get Gloria to help."

The very personification of the Spanish Inquisition, Charlotte realised very quickly, was her neighbour Albert. All she could feel was great heartfelt relief, although on a day to day basis she loathed him ever since the bikini in the garden situation the previous summer. At least, despite his personal drawbacks, in this situation he looked like just the help she needed. What she wanted to do was to try and stop him from waking up the long-suffering Gloria at this ungodly hour. Whatever time it was she knew it was certain to be ungodly.

"Albert don't do, don't go, Gloria not fair too late. Don't..." was all Charlotte actually managed before her head fell back to the pavement.

Albert reacted to Charlotte's various splutters by deciding to abandon any attempt to raise Gloria from the dead and concentrate instead on getting his neighbour safely installed back at home. Ignoring all her protestations, "Get off Albert you're hurting – get off you bastard etc," he grabbed her right arm rolled her gently, or as gently as he could, amidst a melee of arms and legs, onto her back before pulling her into a sitting position. By this time Charlotte had quietened down considerably and was even beginning to co-operate. With one final heave Albert managed to get her into a standing position even though she was draped somewhat indecorously over his shoulder.

"OK, here we go." Albert enthused as he carried the semi-comatose Charlotte towards her door. "Not far now. Have you got a key handy?" At this stage there was very little handy about Charlotte who was beginning to feel the need to retch all over her doorstep. Hearing the word key made her very agitated.

"Key, key where's my fucking key. In my bag. Must be in my bag. Where the fuck is that? Had it in the taxi, paid the bastard. Must have left it there or it could have..."

"Just stay there," Albert had suddenly become very assertive. "Just stay there and I'll have a look on the pavement. See if I can find it for you. Won't matter though because...." By this time, his voice was becoming indistinct as he reached the end of her path.

Charlotte looked an utter mess. Bringing an utterly new dimension to dishevelment she sat somewhat meekly sipping a cup of tea hastily curated by Gloria who, hearing the commotion, largely Charlotte vomiting outside her bedroom window, had come down to bring some order to the situation which was clearly beyond her hopeless husband.

"You look as if you've had a bit of a night of it," Gloria cooed. "Now just drink your tea and we'll get you in bed. Better wait till tomorrow for a shower. You'll feel a lot better when you've had a sleep. Grief is a funny thing, affects people in different ways."

Charlotte vomited again into their carefully placed container which must have been the very first thing Gloria could grab as it was previously an unoccupied goldfish bowl.

Chapter 4: George

Charlotte could not be sure what woke her up – a knock on the door, the binmen noisily emptying Lediard Avenue's mixed recycling bins or the loose fencing panel, which Joe had been meaning to fix, rattling in its concrete prison. Whatever it was that did wake her was of much less concern than the awful pounding headache she became all too suddenly aware of as soon as she regained consciousness. Quite definitely the mother and father and possibly grandparent of all hangovers. Not only did she have a dreadful headache she also realised that she had a quite undeniable, even overwhelming, sense of the need to be sick. Aware of the need to be quick in these matters she began to push herself up in her bed realising as she did so that, very regrettably, she had, during the course of the night, already vomited all over herself, and the bed, without even having the decency to wake up. As soon as she swung her feet over the side of the bed a wave of nausea overcame her and she deposited whatever was left in her stomach over her feet and the rather threadbare carpet of the Brunt master bedroom.

As she hurried to the family bathroom, she realised she had gone to sleep fully clothed, something she seemed to be making a habit of lately. She turned on the antiquated over the bath shower and delicately peeled off her various sticky layers while the somewhat ineffectual boiler did its best, with a series of fits and starts, to produce a decent flow of reasonably hot water. Her headache seemed to ease as the water cascaded over her and she began to try and recall at least some of the events leading up to her falling asleep fully clothed in her bed and, more importantly, her pounding headache. Vague memories of lots of wine and shots were mixed with flashes of George, intermixed, for reasons she could not fathom, with those of thingy whatsit from the funeral directors.

By the time she had finished showering she had arrived at the part where she had had immense problems negotiating the door of the taxi leading to her rather unceremonious exit. After that it was all a blank – a fortuitous blank, but also a warm memory or two of George, so unlike his brother, so kind and considerate. The sound of her telephone breezily announcing an incoming call broke her train of thought.

"Hey!"

"Hey it's Laura. How y'doing? Not heard from you! How did yesterday go?"

"Yeah well I've been a bit busy really," Charlotte was trying to stall Laura because she knew she would want to know everything that had happened, and she wasn't really sure which parts of the story she wanted to reveal. "Well, it's a long story, don't know where to start." Laura knew about the meetings she'd arranged so she knew she would have to give some details about Hannah and Alice although she wanted to hold back on George until she was clearer about her intentions. Charlotte was also rather worried that even at this early stage Laura might muscle in. She loved her to bits, BUT there had always been issues with Laura. Issues with her and Joe, and even before that, where she was never absolutely sure that she hadn't managed a quick knee trembler with some of her exes before they were actually her exes although she had absolutely no proof. Even though she had her doubts the two were always there for each other and had some of the best times ever when they had been out together.

"So, what's been going on. Meeting two ex-wives must have been weird..."

"It was," Charlotte interrupted, anxious to get her day started. "Yeah they were both very different. Neither of them had much good to say about Joe. I suppose that's natural when they both divorced him. You know you were always having a go at me because I didn't know much about Joe – where he worked how much he earned that sort of thing..."

"Yeah, I know I always thought he was playing you, but you never..."

"Well, now this will really blow your mind, it did mine anyway. He always told me he was 42 and it turns out he was 62!"

"Shit, why would he lie to you about something like that? He was a devious bastard. Why would he hide that from you? Why pretend he was so much younger than he was?"

Charlotte was quite relieved to steer the conversation on to how old her late partner was rather than explaining any of the more detailed aspects of Joe the twice married devious misanthrope's past life. She hoped that feeding Laura that information would satisfy her curiosity at least in the short term

"Look, just before I go, been meaning to say, I'd be happy to come round and help sort things out: planning the funeral, sorting stuff out generally. You know me and annual leave, well I've got loads to take so we could have a proper sort out and catch up at the same time."

Charlotte's initial reaction was to keep Laura at arms-length in view of the amount she was finding out about Joe on a daily basis which she was finding difficult to process. She didn't really want anyone else coming along who might just satisfy their vicarious interests but not add much to progressing the funeral. Having more or less decided to snub her offer she remembered just how lonely it was ploughing through everything. She had a long list of things she needed to do and she decided, on balance, Laura, even with all her inbuilt drawbacks, was just the person who would be able to help out. After all, who else could she turn to?

"Are you sure you don't mind? Absolutely sure?"

"Wouldn't have offered if I wasn't serious. I'm guessing you're feeling the pressure. I mean it was really unexpected. It'll be like being a detective sifting through all the clues." Laura had started to use a spooky voice-over type voice as she was speaking which made Charlotte immediately regret her decision to involve her as Dr Watson to her Sherlock Holmes. Nevertheless, she reckoned it would be much more fun with two as it would undoubtedly involve some prosecco, never a bad thing, some laughs and someone to share things with.

"Well, I'm still not sure that there won't be some more surprises to come leaping out at me. There's so much stuff still to go through. Shall we start tomorrow? I'm not up for it today. Still suffering from yesterday. Tell you all about the wives tomorrow. Bring some prosec!"

"Of course, can't imagine not. Should be fun!"

Fun was not the first word that came to Charlotte's mind when thinking about dealing with Joe's shit. She had already spent a lot of time ploughing through some of his filing cabinets. What she really needed to find was whether he had left a Will, because they had never had a 'Will conversation,' any life insurance policies or any information as to how to get access to his bank account. There were a lot of expenses coming down the track and Charlotte knew very well that she would not be able to afford them on her own, neither did she want to waste her money on such an enterprise if she could avoid it. Laura, she decided, would be an excellent sleuth because when she had been to Laura's flat, she'd been amazed at how phenomenally well organised she was.

"Did you get home OK? As soon as the taxi went off, I realised you were in no fit state to get yourself home. I kept ringing your phone, but it must have been switched off. I thought you might have dropped it somewhere."

Staccato George stopped gabbling long enough for Charlotte to make a contribution.

"Yes, I'm fine. Bit of a drama though. Fell out the cab. Puked all over the place in the bedroom – still need to clear that up, to be fair. Had a banging headache this morning but I've just been pottering about, feeling better now."

"Great that you got home. I was really worried about you. Shouldn't have let you go."

"Yes, that was my own fault. Can be quite headstrong you know. As soon as I sat in the cab, I felt dreadful. Head spinning and all that. I think the driver just wanted to get rid of me. Left a load of stuff in the cab as well, I need to check up on where that is. Anyway, were you OK? You weren't driving, were you? Things got a bit out of hand in that restaurant, didn't they?"

"Look don't really want to dwell on that. I've been thinking about what we were talking about and I feel really guilty..."

"Guilty, why what have you done?"

"It's not me, it's Joe. He seems to have led you a merry dance and now, this, has left you in a really bad place – as I said last night I want to help and we never got round to seeing how this could work out. You see I want to try and make things better. I think you're a really together person and you shouldn't be in this position. Do you see what I mean?"

Charlotte was confused. The tone of George's voice was undoubtedly sympathetic, he seemed to be genuinely concerned and yet how could she be sure he wasn't looking for more – why should he take on the burden of his brother's bad behaviour. They hadn't even been close, so he could hardly have known what he was up to. Charlotte's first impression, the previous night, had not been good. After all he came across as a complete fool at the start of their meeting, it was only as the wine flowed that she saw him in a different light, but she didn't want him to get all soppy and be sorry for her and endear himself to her by preying on her low spirits. It was too soon for that, far too soon for anything.

"I know what it's like, being lonely, tackling an overwhelming problem and needing help and not being able to see it because of grief or a sense of responsibility, so I really think I can help."

George's rather more insistent tone was beginning to annoy Charlotte. She had already enlisted Laura to help with the immediate challenges and George trying to ingratiate himself was not what she wanted now although she did not want to put him off completely, not yet anyway.

"George, look thanks. Thanks for your concern and everything but..."

"No, I realise that maybe I've approached this the wrong way. It's tricky on the phone as well. Look, I know you must be busy. I know I can help but you've got to do all this in your own way and in your own time. So..."

"Thanks, George for your understanding. I've got Laura involved at the moment. She's coming round tomorrow and we're going to look through some of Joe's stuff. So maybe when we've done some of that we could see where that gets us and maybe you could pitch in then."

"Well, if that's what you want. I mean I can still join in now. More hands etc but..."

"No, I really need to get shifting now. He's been gone 3 days now. I need to get my head round that for a start off and then there's everything else." Charlotte knew she wasn't making much sense, but she didn't want to let George too close, too soon. She didn't really know what his agenda was. She wanted to believe he was going to act in her best interests but there was a nagging doubt. Anyway, after one drunken night she still didn't know much about him.

"So, I tell you what, let's see how Laura and I get on and then I'll text you or we could FaceTime and see how things are going."

"OK then," George sounded distinctly disappointed. "We'll leave it like that then."

In response to George's deflated tone Charlotte signed off breezily: "Thanks for phoning, means a lot and I will be in touch. Bye. Bye."

"Bye."

After a quiet morning trying to establish some sort of order in the house: putting out the recycling, loading the dishwasher, hoovering and cleaning, particularly in the master bedroom. Indeed, anything other than addressing the matter in hand, Charlotte felt marginally more certain that it would be better, easier, to wait for Laura rather than getting overwhelmed by the detritus of Joe's life too soon.

However, apart from feeling a lot calmer, her major achievement of the day was to establish another list of all the things she needed to do regarding the funeral some of which she was looking to delegate, and a further list of all the information she needed to find out in order to move forward: where he worked, how much did he earn, bank statements, credit card bills, loans. How she dreaded the possibility of finding out he owed zillions of pounds to a loan shark, especially in view of what Hannah had said about him running up debts back in the day; and, ultimately, whether there was any indication he may have taken his own life, after all, she reasoned, he was on his own, no other car was involved she had no idea what might have been going through his head.

Laura's arrival was exactly what Charlotte needed. As she opened the door to her friend, she found herself involved in a confusion of flowers, prosecco, chocolates, nibbles and Laura who was giggling, a little inappropriately. It was only 3:30pm and it felt to Charlotte as if her friend had been imbibing to a not inconsiderable extent before she had set off on her rescue mission. Having established some sort of order from the profusion of gifts, the two friends sat down each clasping a mug of strong tea.

"Now," Laura began in what sounded like a very authoritative fashion, "tell me what you want me to do and then we can crack on. How far have you got up to now? I'm guessing what we really need to do..."

"Hang on Laura, just hang on please," Charlotte felt she had to call a halt to Laura's stream of consciousness. "You can really help me here, but we've got to be focused. I've spent quite a lot of time being overwhelmed by stuff, reading stuff, putting it in order and it's a waste of time and we don't want both of us to be sucked into that. It's all **his** stuff, he's gone, so just sift through to see if there's anything relevant, and I'm going to tell you exactly what is relevant, so we can get the job as quickly as possible. I know next to nothing about Joe – jobwise, moneywise – virtually nothing. I mean he did go on about logistical stuff whenever I pushed him but I could never make any sense of what he was saying. Anyway, it didn't seem important, then. Don't look at me like that I know you kept on moaning at me because I didn't know more but that's done now so let's concentrate on what we need to do."

She led Laura to Joe's study to show her the scale of the problem – serried ranks of filing cabinets which, somewhat fortuitously, Charlotte had found the keys for.

"I've only started looking through this stuff for a few hours and got nowhere. We need to find anything to do with work, pay – anything financial, life-insurance, you know the sort of thing. Now I can tell you some of this stuff goes back for ages. But we just need recent information. Go through the files and identify anything that might be relevant and then when we've been through everything, we can bring all the relevant stuff together for further consideration. We'll need to get some stuff together for the Executor as well I suppose."

"OK boss got that! This shouldn't take long just needs a bit of focus."

That's why Charlotte wanted someone else, someone with more objectivity involved because she wouldn't be allowed to wallow in memories, regrets and odd bits and pieces that Joe, as an inveterate hoarder, had squirrelled away.

Several hours of searching, several glasses of Prosecco and amidst much giggling and chatting the investigators pronounced themselves satisfied with their work. Aided in no small part by several files in a code number protected box labelled: utilities, work, money – which was neatly subdivided into payslips, credit cards and investments; and passwords. Regrettably, they had only been able to access that file which had of course contained the code to the box after they had virtually destroyed the aforementioned box by way of an industrial size hammer and a large chisel. Never one for doing things by halves Charlotte had raided Joe's toolbox for what she thought would probably be the most suitable implement. For the first time since she had met Joe, Charlotte knew where he worked, how much he earned, what his pension entitlement was and that he paid off his credit card bill, in full, every month.

Charlotte's amazement at just how meticulously in order everything was, far outweighed her happiness regarding the abundance of knowledge she had learnt about her deceased partner. She had always thought of Joe as a sloppy person, whether it was tidiness, personal hygiene or, as far as she knew, keeping track of his affairs. When she thought he had been wasting his time watching late-night movies it now dawned on her that that must have been a cover for his squirreling activities. Otherwise, how could he have assembled so many bits of paper in date order and, from a cursory glance, always paid his bills just before the overdue date. In his other life Joe was nothing short of a paragon of virtue. He had clearly paid well over the odds into the cumulative pot for food and outings. He had always insisted on paying the rent in full, arguing that he would have to pay it anyway even if Charlotte had not been there. Charlotte felt this put her in the rather invidious position of the guest who could be evicted/replaced at any time whilst at the same time appreciating the gesture. Judging from the statements they had just discovered that also applied to utility bills, something that Charlotte had not really been aware of. The further they delved into the finances of the Brunt/Summersby alliance the more obvious it was, at least to Laura, that Charlotte had managed to land herself an extremely easy ride.

"How come he paid for so much?" Laura asked incredulously after they done some initial totting up. "You were getting pretty much a free ride. What was in it for Joe?"

Charlotte decided, that in the interests of decency, she wasn't going to reveal the innermost secrets of the couple's sexual activities. She knew only too well Laura's voracious appetite for any lurid stories which she could explore to her best advantage and enjoyment. Charlotte was also well aware of Mr B's requirements and, although it was never discussed in the same light, it was clear that this had been Joe's quid pro quo. Frequent, pedestrian and perfunctory were all words that came to mind when reviewing Joe's performance in the sexual arena which was partly the reason for Henry with his, until recently, excellent performance and, possibly, why Charlotte derived quite so much enjoyment from the situation. Although Joe was totally predictable, as long as money matters were always taken care of, then Charlotte was quite prepared to go with the sexual flow.

"We never really talked about money. He always said he would look after me. There was nothing to worry about. So, I never did. Joe was Joe. You knew what to expect with him. No real airs or graces, but it suited me. Not sure what I am going to do now though. I wasn't planning to move on." Charlotte realised as she spoke that she wasn't being absolutely truthful with her friend as she was neglecting to refer to the fact that immediately prior to Joe's death she had in fact been thinking of doing just that and hitching a ride on Henry's wagon. "Yes, I can see that. By the way what are you going to do about that solicitor's letter?"

During their search of Joe's personal papers, predictably tucked away in a file labelled 'Wills', Charlotte and Laura had found an envelope containing a letter from Jarvis & Sons, Solicitors stating that they held a certified copy of the Will of Josiah Thomas Brunt dated, ominously they both thought, five years previously. Charlotte realised immediately that Joe would still have been married to Hannah at that time, so the discovery of this letter was an immediate cause for concern. Up until that time Charlotte had not really thought much about Joe's possible assets, she was much more concerned about any debts that he may have accrued which she might have been responsible for. However, she realised the existence of this document could change everything.

"I'll have to get in touch. We've got no alternative. We need to find out what we need to do and what's in the Will."

"What if he's left everything to Hannah, that wouldn't be fair would it? She'll already have got a settlement after they divorced. Good job this place is rented.

"You're right, it wouldn't. Anyway, as far as I know she didn't have a very high opinion of Joe so she can sing for anything from his estate if it's up to me."

Laura looked at her friend and not for the first time she wondered just how she had managed to reach such a senior position, in the debt collection business, when she was so naïve. After all she had known Joe for two years and was completely astounded that two ex-wives could emerge from the woodwork in such short order. How could Joe have managed to deceive her in such a fashion. She thought he was much younger than he was, he had been married twice and yet she was totally unaware, to say nothing of a brother. Realising it was too late to change things now she decided to be as supportive as she could to her perplexing friend.

"Well, the only thing to do is to see what's in it, his Will, in the worst case scenario you'll have to contest it. People can't get two bites of the cherry, can they? It would be really unfair if they could."

"I have literally no idea what to do. I'm in a situation where every day brings new mountains to climb. I've absolutely had this now with funerals, wakes, wives and now Wills – I wonder what could possibly top that lot."

Barely had she finished uttering these words than the Brunt doorbell began to jangle with a certain degree of urgency.

"I'll get it, probably Jehovah's Witnesses or a meter reader. Leave this to me."

Charlotte heard a muffled greeting before George walked through the study door bearing a plethora of gifts – flowers, chocolates and, to Charlotte's horror, a huge cuddly bear.

"Hi Charlotte, just thought I'd pop round to see how you're getting on with the detective work."

Laura followed him through the door mouthing, 'Joe's brother', to Charlotte and seemingly, and highly inappropriately, indicating she thought he was fit.

As George was talking, he became aware that something was going on behind his back. Turning round, he caught Laura in the middle of giving a thumbs up to Charlotte. He looked back quickly and chose to ignore what he might or might not have seen.

"Have you made any interesting discoveries? As I say I've hardly had any contact with the old bugger recently. Never really talked about work and that sort of stuff..."

"Yes, been good really. Think we've worked out most stuff especially the finances – I was really worried about that after I spoke to Hannah, didn't want to find out he owed zillions – and where he worked. Still can't believe..."

Laura's reaction to Charlotte's admission of her naïveté regarding Joe manifested itself as a loud guffaw as she tried to control her laughter.

"Charlotte I was on at you for ages. You know that. You were just wilfully negligent and look where it's got you."

Charlotte and George rounded on Laura simultaneously.

"Laura you don't have to make such..."

"My brother was a bit of a dick you know."

As they spoke together Laura felt as though she was under attack.

"No, sorry you carry on."

"You don't need to make a show of me in front of George. I'm not so stupid that I hadn't realised where I went wrong – even though I was a bit late in doing so."

"OK, sorry that was a bit below the belt. Sorry!"

"Anyway," Charlotte was scowling at Laura as she spoke, "Laura has been really helpful although even with that I'm not really sure how far we would have got if Joe hadn't been so meticulous about his filing system. It was amazing, and we found out he was working as a senior manager in a call centre for a logistics firm. Been there for a few years. We still don't know why he was away so much though. There is no reference to making any journeys, hotel bills or anything so that all remains a mystery, a complete and utter mystery."

"What about phone contacts did you check through them to see if there's anyone you don't know?"

"It's almost like there's a whole section missing," Laura chimed in. "As if one section of the filing cabinet has been removed. We know that he was away once a month for a few days and that sometimes he stayed away a bit longer, and yet we don't know what he was doing. He told Charlotte it was either business or football or cricket but, where's all the memorabilia – programmes, tickets, scarves – just doesn't make sense."

"Yeah and the other thing is we found a letter saying Jarvis and Sons hold a copy of his Will dated five years ago so I have no idea what impact that could have. Do you know anything about Wills? Do I have any rights? What if he left all his worldly goods to one of his ex-wives? Surely he would have updated things after he got divorced? Wouldn't he?"

George opted for a pragmatic approach: "Best thing has got to be to contact the solicitors we…" Charlotte was a bit doubtful about the idea of them all somehow being involved in this together, but let him carry on, "…don't know what might have happened since that letter was written. Only they will know, and they'll be able to give you some advice, I should hope."

"You're probably right George," Laura smiled approvingly. "Changing the subject, George, hope you don't mind me asking? What pays your bills at the end of the month?" Laura was getting a bit skittish. "You don't have to say. Just curious."

Charlotte often had issues with Laura regarding men friends. Laura always seemed to think one of the perks of being Charlotte's friend was that she had the opportunity to flirt with, cuddle with and even, when she was really drunk, smooch with her man. In this particular case the demarcation lines had not even been drawn and Laura was entering the field of play with her simpering, flirty ways. George seemed unaware that he was being played: "I work for a firm of accountants actually. I'm a partner," he volunteered. "Was never any good at maths at school then a mate of mine really got into it and I realised it could be pretty lucrative as well as being quite interesting. I moved into forensic accounting recently, whole different world from what I was doing before…"

Laura and Charlotte looked at each other with puzzled expressions as George continued to highlight the ramifications of forensic accounting. Neither of them really knew what he was talking about nor did they particularly want to.

"….a couple of weeks ago I attended court for the first time in my new job."

"Wow, that must have been really cool," Laura tried to inject some enthusiasm into her voice but was hardly able to disguise the fact that she really wanted, desperately wanted, to change the subject of the conversation.

"Was that a bit scary, being in a court and that?" Charlotte had not picked up the signs from Laura and made a half decent attempt to prolong the topic unaware that her friend was just about die of boredom.

"No, it was OK actually because we spend a long time preparing for a court case so we know, or are pretty sure we know, all the answers to the likely questions that are going to be fired at us. Actually, I got a lot out of that court appearance, especially when we won. I felt I was playing a full part in the process rather than just doing the preparatory work and leaving the presentation to someone else." As George spoke Charlotte was beginning to see another side to Joe's brother apart from the somewhat bumbling dunderhead she had first met. When he arrived, although he had overdone the presents, she had been impressed by his Lacoste polo shirt and a smart pair of black jeans: even his trainers looked quality.

Laura decided that her original approach had not really achieved what she wanted so she tried another, somewhat tangential, chat up line, "What sort of music do you like? Y'know bands, singers? D'you go to any gigs?"

Laura's new approach seemed very intrusive to Charlotte but again George was quite happy to oblige with plenty of detail such that he and Laura began to develop a separate conversation. In such situations, faced with Laura's superior skills in the flirting department, Charlotte did what she usually did which was to find something else to do while they chatted inconsequentially.

George's fascination for Laura bemused Charlotte rather more than slightly because, ostensibly, he had arrived with presents for her and to pick up from their previous meeting. She was more than a little disappointed that their burgeoning friendship had been rather rail-roaded by Laura's over enthusiastic attention. When she arrived back in the study having busied herself in the kitchen and visited the toilet she found her two guests getting ready to leave as George had offered Laura a lift home as it was on his way to a late meeting he needed to attend.

After a brief hug and a kiss on the cheek from George and a hug from Laura the pair parted with George shouting over his shoulder: "I'll be in touch about the solicitor stuff. I'll see what I can find out about the rights and wrongs, so you know what to expect." His facial expression and his body language seemed rather contrite to Charlotte, as if he were being ushered away against his will and was unable to extricate himself from the situation without making a scene.

"Yes, that would be good. Give me a ring George. See you Laura."

"Will do!"

Charlotte had tried to sound cheerful even though she felt anything but, as she felt Laura's intervention meant that she had been unable to have a proper conversation with George.

"Lots of people here tonight. I thought you said it was just a few friends."

"Well, I thought it was. I mean it's not a special birthday or anything, so I'm really surprised."

"Who's that talking to Laura? Not seen him before. They seem rather close."

"Don't know. Don't think she's seeing anyone at the moment. Not that she said anyway."

"I'll go and get some drinks. Usual?"

"Rhubarb gin and tonic please. No ice."

Charlotte saw Joe make a major route adjustment as he walked to the bar to ensure he had a chance to not so much say 'Hello' to Laura but to subject her to a full-frontal assault. They seemed to be clinging to each other for an indecently long time before Laura belatedly extricated herself from Joe's clutches. As he continued his journey to the bar Laura left her companion and tottered towards Charlotte in her 6" heels. She looked stunning, Charlotte felt rather dowdy in comparison, she must have been to the hairdressers on her way to the party, every hair was in place. She had a loose ponytail with, she was reliably informed by a recent perusal of a Heat magazine fashion special, 'side bangs' and some awfully expensive earrings. She was wearing a red dress with a drape neck and an open back side split which, as far as Charlotte was concerned, left far too little to the imagination of the many men whose eyes were glued to her as she shimmied towards her. Charlotte felt Laura's outfit would not have been out of place on the red carpet at the Oscars and felt even more dowdy in comparison.

"Wow! You look absolutely stunning. Gorgeous. Are you with somebody? That guy you were talking to?"

"No, it's someone I know from work. I just felt like splashing out for a change. Makes me feel great. Bit weird all those people looking at me though."

"You've certainly got the eyes of the room. When you were walking over just then everyone was watching you. Everyone!"

"Y'don't look bad yourself. Y'know. Blue really suits you," Laura was trying to deflect some of the attention from herself, aware that her friend might be feeling a bit overwhelmed at her effect on the assembled company. "Like your hair as well."

Joe's return with the drinks, including a gin and tonic for Laura, precluded any continuation of Laura's attempt to offer any further moral support.

Joe was in overdrive: "Laura, you look amazing. Doesn't she Charlotte? That dress – wow!" He hurriedly divested himself of the drinks so he could give Laura another unnecessary and overenthusiastic cuddle. He had managed to slip his arm around Laura's shoulder and pulled her towards him with such enthusiasm he nearly caused a dress malfunction in an area where there was very little more to be revealed.

"So, what's this in aid of Laura? You hoping to pick up a new partner tonight?"

Laura giggled as she lapped up the compliments and the attention: "Not really, just fancied dressing up for once. Got a bonus at work and thought I'd go the whole hog – new outfit, hairdo, shoes you know." As she once again prised herself from Joe's grip she smiled at Charlotte as if to say: 'I didn't ask for this y'know. Keep him in his place'. Having achieved her aim, she edged towards Charlotte, and out of hugging range of the energised Joe who had finished his drink in record time and, having excused himself, had headed back to the bar.

"Look Charlotte I'm sorry but..."

"You don't have to apologise he's a bugger like that. Doesn't seem to realise what he's doing – he makes everyone feel awkward. I mean you really do look good, but he didn't need to go so over the top. All that hugging and stuff..."

"I know, he's got a proper eye for other women. We said that before, but he's a bit out of control tonight. Are you two OK? Have you had a row?"

"No, no, we're fine . He's been away again. It's often like this when he gets back from one of his trips. He's really nice with me at home – brings flowers etc, but if we go out, he just seems to forget who he came with. Just look over there, now at the bar. Harriet King, next to the tall black guy."

"Oh yeah, I see her."

"Well, he's got his hands all over her as well, making a big fuss of her. He's old enough to be her father, easily. I don't want to have a row while we are out, but it really makes me feel uncomfortable. I didn't really want to come out tonight, but he insisted."

"Maybe he'll calm down when he's had a few drinks. I think they're opening the buffet so that'll keep him occupied for a while."

"Yes, but then in his current mood he'll probably want to start dancing." Charlotte pulled a face.

"You're OK, flower. If you want to sit out the dancing, I'll keep him occupied. There's always a crowd that like to dance. I'll get him to join in with them. Give you a break."

"But then he'll think I'm boring for not joining in the fun. I don't want to be a wet blanket, put a damper on things. He's always the life and soul of the party..."

"Look, Charlotte, you're OK. I've got your back on this. I'll keep him amused for you. You can't help not enjoying dancing."

"But..."

"There's no buts. Wait till he comes back and see what happens. You don't need to make yourself do anything."

"But..."

"He's coming back looking all pleased with himself."

"Hi girls. Got some more drinks. Just talking to Harriet, you know her, over there," he pointed to the bar where Harriet was still standing. "She wanted to know if you'd like to come for a few more drinks at her parents' house after this finishes. If we want to make a proper night of it."

"Look Joe, Charlotte looks bushed so why don't we see who's going later and if we fancy it, we can go as well. Give Charlotte a chance to get an early night."

"Well, if you don't mind Charlotte?" Joe was wheedling, using his childish voice to get what he wanted. Charlotte knew she would suffer for a late night but was equally sure she didn't really want Laura in her skimpies to spend too much time dirty dancing with her partner. She had been offered an easy way out of a late-night and a banging headache but, but...

"OK, why don't you kids dance the night away. Might have one of my migraines coming on anyway," she replied. "Sorry Joe, I would come if I could, but you know how these things develop," she slipped her fingers into Joe's hand and squeezed while giving him a needy look and a rueful smile. "I think that settles it, Laura. I'll go and get myself sorted out with a cab in a bit and you can get off and enjoy yourselves. Don't know where Harriet lives but if it's easier, Laura, why don't you stop over at ours, we can sort cars and stuff out tomorrow."

"Thanks Charlotte, yeah that would be good. We'll try and be quiet when we get back."

"As if!"

"You sure you'll be all right getting home? How's your head?" Joe was showing his well-practised minimalist concern for Charlotte's well-being in order to assuage his guilt at going off gallivanting when she wasn't feeling very well. Charlotte knew of old that now he had got permission to carry on the party there would be no dissuading him so there was no point in trying to get him to go home with her.

"You go ahead. I'll be fine."

The drinks flowed for a while longer before Charlotte took her leave, having taken her usual dose of placebo Migraleve in order to look the part of a wounded heroine reluctantly leaving the party.

Just before she fell asleep, she briefly reflected on what had happened but decided that she would have to trust Laura not to let things get too out of hand. After all she was her best friend, it had happened before.

And now in slightly different circumstances it was as if history was in the process of repeating itself, as far as Charlotte could see, with Laura having waltzed off with George in such a flagrant manner. The positive vibes from spending time with Laura and coming to terms with so much about Joe that had been a mystery, had dissipated slightly. Charlotte began to look through her to-do list and to annotate some of the items, so she knew what she had to do first and how she thought she was going to do it. Number one was to contact Joe's former employers to let them know formally that he had died and to enquire solicitously about her rights in regard to his pension. This was crucial as she had no doubt that as far as XXL Logistics (UK) plc were concerned she probably did not even exist. She needed to know where she stood ASAP so she could work out what to do about the rent on Brunt Villa. Without wanting to appear in any way mercenary Charlotte did rather regret any evidence of a life insurance policy she might have been able to lay claim to, which would have tided her over until everything else was sorted out. Although both Laura and George had been extremely helpful, she was becoming increasingly aware that she needed some expert help to steer her through this minefield and to make sure she understood exactly what she was entitled to.

As she walked around the house clasping her empty mug her phone pinged:

> Sorry about that. Are you OK? Laura suggested it might be a good idea to leave. Said you were getting upset. At home now. Phone?

Being made aware, for the first time, of Laura's special power of mind reading, reduced Charlotte's anxiety a touch. Her first response to Laura shepherding George away was that she was allowing her predatory instincts to negate her duty of care to her friend. Could she now believe that her sixth sense had alerted her to a need to give Charlotte some headspace? The only way to resolve the matter, she decided, was to have a discussion with Laura, if possible before the funeral, so that she could clear the air relating to Joe and lay down some ground rules for the future.

> Hi George, you didn't need to have disappeared so soon. I'm fine. Going to do a few things. I'll ring you later xx

After a very productive time checking and replying to emails, opening the latest tranche of sympathy cards, and establishing a list of people who wanted further details about the funeral/after party, Charlotte was feeling much more in control of the situation. Three days and counting and things were shaping up: she was hoping George might have made some progress on the Will front; someone from XXL Logistics had responded very quickly to her email suggesting a meeting to discuss the way forward regarding Joe's pension; and she hadn't broken down today, yet, which was a major improvement. She was also feeling quite hungry which she took as another good sign. More tea, a sudoku puzzle and then she was going to phone George.

Somewhat later than planned after a Sudoku induced nap Charlotte decided to phone George. She had been very impressed by George Mk II, much less dithery, spruced up and helpful, at least so far. She was keen to discover more information about Joe. A lot of what had been said during their previous meeting had been washed away by an excess of alcohol, so she needed to check things out. She was grieving her loss, but she was also realising that a lot of the Joe she knew related to some fantasy world he had created. She had trusted Joe and been failed badly, but did the fact that Joe was deceitful mean she should not trust his brother? He seemed very sincere, but with only three days since the fatal accident her head was still in a mess. She didn't want to make any more mistakes. She needed to know what George Brunt wanted, what he had to offer and whether he could help Charlotte to, not only survive this catastrophe, but also, perhaps, build a better future

"Hi Charlotte."

"Hi. Sorry for taking so long. Is it OK to talk?"

"Yeah. I'm home. I'm getting a takeaway later so now is as good a time as any."

"Good. I've had a really successful time since you left. By the way thanks so much for coming. S'funny but..."

"Well, I thought I might be able to help. Offer some support. In fact, I thought you'd be on your own to be fair. Laura's fun but she's a bit bossy, isn't she? The way she just decided we were going, now I think about it, was weird. I just assumed because she was your friend that she knew what you were feeling, and I didn't want to upset you..."

George was beginning to retreat into apologetic mode George, Mk 1 George, Charlotte wanted to avoid any repetition of that persona. A retreat was not to be encouraged just as, what Charlotte fervently hoped, was 'the real George' was beginning to emerge.

"...so, I just went along with it."

"No, I was fine, but Laura was probably right to whisk you off. We'd had a few glasses of Prosecco, always makes me a bit emosh, and we'd got as far as we could really. By the way, thanks for the flowers and the chocolates, that was really generous. Quite unnecessary but lovely."

"No problem. I suppose I brought them for two reasons..."

Charlotte could feel an apology coming on. Maybe default George was not the person she wanted him to be. She needed to sort this out -

no use building a friendship, trusting someone, if they couldn't deliver the goods. Strong, decisive and ready to offer worthwhile support was what Charlotte required.

"... firstly, because I know most women love flowers, the bright colours, the scent lifts the spirits and I wanted to do that for you; and secondly, well the way we parted after the meal was awful. You were so pissed, and I just pushed you into a taxi. Hardly very chivalrous and I wanted to refocus things and re-establish my positive credentials. Make you smile and appreciate me just in case you thought I was not to be trusted – getting you bladdered and then deserting you. Not a good plan really."

"It got a lot worse, actually, the taxi driver just left me for dead..."

"Oh, I'm so sorry!"

"Don't go there George it wasn't your fault. Don't ruin it. It was me that tripped up. Silly fool. No one to blame but myself," Charlotte needed to keep talking to make sure George did not relapse into his alter ego again. "No, my neighbours Gloria and Albert came to the rescue. Thank goodness! No bones broken or anything. Only my dignity suffered. Don't know what I'll say to them when I see them again though!"

"Good I'm glad to hear that. Now I don't know whether you remember when we met, I mentioned that I wanted to help in any way I can. I mean I don't know how you're fixed for money for the funeral etc? What about the rent? You see – well cards on the table I've got a good job, quite a lot of savings and well, you're in a bit of a mess, so being related to Joe and stuff well, I feel, I think I said this before, a responsibility to you."

Charlotte didn't want to be a liability or to have someone who was a complete stranger a few days ago feeling responsible for her, just because she happened to be in a relationship with his brother, who, to make matters worse he was more or less estranged from. However, she could be in a real mess if things did not go right for her especially in relation to the Will. She wanted any rescue plan to be on her terms though. She would not be able to countenance any repeat of her previous relationship with Joe or for that matter her previous lovers. Her ability to choose reliable partners in the past had been severely lacking and that was being more than kind to herself.

"Why are you always like this? I've been at work all week 12 hour shifts. Stop on the way home for a few beers and then this..."

103

"How dare you. You're pissed Mark Jones. It's 8:30pm and I've had your dinner ready since six when you promised me, faithfully, you would be home. What is the point? Why do you behave like this and then try and blame it on to me? What the fuck is going on in your head?"

Mark slumped into an armchair. He knew he was in the wrong but refused to admit it. In his drunken haze he could only launch an attack, it was his best means of defence, at least with Charlotte it was. "Look I had a few beers and then you..."

"Mark don't you realise how pathetic you look slumped there? I have every right to be annoyed with you. I told you I was cooking a meal for you. Thought it would make a change from your Fray Bentos pies in a can or your tins of chicken curry. So, I make an effort for you and you decide to mess it up by staying in the pub until you can barely stand. Anyway, how did you get home? If you've driven here, I swear I'll find your keys and chuck them in the river. You're just so disrespectful – you make me sick!"

Mark had listened to streams of invective from Charlotte before, but this seemed to be reaching a new level of vitriol. Having made the decision to escape from her verbal battering he pushed himself up from his slumped position and succeeded only in propelling himself with some force straight into a rather sturdy television table thereby knocking himself out, causing a severe injury to his head and bringing the TV crashing down upon him.

Not for the first time Charlotte found herself ferrying her irresolute partner to A & E to sort out another self-inflicted injury.

As Charlotte remembered this traumatic incident it served as a poignant reminder of the result of her poor taste in men that she was so desperate to improve upon in the future.

"...I've been looking into the Will situation..."

Clearly Charlotte had missed some of what George had been saying but was relieved that he had come to something which sounded really important.

"... and there are all sorts of opportunities to vary things and challenge things, so I think the best thing is to contact the solicitors, find out who the executor is, sort out probate and work from there. As far as I know we are the only two parties with a direct interest. So may as well go together to start the ball rolling. If that's OK?"

"Well, yes I suppose that makes sense then. Although I'm a bit worried Hannah might come into the reckoning as he was still married to her when he wrote this Will. Anyway, I think you're right, it's important to go together so we'll both know where we stand from the horses' mouth as it were, rather than having to repeat everything and maybe getting it confused."

George raised the matter of his involvement in any Will Joe might or might not have written in what Charlotte at first thought was a very casual manner of the type, 'well we have a common interest so might as well do it together'. Subsequently Charlotte was not so sure. Having met two of Joe's ex-wives who had appeared from nowhere she began thinking that she might have let George get too close, too soon. He was Joe's only real living relative, as far as she knew, so he was de facto the only imminent threat to her future financial well-being, although even that could be compromised by the possible involvement of the ex-wives. So, having already admitted that he was in a position to offer her financial support then she was intrigued to know why he wanted to be so closely involved at this stage.

They had agreed that, in the first instance, Charlotte would contact the solicitors and make arrangements to find out what the procedure was to ascertain the contents of Joe's Will. George's direct manner had endeared himself to Charlotte. Although she still felt slightly wary, she also felt he probably did have her best interests at heart though that approach may be tempered slightly by his own self-interest. At this stage Charlotte did not feel the same desolation that threatened to engulf her during the first few days after Joe's death. When the funeral was out of the way she felt quite certain she would be able to rebuild her life without Joe and, in fact, with all that she now knew about him she could see a brighter future as she learned from the pitfalls of her extremely naïve approach to her relationship with him.

Chapter 5: Viewing

Charlotte's connection with nature was, as she had become increasingly aware, somewhat tenuous to say the least. As a child she had lived in a high-rise block with her only access to fresh air being a junk-filled balcony on the 17th floor. Her mother had never been one to embrace the countryside, so trips to the local park were rarely undertaken even though she and her brother were always whingeing about not being able to go out and play.

Even when she left home she remained a Townie, living in a city and concentrating mainly on the cultural aspects of city life and, even then, eschewing walks in the variety of green spaces and countryside that surrounded her. Physical exercise was not on her agenda. She had tried that at school and had not enjoyed it and, as with so many things, having taken against them at a young age it was very difficult to rekindle any interest in later years. Cross-country running in the mud and torrential rain had had a highly traumatic effect on Charlotte. She still, nearly 20 years later, suffered horrific flashbacks if she saw someone out running, hence the reason she avoided any open area which might mean she was surprised by a runner without her having been given proper prior notice. Getting wet, thoroughly wet, and covered in mud for no reason other than the whim of a sadistic sports teacher had left an indelible mark. Her nickname at school had been Penguin for the fairly obvious reason that she did in fact walk like one. Cross-country running had always been resorted to when the hockey pitches become too waterlogged to allow play to take place. No one seemed to have realised, much to Charlotte's chagrin, that if it was too wet for hockey then it was, in all probability, also too wet for running. Charlotte was never very impressed with the mental acuity of her teachers, something which led to many confrontations over the years as her troubled school days continued.

Seeing runners anywhere, even on the TV, induced Charlotte's flashbacks and her reaction to rain, particularly if she was ill-equipped, was even worse so that even on the warmest summer's day she would often be seen with a poncho and an umbrella in her backpack. 'Just in case' was always her motto. Like a well-trained Girl Guide she always reasoned that it was best to be prepared.

The traumas associated with outdoor sport and weather had had a further deleterious effect on Charlotte's life view in relation to her lack of enthusiasm, put more clearly, her hatred of gardening. As a child her numerous trips to her father's cherished allotment left her feeling that she was only really invited along to help carry the necessary tools backwards and forwards because the allotment society, run by Ubergruppenfuhrer Jones, had a no shed policy. Her father made every effort to engage her in the process of digging: even with a child spade. This did not work for Charlotte; sowing: far too fussy for her and the delay between sowing and any signs of life was also far too long; weeding: Charlotte was not particularly good at sorting weeds from seedlings, a fact which caused endless arguments and a need for a not inconsiderable amount of re-planting; and then of course there was the weather. Having traipsed around three quarters of a mile to the corporation allotment her father was loth to abandon ship unless the weather was truly awful, gale force seven or eight in seamen's terms. Of course, at the first sign of proper rain Charlotte would don her best school raincoat, in fact her only raincoat, put up her umbrella and proceed to stamp up and down the path separating the Summersby plot from the adjacent much-loved oases amid the urban clutter.

As if stamping was not enough to get her dad's attention whilst he worked systematically through his tasks for that particular day, Charlotte would also shout with increasing volume and intensity such things as: "When are we going home Daaaaaad!" "It's raining it's pouring the old man Is snoring," and if the situation deteriorated, "DAD! I'm going home now don't try and stop me because you can't!" The last sentence was screamed at a volume sufficient to wake the dead and was usually timed at the tipping point when her father had really had enough of gardening, of the weather and of his daughter creating such a fuss. The walk home was always accompanied by a plaintive lecture which rarely varied from a fairly constant ecological theme: "Look Charlotte I know you're fed up, but we need to take every opportunity we can to get out in the fresh air, look after the crops, help the environment. There is a lot of evidence to say that the way we are going with the world, it's not going to end well, not at all, and your generation," this part of the lecture was usually accompanied by pointing gestures, as if her dad could actually be mistaken for addressing someone else, "will be the ones who'll suffer unless we change…"

Fairly early on in the lecture Charlotte would have effectively switched off and resorted to humming and uttering the occasional misplaced 'ummmm' or 'ahhh' which her father would completely ignore as he rehearsed his core arguments all the way back home.

Cordelia Summersby's attempts to calm her husband as he proceeded to 'humph' his way around the house after his arrival, having left muddy footprints in most of the places that he knew very well he should not have left them, rarely worked, and Mr Summersby was left fuming into his Daily Mail drinking an emollient mug of drinking chocolate.

Having survived the allotment years Charlotte embarked on a community garden initiative at University hoping to put behind her the various phobias she had accumulated in her formative years. She foolishly joined a university society with the grand title of University Students for a Greener Future. This was during Charlotte's Friends of the Earth phase which up until joining the society had been an unknown quantity to her. She was gradually seduced by not just the flame haired and bearded leader of the group, one Jamie Hughes, who she thought bore a passing resemblance to a Viking sailor, but also by the whole idea of saving at least a small part of the neighbourhood rather than the more altruistic aim of saving the world, which absorbed so many of her fellow members. However, despite her emotional and often physical entanglement with the leader of the gang Charlotte's involvement had caveats concerning, as ever, mud and rain.

Unfortunately, this honeymoon period in Charlotte's relationship with things environmental did not last long. Her discovery that Jamie's interest was not confined to her made any further battles with the elements rather superfluous. As a result, with her romantic association having been laid bare, Charlotte decided to dump Jamie and hang up her Wellington boots as she sought other activities which better suited her aversion to any over involvement with earthy matters.

Her association with Josiah Brunt began some years later and constituted her next brush with eco-friendly matters. The intervening years had principally focused on a string of relationships varying from the ultimately unsatisfactory to the didn't last long enough to really form an opinion. Charlotte was not averse to getting straight to the point when she met someone who she was attracted to. Her main problem was that depending on her state of inebriation she, on some occasions, could hook-up with some, in the opinion of onlookers and friends, very devious people, which meant her being persuaded to participate in a number of quickies in pub car parks, on landings and, worst of all, on one occasion over a car bonnet in a lay-by immediately adjacent to a busy dual carriageway. At least, she was pleased to recall, this last involvement was under the cover of darkness which probably protected her identity but even so attracted a number of lewd comments from passing cars accompanied by a fusillade of tooting horns! Charlotte had to admit to herself that she was in no way proud of her licentious period although she blamed most of her ill fortune on the calibre of the men she came into contact with. Her blissful ignorance of Shakespeare's Julius Caesar meant she had no knowledge of Cassius' line where he says: 'The fault dear Brutus is not in our stars but in ourselves that we are underlings'. As a direct result she gave scant regard to the fact that the fault in these circumstances may actually have lain with her. Self-analysis was not one of Charlotte's strong points, after a disastrous couple of years studying a psychology option at university. The lecturer did not make a very good impression on her, although he did have a very significant impact on several of her compatriots who were keen participants in, albeit brief, relationships with him. She also was no great fan of Freud, Piaget, Rogers or Pavlov whose work on classical conditioning she found far too deterministic and totally ignored the role of the free will of the individual. Her eventual falling out with the aforementioned lecturer was largely based on the fact that, far from nurturing individual students and guiding them towards new discoveries, he was a more or less total throwback to the rote learning for which Charlotte had no time for at all. Their final showdown was in a lecture theatre where after asking an innocuous question about the superego she launched an amazing tirade against his fundamental knowledge base, his lecturing style and his overfamiliar way with female students. Her subsequent flounce out of the lecture theatre was warmly applauded by many of the attendees. Not only that, but it also led to her being summoned to meet with the Dean of the Faculty, a full enquiry and the eventual parting of ways between the University and the unfortunate/unsatisfactory lecturer.

Josiah claimed to be an in-the-DNA eco-warrior and, according to him had been fighting this particular battle for many years. Initially, of course, Charlotte's previous experiences weighed heavily against the success of their relationship until he managed to persuade her that her previous traumas need not be repeated, nor did they have to mean a total aversion to green issues. Joe refocused Charlotte's attention away from the nitty-gritty of the environment towards an appreciation of natural beauty and in particular trees. He proved to be a bit of an arborist in that as far as Charlotte could discern in the early days he was an expert on the cultivation, management and study of individual trees. His expert status, as with everything about Joe, came into question the more interested Charlotte became in the subject. Even at this early stage she was able to challenge some of his assertions, particularly in relation to the classification of trees as his knowledge was rather confined to the more obvious indigenous types: oak, ash, chestnut etc and he had very little knowledge of imported trees and their influence on changing habitat for native species which were causing problems in some areas of the country.

The one thing that had the most impact on Charlotte's attitude to things natural was an early present of a book on historic trees throughout the UK. Charlotte's lack of involvement in things environmental meant the real importance of trees to the well-being of the planet had passed her by, as had the incredible lifespan of trees even those quite close to where they lived

Gifts from admirers had usually meant wine, flowers, chocolate and the like for Charlotte. In fact, Joe was the first male friend to have ever bought her a book of any type at all. She was impressed with Joe's gesture for three very important reasons: one, it was, by her reckoning, awfully expensive — Joe had forgotten to cut off the requisite section of the sleeve which advertised the price; two, it was a beautiful object — high quality paper, beautiful pictures; and three it was full of fascinating information about trees which, for some reason, that she could not immediately understand, she found very interesting. From the day she received the book she developed an entirely different relationship towards trees which in no small way led to her developing a very close relationship with Joe. Their mutual fascination gave the early stages of their relationship a unique focus. They began making trips to churchyards where many really old trees reside, as well as the forests and woods highlighted by her highly prized guidebook. Charlotte would be the first to admit that beautiful old trees were not the only reason for their expeditions although, mercifully, both of them respected the sanctity of churchyards throughout the period of their exploration.

"There's something very peaceful about trees. Especially really old ones. This one," Charlotte was pointing at and addressing a tree which was over 500 years old, "has been here for hundreds of years. Can you imagine what she'll have seen? The changes in fashion, in transport. This road has probably changed beyond recognition, from the track that used to be here."

A frequent occurrence during their tree stops was Charlotte waxing lyrical. She would always have THE book in hand and would sometimes, if so moved, read a passage about a particular tree that they were looking at. Charlotte's worshipping of trees did try Joe's patience from time to time, especially when a quick visit lasted upwards of an hour. In his view there was only so much attention required per tree.

"But Joe, can't you see how gnarly that tree is. It's bristling with potential. As soon as winter is over and the sap starts to rise can you not feel its power to create, to grow..."

"I think you're going a bit over the top there Charlotte, getting all poetical. I see trees more practically than you. They absorb CO_2 which is brilliant in the current climate. We need this. I get that. We need to revere them, I get that..."

"But can't you see just how impressive a tree this is. How strong it is. Also, in 500 years think of all the storms it has withstood. You can see all sorts of bits have been snapped off. Just imagine how strong it must have been, and still is, to withstand such onslaughts, and more to come I don't doubt."

"I still come back to how important they are to the planet. In our battle to limit the CO_2 in the atmosphere they are of paramount importance. You'll become a tree hugger next. That would really be weird. Don't think I could cope with that."

"S'funny you should mention that because I have been reading up on that very thing. Well, you know I get a bit emotional sometimes when we are looking at trees. Well, it turns out hugging trees is good for your health..."

"Says who? That sounds like a load of hippie bollocks. Where did you get that from?"

"There's lots of books about how trees can help with mental illness, particularly ADHD and depression. You need to read Blinded by

Science. Apparently when you hug a tree it leads to an increase in your levels of the hormones serotonin and dopamine making you feel happier. There's forest bathing as well. The Japanese swear that it enhances the immune system. They call it shinrin yoku and apparently have been using it in companies to promote a healthier lifestyle for employees. In forests the essential wood oils in the air that are emitted by the trees, they're called phytoncides, increase the number of killer cells in the body. These cells help fight sickness and disease. Not only that the five senses are strengthened..."

Joe looked on incredulously as Charlotte got into her stride. "You sound as if you've swallowed an encyclopaedia, Charlotte, and a hippie one at that. You're getting all preachy as well. We'll be stripping naked and cavorting through the fields in a minute."

"Don't you mock me, Josiah Thomas Brunt," Charlotte always used Joe's full name when she was getting cross with him. "The Japanese take these things really seriously and they reckon the more you forest bathe the stronger your senses become. I think there's a lot to learn from exploring other people's views of working with nature. We are so wedded to cars and profits and exploiting natural resources rather than working in harmony with each other and our environment. We can't go on like this forever, you know. We'll reap what we sow. Some pandemic will come along and teach us a very severe lesson. We can't just go on polluting and extracting regardless. We need to be much more careful of the world's finite resources."

From incredulity to respect in the space of a few minutes, Joe stood up from the bench on which they were sitting, bowed towards Charlotte and started clapping. Charlotte stood up and pushed him away. "Now you're taking the piss. Bastard! I'm only trying to get you to see that there are other ways of working where we are more in harmony with our surroundings."

"No, no I'm not laughing at you Charlotte. That was a really good argument there. I mean I do get nature. I've said that and if you take that to its logical conclusion we do need to change. I'm not so sure about tree hugging and forest bathing, they sound a bit strange, but I do understand what you're saying."

"Good, and so you should."

So, although Joe started off as the environmentalist in the relationship, it was Charlotte who soon became the most enthusiastic of the two to the extent that she went to talks at the local library although she still managed not to get so involved to ever have to consider the perils of mud and rain. She was also glad that, as they were always in Joe's car when they were making their trips, at the first sign of inclement weather they could beat a retreat, although she did always pack emergency clothing just in case the car broke down. Being extremely risk-averse her emergency pack also included a cornucopia of nibbles, savoury and sweet, as well as a variety of flash lamps both solar and battery powered with a butane heater as the icing on the cake.

Charlotte's reawakening to all matter's bucolic was in part the reason for her motley crew's arrival at the entrance to the Green Acres Memorial Park. She and Joe had spent several memorable afternoons making love in the countryside, gambolling amongst the rapidly ripening ears of corn or treading carefully over the spiky remains of harvesting depending on the season. As to why both George and Laura were on the excursion, Charlotte was not sure whether it was happenstance that brought them together or that one of her guests was manipulating the situation for their own advantage

As part of their discussions in relation to Joe's Will, George offered his assistance in checking out locations for the eco-funeral. Not that he had any particular interest in such funerals per se, but he did have a particular interest in Charlotte and, recognising her vulnerability, decided that by offering help at strategic moments he would a) make himself useful; b) ingratiate himself with Charlotte; and c) occasion opportunities where they could meet up in a non-threatening way and, apart from achieving their business objectives, could also get to know each other better. He had also offered to give the eulogy for his brother, something that Charlotte had not even thought about apart from wanting to avoid the toe-curling bit where the vicar or celebrant tried to make out that they knew the deceased when they had normally never met them.

"You don't want to waste your time and your days off following me around woodland sites. Surely you've got better things to do?"

"Oh yes, I probably have, but you've got so much on. Perhaps an extra pair of eyes and ears might come in useful. Besides I'm the only family member concerned so I really think I'm obliged to help."

That guilt thing again. Charlotte could feel that justification feeding in. Obliged to, ought to, assuage my guilt etc etc. Charlotte didn't want to hear any more of that sort of talk. "Yeah, I get the bit about being family, albeit estranged, but just in case you are thinking it, I don't need protection, you know. I don't think it's gonna be anything like buying a second-hand car or buying new uPVC windows. They won't be crooks. This is eco-stuff – there won't be any hard sell."

What had Robert Piggott said, "It'll be very alternative, you'll need to be ready for that." Even though he had never done an eco-funeral, he was still able to sound like the guy on TV, moneysavingexpert.com, nothing he didn't know and always knew the best way to do everything. "There won't be any expensive add-ons or anything like that. One price, one box, one ceremony, tailored, of course, to your needs."

"But anyway, as I've said I'm between jobs, so I'd be really happy to come along for the ride. I won't get in the way."

The same, unfortunately, could not be said about Laura's involvement. As soon as she heard that George and Charlotte were planning a trip together all hopes of a quiet day pottering in the countryside with a pub lunch thrown in went out of the window.

"That's nice of him to offer to help though isn't it? But I'm a bit worried he might try and influence you too much. D'you get what I mean? You want your send-off for Joe, you won't want to have to compromise because someone you hardly actually know, who is his brother, rocks up with his size 10 feet."

"Look, I wasn't planning a big expedition you know. It'll probably be quite boring actually. I've got two places in mind and I just want to get a feel for them – how they do things, whether it will feel right. George can help with that, I think. Not sure where you fit in, Laura?"

Charlotte was in wary mode. On the basis that she was really gate-crashing her arrangement she was reminded of a conversation only a couple of days ago. Was this really friend Laura or rampant man devouring machine Laura trying again to inveigle her way into George's life. Lacking a really strong put down Charlotte decided on damage limitation.

"OK, if you really want to come you can, take your cues from me, don't try and take over."

"As if I would. I think three heads will be better than to one on an occasion like this. We can both cheer you up as well!"

Charlotte was well aware that she felt in need of being cheered up but felt rather uneasy as to what Laura might have in mind.

"Let's get the tunes on, then!" Laura had barely been in the car for a minute and she started trying to inject some energy into the proceedings. Charlotte and George who had up until then been driving in silence, grimaced at each other. Charlotte feared the worst for the rest of the journey.

"What 'tunes' do you want?"

"Got any on your phone? Can't you just stream them to the car radio..."

"Sorry Laura I really don't feel like listening to music today...."

"Oh OK then I'll just have to use my headphones." For the rest of the journey Charlotte and George exchanged occasional comments about the countryside or the number of potholes or the lack of any road sense of their fellow motorists: "Did you see that the absolute twat. Could've killed herself then," or "How did he manage that. No place to overtake there. How did he squeeze in. Lucky bastard!" etc etc was the extent of their exchanges.

As they walked into the modern single-storied building just inside the gates of Green Acres Memorial Park an immaculately dressed woman, late 20s early 30s, Charlotte thought, greeted them cheerfully: "Are you alright there?" Charlotte pondered an existentialist conversation about what feeling alright would be like when standing on the threshold of a funeral establishment about to discuss the funeral of a dear departed partner but decided it would be both too much trouble and might not be well received.

"Hi, I'm Charlotte Summersby. I phoned earlier. This is George brother of the deceased and my friend Laura. I said I'd seen your brochure, but I wanted to look round to see what your offer is. I want to..."

"Of course, I understand that completely. May I call you Charlotte?"

"Of course. That's fine."

"My name is Abigail Forbes I am the Assistant Manager here. Now I don't want to beat around the bush. We offer an extremely reasonably priced environmentally friendly funeral experience tailored to exactly what you, the customer, wants. We have been in business for...celebrate a life lived as well is to mourn a life lost...our concept of a natural woodland burial is based on four core tenets: sustainability, biodiversity, quality of service and customer choice...burial process incorporated in plan to restore the woodlands here to native broad leaf species... essentially, we offer a different way to bury the deceased that respects both the environment and the customer's desire to choose." Charlotte had drifted in and out of the lengthy introduction which seemed to contain far more funeral speak than actual information.

"Any questions?"

Charlotte leapt in before either of her companions had a chance to react: "No, not really. Thanks for the background. It's useful to know where you are coming from." So much for Robert Piggott's idea of a hippie love-in. As far as Charlotte could tell this was business as usual in a forest. Simples.

"OK, let's have a look at the ceremony room and our woodland walk where the graves are located so you can choose the spot where your loved one can be buried. Shall we go?"

"Just one thing before we have a look round."

"OK."

"Can we talk in private?"

"Of course," Abigail ushered Charlotte into an adjoining office.

"Well, it's a bit awkward really but..."

"It's OK, do you have some special requirements? We can usually accommodate anything people want within reason." She gave Charlotte a rather coy look.

"Oh yes, I mean, what I wanted to ask was: what if we wanted to be buried together? I mean, well, of course I'm not planning to die anytime soon, but we always said, Joe and me, that we wanted to be buried together. So, would that be one on top of the other or would we be side-by-side like. Just wanted to get it clear in my mind really."

Abigail turned away from her suddenly and her body started shaking. To Charlotte's amazement she realized she was having a fit of the giggles.

After a few seconds, which in the room seemed to stretch for ages, Abigail turned back dabbing her eyes with a tissue she had hurriedly dredged from a pocket and immediately began apologising.

"Charlotte, oh dear, look, I'm really sorry. I just got this picture in my mind of you and the deceased on top of each other. D'you know what I mean? Sorry, very unprofessional. Really, really sorry!"

Charlotte really had no idea what Abigail meant so she smiled as sweetly as the circumstances allowed and waited for her to continue

"The best we can do for you here is if you pay for two adjacent plots the unused plot will be held for you in perpetuity. That is to say, until you require it."

"OK. Another question then, don't get me wrong here, but is there any discount if you buy two plots?"

The assistant cemetery manager was taken aback by this question. In fact, if her face was anything to go by, she was repelled by it. For a moment she lost her composure and smiled derisively at the back of Charlotte's head. Charlotte, who was embarrassed to ask for a discount in such circumstances, had turned away as she was speaking in the hope of giving her question more emphasis whilst also not displaying her embarrassment.

Having regained her professional air Abigail was able to recite from her cemetery price list the exact situation regarding multiple burials.

"Well Charlotte," she began rather disdainfully, "at Green Acres we do encourage forward planning. After all none of us know what is going to happen next so if you wish to be buried next to the departed it would make eminent good sense to pre-purchase the adjoining plot. However, I need to make it clear to you, as I do to everyone who is in this situation, that there are no discounts available because, of course, the costs associated with the second burial are exactly the same as they are with the first. I'm sure you can appreciate why that would be the case?"

Turning to face Abigail, Charlotte smiled meekly: "Well things are a bit tight at the moment, moneywise, so I thought it might be worth a try."

"Indeed. Well, we can sort everything out once you have had a look round. We normally use a golf buggy for visitors but that's going to be a bit tricky for three of you. Is it vitally important for everyone to do the full trip? Could one of your guests walk round? It really isn't far, but it's going to be a bit of a squash."

"It's OK. I'll ask Laura if she can walk. It's important for George to see everything."

Duly sorted, Laura tottered off in the direction of the ceremony room while she and George managed, not without difficulty, to squeeze into the rear seat of the aforementioned buggy. It seemed to Charlotte that using the buggy was more for Abigail's convenience than anything else. On arrival at their destination George, very chivalrously, offered his hand to support Charlotte as the stability of the charabanc was threatened by the disembarkation.

The ceremony room, referred to as the Woodland Hall, was light and airy with around one hundred chairs arranged in a wide arc facing towards a podium with a curtained off area to one side and a series of full-length glass panels, which the brochure described as bringing the woodland and the meadow into the room with breath-taking effect. Entering through the wide glass doors Charlotte was aware of a calm soothing ambience inside. All the woodwork was exposed which gave the room a rustic open feel. Laura's stilettos clattered across the floor as she marched around giving a running commentary: "This is really nice Charlotte so peaceful isn't it? Just right, I think. Do Joe proud. Can you have your own music Abigail? I mean that wouldn't be a problem would it I hope?"

"No, Laura, everyone using the cemetery is encouraged to bring their own music. Particularly if you're going for the humanist option, because music allows people in attendance time for reflection and it breaks the ceremony up into sections. We always find music works very well."

"Oh good," Laura sounded a little too excited for the seriousness of the context. "Have you got any ideas for music Charlotte? We could always think about it on the way back?"

"We'll need to make sure they fit the occasion though," George contributed a note of caution to the proceedings probably based on his experience of listening to a muted version of Laura's 'tunes' emanating from her headphones in the car earlier.

"I've got a few ideas based on our discussions," said Charlotte.

"That's always handy if you know the deceased's wishes. Makes it easier all round. We finished here? Then we can go and have a look at the burial grounds. You will notice as we go round – I'll stop and show you one or two and wait for Laura to catch up – we have special dedicated burial trees and burial areas, and you can choose which suits you best. Of course, if you would like to consider one of our Prestige options then we can talk about..."

"Now it's OK thanks we'll just go for the basic one, I think. As I mentioned I've not got a lot of money to spend on this and we've got the wake to..."

"OK let's get going then." George was keen to keep things moving and was also acutely aware that Charlotte was beginning to burble.

For the second part of their journey George offered his seat in the buggy to Laura as he had become painfully aware that she was not best prepared for walking long distances, more than 10 – 20 yards was pushing it. Without exerting himself too much he was able to keep up with the buggy and was also able to look round and appreciate the fabulous woodland setting and join in at each stop on the route to personally examine each of the options that Abigail was anxious to display to her prospective customers.

"It's nice this place. Very peaceful. You wouldn't realise there were loads of people here would you. I mean dead ones of course, not that there's loads of people looking round!"

"Yeah, I know, you said that before, Laura. I think it's got a good vibe, but the issue is going to be how much is it going to cost. Can't think it's going to be cheap."

"What about George? He *is* his brother. Doesn't look as if he's short of a bob or two. Why not ask him to put his hand in his pocket. It's worth a try."

"No, I couldn't do that. It wouldn't be right just springing it on him. What would he think?"

"I know you're struggling so maybe; you know, he might want to help."

Laura had started nudging and winking at her friend as she spoke: "He might want to contribute to, you know, get on the right side of you."

"Get on the right side of me for what? Not sure what you're saying."

"I'm just saying George might want to get more involved with you, like, and paying for the funeral, or at least paying for some of it, might be his way of showing his feelings."

"I couldn't accept his money on that basis. Then I'd feel obliged to him and I don't want to get in that position. I don't ever want to be obliged to anyone again."

As they were speaking the buggy had glided to a halt outside the cemetery office. Abigail, who was aware that the two friends had been talking, headed to the office calling behind her: "You two take your time. You probably have a few things to talk about."

Charlotte was not at all happy with the suggestion Laura was making so without saying another word she made for the office as well. In the distance she could see George was making no effort to catch up.

As she got into the office Abigail was laying out several sheets of glossy paper on the table along with some glasses and a big jug of iced water.

"Help yourself to a drink. I'm just setting out the options we offer with regards to a woodland burial – with a tree, without a tree or in a woodland glade. I pointed out a couple of examples as we went

round which I hope gave you a good idea of what was on offer. I've already eliminated the Prestige option as I'm aware that is not in your price range and I understand that. Perhaps you want to have a look at the details before the others catch up."
"OK, that's good. Thanks."

A few minutes later Laura and George burst through the door in quite an agitated state, looking rather wet.
"Just started pissing down so we had to run over. Absolutely poured down. Sorry we're making the floor a bit wet."
"Not a problem. Fully understand." Abigail clearly wasn't to be put off by a little precipitation as she moved towards clinching a deal. "I think considering everything you said today, Charlotte, that you are going to be looking at £2 to £2.5k including everything that we talked about and, one thing I forgot, the use of the electric hearse should you require it to take the deceased's body from the ceremony to the woodland site. I know you said you're on a tight budget, so how does that feel?"
Charlotte's first impression was that it felt awfully expensive for what it was. All extremely cute and eco-friendly but a lot of people were making a living out of burying people in pleasant surroundings rather than the council run crematorium.
"Well Charlotte, I think..."
Charlotte bristled at the idea of George butting in on her conversation. She was absolutely sure now that she shouldn't have invited him. She knew now it was going to be really difficult to make up her own mind. Why couldn't he keep his big mouth shut. She turned on him glaring, "George first and foremost this is my decision," Charlotte was angry, and she needed George to see that. She continued in the same vein, "and as such I would appreciate it if you could let me decide what I want to do. I'll ask you for your help if I need it. Thank you now..."
"But Charlotte. I was only..."
"George please, please. This is my money. I'm honouring a commitment to a guy who kept so much from me – who I thought he was has completely unravelled over the last few days. I'm struggling with that, it's really difficult from my standpoint to see if I can afford to go through with our agreement given how he deceived me. Whether I can honour that. I need some time to think about it."

Abigail was looking increasingly embarrassed as events unfolded and was unsure how to take things forward.

"Look Charlotte the rain has stopped. Why don't you and me go for a walk just so's you've got a bit of time to weigh things up," Laura had seen her friend getting more and more upset and jumped in to try and ease the situation by extracting Charlotte from what was becoming a major confrontation.

"Thanks Laura, I don't need to go for a walk. I had planned to have a look at another woodland setting today, but I'm really impressed with what you're offering here Abigail and I actually think the numbers will add up." Charlotte decided that rather than have a public disagreement or a cosy chat she should make her own decision. She didn't need any help. George was not going to take over her funeral. "So, if you could send me a detailed quotation. I'll get back to you straight away to confirm things."

After Charlotte had made her announcement, she gestured to Abigail that she wanted to have a further word in private. She wanted no further interruptions at this stage. A few minutes later, having arranged a date for the funeral 10 days hence, she re-joined her companions who were standing by the exit obviously enjoying a joke. As soon as they saw Charlotte approaching, they exchanged embarrassed glances, stopped laughing and started looking rather vacantly at their feet.

"Right then that's sorted. I'm pleased with that. I think they'll do a good job here. Got a good vibe, I think."

"Yeah, I like the idea of the woodland. Works well and if it was what Joe wanted then it's got to be right, hasn't it?" Laura was chattering on to herself such that George and Charlotte barely even heard the question, let alone bothered to reply.

Charlotte was silent as she led the way to the car. George was just behind her making no attempt to catch up or engage in conversation. The pathetic figure of Laura tottering in their wake amused Abigail who was left wondering exactly what was going on between the departing visitors. She had had lots of experience of emotional outbursts as people became overwhelmed by the situation but never a flareup like that. She decided to make sure she booked a day's leave for the day of the Brunt funeral as she felt she had seen enough of the two main protagonists to last her a lifetime.

Hardly a word was spoken on the return journey. George was concentrating on driving as fast as he could, Laura was absorbed with her phone and Charlotte spent the whole time staring out of the window.

As George pulled up outside Laura's residence he said: "Good to see you again Laura."

"Thanks for driving George. Glad I went, good to know you've got a date now. I'll put it on my calendar when I get in. You OK Charlotte? You've been very quiet all the way back. Want to come in for a brew?"

"Yes, I will if it's OK. Thanks. Thanks for driving us George it was a great help. I'll text you later. OK?"

"Yeah, that's fine. Glad you got the venue sorted. That must be a weight off your mind?"

"Yes it is. Thanks George."

"See you girls."

"I really don't know what to make of George..."

Laura and Charlotte had settled on Laura's massive Sofology three seat settee which had a recliner at either end. Needless to say, they were both making the most of reclining at this moment in time.

"When I first met him. You know he made contact. Joe's secret brother and all that. Well, he was so nervous and needy I nearly decided to blank him. He just didn't seem as though he could be any help at all but since then..."

"I've got a strange feeling about him. About like, his motives really," Laura had suddenly become a motivational expert – not her usual approach to men, as far as Charlotte was aware. "You see he's dead attentive to you, obviously really wants to help, but then he's also been dead chatty with me. Asking all sorts of questions about me and boyfriends and interests and how long we've known each other. It was like being interviewed by a policeman. You know, a bit threatening. Made me feel uncomfortable to be truthful."

"You did drag him off last time you were both here. Poor sod, maybe he was just making conversation. It wasn't his idea..."

"OK I get that. I made a mistake, but you need to think about this. Joe's only been dead for a few days and his brother's on your case. You need to ask yourself why is he doing it? – spending time at a burial site, helping out with his estranged brother's affairs, and don't give me that stuff about guilt. You need to decide if you can trust him before he gets much more involved, otherwise..."

"Laura!" Charlotte put her cup down on the table rather forcefully and rather loudly as she continued, "I know you have your own views about my relationships with men, but I think you're reading too much into this. I know I lost it with him back there, but I'm struggling with him getting too close to me even though I know he's trying to be supportive. He's in a very difficult position."

"OK you can ignore me if you want," Laura sounded a bit peeved, "but I think you'll regret it. I really do."

"Don't get me wrong Laura, got lots on my mind at present. Can't be bothered with motives. Now I'm just so grateful to both of you for helping which brings me to this, I need to ask you another favour. I've got a sort of list of all the people who said they want to come so far – need to send a formal notice. It's not an invitation is it. I don't have to invite them for God's sake. And I need to confirm the Crown & Anchor for the bash afterwards and to add that in. Just need to get the wording right..."

Charlotte's phone pinged for the nth time since they had been talking. She had been trying to ignore it, but curiosity got the better of her, "I'd better check," as she retrieved her phone from her pocket. "OMG can't believe that, 15 messages. Look I'll just flick through them and then I'll be right with you."

"More tea,"

"Yes please."

Laura retreated into the kitchen leaving Charlotte scrolling through the messages on her phone

When Laura returned with two cups of builder's tea Charlotte was still absorbed in her task. As she caught sight of Laura she looked up.

"Thanks love. Lots more sympathy – think I'm suffering an overdose of sympathy. Just makes me feel all weak and wishy-washy. The big problem is I don't know who most of them are! Anyway, there's a bit of good news – well it better be good news! The solicitor has texted to say he wants to read the Will this afternoon. George replied straightaway. He can make it, so we are on for 4 o'clock. Oh my god Laura this is so important. I have no idea what I'm gonna do if he's left it all to someone else. I'll be screwed. I'm sure I'm in with a chance. Don't tell me I'm clutching at straws, all his finances were so tidy..."

"Yeah, I know not like the Joe we both thought we knew."

"Exactly so I'm thinking," Charlotte's voice was quavering as she became unusually animated, "he won't have left things as they were, would he? Like leaving everything to one of his wives – he'd have kept things up to date. Wouldn't he? Laura, wouldn't he?"

Laura was not responding to Charlotte's questions. In fact, it looked as if she was in a trance, deep thought. In response to Charlotte's shrieking, she finally turned round to look at her friend. She grabbed hold of her flailing hands and held them tightly for a couple of seconds.

"I've got it," she said solemnly. "I know why Joe's brother is all over you. He thinks Joe must have had a bob or two, for reasons we cannot even guess at, and that he'll have left it all to you, so his only chance is to get on the right side of you, so you'll share it with him. Sneaky little bastard, making out he's all for you and what he's really interested in is Joe's money."

"Well, trust Laura to think the best of everyone eh, eh? You seem to have forgotten we've been through the file and what was it £6k in an ISA and a few hundred in his current account? Not really worth getting excited about really. Is it?"

"There must be some more money. I mean loads of money that George knows all about. You see you are being conned again by all his charm and stuff and really all he wants is the cash. That's all he wants. Can't you see that, Charlotte?"

Charlotte was getting impatient with her friend and her inability to, at least at the outset, give someone the benefit of the doubt and angry that she was trashing George's intentions without actually having a clue what they were. Despite what had happened earlier at Green Acres she found herself defending George against what she perceived as Laura's unwarranted slurs.

"You need to back off a bit here, Laura. You'll be calling the police next. The guy's actually done nothing wrong and you will have him on a list for deportation in a minute. I get that we need to be cautious but don't just write him off!"

"D'you fancy him? Is that why you're being so defensive? Charlotte Summersby, the poor lad is not in the ground yet and you're lining up a successor. You're dreadful, awful I..."

"Laura stop it, stop that right now. Can't believe what you're saying." As she continued her voice became louder and she began jabbing her finger towards her friend. "Just listen to yourself condemning the man without a shred of evidence. All we know is he offered to help. That is all we know so let's work on that basis shall we, and leave all your mumbo-jumbo third-rate soap opera plot conjecture for another time. So just shut it OK? OK?"

Laura, amazed by this tirade, nodded meekly as she stared resolutely at a vase of flowers on the table next to where she was sitting.

"Look, I don't want to fall out with you, but you do come up with some stuff. I need your help tomorrow so let's leave all the dreamed-up stuff for now, see how things develop and move on."

"OK, sorry but I thought..."

"I know you did but that sort of thinking is not going to help. I'll try and sort out the pub when I get back from seeing the solicitor. Then tomorrow we can just concentrate on making sure everyone knows what is going on."

"OK sorry, I got a bit carried away," and trying to redeem herself she added, "George is a nice guy, I'm sure he is, but it does..."

"I'm not listening to any more Laura. I'm going to phone for a cab."

As she entered her lounge, well the lounge formerly rented by the deceased J Brunt and shortly to become the sole responsibility of Charlotte Summersby, she headed straight for the drink's cupboard and more specifically the rhubarb gin therein. She tried to estimate a double before she went in search of some tonic and ready-made ice courtesy of Joe's double fronted American fridge. Whilst It had caused many rows and led to the banishing of the dishwasher Charlotte had to admit now, when it was too late to inform her late partner, that it was bloody marvellous – gin without ice was definitely not happening. Her first toast was to Joe for his foresight and the second was to Laura and the support she was offering. Charlotte could tell it was really difficult for Laura not to offer her opinions, so she knew she was treading a fine line when she clearly was not happy with what was going on, but even so was still warning Charlotte of what she felt. They rarely had any discussions about men and their suitability, or otherwise, before because of their divergent views of what was 'best' for Charlotte. They were anxious not to fall out over men especially as in many cases, up to Joe and Charlotte's relationship, they had not lasted long enough to have warranted intense scrutiny. After a drink fuelled one-night stand Charlotte often couldn't even remember the guy's name let alone any of the finer details.

So, Charlotte concluded, if Laura was really worried about George, she owed it to herself and her best friend to be cautious and not just rush blindly into trusting him completely before being very sure she was doing the right thing. As she settled back in her chair sipping her gin she realised she needed to be going out. Wanting to make the best use of her time she reached for the house phone to check whether anyone had left a message. As she did so it started to ring, and an unknown number flashed onto the screen.

"Hello."

"Hi Charlotte, it's Hannah."

"Oh hi, thanks for calling. I was thinking I'd give you a call actually..."

"Well, I was just phoning to see how you're getting on. I mean I think you were in a bit of a state when I was talking to you last. I know it must have been a shock."

"It certainly made me think very differently about Joe. Very differently indeed.

"Well, I worried particularly about all the debt he'd run up. Not that I can help with..."

Charlotte felt Hannah had slipped that proviso in unfeelingly quickly. So, she was just basically ringing to see what else happened, after she left the scene, for her own vicarious pleasures

"Well, it's OK," Charlotte interrupted rather firmly. "You've no need to worry on that score because I've been through all this stuff and there are no nasty surprises at this stage. I'm not counting my chickens yet though because I've got to go to the solicitors later on to see what is in his Will and I don't know what he's going to say. I'm going with George..."

"His brother?" Hannah broke in, her voice breaking with emotion. "That bastard. He's turned up has he? I hope you haven't got in too deeply with him. He's so devious. Has he told you why he and Joe hadn't been speaking? Obviously, I don't know about recently, but while Joe and I were married George was one of the biggest issues we had to deal with. He was constantly on the cadge for something, usually money, to get himself out of hot water with his 'investments' which always seemed to go tits up. Oh my god I'm really sorry to hear that. Is he sniffing around for money from you? Cos if he is just tell him to do one. Honestly that guy is trouble."

Whilst Hannah ranted, Charlotte had a fleeting memory that George even phoned her after the split to commiserate and now she was sure he was after Charlotte in much the same way. Hannah's diatribe caught Charlotte completely unawares but added to her problems coming so soon after Laura had issued her own amber alert. George had proved to be quite helpful so far, indeed he had offered money to Charlotte rather than trying to get one over on her even though on the downside she was struggling to keep him at arm's length. He had claimed to be doing quite well rather than pleading poverty. Charlotte was backed into a corner. She knew very little about Hannah. She did not, as a general rule, take to over-opinionated people, but as she tried to rationalise the strange world she found herself in there were always so many buts. Charlotte wasn't sure how to react. She hardly knew George, Hannah seemed have a major problem with him, but she wasn't giving her very much space.

"Look Hannah. I hear what you're saying..."

"But you..."

"No Hannah, no listen to me please," Charlotte absolutely hated being told what to do especially when the person who was telling her was someone she hardly knew. "Look you're entitled to your..."

Joe and Charlotte were always rowing about opinions, who was entitled and who wasn't, on whether one person's opinion necessarily countermanded another's. Human rights came into it as did various UN Charters, the fact that the UK didn't have a written Constitution and when it came to Brexit that wasn't just an opinion, In versus Out, it was a declaration of war one against the other. Charlotte was always on the back foot in the past. Not now, not in the newfound future of Charlotte Summersby as she set sail in life's strong and as yet uncharted seas.

"Listen Charlotte, please listen this is..."

"No, I'm sorry Hannah I'm not going to listen. Let me just explain. I don't know what experience you've had of someone close to you, very close to you, dying. I would just say, I don't recommend it. Not for one minute. It leaves you numb, angry, isolated, an emotional wreck. It's not easy being like that and..."

"I really need to butt in there..."

"No, you don't Hannah, you really don't," shouted Charlotte. "I haven't finished. When I have, I'm going to hang up. So just listen to me please and then we can go our separate ways. Now where was I – when you're at your wits end with grief, worry and loads of other shit you need support, Hannah. You really need support. I didn't want to ask my older sister, so I had to lean on Laura, we go way back, she's been brill for support, y'know a shoulder to cry on. Now, and this is where you really need to keep quiet, this is where George comes in - he obviously heard about Joe and he got in touch. Now he said he wanted to help and that's exactly what he's done. At no time has he made any demands on me, he's just been very supportive. You have obviously had a quite different experience and no doubt when I mention your name to him, he'll have some equally strong views about you. At the moment I'm not sure I give a toss to be honest. I'll make up my mind who I accept help from. I'll make up my mind how to deal with people. I will not be told what to do by anyone. I just want to make that very clear."

"I only want to save..."

"Hannah, I'm done with this. I'll be in touch regarding the funeral details and, if you can make it, I look forward to seeing you then." With that Charlotte replaced the phone in its cradle realising as she did it that her hand was shaking. She went to compile another gin before she started pacing up and down the kitchen. "What a bitch, all that shit about George. What does she know? She and Joe fell out over money, I've never had any issues. Never even heard of the guy while Joe was alive so how bad could he have been. Interfering bitch!" Charlotte was working herself up into a frenzy as she began kicking the waste bin and fridge door, all the time berating the overbearing Hannah.

Weekday evenings in the Brunt household were often solitary affairs. Mostly it was Joe who was out. Either he was late back from work or he had a social activity to attend. All he would say to Charlotte was that he was a great believer in building team spirit which seemed to be very time consuming as far as Charlotte could see. It also involved most often getting drunk which meant that by the time Joe got home Charlotte had long since drunk her hot chocolate and gone to bed. This was a clear signal to Joe that she was not to be disturbed although it was more or less a guarantee that at some stage his snoring, on such nights, would be sure to wake Charlotte up to enable her the opportunity to savour the delights of sharing a bed with an inconsiderate drunk. Being alone in bed since Joe's demise had differed in one joyous regard and that was not being woken up by said sonorous snoring. Charlotte still woke up and notwithstanding previous not insubstantial drawbacks, she did miss her hairy snuggles; his firm hands on her breasts; or his reflex jerks as she lay her ice-cold hands on his bum. As she reached into the empty space next to her, she started thinking about the life they had shared. Prior to Joe's passing she had always enjoyed the thought of falling asleep, letting go clearing her mind and embracing the peace. Recently that calmness and serenity had deserted her, and she ached for that peace to return and ease her pain.

"What did you say? How much? Can't believe it! Charlotte that's unbelievable! What did George say? Was he gobsmacked? I would have been, too bloody right I would have been. Wow good old Joe's come through at last!" Charlotte had barely said goodbye to George outside the solicitors than Laura had texted to ask how she had got on. With too much to explain in a text she had found a quiet corner of a nearby park to phone her back and break the news.
"He's left me £100,000 Laura! 100,000 fucking pounds! To be honest I'm still in shock. I mean you should have seen George's face, he obviously had no idea what was coming, no idea at all..."
"Where are you? Need to meet up – need a celebratory drink. That's wonderful news..."
"Yeah, but don't get too excited, Joe's not coming back, not sure £100,000 really replaces him y'know. I've not buried him, yet you know."
"I realise that, but you were dead worried about how things were going to work out weren't you and now, well you know, don't you? And like that's good news, isn't it?" Silence. "Well, it is, isn't it?"
Charlotte was in shock firstly because she never imagined Joe would have such a stash of money and secondly because of the source of the money. An Aunt Agnes had apparently left him a not inconsiderable amount of money, as far as Charlotte could remember, Mr Jarvis said £500,000 some 20 years previously. All Mr Jarvis would say was that there was £200,000 left which was to be split 50-50 between her and George. He gave the two beneficiaries no further information not, and he made this very clear, not that he didn't want to but because he actually did not know. He didn't know who Aunt Agnes was, didn't know where the other money had gone and, in answer to a particularly aggrieved question from George, he didn't know why George had not been left any money by the previously unknown Aunt Agnes.
"It's amazing isn't it? and he kept it quiet. Mr Jarvis has all the details of the account and everything and when it's all gone through probate, he can pay us both out. Apart from that he's left everything

in the flat to me. Mr Jarvis was a bit funny at the end. He gave me a letter which Joe had entrusted to him and then said that although it was a matter for an inquest, he wasn't too sure that Joe hadn't taken his own life."

"What you mean? What could have made him think that? He hadn't gone funny before he died, had he?" Laura's understanding of mental health issues was not very comprehensive, so she had very little idea regarding the tell-tale signs that someone was intending to commit suicide.

"Well, he said, and he told us both this, it wasn't a secret. He said that Joe had been to see him two weeks ago to as he put it: "To put my affairs in order – just in case." I mean he didn't elaborate, but that was really weird what he said: "Just in case." And the other thing was he said Joe had asked that I should not read the letter until after the funeral, whenever that occurs. He gave me a really curious look when he said that and then he added like, as an aside: "Of course you'll have to make your own mind up about when you open it. Won't you?" Really odd though – if Joe hadn't wanted me to read it why has he given it to me now, it's almost as if he was defying him. Going against what he said."

"What y'going to do then?"

"I've not taken in the money stuff yet – I mean I might be able to buy my own home. Never liked renting – it costs a fortune, and you don't get anything back. 42 Lediard St is such a barn. If it was only for me..."

"For how long though, Charlotte? How long you gonna be on your own?"

"I'm not exactly going to be rushing out to find a replacement you know. I think it would be quite nice to set myself up in a sort of cottagey place. Not in town but more in the country if I can."

"Hope you're not going to be too far away though."

"Well, no, of course stupid I'll still need to get work and that."

"OK just so's you remember me. Anyway, what did Georgie boy say? Are you absolutely sure he didn't know beforehand?"

"No."

"Are you positive?"

"Well, if he did, he's a bloody good actor. He just started laughing great big bursts like proper guffawing. He nearly lost it. Hysterical like. I mean he said before that he was there to help me sort things out. I think he feared the worst and that his brother wouldn't have updated his Will after his last divorce. I think that's why he came. I don't know much else 'cos at the end of the meeting he said he'd catch me later because he wanted a few words with Mr Jarvis in private. No idea what that was about, so I just left them to it."

"Not so sure that was a good idea, y'know. Leaving him on his own with the solicitor. I mean he might have been up to all sorts."

"What d'you mean 'all sorts'?"

"Well trying to get things changed. You just don't know. I told you before I've got a feeling about your George."

"Come to that you're not alone. Not sure I should be telling you this. I'll never get any peace. Well, I had a phone call from Hannah yesterday."

"Ex-wife Hannah," chimed in Laura.

"The very same. Well, she was going crazy knowing George was on the scene. OMG she was really going on with herself, more or less telling me to have nothing to do with him as if he was the devil incarnate or something. Apparently, he was always in money troubles in the past. She was absolutely terrified he was going to rob me blind. Had to tell her to piss off in the end as she was coming out with all sorts. I told her that I'll make up my mind who I talk to, who I trust. I don't need lectures etc. She obviously had me down for a proper fool."

"She won't be very welcome at the bash then?"

"To be fair I left it with her. I just said I didn't want to talk to her anymore and it was up to her if she wanted to come to the funeral."

"Well, you're certainly learning to stand on your own two feet lately. Not a pushover any more eh Charlotte?"

"Well, stupid bitch – that was then, and this is now. Up to now George has been a great help, as I told you, and we'll just have to see how things develop just so long as he doesn't overstep the mark."

"OK, back to business. You've had a rough couple of days – how about a couple of drinks, local? Just a nice relax, won't be late. OK?"

Silence. "Charlotte don't go all quiet on me now."

"Just thinking," Charlotte was weighing up whether the inevitable blinding headache would be doable in order to have a bit of light relief from her new temporary job as a funeral organiser. She still needed help with that so decided to make a deal.

"OK you're on..."

"Great I knew you'd see sense..."

"...but I still need your help tomorrow remember. After lunch be OK, to go through stuff and make sure everything is moving in the right direction?"

"How long do you need?"

"Only a couple of hours. OK, deal?"

Demure but not dull was the look Charlotte had decided on for her evening out. She had opted for a dark red dress with a hint of sparkle, matching shoes – she had had the whole outfit for the duration of her relationship with Joe and never had the chance to wear it – and pastel lippy and a bit of eye shadow just to hide away any residual puffiness. It certainly worked for Laura who was gushing all over her as she joined her at the table in Chloe's Dine & Dance bar.

"You look great lovey, really good. Glad you made the effort – makes you feel so much better."

As Charlotte settled, she was aware that other people in the bar were looking in her direction. If she caught someone's eye she smiled and nodded hoping that would be sufficient to keep them at bay. What she really wanted to do was have a natter, a few drinks and maybe a dance, not a recurring series of conversations with Joe's acquaintances who felt obliged to offer their condolences. She was holding the line quite well until Harriet brushed past her on the way to the bar. As she glanced back to apologise she recognised Charlotte, smiled affectionately, and walked back towards her.

"Really sorry about Joe. Not had a chance before, but..."

As Harriet was about to stray into forbidden territory for her relaxing night out Charlotte interrupted her: "It's OK, I realise it was very sudden but I'm getting there thanks."

"OK, that's good. I've never spoken to you before have I?"

"No, I've seen you chatting to Joe a couple of times."

"Yeah, s'funny. I used to go out with George, Joe's brother."

"Yeah, I know George. He got in touch as soon as he heard about Joe's death. Been very helpful."

"Not seen him for ages. Real diamond though. I used to ask after him, but Joe was never very forthcoming. I knew George when I used to live in York. That was when Joe was married to Hannah, what a bitch she was. I think she fancied George at one time, and he kept on blanking her and she really didn't like that. He even told Joe about it which, I think, is one of the main reasons why they got divorced if I remember right. Anyway, if you see him give him my best. Have fond memories of George."

With that Harriet considered the conversation finished and continued in the direction of the bar.

"What did she want? Seen her talking to Joe in here before. Never sure what she was up to. Bit too brazen for me."

"Told me she used to go out with George a few years back..."

"Oh, sounds interesting..."

"Yeah. Think she's still holding a torch for him as well."

"How d'you know? She was only talking to you for a couple of minutes."

"She was a bit intense, not just passing a comment, and she was very keen for me to mention her name next time I saw George. Not sure I want to get involved. Anyway, going against what you and Hannah have been saying she said he was a really good bloke. Very generous apparently as well," Charlotte decided to embellish George's reputation, hoping Laura might back off somewhat in her criticism.

"Fascinating! Well, I'm about ready for another drink. You?"

"OK, but don't forget we've things to do tomorrow so not going to be having loads, OK?"

"We've not exactly been racing along up to now, so I don't think you've got too many worries there." Laura tottered to her feet as if to go to the bar and then leant on Charlotte's shoulder. "Have you noticed how many people are looking over here. I'm getting a bit uncomfortable. Shall we go somewhere else where they're not so nosey?"

"No, I'm set here now. Anyway, I'm getting lots of sympathetic smiles. Feels quite supportive really. Providing we don't make fools of ourselves," she accompanied these words with a stern look in Laura's direction, "we should be fine."

The last thing Charlotte wanted to do was traipse round the local bars worrying about whether people knew her or not. She reached for her phone to check any messages before Laura got back. She spotted one from George but didn't want to get involved in a text discussion in front of Laura, so decided to delay her reply so she could just enjoy a natter and catch up with her friend as planned. George could wait until tomorrow after she had made sure her funeral preparations were on track. She had a nagging doubt as to whether everything was going as planned or in fact, as the alcohol began to take effect, whether she had a plan at all

Chapter 6: Variations

Charlotte was feeling very pleased with herself. Her trip out had gone as planned, no banging headache, no lethargy and, for the first time since Joe's passing, she had not cried herself to sleep. In preparation for Laura's arrival, she had spent the morning tidying the house, checking all her messages and emails, as well as letters and cards, so she had got the most up-to-date list of people who had said they wanted to attend. They had set the date for Friday 27 September while they were at Green Acres Memorial Park. The Crown & Anchor could accommodate the wake and, taking into account her recent good news on the money front, so far things were not looking too expensive.

What she wanted to achieve with Laura was to check through her thinking, design an e-invitation card, which she was going to print out for the technophobes, and go through the funeral director's checklist because she knew she would have to make contact with him again soon and didn't want him to have any 'issues'.

Charlotte was feeling as happy as she could be in the circumstances, more so because the house looked tidy which always made her feel relaxed. Not having to wonder which room was best to invite people into because she had forgotten! Although she missed Joe, lots, there were issues every day, sometimes more than once, when, love him to bits, Joe memories flashed through her thoughts although some of them were not very good.

"Look I meant to do that before you got back. It's just..."

"Joe – it's 'just' again. 'Just' is not good enough, is it? I mean, really, you've not done anything since I left this morning, have you? Cups and plates all over the place. Couldn't you just have put them in the kitchen? That would have been a help." Even as she ranted Charlotte knew she was wasting her time. Joe was just untidy and no amount of rows were going to change him. It was just that she despaired every so often, mainly after a long day when she was hungry, the mess was just too much and she railed against the man who caused her so much distress.

Later, after he got his arse in gear, and apologised and made her laugh she forgot all her annoyance, until the next time. Every so often he did try and let his charming side come to the fore, which was really appreciated, Charlotte just wished it happened more often. Cleaning and clearing up were, Charlotte reasoned, most of the time, a small price to pay for living rent and rates free. She only put in for her food and towards holidays so she had little cause to complain, except that she did!

Charlotte was rather worried that the bad stuff kept coming back. However she was also finding that some aspects of living alone were rather appealing – being in control covered a lot of situations – but she also recalled some of the better aspects of not being in control and she really missed those, for quite different reasons.

As she thought more about Joe she remembered his brother and how she had left him the previous afternoon and realised she had not responded to his text. Mindful that she needed to check out a couple of things with him she found his number on her phone.

"Hi Charlotte, what kept you?" George sounded a bit irritated as if Charlotte should have been in touch more or less immediately. She had expected a warmer greeting and this put her very much at a disadvantage.

"Oh, sorry didn't think it was urgent. Look I've got a lot on here. I was..." Charlotte was beginning to sound a bit petulant so she tried to catch her breath and calm down, but before she could George interrupted: "I realise that, sorry! I was looking forward to hearing from you," George's tone had changed now. "How are things going? Is everything falling into place?"

"Yes thanks. Going pretty well as far as I can see. Difficult to know – never having done anything like this before!

"Obviously. Good news yesterday about the Will wasn't it? I was completely blown away. Don't know about you?"

"I had no idea at all. I mean Laura and I had been through all his paperwork and there was no clue. I had in the back of my mind it would be bad news, to be fair. When I heard from Hannah she was going on about how much he had owed, when she knew Joe, so I didn't have a lot of hope really."

"Well, I had no idea about the inheritance. He kept that a very close secret from me and I don't know why he would have done that for all those years?"

"Well," Charlotte really wasn't sure whether to delve into Hannah's views with George at this stage, but he had brought up money so she decided to push at the open door, "perhaps he thought you might want to borrow some of it or dispute the Will even..."

"No, I really doubt that. We never spoke about money, ever. So, it wouldn't have happened."

"S'funny because, well, I'm not sure I should say this..."

"Say what?"

"Well, Hannah phoned again yesterday."

"Oh, did she?"

"Yeah, wanted to know how I was getting on. She sounded really concerned, especially when I mentioned that you had been in touch."

"OK."

"Well, she went mad..."

"What d'you mean?"

"Well, basically, she was saying you were altogether untrustworthy and that I should have nothing to do with you. She said you'd only be interested in me for any money you could get from me. She was adamant that you were up to no good."

"Don't know why Hannah should have it in for me. When she and Joe were married I didn't have very much to do with them."

"Well, that's not what she said, you know," Charlotte was trying to keep her tone as light as possible, she didn't want to give George the impression that she believed Hannah, but she did want to hear his side of the story. "Apparently, and this is what she said, you were always round asking for money for various bright ideas which never came off. At least..."

"That's bloody ridiculous – I've never wanted to get involved in get rich quick schemes. Why would I? I've always had a steady job. She must have got the wrong person. I can't think why she would want to say such nasty things about me."

"She reckoned you were one of the main reasons Joe and her split up."

"That's outrageous! How dare she say that! Joe dumped Hannah because she couldn't keep her hands to herself – that's what he told me. I remember going round there for meals over the years, we met up at other do's and stuff. They were usually fine together, but as time went by they seemed to snipe at each other a lot and I just kept out of their way really."

"What a bitch, and she sounded as if she was only saying all this stuff to help me. You told me before that you had fallen out with Joe some years ago. What was that over?" Charlotte realised she was putting

George in an awkward position. She had already told him about Hannah's accusations and now she was prying into his past life. She was expecting a rebuff.

"Well, it's a long story really. Do you really want to go into the gory details now?" George sounded quite relaxed about the issue. There wasn't even a hint of annoyance, but instead he seemed genuinely interested to know just how bothered Charlotte was about the detail.

"It was just that after what Hannah had said, y'know, it made me wonder exactly what was going on. I'm getting to know so much about Joe since his passing I could write a book, but it still seems as if there's more to find out. I'm getting more curious."

"It's OK I'm happy to talk about it at some stage. Perhaps not now though, so can we move onto why I texted you, please. It was because I wanted to talk to you about something else, altogether."

"Oh. What was that? Sounds interesting."

"Well, you know our visit to the solicitor's yesterday," George paused. Charlotte was not sure whether or not to respond.

"Y-e-s."

"Well, you know I stayed behind after you left." Another pause. Charlotte suspected George was stringing her along to build up the suspense and it was working.

"Y-e-s," Charlotte could feel her heart beating faster and her mouth was very dry but she had no idea why. Why was she so excited? Why was George teasing her? Her hesitant responses just seemed to encourage him and he was laughing almost giggling to himself at each stage.

"Well, I had a very interesting conversation with Mr Jarvis." Pause — Charlotte could almost feel the smirk on George's face down the phone line.

"Y-e-e-e-s."

"And he was saying that it might be a good idea."

Pause

"George what are you going on about? Stop teasing me! My heart is nearly beating out of my chest here. Stop it please!" If George had been in the same room Charlotte would by this time have been punching him and swearing at him. However, the verbal assault was a different matter: "You bastard why are you winding me up. Just tell me what you are talking about." Charlotte had lost it and she was shouting full volume at George.

"If you let me get a word in I'll try to tell you. OK?"

"OK."

"You know when we first met, I said that I wanted to help you in any way I could? Well, when I heard about the way Joe had split the money I realised I could make a real difference. I've told you before I'm OK for money so I really don't need any more, so I asked Mr Jarvis if there was any legal way that the Will could be changed so you got more of the money. He suggested varying the Will."

"Varying it? What does that mean? Don't you want your share? Is that what you're saying? I get your share?"

"Well more or less."

"More or less what?"

"Well, what we decided would be if you got £75,000 and the remaining £25,000 stayed in trust for you. For you to..."

"You mean you're going to give me £75,000? Really? You actually don't need the money so I get it? What's in it for you? You're either a major twat or so generous you'll hurt yourself being so nice. I'm speechless," Charlotte burbled.

"Well not exactly. You seem to be saying quite a lot actually. No, there's no catch at all – I want you to have the money. End of."

"But I can't agree to that. I hardly know you and you want to give me a fortune that is rightly yours. And you don't want anything in return?"

"Not really, no I don't. It's not a condition, so don't see it like that, but what about if we spent some of the money on a holiday. We could both do with a couple of days away before the funeral. Make a change, you've been under a lot of pressure and it will give us an opportunity to get to know each other better."

"So that's the catch. A dirty weekend with you and I get..."

"No, nothing like that at all. Not at all. We can keep as separate as you like, but just spend some time together away from this place and curious eyes."

"D'you think that's very appropriate? 'Recently widowed woman splashes out on weekend with deceased's brother' wouldn't read..."

"Hey, it's not such a bad idea. Just a thought. If you don't fancy it then we won't bother," George sounded hurt at being so comprehensively snubbed. "Where we go, what we do, everything is down to you and what you want. All we do is use some of the inheritance to pay for it. If all you can think of is impropriety then I'm really disappointed, I thought you had more about you than that."

"Don't know what to say really. I mean I didn't fix the funeral for next week so I could sneak off on a romantic idyll with you. I just wanted to have enough time to sort everything out so that I..."

"Wouldn't get anything wrong. Y'know you're really too hard on yourself. My brother would have been very impressed by everything you've done so far. I'm not sure he could have done the same for you." Charlotte felt she ought to leap to Joe's defence but chose silence instead. "Now I'm not being nasty, honestly, what I'm saying is that, even at his best, you know what I mean, he'd have made a balls of it just because he was Joe. I'm right aren't I?"

Charlotte smiled to herself partly because of the astute analysis from Joe's pop up brother and partly because of a memory he had triggered of a 'surprise' Valentine's treat Joe had arranged for her only a couple of months after they had met. He had booked a very expensive restaurant for their meal and then made every effort to keep the venue secret to the extent that, as of the late afternoon of 14 February, Charlotte had no idea if, when, or where she might be going for Valentine's evening. She had in fact, given up, she was so pissed off that she had decided to end their relationship as soon she saw him again.

Arriving home from work she had flounced into the house, looked wildly round for any clue as to what was supposed to be happening and then, having exhausted herself emotionally, she raced upstairs and threw herself on the bed. She was distraught, completely and utterly at a loss as to why this man, who had begged her to move in with him so recently, could mess up so badly.

She had made sure he had had his card before he went off to work, expecting some level of reciprocation when she herself arose. The absence of any sort of card, home-made or not, or any flowers got Charlotte off to a bad start which had not got any better, in fact it had got worse, much much worse.

"Charlotte! Charlotte are you OK? Love, wake up! It's Joe. Where've you been?"

"Geroff you bastard," Charlotte flailed her arms in the general direction of where she thought Joe's voice was coming from. "Are you pissed? Have you been out with your mates? Decided to come home now have you," each phrase was punctuated by Charlotte's continued attempts to land a good punch on her errant partner. She wasn't bothered where she hit him, she just wanted to cause him some pain – the worse the better.

"What happened? I waited ages for you, phoning, texting, you didn't pick up. I paid for the meal, ate mine then came back..."

"So, you've had your meal have you? Thank you very much. Selfish bastard. Where's my card? Where's my flowers? And how the fuck was I supposed to know what was happening?"

Charlotte had stopped flailing, she was just sobbing, big tears rolling down her cheeks. Joe could feel her pain but inwardly he felt quite justifiably that he was the injured and, considerably poorer, party.

He sat on the bed, wrapped his arms round her and held her closely feeling her wet face against his as he tried to stop her shaking.

"Look, I'm sorry, I'm really sorry – I thought it would make a really nice surprise."

"What would? Me getting really upset and crying myself to sleep? To be honest that's one surprise I could have done without..."

"No, come on, come downstairs. I want to show you something."

As they entered the kitchen Charlotte started laughing. Propped up by the kettle was an enormous envelope, next to that was a box of chocolates and to top the lot off standing in a vase immediately adjacent was what looked like, to Charlotte's tutored eye, an M&S £25 bouquet of flowers artfully re-priced at £50 for Valentine's Day.

Charlotte started battering Joe again. This time her flailing arms made connection as she began shouting again: "You stupid bastard. Went to all this effort and didn't bother to tell me. You know I never come into the kitchen before I go out to work. You know that because you're always moaning about how much I spend at Costa! You and I were finished a few hours ago y'know. I was in such a mood with you I never even looked in here when I got back." She sat down heavily on one of the breakfast bar chairs. "Oh my god what a pair of fools... Couldn't organise a..."

"I thought I'd done really well actually. Trouble was I managed to make it a bit too much of a surprise."

At that they both embraced and laughed together at the hopelessness of the situation they found themselves in.

Charlotte was able to smile, with the benefit of hindsight, at how stupid she had been thinking the worst rather than in any way giving Joe the benefit of the doubt. He had never arranged another surprise since then which was probably just as well. Charlotte's nerves would never have stood the strain

"You've gone quiet," said George after a long pause

"Just remembering Joe's organisational skills. That's all."

"Any details?"

"Nah, just memories," Charlotte sounded rather wistful and George decided he needed to break the mood.

"So, is it Butlins or the Costa del Sol?"

"You're dead pushy, Mr Brunt. I'm still trying to come to terms with all this money you're trying to chuck at me and now you come up with a no strings attached holiday offer. I'm overwhelmed by all this but can I trust you? What's to stop you taking advantage of the grieving widow? Eh?"

There was another long silence tempered only by the distant sound of music playing, somewhat ironically or deliberately, 'You are the sunshine of my life'.

Eventually George took up the conversation again: "So here's the thing. You keep knocking me back OK? Now I get that we've only known each other for a few days. Mind you it seems more like a few weeks, at least. As you come to know me better you'll realise all of my behaviour is in character. I don't want to boast, I know that wouldn't help, especially on the phone, but I could give you a list of stuff..."

"Don't push it any more George, please. I'm sure you're a really nice bloke. We just seem to be going round in circles here, so can you give me a bit of time, please. I need to check out what is going on. I've told you before my emotions are all over the place. You might think I'm born to be a funeral planner, but I'm really not sure. I need some space, that's what I'm saying and I don't think you've got that yet. This is my situation and I need to decide who can help and who might hinder..."

"I don't want to be a burden. Really, just let me show I can help. Please!"

"OK!" Charlotte jumped in, too sharply she later realised. "OK just leave me alone for 24 hours – no phone calls, texts, emails or visits," that seemed to have covered most bases, "and I'll get back to you when my head is a bit clearer. Don't get me wrong, this is not a brush off, not at all but..."

"You want some space OK? I'll wait to hear from you, Charlotte. Don't leave it too long though."

Abruptly the line went dead and after a brief pause Charlotte started sobbing gently. Joe had only been dead five days and here was this guy, George Brunt, who had popped up out of nowhere wanting to 'help', throwing money in her direction. While Charlotte was very grateful she was also no nearer now than she had ever been to working out whether all this 'help' came with any conditions. She had an uneasy feeling about the Brunts. She had only met two, she had no idea if there are any more, she had a terrible premonition that there might be, but she was almost certain two was enough. Actually, literally more than enough. On one level she'd enjoyed, benefitted, from all his expertise but there seemed to be an underlying tension, a dreaded quid pro quo – I do something for you and you, grieving my brother or not, do something, something that she was beginning to feel was a Brunt obsession, for me.

Charlotte was certain of one thing. If she kept busy she was fine, but when she stopped and let her thoughts drift, Joe was everywhere. His words still echoed round the house: "Hi babes!" Charlotte hated being called 'babes,' "I'm back. I love every bit of you, constantly. Is there a cup of tea in the pot?" "Are you cooking tonight, love?" Such common words, all with their Joe interpretation. Charlotte's problem was that, as she was so completely surrounded by Joe's isms, she could not imagine how she could let someone else, however ostensibly platonic, let alone another Brunt, into her life.

After she had finished crying this time, Charlotte decided to check her phone. Mercifully, she was well down on the commiseration texts, but instead she was getting a good number of positive RSVP's including one from The Team:

Looking forward to meeting you Caz – lots to talk about.

Her first thought was: who the hell can The Team be and why are they calling me Caz. No one ever mentioned the Caz word, not in her presence anyway. Their arrival would no doubt add a bit of frisson to the day although from this distance it would not be very welcome at all. On the day it could mean chaos or worse.

Hi Charlotte – not heard from you since. Here for you, love Henry xx

was the next message on her screen. Fleetingly Charlotte thought "Poor old..." But then reality kicked back in two Brunts and Henry were already more than Charlotte could deal with especially if she was going to start apportioning guilt to members of the group. Joe was definitely enough for now so she clicked on the dustbin and consigned Henry's latest message to her deleted file, never to see the light of day again. Dear old Henry, convenient, comfortable and safe. One conversation that would never take place was explaining to Henry his place in the Summersby plan. Charlotte felt certain he'd be better off starting again with someone who at least might try to show him some respect rather than exploit his goodwill.

Hi Henry, late availability – any chance of meeting up at mine tomorrow?

Charlotte knew the answer. Henry was like a lapdog. She clicked her fingers and he would come running. Even though he was in work less than a minute later came his response:

Yes of course, darling Charlotte.

Joe usually went away at least once a month which gave Charlotte a good opportunity to choose whether she wanted some time on her own or whether, much more likely, she wanted to unleash her inner tiger and brush off the Kama Sutra one more time. She wasn't sure whose bright idea it was to delve into the ancient Indian volume but had a sneaky feeling that it was an article in Cosmopolitan magazine which had started her off. Having dealt fairly comprehensively with the five easiest positions Charlotte and her faithful disciple had started trying some of the trickier ones which, at times, had made her wonder whether they would need the assistance of a third party to bring them to complete fruition.

The phone ringing in the hall broke her train of thought rather abruptly.

"Hello."

"Hi Charlotte!"

"Yes.

"It's Robert, Robert Piggott ..."

"Yes I know which Robert you are, Robert," Charlotte broke in as calmly as she could. She really didn't need any spiel from the FD. A quick Q&A would do nicely. "How can I help?"

"Well, I just wanted to check some details about the funeral next Friday. I gathered from Abigail at Green Acres Memorial Park that you were v. impressed with their facilities and were happy to go ahead. So, I need to sort out a few things from our end."

"OK."

"Namely is it still one car, no flowers, no pallbearers and the car to take you to the Memorial Park and the pub and you will make your own way home from there?"

Charlotte's response was rather unexpected, she could not help it. She laughed. Not so much: 'Ha ha' as a splutter containing a fair portion of the tea she'd been sipping followed by a guffaw. A wicked thought had flashed into her head.

"Well Mr Piggott things have changed a bit here. Well, they've changed massively actually. So...well I'm not sure. You've just made me think of a completely different approach."

"Oh," Robert Piggott sounded very anxious. "What sort of change would you be considering?" he continued ultra-cautiously. "What can we do to help?"

Robert was desperately trying to position his firm to be in a pre-eminent position to make the most of these changes at the same time as remaining unsure that they weren't about to be swept aside by some "bright idea" on the part of the irascible Ms Summersby. "I'm sure that we can accommodate any changes you may have in mind," he continued in the absence of any sound from the other end of the phone. "Just tell..."

"It's all right Robert – I'm not kicking you off the job. You see I've inherited quite a lot of money or a heck of a lot of money depending on what I decide to do." Charlotte babbled as a curious Mr Piggott chose to keep silent and listen to Charlotte as she kept talking. "You see before, in the no this and no that days, I was trying to do things on the cheap. Now in the days of Wine and Roses we could go horse-drawn carriage, gun carriage or even a 24 gun salute if you like. I mean I really need to think about the implications of what Joe has done. His generosity. I'm sure he'd want me to make sure he went off with a bang if you know what I mean, you know?"

"Well Charlotte not sure where we are going here. Of course, my firm will be only too pleased to accommodate anything you want in relation to making the funeral special, but can I ask, I don't want to pry of course but..."

Why is it, Charlotte thought, that the minute someone says they're not wanting to do something that it becomes abundantly obvious that that is exactly what they are doing because it is essential for their continued well-being to have full details of the information that they indicate they don't actually need.

Charlotte's flight of fancy had ignited Robert Piggott's entrepreneurial zeal. He could sense the possibility of a Spartan ordeal being replaced by an overindulgent orgy of expensive white horses, doves, dozens of them, orchestras, singers. He had done them all before, but not at the same funeral unfortunately, but at a push he was quite sure he would be able to deliver all this and more.

"You see it's not too late to have another sit down, with your friends – they were quite helpful before," funeral director code for we could work on them to increase the extravagance and thereby the take for Piggott & Sons, "then..."

"I think this is all getting a bit too much for me you know. Me shouting my mouth off about my inheritance and pissing it up the wall on a funeral. Getting a bit giddy there. Don't want to raise your hopes too high do we." Robert felt he was being patronised as Charlotte's tone of voice changed. He half expected her to start virtually patting him on the head if she carried on much longer. "What I'm trying to say is that I still need to be careful. Never really sure what's gonna happen next and I know you want me to spend as much as possible. It's..."

"Now, now Ms Summersby that's really not fair," Robert sounded hurt that his professional standards been impugned. "We are here to serve you Charlotte, never to exploit. I..."

Back to patronising Charlotte: "Look I don't want to ruffle your feathers. Let's just say can you put a second car on standby. I'm not at all clear on numbers yet, but if we've got an extra six seats if we need them, then I think that'll be a good idea. Don't you?" By seeking his advice on an issue central to Robert's skill set she changed the mood of the conversation to much a more positive one.

"Of course, that's very sensible Charlotte, having something in reserve. I would always recommend that and you can always cancel up to 24 hours beforehand and you won't incur any additional costs. Of course, this is another one of the reasons why it always make sense to use a reputable firm for all your funeral requirements," Robert could never resist the opportunity to embrace his sales-speak which served to enhance every aspect of the funeral experience and, hopefully, encourage customers to recommend the services of R Piggott & Sons to anyone they knew who found themselves in a similar position, "because we are able to adjust to our clients' needs right up to the, well, more or less the, last moment."

Charlotte was getting fed up with Mr Preachy Piggott. She had had her fun teasing him, enough was enough. In any event her arm was beginning to ache and her ear was ringing wet with sweat or condensation. Whatever it was it was unpleasant so she really needed to get rid of Robert, at least for the moment

"OK, so we know what we're doing here, Robert?"

"Yes, I'm very clear Charlotte."

"Good, let's leave it there for now. I've got loads of stuff to do and so I'd better crack on if you don't mind." Charlotte had been longing to use that term. It was like 'for the avoidance of doubt' an immensely attractive phrase but, so far at least, with a fairly limited usage quotient as far as she was concerned and yet here she was 'cracking on' and it felt good.

Shopping, food shopping, had always been a contentious issue in the Brunt/Summersby household. A list was kept in the kitchen held to the fridge by a magnet with the inscription 'A journey of 1000 miles begins with a single step'. Helpfully it was sturdily mounted and came complete with a pencil attached to the mount with a piece of string. The idea was, and it had been agreed and re-agreed at countless 'we need to talk about this' sessions, that as soon as stocks of a particular item ran out or were running short then it should be added to the list using the ever present pencil. Subsequently whenever either party needed something from the Co-Op in order to cook a specific meal they would detach the front page from the stack and take it with them and buy everything they could from the list. Anything not purchased would then be added to the clean shopping list upon return. This perfectly straightforward plan had utterly failed on so many occasions, not least because the pencil continually went missing, and one or other of the partnership forgot to add essential items to the list. These failings gave rise to so many rows neither party dared mention it again for fear of causing a complete meltdown in their relationship.

Up until Joe's death shopping duties had been performed almost exclusively by Joe because then, when there were 10 tins of tomatoes, 5 kilos of rice and dozens of recycled waste sacks and no beer or wine, he only had himself to blame. Charlotte became rather smug about the shopping situation more especially when, usually on a Friday night, a plaintive cry emanated from the utility room: "Charlotte, where's the beer gone? It was on the list."

With the utmost self-control and in her chirpiest voice Charlotte would call back: "Sorry no idea. When did you last go shopping?" Having put the ball firmly back in the server's court Charlotte continued whatever task was consuming her attention be it willow basket making, ironing, silver earring making or cooking or any of another 50 or so jobs she had always meant to do or to take a course on.

Not long after similar exchanges regarding the absence of beer the front door would slam and the car could be heard reversing noisily into the road prior to the 200 yard drive to the nearest Bargain Booze. Joe preferred what he referred to as 'proper' beer, but in extremis he would drink almost anything

As Charlotte prowled cautiously round the Co-Op she was wary of not forgetting anything she needed, the list was, as so often before, firmly attached to the pad in the fridge with the dangly piece of string indicating that the integral pencil had been 'borrowed' for some other purpose much more important than noting grocery requirements. This meant that she would be shopping from memory which always led to problems.

Whilst the failure ratio was probably 3:1 in Charlotte's favour a number of embarrassing situations had occurred over the months – a lack of toilet rolls at a crucial moment; no soap, anywhere; and worst of all a lack of tampons which Charlotte freely admitted was her responsibility. No mistake this time as she made sure to buy a large box.

Looking at her watch she realised she'd been circumnavigating the store for over an hour and only managed to source four things for her basket. As she realised this she also became aware that she seemed to have come to the attention of a member of staff and a security guard who were approaching from opposite ends of the aisle in which she seemed to have dropped anchor.

"You all right there, Miss?" asked the approaching security guard. "You seem to have taken root."

Charlotte looked round and was immediately aware of the ultra-concerned look on the female member of staff's face.

"Yes, just taking a minute thanks," was her only contribution at this stage.

Charlotte was confused firstly because for a moment, deep in her own thoughts, she had no idea at all where she was and secondly because it appeared, in the half reality of her moment, that she was under threat of attack. Why was she in this tunnel surrounded by cereal packets being approached by two overly curious 'people' or were they aliens? Then everything went fuzzy and the next thing she knew she was lying on the floor being tended to by more masked aliens although fortunately she realised, quite early on, that they were actually paramedics.

"OK Miss, stay with us now. Just keep looking at me. Take some deep breaths for me. Just stay with us. What's your name?"

Charlotte heard what the amazingly attractive lady in green was saying but was unable to formulate a reply. She desperately wanted to stay with them so she kept breathing steadily, stared into the warm voiced lady's eyes, willing her mouth to utter a response.

The green lady was patience personified as far as Charlotte was concerned as she waited for her to respond.

"Good girl you're breathing well. Just ease up a bit, I'll help you up then you can have a drink. Maybe a bit dehydrated, love."

Charlotte managed to get herself, with help, into a seated position and promptly gulped down the whole of the small bottle of Volvic which she'd been offered, even though she would have preferred sparkling rather than still. As she finished drinking she spluttered as she started trying to talk as well as taking big breaths of air.

"Sorry, I'm so sorry. Don't know what came over me there." As she tried to gain control of the situation she was experiencing flashbacks of being pursued by aliens down a labyrinth of tunnels toward a massive 64 story high stack of Cornflakes. Charlotte knew she needed to avoid any references to these unlikely events. "I was just shopping and..."

"OK you're doing really well now," green lady was using her most soothing voice. "Really well. Now can we just get a name here please?"

"Charlotte Summersby 42 Lediard Ave."

"OK, fine thanks Charlotte. Now let's see if we can get you somewhere more private because we are rather getting in the way here I think."

Looking round Charlotte could see groups of gawping customers blocking either end of the aisle where she had temporarily taken up residence.

"You can use the manager's office if you need to," one of the original inquisitors offered generously. "They can usually find somewhere else to go if there are pressing needs."

Charlotte was rather clumsily bundled into a wheelchair for what turned out to be a relatively short trip and she began to muse on what variety of ills could be covered by the term 'pressing needs'.
Her analysis was abruptly halted by their arrival at what could at best be described as a cubicle and at worst a hovel.
"Here we are then. Take as long as you need." The previously alien and now very helpful person ushered the small party of medics and Charlotte into the room and left them to it.
"Now Charlotte, it was Charlotte wasn't it?"
"Yes that's right."
"OK, Charlotte how are you feeling now? Do you need anything more to drink? Are you hungry, I'm sure we could get you a sandwich."
"No, I'm OK thanks. Just wanna finish my shopping and get home really. I'm rather busy at the moment. My partner died recently and I'm arranging the funeral – lots to do."
"OK we'll just do a few checks – blood pressure and stuff and then you can carry on but I think, as far as possible, you need to take it easy for a couple of days if you can. Your body's had a bit of a shock."
"Yes I can see that. I'm sorry to have caused all this trouble for you."
"Now don't worry about that. All part of the job. Just to check, have you fainted before – recently I mean?"
"No, not that I can remember, although I have been feeling a bit tired lately I just put that down to the stress of the funeral. Apart from that I've just been coping as best I can."

"Well, everything seems OK, your blood pressure is OK, I've checked your heart and that's OK. Have you been eating OK?"
"Not been quite as careful as I should. Probably eating too much junk food as I've not had time to cook."
"Having any nausea or headaches Charlotte? Just trying to see if there's any underlying reasons to what has happened."
"Yes I understand that. No not had any nausea and I never have headaches, never." Charlotte felt this wasn't a good time to reveal her post prosecco headache problem. Obviously, they weren't talking about **those** sorts of headaches.
"OK, we think you're good to go now but it might just be a good idea to make an appointment with your GP so they can give you the once over just in case something is going on."

Charlotte hated going to the doctors. Always made her feel inadequate and ended up costing a fortune for a prescription. Hated sitting in the waiting room with hordes of ill people. Never knew what you might catch. For Charlotte, a doctor's waiting room was only, very marginally, better than a dentist's, but only just.

"All right, if you think I should then I'll try and get an appointment – just in case."

"Yes I think that would be best Miss Summersby."

With perfect timing the shop assistant opened the door as the paramedic finished speaking: "You all OK here? Just wondered if anyone wanted a drink or any food?"

"No, we're all finished here thanks," said green lady who Charlotte realised had never introduced herself. "So, we'll be on our way. Thanks for the offer."

"OK, well I've got your trolley outside love. Do you want any help with your shopping? I can easily come round with you if you'd feel happier?"

"That's very kind of you, thanks. I've really only got a couple more things to get so I don't need to bother you, thanks."

By the time Charlotte arrived home she felt much better. The rest of her trip round the supermarket had been uneventful, thank goodness. Her experience with the alien zombies had proved to be very unnerving, not to say calamitous. She had never fainted before, at least not since she had had her belly button pierced as a teenager. Checking through the paramedic's questions she realised that actually she had felt a bit nauseous the last couple of mornings but she had put it down to her nerves and having to deal with all the pressures of the funeral and particularly trying to sort out what George Brunt was up to.

After a long sit and several cups of tea Charlotte started putting her meagre collection of shopping away. She had clearly forgotten most of the things she intended to buy which was no real surprise given the lack of a list. What was a surprise for her was when she came to replace her stocks of tampons in the bathroom cabinet she discovered there was no room. She started to feel nauseous and faint, the room began to spin as she clutched onto the towel rail. As she sat on the side of the bath she was filled with dread. If her period had not started, and it hadn't, obviously, then... She dared not continue the train of thought. If, then, what if? Her head felt fuzzy again. Tiredness, nausea were not symptoms of grief but she suddenly realised something far more unnerving. Charlotte had never been in a situation where circumstances were amenable to thinking about having a baby. She had never really definitively decided whether she ever wanted to have a baby or on the other hand not to have a baby. Maybe she was jumping to conclusions too early, without any real evidence. Charlotte Googled pregnancy symptoms and at first glance she was convinced that grieving, racing around like a headless chicken, doing the right thing etc had masked some glaringly obvious pregnancy indicators. Reading the list Charlotte realised, not for the first time in her life, just how naïve and unaware she was even when it involved changes to her own body, which she had just ignored, failed to check out and plainly not realised what was going on.

Charlotte raced downstairs, grabbed her keys, and drove off to the nearest chemists which was only 200 yards further than the supermarket where she had caused such a commotion only a short while before but was also somewhere she never frequented. At this stage, the last thing she wanted was people gossiping about her purchasing a pregnancy testing kit so soon after creating a scene necessitating the attendance of paramedics.

No mistake about that then. Shit, shit, shit. Charlotte was having a meltdown. Having used her hastily purchased test kit she was responding to the incontrovertible thin blue line. She was absolutely clear — negative has a margin of error but a positive result has no get out clause — you are what you are — she, Charlotte Summersby, was up the duff, in the pudding club or as she had recently heard in a French language film — 'enceinte'. Awful situations, she felt, or indeed any situations, always sounded better in French. Charlotte's predicament was bad enough without the added complication that she had absolutely no idea whether Joe or Henry was the father. Owing to her over enthusiasm for sex she had fairly recently managed to engage in sexual relations with two partners on successive nights. Hardly morally acceptable at the best of times, but in this case, with the advent of a possible child, morals were of very little concern and the overriding consideration going through Charlotte's mind was PANIC!

What Charlotte needed to do most of all was to do one of her regular phone and email checks to ascertain the latest attendance figures for the forthcoming funeral and the after party, but she was finding it very difficult to prioritise this event as she processed the unimaginable realisation that she was literally pregnant. Pregnant without any known means of support. One candidate, for a supporting role, was deceased and the other had shown himself wanting in so many ways that she could never countenance spending time in a relationship with him regardless of whether or not that would be considered as being 'good' for her as yet un-sexed and unborn child.

Having managed to put enough of her fears about the other upcoming and also unwanted event to one side Charlotte began the process of updating her funeral database. All the results were in, she deduced at the end of her methodical digital research, so she now had final numbers for the actual funeral which would easily be accommodated by the ever persistent Abigail, who had left a minimum of two messages every day seeking reassurances on either numbers of attendees or car parking space requirements. Green Acres would not be full but as long as everyone turned up there would be a good sprinkling of people on the highly polished solid beech benches. The Crown and Anchor, on the other hand, looked as if it was going to be uncomfortably full if everyone turned up which troubled Charlotte briefly. However, she decided that as there was nothing she could do about it, it would be best to leave it to fate. Hopefully, if it was too uncomfortable some of the more peripheral mourners would only stay for a short time or they would spill into the extensive outside seating area. The worst that could happen was that the vol au vents or Scotch eggs would run out. Charlotte's initial thought was that she would be pleasantly pissed by then until she realised that, on top of everything else, she would, for the foreseeable future, be abstaining from excessive alcoholic consumption if at all possible. Unable to deal with that she thought she would just hope that the true British stiff upper lip tradition would prevail.
Having finalised all the figures Charlotte sent a series of emails to the various interested parties including a confirmation to Robert that she would indeed be requiring a second car. While not wanting to spend all of her inheritance in one go she felt a bit tight only using one car and decided the additional vehicle would make more of a spectacle for her Joe and probably put a few people's noses out of joint into the bargain. She imagined the stir that would be caused on Lediard

Avenue at the site of three black limousines cruising past with the casket containing Joe Brunt leading the procession. Curtains would be twitching as her nosy neighbours peered and pried to see what was going on. She hardly knew any of them so that the fact that the name JOSIAH spelt out in multi-coloured flowers would be resting on either side of the casket would have left them none the wiser as to who all the fuss was in aid of.

Neither Charlotte nor Joe had ever been very careful about drawing curtains, turning off lights or, for that matter, being overly fussy about walking around naked. They had often joked that the occupant of number 63 who lived directly opposite must have had a field day trying to accidentally catch them out as they often caught her looking 'innocently' out of her bedroom window in their direction only to turn quickly away hoping not to be noticed. In fact, these occasions were one of the main causes of Joe becoming even more daring such that he often paraded naked in front of their bay window with his modesty only being protected by the height of the window ledge. Mrs Whateverhernamewas would be another on the list of people who would miss Joe's presence although in her case she would not be able to put her thoughts into words for inclusion on a sympathy card! Charlotte had been really comforted by the messages on so many of the cards that had arrived in the aftermath of Joe's passing. They depicted Joe in the way she wanted to remember him, kind, generous, prepared to go the extra mile etc which helped to counteract some of the less well-known aspects of Joe which led to the necessity for Henry in the first place.

When Laura arrived, she was pleased to have someone to talk things over with even though she had decided the topic of baby Summersby was definitely not up for discussion, not yet anyway. Long before Laura got involved Charlotte had decided she needed to know exactly what she was going to do. She wanted no pressure one way or the other as to how she should proceed before she had decided.

"Hiya, come in."

"Thanks. Sorry I'm late, couldn't get away from work. You OK hun?"

"Yeah, well not really. I think all this funeral stuff has got me down."

"What d'you mean?"

"Well, before, this morning I passed out in the Co-Op. They called an ambulance and everything. Proper showed me up, I can tell you."

"What happened?"

"Well, I just felt all funny. Thought I was being chased down these tunnels," as Charlotte spoke she had a vivid flashback and started shaking. "Oh, I need to sit down just thinking about it. Well anyway I felt all woozy and stuff and the next thing I knew I was lying on the floor and a couple of medics had come and there were crowds of people gawping at me."

"Must have been awful."

"It was, I can tell you, and then they started asking all sorts of questions and gave me a thorough once over and made me promise to book a GP appointment."

"That's not like you though. Can't ever remember you fainting before."

"No, I told them the last time it happened was in Claire's when I went to have my belly button pierced, not sure when but I was like 15 I think. I caused a right commotion there as well. I seem to remember after I fainted I slid slowly down the inside of the front window of the shop. "Gathered quite a crown though!"

"Why did you faint?" Laura's questioning was becoming a little intense for Charlotte by this stage, but she wanted to allay her suspicions that anything more serious was involved.

"I think I just got myself a bit confused. I'd been wandering around the store for ages, apparently, without buying anything. Maybe I was dehydrated and I'd missed my lunch, always a mistake. A combination of things to be honest. Feel a lot better now though. I've got my glass of water and whenever I go out from now on I'm going to take a bottle of water with me. The whole thing was horrid."

"Well, I've obvs not been doing my job properly letting this happen on my watch! I'm glad that it was nothing more serious anyway but just take it steady now - funeral next Friday and then you can move on."

"Well, you'll be very pleased to know all the arrangements are sorted out with Green Acres, the Crown and Anchor and Piggott's! I've decided to have a second car. I'm not bothered..."

"Sorry to interrupt you but I need to tell you something, nothing serious, but I'll forget otherwise. You remember Richard from our days in Scarborough?"

"Richard, was he the one you really fancied, that I went out with. Dumped me right out of the blue. Bastard!"

"Yeah. Well, I had a Facebook message from him yesterday. Apparently your name popped up as a suggested friend, he sent you a friend request but he's not heard anything. He's asked me to remind you."

"Can't say I've seen anything. Were you still following him after all this time?"

"Not avidly," Laura was trying to sound disinterested, "but you know how it is, people just get added to the list. Can't ever remember doing a Facebook cull on my phone!"

"So, he wants to be friends now. That's a bit weird. I was really upset when he broke it off. I never really understood what went wrong. You know it's difficult, sometimes, people don't explain these things. Too busy moving on."

"Maybe he's reached the point in his life where...You know, a turning point, where he feels the need to re-engage with his past and reach out to someone who he feels..."

"God you're sounding like a psychoanalyst there. All 'turning point' and 'reaching'..."

"Don't take the piss I'm just trying to help you understand his motives. He was a really nice guy. As you know I fancied him myself."

"Another one to add to the list eh," Charlotte tried to sound as unconcerned as she could as she struggled to hide her astonishment at this brazen admission. She was beginning to compile quite a long list of names where she and Laura had a shared interest. Now she knew this unwanted attention stretched back even further than she had previously thought.

"Don't need to get jealous. Anyway, I wouldn't want any of your castoffs I can tell you. By the way have you heard from George lately? You know your new squeeze," with these words Laura lunged at Charlotte to nudge her as she sat at the other end of the settee.

"Well," Charlotte paused for effect, "I'm glad you mentioned him, but he's not my boyfriend. We just..."

"Oh, come on Charlotte you can't fool me. I know the way things are heading."

"I'm trying to be really careful here Laura. I'm not just going to dive into another relationship so soon after Joe's death. It wouldn't be right."

"It's not about what's right. It's all about opportunities I think. You have to make the best of things."

"A minute ago, you were all for me getting back in touch with Richard and now I've got to get fixed up with George. There's too much pressure here. I need time to make up my mind." Charlotte was glad, in view of Laura's attitude, that she had not raised the topic of baby Summersby. At least she could discuss Richard and George fairly dispassionately although some of the memories that the mention of Richard's name had brought back to Charlotte's mind were actually making that sort of analysis rather difficult. "Anyway, I've got some good news. I said good news, right, so don't start upsetting me by pissing on my chips!"

"As if!"

"Don't, just don't. George phoned me yesterday to say that he was going to apply to vary Joe's Will so that I'll get £75,000 more than before. I'm still really in shock, so kind..."

Laura's face indicated she was utterly gobsmacked. She tried to speak and failed dismally. After several attempts she managed: "What's he after?"

Charlotte reached towards Laura and thumped her on the arm: "I told you NOT to start! I told you and what do you do? 'What's he after?' Is that all you can manage? He wants me to have more of Joe's money. He feels that I deserve it. He is well sorted. Doesn't need it and so wants to share. It's called generosity Laura. He's not after anything. Even wants me to have the other £25,000 as well. When I need it."

"I'm sorry, shouldn't have said that but bloody hell – he's a proper bloke giving that much away. Wowsers!"

"I'm still in shock to be fair. I mean he's been very helpful – he was very supportive at the funeral place, even though he did overstep the mark a bit. Then he's been super good at the legal stuff and now this. I know what your reaction is. I can see where you're coming from but there is a big part of me that really respects what he has done and yet..."

"Well, are there any strings attached? I mean like he wants to start a relationship or you don't get the money or if it's, I don't know, a tax dodge..."

"The only thing is he wants is to go away together for a couple nights, separate rooms and stuff, before the funeral just to have a chill and so we can get to know each other better. If he does want 'a relationship' he seems to want to take it slowly. We're going to use some of Joe's money – have I got anything to lose? Actually, the medics said it would be a good idea to get away for a couple of days rest to get over my fainting. I mean..." Charlotte stopped talking and left her sentence unfinished. She wanted Laura's opinion desperately as she genuinely could not decide whether or not to trust this guy who she hardly knew.

Laura was sitting at the other end of the settee staring at her hands with an unusual intensity. Still staring down, not wanting to have any eye contact she started to speak: "Dunno really, if you're not sure what can I say. I mean it's not my life. He's Joe's brother right. Does he have issues? Does he want to get revenge or is he just feeling guilty because his brother messed up and left you in the lurch with all sorts of secrets being revealed? He must have known that the shit would hit the fan and yet nowhere has he made provision to give you a warning or something."

As Laura spoke Charlotte remembered the letter the solicitor gave her, maybe the answers were there. However she decided at this stage not to remind her as she wanted her advice based on what they knew now.

"You know what," Laura smiled at Charlotte. "You know what I think, I think it's a guilt thing. He's been a perfect gentleman so far; I think he's embarrassed by his brother's legacy and actually wanting to make amends. Reckon I've cracked it. You go on holiday, make sure you spend Joe's money wisely and if it doesn't work out, well, apart from the funeral, you never have to see him again."

Charlotte and Laura had inexorably moved closer during their conversation and as Laura finished speaking she reached across to give Charlotte a hug of reassurance. They remained huddled together patting and stroking each other, murmuring words of affirmation.

Disentangling herself finally Charlotte pushed up from the settee, very purposefully, and headed towards the kitchen.

"Tea?" she asked as she retreated.

"Yes please. Feeling really dry!" was the response.

Amidst their usual chatter the pair soon agreed the running order for the celebration and Laura had designed a very respectful but still pzazzy e-invitation which she showed Charlotte how to send to her database of would be attenders. After she left, Charlotte checked her friend requests and as expected found Richard. She quickly clicked on confirm, and closed down Facebook and, unusually for her, turned her phone off. She needed some space before she phoned George to arrange their break. Although she was far from convinced by Laura's explanation of his behaviour she did think it was worth taking him up on his offer. Joe's death had made her realise that their relationship had been far from perfect both in terms of the lack of transparency relating to Joe's affairs and also in terms of her well-being. She was with Joe in every respect and yet still felt the necessity of having Henry in her life. She was feeling rather ashamed that instead of calling out what she imagined was Joe's double life she had used it as an excuse to have a double life herself. Another life which had, in many ways, been just as unsatisfactory as her life with Joe. Whilst Henry was a remarkable sexual partner he was significantly lacking in many other areas. She saw his role in relation to her as being the opposite of her relationship with Joe which explained why, whilst she could, she held onto them both in spite of the scheduling issues she had to deal with!

At 37 Charlotte felt Joe's death offered her a chance, another chance, to get some order into her life. Find a man who loved her for who she was, who was going to be reliable and open. She fully appreciated that this might well not be George, but if she approached their quality time with a clear agenda then she felt she would be in a good place to see if she wanted to form a relationship that would be more solid than the one she had had with Joe. She knew she had to be careful because emotionally she was still all over the place – crying for no reason, fainting in shops which could be construed as pregnancy-related, but she still felt had an emotional element, and her ongoing reaction to Joe's death. At one and the same time she could be very calm and in organisational mode looking at the minutiae of the funeral, and on the other an underlying annoyance that the responsibility for it had fallen into her lap in the first place. As she planned and reflected she began crying, softly at first, but slowly the tears gathered momentum as her body began convulsing, again.

After wiping away the tears with the back of her hands and sitting silently for a few minutes she decided to turn her phone back on and call George to discuss their holiday. However, Charlotte's best intentions were subtly subverted by an image that had magically appeared on her screen demanding immediate attention. The circle contained a picture of a handsome male whom Charlotte did not recognise. Ever curious and completely forgetting her original mission she tapped on the image which initiated the launch of the following message: Hi Charlotte its Richard. I'd heard that you've suffered a tragedy in your life. I exchanged a few messages with Laura and felt awful remembering how we split two years ago. I really want to apologise and explain. I think it would help you. I know it would help me. I have so many happy memories of our brief time together. Can we talk?

Charlotte was sitting in the bar of the Peasholm Manor Hotel overlooking Peasholm Park in Scarborough. She and Richard had just finished a four course meal in the restaurant and were feeling rather full and a bit drunk having shared two bottles of wine during the course of the meal.

"You know I said I was going for a new job?" Richard sounded anxious as he blurted out this news. The evening had been spent discussing future plans including possible holidays and historic sites which they wanted to see together. Charlotte had a lot of experience of the north-east and Yorkshire whereas Richard knew more about the Midlands and North Wales. As they spoke they took turns to recommend favourite locations, laughing as they became more competitive and outrageous pitching their particular favourites as somewhere they MUST visit. Charlotte was startled at this new direction for their conversation which had immediately taken the sheen off their previous plans. "Look I should have mentioned this before. I just got a bit carried away. The wine probably gone to my head, but the thing is if things go to plan, and this has only come up in the past couple of days, I'll be moving to Kent to start this job in about three weeks."

"OK," Charlotte spoke slowly as she tried to assimilate the new situation. "So, this means what – you're going to be moving to Kent? Will this mean our relationship is going long-distance? How long are you..."

"Well, actually it means this is like our last date. I've had experience of a long-distance relationships in the past and they, from my point of view, just don't work out – lots of travelling for a date doesn't really suit me I'm afraid."

There was a long silence, Charlotte was speechless. Ten minutes ago, they had been mapping out their lives for the foreseeable future and now Richard had dropped the bombshell that he was moving away from Scarborough and, by implication, from her, totally.

"What the fuck are you talking about?" Charlotte shouted much to the consternation of her fellow diners. Realising the stir she had caused she lowered her voice as she continued her harangue. "Richard, what are you on, you pillock? We've just been talking about the future as if everything is going fine and then you're coming out with this shit.

You're moving away and we're finished. Am I right?" She scowled at Richard and without allowing him a chance to reply she grabbed her bag from the table and stormed out of the bar leaving a number of bemused drinkers watching her red capped sleeve skater dress disappear through the double doors leading onto the street.

That was then, thought Charlotte, and now Mr Wyatt wants to apologise because he thinks it will help her. Their acrimonious breakup had left Charlotte devastated, completely distraught. No follow-up text, nothing at all. Complete communication blackout and now he had heard about a tragedy and wanted to get back in touch.

Having so recently had her trust so comprehensively trashed by Joe she was now in the position where two men were queuing to either gain or re-gain her trust each, obviously, for their own reasons whilst making clear that their motives were entirely altruistic. Charlotte had already decided that any future relationships had to be on her terms and open and honest. Her head was definitely going to rule her heart and, unlike previously, she was utterly determined that she would not be seduced by either of these suitors on a whim. She was pregnant and had no intentions of returning to her former ways of leaping enthusiastically into bed with pretty much anyone she fancied. In future she was going to be very clear about their intentions before getting involved in such activities. As far as she could tell both George and Richard were nice guys – she'd actually had a sort of reference for George from an ex which she felt augured well. She also knew Richard of old and until his, as yet unexplained behaviour, he was first in line to take her hand in wedded bliss. All this excitement and uncertainty in the midst of the saddest occasion of her life was causing her considerable extra worry.

For once in her life Charlotte decided to make her own decision. No checking with Laura and definitely no mention to her sister Francesca. She had used her to bounce ideas off before, notably the Joe problem, but that had not ended happily and as she had not been in touch except to say she'd be able to pop in on the funeral, whatever that could mean, now was obviously not a good time to look for sibling support.

"OK, so I'll meet you at the Peasholm Manor Hotel for dinner at 7pm tomorrow and I'll book two single rooms for two nights including breakfast. Is that OK?"

After a lengthy conversation George had agreed every particular of the arrangements for their toe dipping trip. He was even quite keen to embrace the idea of the Yorkshire town of Scarborough as the venue. Charlotte told him it held fond memories for her and, despite the fact that he had suggested York or Sheffield, he soon agreed sounding as if he was much more concerned that the venue for their tryst should be absolutely what Charlotte wanted rather than anything else. As he put it so succinctly: "This is for you – I'm just the facilitator, remember that."

Charlotte was delighted when she put the phone down. It sounded as if George was going to make sure they had a good couple of days away, no expense spared. He'd even asked Charlotte to research all the things she wanted to do during the time they were going to be in Scarborough so they didn't have to waste time sorting out their itinerary while they were actually there.

Charlotte decided from the start that it would be better to travel separately so that if things did not work out then there would be no embarrassing silences on the journey home and if they had worked out then there would be plenty of other times to meet up afterwards. In any case she really enjoyed travelling by train and as part of George's mission was to make everything ideally suited to Charlotte's requirements his only reaction was: "Enjoy. I'll take the car so that we can get about easily. Makes sense."

With one unalloyed success to her credit Charlotte was just left with the Richard factor to be dealt with. She felt she would be quite keen to re-engage with the man with the laughing eyes and enquiring mind if that was what he was interested in. If he just wanted a shoulder to cry on then this was the wrong time for that – she was looking for support from almost any source but only on her terms. As she tapped his number into her phone she was looking forward to what promised to be an interesting exchange.

"Where are you anyway? When I last saw you were moving to Kent. How did that work out?" Charlotte and Richard had been exchanging pleasantries for the whole of the conversation when Charlotte decided to inject a sense of purpose. She was never very keen on small talk and with all her high hopes, at least initially, the level of conversation so far been unfortunately banal.

"That's what makes me feel rather foolish actually. After all that fuss and the rest of it I never did get to Kent. Stupid I know, I just lost my focus and stayed in the same job ever since."

"Jesus, you're some kind of freak. You've left it 3 years to get in touch and just stayed put. You broke my heart. I was in a terrible state for weeks afterwards. Probably the reason I got involved with Joe to be honest. I was at such a low ebb and then after a few, I think quite a few one night stands, Joe turned up keen to lift my spirits and..."

"Look I'm sorry. I meant to say that before but we just got off to a good start and I forgot. Sorry. They really wanted me to move down there and moving with my job seemed like a good idea. What wasn't a good idea was getting drunk with you over dinner making all sorts of plans and then..."

"Trashing them without any explanation. You could have thought about a way of letting me down gently, couldn't you?"

"Of course I could but I think the drink, mixed with the medication I was taking, was a perfect storm actually. Not to make it any easier for you I was on anti-depressants for months afterwards. Then my sister committed suicide..."

"What, not Martha? I really like her – what made her do that?"

"No one knows. She didn't leave a note or anything. It could have been an accident, you know, a cry for help – we'll never know. Of course, that didn't help my state of mind at all. Really I was lucky to keep my job. I got in a lot of trouble because I assaulted a colleague who was winding me up. Dead lucky the union rep managed to get me off with a letter from my doctor and character witnesses. After all that..."

"You should have got in contact before then, you bloody fool. I really loved you y'know. I wanted to..." Charlotte stopped in mid-sentence as she realised her previous resolution to keep everything under control was being undermined by her unnecessarily providing far too much information. He was supposed to be making his case to her, not her offering herself virtually on a plate to him. What had happened before did not automatically mean anything was going to happen now. She decided to change gear in mid-sentence to, "...well I'm not sure now where we are up to. I was in a bad place myself, but obvs nowhere near as bad as you.

After Charlotte had regained control of herself, and the direction of the conversation, Richard managed to convince her it would be better for both of them if they could meet up and talk things over. Charlotte, in a gesture which she later regretted, volunteered that she was in Scarborough in a couple of days time and in no time at all they had arranged to have lunch shortly after George would be returning home after their luxury break.

Chapter 7: Seaside

Arriving in the middle of the afternoon at Scarborough Station Charlotte's first thought was to get a taxi to Cayton Bay Beach. She had not been there since her hurried departure from Scarborough in the aftermath of her split from Richard. She loved being close to the sea, listening to the soft rolling waves, watching the wheeling seabirds and feeling the sand squishing between her toes. Cayton Bay had been her favourite beach during her time on the Yorkshire coast because, apart from sunny summer days, it was relatively deserted and an ideal place to while away time reading a book, a voluminous weekend newspaper or people watching. Today's plan was to walk along the beach, after descending the steep winding path, and to mull over her plan to deal with both George and Richard. Charlotte was relatively relaxed about pop-up brother. She was looking forward to spending some time showing him around some of her favourite haunts particularly the Castle, Peasholm Park, the Rotunda Museum and, if he was up for it, the North Bay Heritage Railway. His express wish was to ensure that Charlotte had an enjoyable time so she was hopeful that he would enter into her tour with a spirit of adventure. Any other reaction would, as far as Charlotte was concerned, indicate that his intentions were less honourable than he had initially declared. Charlotte was cross with herself for the way she had started gushing over Richard at the first opportunity which made her even more determined to hold back in the enthusiasm stakes with George lest the same thing should happen. The way forward was for Charlotte to be in control – if she decided in the fulness of time she wanted to spend more time with George, have sex with George or indeed do the same with Richard then it had to be on her terms not because she had cast her scruples to the four winds. Although she was in a bad place emotionally she had also realised that after the funeral there were going to be opportunities for a new beginning with baby Summersby, utilising her new wealth, and new friendships to establish Charlotte Summersby as someone who was in control of her destiny for once, possibly, for the first time ever.

Charlotte had walked and thought and talked to herself until she reached a rocky area full of pools where a handful of children were excitedly jumping from rock to rock shouting with delight at each fish or crab that they saw. She dipped her fingers into the crystal clear water of the pool nearest to her perch. Ice cold. The pool was in the shade so out of the warmth of the sun. She watched the water trickling from her fingers and splashing back into the pool. She felt perfectly at peace as she sat and tickled the water remembering happier times. She started to question why she had reacted so unequivocally in leaving Scarborough. To swap the countryside, this idyllic spot, for the big city, really on a whim, in what, she now realised, was an overreaction to one person's ill-judged decision. Her emotional turmoil, at the time, must have been so strong that she could not see any other alternative because, having only been back for a couple of hours, she was already making plans to stay. To start a new life somewhere she should never have left in the first place.

"Charlotte? Is that Charlotte?"

Charlotte looked up from her reverie and spotted the source of the booming voice. A sandy haired, tall man with a Barbour jacket and green wellies was approaching her dragging two small children behind him. Some way behind the advance party trailed a smallish woman encumbered with a pushchair and all the paraphernalia of a family beach trip. As the party got nearer Charlotte recognised Rex Sliborne, one of Richard's friends. Someone who she had neither expected nor wanted to see at this particular time or at any other time for that matter.

"It is Charlotte isn't it? There I was right. Never forget a face or at least..."

"Yes, Rex you're right. Big surprise!"

"Well, where have you been hiding all this time?"

"I moved to Manchester a few years ago. Not been hiding. Been working as an Arrears Assessment Executive for a firm of Debt Collectors," Charlotte was not sure how much Rex would know about what had happened between her and Richard so she decided to gloss over that. "How are you doing? See you've got a family now."

"Yes these are Sophia and Eleanor and this is Mary Grace, my wife."

"Hi kids! Hi Mary Grace! Lovely names."

"You married yet?"

"No," Charlotte decided to go for the easy option and continued, "not really looking at the moment. Enjoying myself too much being single to be honest." Stay in control, be strong. Charlotte's mantra to fend off the audacious questions from Rex with a Filipino wife.

"Each to their own. We're very happy, aren't we lovey?"

"Yes, Rex. Two lovely children too. Very pleased to be here."

Charlotte didn't really want to continue the conversation. Rex and his family had burst in on her peace and quiet and she wanted that back as soon as possible.

"Very lucky," was her only response.

After an awkward pause Rex, who seemed have anchored himself to a spot about three feet from Charlotte said, "See anything of Richard recently?"

"Well actually... No not since I left Scarborough two years ago," Charlotte had hauled herself adroitly back from revealing all in one sentence. There was no reason at all why he should get to know any of her secrets, whether innermost or not, so she stuck to the truth as far as she was prepared to acknowledge it – speaking is not seeing, she reasoned.

"Yeah I see. We meet up every couple of weeks at our local for a catch up. Of course, he was going to leave us and go south, must have been about the time you left. Job fell through and soon after both his parents died so he stayed put. Shame about you two though..."

"That must have been a blow. They were close but it's always difficult as parents get older if they don't live nearby. I never met them, he often talked about them."

"You never know, if you're staying for a while you might bump into him. I'll mention I saw you when we meet up next."

"You don't need to bother," Charlotte tried to sound noncommittal, not against being mentioned, but not massively for it as if there was little purpose for him to speak on her behalf – if that was what he was intending.

"OK well we'd better be going," for some minutes Sophia and Eleanor had been getting increasingly restless as they ran around their father's legs, splashed in the water and generally became more out-of-control. Mary Grace was playing no part in the childcare as she had set her burdens down on some rocks and was taking what looked like a well-deserved rest, "These two need feeding. Good to chat after all this time Charlotte. Enjoy your stay."

With that, and without a word to his wife, he grabbed each child by the hand and headed off to the steps. As Mary Grace began to gather her belongings Charlotte fleetingly considered stepping in to help but just as quickly decided, in view of her condition, and the fact that she didn't actually want to prolong her contact with Rex, that she would wave sympathetically towards the slowly receding figure of Rex's servant/wife.

As she resumed reminiscing about her past involvement with Scarborough a number of incidents came to mind concerning Richard. The closer their meeting was getting the more nervous Charlotte was feeling as she remembered some of their more memorable escapades. For three years she had managed to put all thoughts of Richard out of her mind. Now she was being engulfed with powerful memories of how happy they had been sharing Richard's hastily arranged adventures: picnics, lovemaking, cinema trips, walks, thrill-seeking at Alton Towers, zip wires or even trips abroad if their mood took them. As more and more memories came to the fore Charlotte worried whether she would be able to keep to her plan.

Remembering the love she had felt for Richard seemed to be overwhelming her, her hands were sweating, she felt as if she was about to have a panic attack. She was over 36 hours away from meeting him and she was feeling faint. How would she react to seeing him in the flesh? She would have to be very careful; he had cast her aside in brutal fashion before, such that she would be a fool to trust him again without clear evidence that he had changed. Charlotte remembered how she looked forward to his phone calls and agonised over a late text as she moped about waiting for their next contact. Rewinding events as she sat in the late afternoon twilight Charlotte could see that what had happened between them might actually have been her own fault – had she pushed him too hard?

It had been a hot summer's day. Richard and Charlotte had been enjoying a quiet afternoon on a secluded part of the beach. Charlotte had been topless most of the time as she wanted to get rid of her strap-marks whilst also pleasing Richard who was always paying her boobs compliments. He had even named them Thelma and Louise after one of their favourite kick-ass movies. They had been reading and kissing and playing with a frisbee as well as consuming two bottles of wine. As their playing and kissing became ever more intimate Richard started tickling Charlotte, wrestling her to the ground and generally trying to 'accidentally' remove her bikini bottom. As they had a large section of the beach all to themselves Charlotte wasn't worried about prying eyes and inevitably, as many times before, their sandy embraces evolved into full-on sex with Charlotte whooping and egging Richard on. As they finished they both flung themselves on their backs on the sand and started giggling.

"I love you Charlotte Summersby. Utterly and completely love you!"

Richard leaned over to Charlotte and kissed her and, running his left hand down her sandy body, seemed to be intent on prolonging their sexual antics. Charlotte, who was feeling hot and sticky, was having none of it, and pushing Richard away roughly started running towards the incoming tide arms aloft shrieking with laughter. Richard ran after her and they were soon gambolling in the surf as they washed all the sand off and, as they were both in a carefree mood, they started kissing and rolling over and over in the surf locked together, laughing and giggling. As they played the sun was fast disappearing over the horizon and as the dusk gathered their figures became silhouettes against the dimming sky.

Realising that it would soon be dark they linked arms and marched boldly towards their clothes only to find that not more than a few yards away a group of young men had set up camp, while they had been away, and were starting to light a fire. Needless to say their delight at catching the couple au naturel led to several ribald comments as Richard and Charlotte tried to hide their naked bodies from public view. It was all good natured, as well as being potentially embarrassing, not that the exhibitionist in Charlotte really cared as she made a big show of getting dressed carefully whilst at the same time flashing her body somewhat drunkenly in the group's direction. She remained blissfully unaware that the young men were in fact far more interested in their weed and cider than in wasting their time on a licentious and rather plump woman flaunting herself in the semi-darkness.

Charlotte could still remember her naughty times, not just with Richard either. Thinking back, she wondered if it would ever be possible for her to settle for one partner, one lover or would she always have a certain restlessness to contend with? George clearly had a lot to do to match up to the variety of delights served up by Richard although she was looking forward to the fact that he may be quite different from previous dalliances. A non-lustful lover perhaps, a concept which she had never encountered before. She had always encouraged and enjoyed an active sex life and didn't really, of her own choice, fancy a relationship based on a sex-lite approach. Her go-to was always based on physical attraction first, reasonably left-wing views second and an interest in horizontal sports third even though perhaps, she mused, attention to the first two categories was rather circumspect on occasions usually involving rather too much Prosecco. However George might turn out she was anticipating that, based on past experience, Richard might want to revive their sexual relationship. She shivered at the thought especially as her head was full of thoughts of Joe's funeral making this particular train of thought seem more than a trifle incongruous.

The incoming tide was by now lapping at Charlotte's feet and, as she looked at her watch, she realised that the time of her meeting with George was approaching rapidly, so rapidly in fact that she might even be late. Having hastily phoned for a cab she rushed across the deserted beach and scrambled up the steps to make a rendezvous with a representative of Borough Cars.

"You first."
"You sure?"
Charlotte and George had settled themselves at their table after pre-dinner drinks in the bar. Charlotte was feeling relaxed after her afternoon on the beach. George had obviously put himself out with a new haircut and what looked like a brand-new pale cream jacket, blue shirt and sharply creased chinos. The waitress, whose name was Anita, according to her over large oblong name badge, was hovering tablet poised.
"I'm starving so I'll go prawns and a 12oz ribeye steak please."
"How would you like your steak, madam?"
"Rare please."
"Any sauces there?"
"No thanks, but can I have some English mustard please?"
"No problem. Sir?"
"I'll have the whitebait and the steak and ale pie please."
"Is that with chips or mash sir?"
"Chips please and can we have a bottle of the Merlot as well please."
"OK, I'll bring your starters over soon as they are ready."
"Rare steak! Unusual for girls?" George was in a playful mood. He had been teasing Charlotte about her dress in the bar, calling her out for showing too much flesh for a first date. Charlotte was wrong-footed from the start having to defend the way she looked after having congratulated George on his attire. She had searched the Internet for

something sexy without being illegal and had chosen an off the shoulder lace-up-back dress in a bright green. It made her feel glamorous, she was hoping for a compliment but this was clearly not the game George was playing. In the early skirmishes George almost apologised for his cheek but Charlotte was going to be ready for him the next time.

"The only way to get a decent steak," was her response. "So few places know how to cook steak that the only way to get anything that hasn't been incinerated is to ask for rare. That's my experience anyway."

"The only meat they can't really fuck up is chicken I think. Always a safe bet you know."

Charlotte would never have thought of herself as a prude. In fact she swore quite a lot herself but only when absolutely necessary but George's wholly superfluous use of the f-word shocked her as she began to think he might have had a few drinks before they met up. Maybe his playful teasing was not his usual demeanour but was the direct result of indulging in too much Dutch courage.

"What've you been up to today?" Charlotte decided to ignore his profanity and try to move the conversation on. She had George down as reasonably sensible and, given his generosity, someone who might be interested in a relationship. However, she felt, perhaps due to nerves, he had got off to a poor start.

"Drove over after lunch. Booked into the hotel and I've just been reading in my room since," George sounded very innocent. "You?"

"Lovely train journey, had a table for four all to myself and then I spent the afternoon on the beach," Charlotte stopped abruptly as she was about to mention Mr Slibourne, but decided against it as that would have taken their conversation in an entirely different direction. "It was lovely down there on Cayton Bay Beach. We can have a look tomorrow if you want. It's hardly ever very busy because of the steps down and back up for that matter. I played in rock pools and remembered past times when I had been there. It was great, the only thing I missed out on was a swim. It was dead calm, but I never even thought of bringing a costume."

"There's a pool in the hotel. Maybe they would lend you a cossie or you could always pop out to get one – we could swim when we get back from our tour."

"That would be great..."

Anita had arrived with their wine and followed up shortly afterwards with their starters.

"Prawns here, whitebait for you sir. Enjoy!"

All further conversation was halted as they both ate their starters.

The wine had flowed as agreeably as the conversation for over two hours, Charlotte realised, as she glanced at the clock on her way to the toilet. The hotel had lived up to her expectations and their table had afforded a fabulous panoramic view of the sunset. After a rather shaky start George had settled down into a more reflective mood as they explored a number of issues: politics – left of centre; sport – football and cricket neither to excess; the arts – keen cinema goer, a definite plus point. Charlotte had given up trying to entice Joe to go to their local arthouse cinema; and whilst not avid gallery attenders they also discovered a mutual liking for the highly complex work of Anish Kapor. Charlotte was in no doubt that taking time to talk to George had been very worthwhile so far and she was looking forward to conducting her tour the next day.

"I think the wine must be taking its toll on me. I'm beginning to feel quite tired. I've been quite busy at work lately as well. It's nothing to do with your excellent company, honestly!" George laughed as he offered what Charlotte considered was a very weak excuse for winding up dinner.

"Oh, OK then. Need to be in good form for tomorrow and I've got lots of reading to do. Give me a chance to check my emails. I'm sure I've got everything covered for the funeral, but I keep worrying I've left someone important off the guest list. I don't think I've ever felt so responsible for anything in my life before. I just feel as if lots of people are watching me, checking to see if I'm doing right by Joe..."

"Don't be silly," George reached across the table and lightly took hold of Charlotte's hand. "Everything is going to be fine. They'll be rooting for you, not judging you – the guests will thoroughly appreciate what you've done. I'm sure of that."

Charlotte gently eased her hand away from George's grasp. Talking about the funeral was making her feel emotional although George's words and his gesture of reaching out his warm hand felt reassuring. Crucially she didn't feel he was invading her private space – it just made her feel closer to him. She didn't want to rebuff him for offering her reassurance but she was wary of dropping her guard as she needed to keep matters firmly under her control. She wanted to nurture George's feelings without throwing herself at him at the first sign of his wanting to offer his explicit support.

"I hope they will, but I can tell you I'll be glad when this is all over. The funeral, I mean, not this weekend." They both laughed as Charlotte tried to relax the rather tense atmosphere that had developed between them. "No George I really appreciate your support. I really do." She patted his hand softly and smiled. "Well let's get this bill settled and get ready for tomorrow."

"All taken care of, remember, this is all on Joe," George was smiling benignly although Charlotte was unsure as to whether or not she detected a paternalistic undertone creeping in. As her emotions were so fragile she was never quite sure how accurately she was interpreting other people's signals. She desperately didn't want to give the wrong impression, but equally she didn't want anyone to get one over on her either. Was it grief or maybe baby hormones which were making her brain turn to jelly.

"Oh yeah I forgot our plan. If you settle all the bills then and we'll sort everything out later. If that's OK?"

"Yeah that'll be great. I'm sure the old bank balance will be able to take it for a short time."

George was defaulting to his pre-dinner persona. The one Charlotte disliked. She didn't want to be tricked into being any more effusive in her comments. She felt she had already said enough. She decided to use a well-worn political strategy – ignore the question and just talk to fill the space:

"So, we'll go to the Bryherstones Country Inn at Cloughton Newlands for lunch then." George was gathering his phone and room key as she spoke. "What time for breakfast?"

"8.30ish? I never like to get up too early when I'm in a hotel. Do plenty of that when I'm at home and needing to get up for early meetings."

"8.30ish it is then. Thank you."

Charlotte and George walked to the lift together and as they reached their floor Charlotte leaned across and kissed George on the cheek and thanked him again for his generosity.

"My pleasure. See you in the morning."

After a full English breakfast and plentiful cups of coffee Charlotte and George set off on their tour of the delights of Scarborough starting in

Peasholm Park which was a short walk from their hotel down a sloping zig-zag path past a number of very friendly grey squirrels. Charlotte remembered that there were dragonhead pedolos for hire on the lake from previous visits and as it was a sunny but cool September morning she was hoping that the season would not have finished; that George would be up for a pedal round the lake; a walk through Peasholm Glen and maybe a trip to the island in the centre which contained a Pagoda and a mystical Chinese garden. As they walked they chatted comfortably enough with each other. George was obviously relaxed, which Charlotte appreciated, as she had already had enough of the rather neurotic facets of George. A casual observer would probably have identified them as friends rather than probationary lovers based on: a lack of eye contact as they talked and a slight awkwardness between them. Most of the silences were broken by George as he seemed anxious to keep the conversation flowing whereas Charlotte was quite happy just to walk, listen to the birdsong and respond to George's remarks. It was clear he wanted to find out more about Charlotte's time in Scarborough although she wanted to stick to her plan of working on a need to know basis. George needed to know she was not a pushover. Knowledge of previous lives was to be a two-way street as far as Charlotte was concerned otherwise she could see things ending up in a virtual cul-de-sac.

"So how many years did you live here?"

"Roughly five – it was work really that brought me here," and then to fend off a possibly intrusive follow-up question, "Remind me, George, how long did you live in York?"

Just as George was about to reply they rounded the corner in the path and they got their first view of a clutch of dragonhead pedolos bobbing invitingly at their moorings.

George laughed, "Now that looks like fun. Shall we?"

Pleased with his response Charlotte smiled, "Of course. They were the main reason I brought you!"

"Haven't been on a pedolo for years. Shame we haven't got any kids with us because we've got no real excuse. We'll have to fess up to being kids at heart," he added rather cheesily.

"Let's get it sorted out," Charlotte wasn't at all sure about the reference to children – it was the first time either of them had made any mention. It reminded her of her big secret and her even bigger dilemma: who to tell and, even more importantly, was she going to keep baby Summersby. Whilst during the daytime, since she had found out, she had not given the matter very much thought, she had had several long periods of wakefulness devoted to the pros and cons of baby Summersby, regarding what she was going to do and when. She had toyed with the idea of, on the one hand, telling no one, not even Laura, and on the other making it very clear partly to get everything out in the open and partly to see if there was any interest in someone taking her on complete with appendage.

"You're deep in your thoughts Charlotte – what's going on?"

"Nothing really, just remembering other trips here."

"D'you want to share?"

"No not really," Charlotte knew she needed to be firm in her determination not to let George know too much about her too soon. She realised he was only being companionable but she only wanted him to learn about her, and particularly her past, at her pace.

By now they had pedalled to the far side of the lake, after a narrow miss with the floating bandstand, and found themselves alone. The only sounds they could hear were birdsong and the muffled squawks and shrieks as fellow boaters were splashing each other and showing very differing abilities at managing the highly temperamental directional control of their vehicles.

"Is this what you needed?" George sounded serious.

"Yes as a matter of fact I think it is. Thanks. I need to reconnect to a fixed point, an immutable part of my history. Gives everything that has happened since a bit of perspective. Meeting Joe and all that has meant and now coming back to a place that has so many memories for me."

"As in what?" George was back in probing mode. Very gently, almost below the radar, he was fishing for information.

Charlotte quickly glanced at her watch.

"I'll tell you later," she smiled at George before continuing: "I think we need to head back now otherwise we'll have to pay for another 30 minutes and mess up our tight schedule."

"OK. Let's get going."

Charlotte relaxed again as they both focused on getting their lively companion back to the shore. Safely moored they quickly explored the island and walked a short way up the Glen before Charlotte realised that time was pressing and if they were going to complete her sightseeing tour they needed to move on.

After a short detour into Scarborough itself for Charlotte to purchase what she later realised was a rather too demure onesie for a lady of her age they set off for Cayton Beach. George's Audi A3 1.6 TD Sportback was an excellent ride so much smoother than Charlotte's somewhat older Kia. Neither Joe nor Charlotte, or for that matter any of Charlotte's previous boyfriends, had been very interested in cars – partly because none of them had enough money and probably, more importantly, that they were more interested in cars as a means of transport rather than as a status symbol. Putting aside every environmental consideration, by the time they arrived at the beach, Charlotte had decided, now she was a woman of means, that she would no longer disregard the idea of buying an Audi or a car of a similar ilk when her beloved Kia finally bit the dust.

After parking the car they walked to the cliff edge so they could better appreciate the magnificent sweep of the bay before descending the steep steps. As they did so Charlotte was hoping against hope they didn't bump into Mr Slibourne. She definitely didn't want to see him again, ever, if possible and never in the company of George, especially in view of their conversation the previous day. Matters of the heart were not something Charlotte dealt with very well at the best of times and this was definitely not one of those: possible baby – father unknown; a funeral – which she was curating with very mixed feelings; not one but two suitors, or friends, or neither – a situation to be at least partially resolved within the next 24 hours; and two ex-wives - Charlotte felt she had the makings of a re-working of a well-known song!

"You must have a lot of things on your mind? Been walking for about 10 minutes and you've not said a word. You OK?" George enquired solicitously.

"Look, yeah, course I am. Sorry if I'm not very good company at the moment, but you're right, lots to think about. It's good you're here though, I do appreciate it. Honest."

"Want to share any of it? I'm a good listener."

There he was again, pecking away trying to get on the inside. Charlotte was trying hard to convince herself that he was operating from the best of intentions, but she daren't let him delve too deeply. She knew herself too well.

"Sorry. I keep on apologising, don't I. Need to stop doing that. As I said, I really appreciate you being here – wanting to spend time with

me and I will…" Charlotte was backtracking, she knew she was but needed to keep George on board, "tell you I promise. I'll share stuff with you but I need to work it out for myself first. D'you understand?"
"Yes, kind of. Doesn't make it any easier though. Should I just leave you here? Come back in a couple of hours say when you've got your head straight?"
"No, no I don't want to do that. Let's go and have some lunch really nice pub lined up. I'll feel more communicative when I've had some food I'm sure."
"It's not that. I really feel for you dealing with Joe's death and everything. You just take your time."
Charlotte could feel a slight earnestness creeping in again. She had knocked George back several times now. She was feeling relatively relaxed in his company but she was mindful that she had lined up a meeting with someone who she hoped could be about to transform her life. Someone who would, possibly, lift the grief from her shoulders and take her with or without baby and enable her to get back to being the old Charlotte. Each day she was re-evaluating her time with Joe and now she compared it with how things had been with Richard she remembered how happy they had been. She just hoped that, against all odds, they could rekindle the joy they had shared.
"Thanks George it must be difficult for you. You're being very patient and that's a great help. I'm sure it will get easier. I hope you're hungry, the pub we're going to does great pies if I've remembered right."
"Sounds the ideal place."

The Bryherstones Country Inn was another venue steeped with memories for Charlotte. Drunken celebrations, birthday parties and quiet romantic dinners with Richard. As Charlotte entered the cosy bar through the door, so gallantly opened for her by George, she could almost see Richard sitting at the bar waiting for her.
She stopped abruptly. Maybe this wasn't such a good idea. How would she be able to concentrate on what George was saying when there was so much of her history all around her."
"You OK?" George had just had to swerve to avoid a suddenly becalmed Charlotte.
"Yes, just wasn't sure about this place. Lots of memories here. Might be better to go elsewhere."

"Well, it's up to you but I bet you've probably been to all the decent places round here, more than once. Let's just get a table. I'm starving!"

Charlotte felt her doubts melt away. George's assertive manner reassured her. He wasn't taking over, as he had been at the cemetery, but rather smoothing out the bumps. Taking the decision out of her hands, but at the same time, deftly, giving her a good reason to see the sense of his suggestion.

Two hearty steak and ale pies, two apple crumbles one with ice cream and one with custard later George wiped his custard smeared lips with his serviette before giving Charlotte a satisfied smile.

"That was brilliant! You see, all you needed was some food. You've been chatting for Britain all the way through lunch."

To Charlotte's immense relief George was a political animal. A left-wing political animal. Lunch had been spent putting the world to rights: Corbyn – pro- or anti- undecided; BREXIT – definitely remainers; and Windrush generation – undisguised embarrassment and bewilderment as to any government that could treat people so callously who, after all, had only come to help the country to help out after the Second World War.

Although the restaurant was quite spacious, and they had been tucked away in a corner, the passion of their denouncements had been disturbing the equilibrium of their fellow diners, quite frequently, such that Charlotte could discern some frosty looks being aimed in their direction. Notwithstanding a certain animosity towards them a general feeling of self-righteous indignation and a shared Ideological standpoint was developing between George and Charlotte aided, no doubt, by the wine they had been drinking. Charlotte had begun to relax her guard more than a little and had started sharing some stories relating to her political involvement over the years and as a result some indication of a rather relaxed attitude towards horizontal negotiations with men with whom she shared a common political outlook. As George left the table for a toilet break Charlotte realised she was not adhering to her previous decision to limit all insight into her past sexual proclivities. She also realised she had not checked her phone for messages since before breakfast. Having entered her pass-code she was horrified to see four missed calls and a number of angst ridden texts from Robert Piggott.

"Piggott & Son. Robert speaking. How may I help you?"

"Hi Robert, it's Charlotte. You wanted to speak to me?"

"Oh, hello Charlotte, thanks for getting back to me. I was panicking a bit to be honest. Got a bit of a problem actually..."

"OK. What's that?"

"Well," Robert was being very hesitant, almost as if he was wanting Charlotte to speak although he had failed to say anything concrete for her to speak about. "Well as I was saying there's a problem. Not here. We're fine. It's just that at Green Acres..."

"Yes!"

"Well to get straight to the point at the moment they can't do woodland burials"

"What! Why the fuck not?" The last thing Charlotte needed was complications and here was Robert giving her complications in spades. "Have they run out of land or something?"

"No, nothing like that. They will be able to do woodland burials, but not just at the moment."

"Robert what are you burbling about," Charlotte had really lost it with the creepy Robert who was just winding her up by his delaying tactics.

"They've had a flood. Apparently with all the rain they've had since your visit the little stream running through the site has turned into a raging torrent."

"OK, so what's the solution?" If her outcome based training relating to debt recovery had told her anything it was a need to look beyond the presenting problem, quickly, rather than just getting bogged down in the detail.

"Well obviously," as far as Charlotte was concerned there was absolutely nothing obvious about this whole situation but she decided to let that pass, "the funeral can go ahead as planned, the ceremony room is well away from the affected area, but the actual interment will have to wait until the water subsides."

"That's all very well Robert, but why am I talking to you? I really need to have a word with Abigail at Green Acres. I don't want my Joe's body and his carefully planted, no expense spared, tree to be washed away whenever another flash flood occurs. I'll need to give them a ring. We might have to rearrange everything unless I can get some guarantees from the cemetery."

"Yes you'd better give them a ring. I was just phoning to give you a heads up because they phoned me about another funeral, can't really believe it, suddenly everyone seems to have gone eco crazy, and I said I would let you know. Mind you there's a few days left before your day. Things could..."

"Robert that's not the point," at this juncture George returned to the table and tapped Charlotte on the shoulder to gain her attention. "OK Robert. Got to go."

"What's going on? Have you had to cancel the funeral? I could hear you from the toilet. It created quite a stir with our fellow diners I can tell you. Don't think they'll want any excitable lefties in here again."

"What do you mean? Was I really loud? That Robert Piggott has really wound me up. There's been a flood at Green Acres!! I've not spoken to them yet, but from what..."

"Calm down Charlotte, you're shouting, everyone can hear, shhhhh!"

"Sorry, sorry but I really lost it there. How the in god's name can you establish a woodland cemetery on a floodplain for God's sake?"

George could sense that their gentle saunter around the delights of the castle, the Rotunda Museum and, possibly, the North Bay Heritage Railway was in peril. So indeed, was Joe's funeral but that was currently of much less importance. Surely that could wait for a few hours at least.

"So, what are your plans then? D'you want to phone – what was that girl's name? The one we met."

"Abigail."

"That's right. D'you want to phone her or shall we leave that for now and get on with the tour?"

"Don't know what to do," Charlotte started crying and, as she did so, reached across the table and grabbed George's hand and squeezed it hard. She looked up at him, tear streaked face, panda eyes, a pathetic figure. "It's totally wrecked the funeral. Can't have Joe and a load of other dearly departeds floating away down the river in their wicker caskets. Can we? Can we George?" She started shaking his hand, still staring straight into his eyes, beseeching him.

George could see no alternative but to address the issue at hand abandoning all hope, temporarily, of continuing their grand tour.

"Let's go back to the car and then you can phone Green Acres and see what they've got to say for themselves."

With Charlotte continuing to sob uncontrollably communication between them became almost impossible. George settled the bill, as agreed, and then with his arm around her shoulders he began to steer her towards his car. Just before they got in George managed to get Charlotte to look at him and placing his hands on her shoulders he shook her very gently both to get her attention and to break the cycle of tears.

"Charlotte, Charlotte look at me!" Charlotte was staring firmly at ground. "Now look," George found himself addressing the top of Charlotte's head albeit about 12 inches below him. "Are you sure you can handle this? You're really upset. Is this the best time to be doing this? Shall we…"

"It's OK," Charlotte straightened herself up, leant towards George and kissed him lightly on the cheek. She had found a crumpled tissue in her coat pocket and was dabbing at her eyes. She had stopped crying and was breathing normally. "I'm really sorry this is messing up our day. Needs to be sorted though. Robert Piggott – bad news, no solution! Just so upsetting. I thought I was on a bit more of an even keel but it's just under the surface – it's still so raw. Thanks George," she reached towards him again and gave him another peck on the cheek. "Thanks for being here."

George, surprised by the level of affection he was being shown by Charlotte, smiled without reacting or responding. He could see the distress Charlotte was experiencing and did not want to misjudge the moment or make things even worse.

"OK let's use the car-phone and then we can both join in if we need to."

"Right – good plan!"

Ten minutes later Charlotte and George were all smiles and determined to continue their tour having ascertained, from the overly apologetic Abigail, that things at Green Acres Memorial Park bore no resemblance to the information being given by the increasingly irritating Mr Piggott. Apparently flooding only affected one of the paths leading to the actual woodland burial plot. According to Abigail this occurred after torrential rainfall and was only a minor problem which could easily be circumnavigated and would be long gone by the time they arrived on Friday. Abigail did also indicate that Mr Piggott was anxiety prone and, although she didn't want this to go any further, one of her least favourite funeral directors to have dealings with. Apart from Abigail's comments reflecting badly on her professionalism Charlotte and George took great solace from the fact that the deluge had been overstated and that not only was the funeral not threatened but also their jaunt did not have to be curtailed.

"Ever since I first met him, that Piggott bloke, well..."

Charlotte was getting overexcited again. George placed his hand on her knee and started slapping her playfully.

"Now, now I think we are both agreed about Mr Piggott. Let's just put that behind us for now." He retrieved his hand which he used to fire up the satnav.

"Where to now?"

"Well, no visit to Scarborough is complete without a visit to," Charlotte was beginning to sound like a tourist guide, "its 12th century castle with over 2,500 years of turbulent history behind it. Scarborough Castle defends a prominent headland between two bays with sheer drops to the sea. This spectacular castle has endured sieges from mediaeval kings, civil war armies and even a German bombardment during World War II. Now you can climb to the battlement viewing platform for dramatic coastline views and take tea in the 18th century Master Gunner's house."

"OK, enough already. I'm convinced – what could follow that?"

"Well sir," Charlotte had fully embraced her tour guide persona now. "I would also recommend the Rotunda Museum which is one of the world's first purpose-built museums built to the design suggested by William 'Strata' Smith, known as the father of English geology..."

"Stop. Where did you learn all this stuff from? Not that I've got anything against the attraction..."

"I used to be a tour guide for a holiday job and used to take tourists on a whirlwind day tour which concluded with a trip on board the world-famous North Bay Heritage Railway which..."

"Well, we need to get going if we're going to manage a decent look at everywhere you've suggested and get back to take advantage of the hotel pool before dinner – do we need to decide now what is going to be possible or we might just be chasing our tails all afternoon?"

"OK let's go to the castle – the views are stunning and then the railway because I just love steam railways."

"Sounds good!"

After a bracing hour in the windy castle ruins and taking in the view from the Roman Signal Station they took brief refuge in the Master Gunner's House to have a look at the array of artefacts which spanned a large period of Scarborough's past. Their windblown day continued as they arrived at the North Bay Heritage Railway after a short car journey. Although the brightly painted carriages afforded some protection they were both glad they had prepared well for their adventure. They had had to run from the car park in order to get their tickets and ended up in a huddle in one corner of the carriage just as the engine puffed into action jolting all the carriages and passengers, such that Charlotte and George ended up in an awkward embrace. As the journey became smoother Charlotte pushed her way out of the pile of bodies, smiled rather sheepishly at George, and began looking out of the window.

"Did you know that the NBHR..."

"Is this more of your guide speak Charlotte?" George was laughing as he spoke, laughing with not at Charlotte

"Yes, but I can tell you some interesting stuff without you having to buy a guidebook. Only if you're interested though?" Charlotte made a sulky face as she paused her infospeak.

"No, please go on," George reacted quickly to Charlotte's change in demeanour. He didn't want to spoil the mood now that they had overcome GreenAcresGate.

"This railway is the oldest attraction at Northstead Manor Gardens. It is a 20" gauge railway and it was first opened in 1931 and is now one of Scarborough's top seaside attractions. This is a great way to travel to the Scarborough Sea Life Centre, which unfortunately we won't have time to visit on this trip, as well as the family orientated Sky Trail and the historic Water Chute, neither of which will be suitable, nor open, at this time."

"Thank you for letting me know. This is great. I love quirky things like this. I remember holidays when I was a child, we always used to go to the big holiday resorts – Bournemouth, Torquay or to a Butlins or Pontin's. Mum and Dad, particularly Dad, used to make sure that we had plenty to do during the day so we'd go to sleep early doors so that he could pop out to the nearest boozer for a few pints."

"My dad was only allowed one day off each holiday. We always went away for a fortnight. Always the same place for years on end, poor food but it must have been the location, not really sure. From what I remember he hated being on holiday with us, especially if the weather was bad as it usually was. You know the Great British Summer before global warming really took hold. Anyway, on his day off he always used to get a packed lunch from the B&B, put his walking boots on, slung his old, battered rucksack on his back and trudged off not to be seen again until we gathered for dinner. He was always a bit happier after his day off but he never actually talked about it much. Mind you, he never really talked at all. He was the epitome of a taciturn person – never ever knew what he thought."

"So he's dead now then?"

"Yes, both my Mum and Dad died within a year or two of each other. They were in their 50s. Shame really, but apart from early on I can't say I missed them," Charlotte was aware that she was letting her defences down again by revealing details of her parents and her childhood but she was happier sharing stuff which didn't reveal any secrets which anyone else, in this case George, could manipulate to their advantage. Joe would often use her past indiscretions to deflect criticisms or analysis of his activities. That was never going to happen again.

As they chatted the little train clattered along affording superb views of North Bay from their vantage point high up the cliff. Whilst they didn't talk all the time they were both at ease with each other now, neither feeling the necessity to fill every gap with a quip or an observation. They were what Charlotte would describe to Laura later as 'easy silences'. Charlotte managed not to reveal any more family secrets prior to their arrival back at the hotel. Even though George had tried to breach her security shield she had been able to fend him off without him really noticing that she was being very protective of her identity, whether that reflected well or otherwise on her. She gave no details about her swimming career or her short time flirting with a career in glamour modelling. If George Brunt was, and it was a big if, going to be a regular feature in her life, his leap of faith was going to be based solely on the here and now not on the basis of knowledge of her misspent life pretty much up to the present day. Charlotte was very anxious to stop the seemingly endless series of relationships based on her sex drive. She was old enough to move on from that and didn't want it to dominate the rest of her life in the way it had so far.

As she moved around in the cramped changing cubicle at the Peasholm Manor Hotel trying to fit into her recent impulse purchase Charlotte wondered what it would be like in close proximity to George just wearing a flimsy piece of material. In different circumstances on a number of occasions, although never as public as this, such an eventuality had in the past led to some very imaginative and pleasurable sex as it appeared that many men seemed to think a woman, particularly Charlotte, in a swimming costume was fair game. Charlotte had to admit she had never been very impressed by her naked body even in her modelling days, she was always in the 'chubby' category, but that never seemed to deter lovers and photographers. However, she had always wished she had the time and the real inclination to do something about the more floppy bits. Hours in the gym had never appealed, nor running or cycling - in fact, all forms of extreme body shaping exercise had never ticked any boxes for Charlotte.

Once ensconced in her new costume she checked herself at all angles, as far as was possible in the limited space available, to see whether she was well covered. The main fear was that either she would have a cossie malfunction or the so far entirely gentlemanly George would appear in a pair of budgie smuggler trunks which she would see as a very direct indication of where he was thinking things might be heading on the second night of their stay.

Much to Charlotte's relief when George eventually emerged from the changing rooms he was wearing a pair of lurid multi-coloured beach shorts which looked a little bit out of place in an indoor pool in Scarborough, but would have been exactly right for a beach in Magaluf.

"Fit's really well," was George's greeting.

In the same vein Charlotte called out, "Rather loud!"

George seemed keen to demonstrate his swimming prowess rather than any other skills and proceeded to swim towards where Charlotte was seated before executing a very proficient tumble-turn which, given the rather small size of the pool, not only succeeded in enabling him to swim off in the opposite direction, but also to drench Charlotte.

"Hey, what you doing?" Charlotte yelled after the miscreant. She was more shocked than angry but after all she was in a swimming pool. She began following him using her much less polished breaststroke.

George stopped, smeared his hair away from his face and smiled: "You OK? Used to be quite a good swimmer. Used to race at regional level. Never went any further, needed to do masses more training to improve my times."

"That was a very impressive turn anyway."

"Thanks!"

Charlotte was beginning to feel uncomfortable standing on tiptoe next to a nearly naked man. They had had a good time together and she felt quite happy to see George again and see how things turned out. She just had to negotiate her way out of the pool without yielding to temptation. She actually wanted to pull George close and kiss him and push herself against him. For the briefest moment she nearly succumbed, she could feel George looking at her as she turned away. She knew what he wanted. She giggled nervously.

"Let's swim!" was all she could manage to break the febrile moment. "It's lovely and warm in here." At that Charlotte resumed her faltering breaststroke only to be overtaken seconds later by George who then proceeded to swim up and down, without stopping, for the next 20 minutes. Long before that Charlotte's recreational swimming fitness had run out and she clambered out to sit in the pagoda style jacuzzi modelled, she was sure, on the pagoda in Peasholm Park although she felt the hotel version was rather less authentic. George was obviously putting a lot into his swimming display, alternating crawl and butterfly, making his tumble turns ever more spectacular and making it impossible for anyone else to have a swim.

When he eventually paused Charlotte took the opportunity to tell him she was going to get changed and that she would see him in the bar around 7.30pm. George shouted something indiscernible and waved before he plunged back into the water to resume his swimming exhibition. As Charlotte left the pool two women were coming out of the training rooms, they exchanged brief hellos and smiles as they walked past. Given their plunging necklines and high leg hipster bikini briefs she thought they would also be more suited to a Mediterranean beach but she was also sure George would be very appreciative of the view on offer, more so than the one she had provided in her maxi-cover onesie.

"Hi!"
"Hey, where are you?"
"In my room. We've just been having dinner"
"Can we talk?"
"Course."
"No one with you?"
"Laura!"

"I know you of old you know. Couple of nights in a hotel and George is a really nice bloke. Back in the day you would have had the 'do not disturb' sign on the door handle. Don't lie!"

"But that was ages ago. I'm not like that now. Anyway I've got a funeral to organise"

Laura was laughing and no matter how hard she tried to muffle the noise it was quite clear. "Not that long ago, lovely. I've got a good memory you know."

"OK OK but I didn't want it to be like that with George. I want him to like me for myself not just be his latest conquest."

"From what I've seen he's definitely soft on you – look how helpful he's been. I don't think he's going to treat you as a pushover."

"That's what I don't want to happen. I've had to be really hard on myself as well."

"How do you mean?"

"Well, after we'd been on our cultural tour we went for a swim in the hotel pool and well he's got a really good body, great swimmer and..."

"You mean you pushed him away?"

"No what I was going to say was that there was a moment, a pause you know as if he was waiting for me... It was really hard..."

"What d'you mean! What..."

"Laura, control yourself! It was hard for me not to get carried away. I mean I know what could have happened but I was determined I was going to avoid any pratfalls."

"Well good for you Charlotte. So what have you been doing on your weekend away?" Laura changed the tone of her voice to make it sound as if their weekend had been a great event. A grand tour instead of a quick look at some of the attractions of a Yorkshire seaside resort.

"Not going to bore you with all the details. I'll tell you when we get back. We got on really well. It wasn't like a date, it was like two mates spending time together. This hotel is wonderful – apart from the swimming pool they have an excellent spa set up with lots of treatments at very reasonable prices, if you've got a voucher. We should come!"

"Sounds good especially if you can get it cheap."

"I've got a voucher cos we've stayed here so..."

The phone in Charlotte's room started ringing.

"Look Laura I need to go. Phone's ringing. Talk tomorrow."

"OK great. Glad you're OK and you've not... you know got yourself into trouble."

"Hello! Charlotte speaking."
"Hi it's George. I just wanted to say thanks again for today. Really enjoyed it. As you know I've never been to Scarborough before – very impressed."
"Of course, I'm sure your experience was greatly enhanced by having the services of a qualified tour guide at your disposal."
"That made all the difference of course. Just wondered if you wanted a nightcap – my room or yours?"
Charlotte was silent, this was the last thing she wanted to happen. She had really enjoyed George's company during their stay. Now she wanted to focus on meeting up with Richard and then finally getting the funeral, flooding notwithstanding, over the line before planning her future with or without baby Summersby and a possible involvement with either George or Richard. She really didn't want any further complications. She had drunk enough and now she just wanted to go to sleep.
"Yeah I enjoyed myself as well but I'm tired now. Don't need anything else to drink thanks. Just wanna go to sleep thanks."
"You sure?"
"Yes George. I'm sure," Charlotte tried not to sound too cold but she also wanted to sound firm. "Night, thanks for my holiday."
"Night, it's been a pleasure."

Charlotte could hear a soft knocking on her hotel room door. At least as she came to that's what she decided it must be. Immediately prior to that she thought someone was knocking on her forehead. She looked at her watch she'd only been asleep for a few minutes but it could have been the middle of the night. She padded across to the door.
"Who is it? What you want?" Charlotte was pretty sure it would be George, who else would be knocking on her hotel room door after all it was a respectable hotel. It wasn't going to be a random stranger.
"It's me. George. Sorry to disturb you but there's something I wanted to say to you – you sort of cut me off before. Can I come in? I won't stay long, promise."
"George it's very late. I told you I want to go to sleep. What's so important?"

"Let me in, Charlotte, it's really difficult standing in a corridor with a bottle of wine in my hand, might attract the attention of security if they come on their rounds."

Again, there was a silence. Charlotte felt vulnerable. Why had George decided to ignore her preference for going to sleep? What was so desperately urgent that it could not wait until the morning? Alone in her warm comfy PJ's in a hotel bedroom she did not want to entertain guests. She was drunk and tired, not a good preparation for what could turn out to be an important conversation, at least for George.

"George you've woken me up. Please go away don't spoil things between us."

"It won't, I promise. What I've got to say. I'm sure..."

Charlotte opened the door suddenly unbalancing George who then fell over and landed in a heap on the carpet. She bent down to help him to his feet as they both started laughing at their strange predicament. As they both stood up George slipped his arms round Charlotte shoulders and gently pulled her towards him.

"After such a great day I didn't want to miss the opportunity..."

Charlotte grabbed his arms and pushed him away sharply.

"Don't say anything else please. This is a big mistake. Trust me!"

"I just wanted to tell you how much I like you. I wanted to show my appreciation," George was stumbling across the room towards her. His speech was displaying signs that he was very drunk. "I really like you Charlotte. I think we go really well together. Don't chou? Don't chou?" George was struggling to make himself understood.

"Look, George, this has gone far enough. We've both had a lot to drink and I really don't feel comfortable with this at all," Charlotte was getting more and more distressed as she tried to deal with George as calmly as she possibly could. For whatever reason George must have thought she was 'available' – perhaps it was the tumble into the railway carriage, that look she had given him in the swimming pool, tiny lapses but had they been sufficient to give him encouragement. George was looking at her with a glazed expression on his face. He must have been drinking in his room after their meal.

"Why don't we just sit down and have a drink. I brought a bottle and some glasses," George paused to reveal two glasses stowed in his dressing gown pockets which had miraculously survived his earlier mishap. "Let's have another drink and get to know each other a bit better. Shall we?"

With this George sat down on the extremely large queen size bed which completely dominated the room and patted the mattress as if indicating to Charlotte that she should sit down beside him.

"George get up! You're not staying!" Charlotte was trying hard not to shout, she was instead using her assertive voice, more often heard when she was addressing troublesome youths or children who were not listening. As George was not moving and was still inanely patting the bed she marched towards him in order to help him up so she could direct him to the door. "Come on then George you've had too much to drink. Need to go to bed now. OK?"

As she tried to help him get off the bed George saw his opportunity to catch Charlotte off balance and pull her onto the bed beside him. However, in his drunken state he overbalanced and ended up lying on top of the prostrate Charlotte.

"Fuck you. Get off me," assertiveness and cajoling had gone clean out of the window and Charlotte didn't care who heard. "I've just told you I'm not interested. What is it you don't understand?" By this time Charlotte had managed to escape George's clutches and was standing over him bawling. "We came here because you, very generously, thought I needed a break after you had equally generously varied my partner's Will. Me agreeing to go to bed with you was not, repeat not, part of the deal," Charlotte was really getting in her stride now as she recalled Laura's doubts about the reasoning behind Generous George's actions. "First of all, my partner died only a matter of days ago. If you remember I, we, are organising his funeral. Second of all I've given you literally no indication that I wanted to have sex with you and third of all something that I haven't told you before, I'm pregnant and I not sure who the father is!"

"Well, that's wonderful news, Charlotte. Best thing I've heard all day. Is it a boy or a girl?" George spluttered.

Bright sunshine was streaming through the window when Charlotte woke. In the turmoil of the previous evening she'd forgotten to draw the blackout curtains. Without moving she tentatively stretched out her hand to see if there was anyone else sharing her bed. She had a vague recollection of lots of shouting, people banging on the door – other residents, the night manager, all wanting to know what was happening and whether the police needed to be involved and then nothing. For all she knew George could have been lurking somewhere in her enormous bed, even though her outstretched hand had not made any contact. He could have retired to the bath or, best of all, he had gone back to his room. Charlotte conducted a quick circuit of the wardrobe and bathrooms of what she now realised was more of a suite than her anticipated single room and was very grateful to find no trace of anyone else within the curtilage. She returned to bed after succeeding in producing a passable cup of strong tea using a variety of sachets and capsules handily situated near the kettle. She propped up her pillows, sipped her tea and pondered.

At first she tried to make sense of what had happened after George had phoned and then arrived unannounced at her door clutching a bottle of wine. The problem was she had no clear recollection of the sequence of events – she remembered being afraid and of being extremely angry. As she pieced together what had happened she still felt that same anger coursing through her veins eight hours after the event. She also remembered announcing, somewhat ill-advisedly in retrospect, her pregnancy, by way of explaining why she didn't want to have sex with George. What was very unclear was his response. She had a very strong feeling that he was delighted with the news although she was unclear as to why that should be. Perhaps she had misheard with everything else that was going on. She wanted to believe that so much that she had an uneasy feeling that in fact her gut instinct was correct. Having been unable to resolve this conundrum she then set about reviewing the events of the day. She was still confident that none of her actions could possibly have led to George believing that he would be welcomed into her bedroom and that she would be, in any way, receptive to the idea of having sex with him. She could not understand how such an enjoyable day came to be tarnished in such a stereotypical fashion.

Charlotte was not a pushover anymore and she felt that she gave George very clear signals to that effect throughout the day. The only moment that she felt she might have let her guard slip was in the swimming pool. Looking back, she realised that was a bad move on her part even allowing for the demure, even uptight nature of her cossie. She had to admit that for a fleeting second she could so easily have slipped her arms around his waist and made a move to kiss him. It had happened so many times before with her making the first move which had been picked up on very quickly by the object of her affections and led to full sex or sex acts in some extraordinary places. That she had so clearly wanted to avoid any such eventuality must have been obvious to George even taking into account that brief moment, surely he could not have been confused. So why had he made the disastrous decision to push his luck in the way he had?

As she tried to make better sense of the previous day's events Charlotte became more and more distraught. George had effectively deleted himself as one of Charlotte's friends by his actions. How could he be so unfeeling – she was a grieving woman who also, just happened, to be pregnant. She was not in the right place for so many reasons to be interested in a new sexual partner. Clutching a cushion to her face she began sobbing .

By the time Charlotte had got control of her emotions and sorted out her make up as best she could, to mask her puffy eyes, it was a scramble to get down to the restaurant before it closed at 10.30. She was a little wary of the reaction she might get but mercifully the room was deserted apart from one table that had been bedecked with a preposterously large arrangement of flowers. Charlotte's condemnation of the gift lasted only until a waitress called out: "Miss Summersby, your table is over here," pointing to the aforementioned flower covered table. Nestled into the top of the display was a note. Charlotte had no illusions as to who it was from.

"Charlotte Darling a million apologies for my behaviour last night. I have no idea what came over me and if I could have my time again I swear...."

Charlotte let the card drop from her hand onto the floor and slumped into a chair. She was stunned She scrabbled around the floor, found the card and stuffed it into her bag without looking at it again.

"Are you OK there? What can I get you for breakfast today?"

"I'll just have toast and coffee please."

"OK. Thanks."

The waitress turned and walked away.

"Excuse me! Sorry." The waitress turned round. "These flowers," Charlotte waved at the table, "these flowers, can you find a good home for them please. I haven't got a car and I've got a busy day so; I know it's a waste, I can't take them with me."

"That's OK Miss I can sort that out for you, they won't go to waste I can assure you."

"Thanks."

"OK I'll go and get your food."

Charlotte had not had to read the card in full, she didn't need to. So now he was making massive gestures and trying to apologise. They

191

were beautiful flowers, no doubt about that, and she hated to have to give them away but they would have been a total embarrassment for the rest of the day – lunch with Richard and then the train journey home. To have behaved so badly then think that an extravagant present made everything right.

Charlotte's opinion of George had sunk even lower as a result of his flamboyant gesture. His message was irrelevant now as she wanted nothing more to do with him. The whole funeral was in jeopardy now – how could he give a eulogy after what had happened and as a result her meeting with Richard, which she suddenly realised was in 45 minutes, had taken on an entirely different meaning. She hadn't seen Richard for three years. In fact, only in the last few days had she thought about him at all. Life with Joe and Henry had taken up all her time and so she had not spent a moment thinking about previous relationships. Now in just a few minutes she was going to reunite with one of the real loves of her life.

"Miss, excuse me Miss." Charlotte's waitress was running behind her as she passed through the bar.
"Yes what is it."
"Miss, the gentleman who bought the flowers asked if there was any message from you? "
"Yes there is, as a matter of fact. Tell him to get stuffed. Thanks."

With all the rushing round and organising Charlotte had had no time to prepare herself for her assignation with Richard. The reason for him making contact was rather vague and Charlotte had no idea what he would look like now. In the taxi to their rendezvous, she managed to exchange texts which at least meant she wouldn't be wandering around aimlessly looking for her date. He was the guy just by the door reading the Guardian. Couldn't be simpler.

"Hi Charlotte! How are you? You look great!" Richard had stopped reading and greeted Charlotte warmly, gave her a quick hug and an air kiss. He didn't seem at all nervous. In fact, Charlotte thought he had changed a lot since she last met him, he was smartly dressed in a pair of sand coloured chinos and a nice blue shirt. He was wearing glasses as well which suited him.
"Hi, it's good to see you. You look different, smarter, more relaxed. I'm good thanks, so what are you doing with yourself these days?"

For 30 minutes Richard and Charlotte chatted amiably swapping stories about jobs, cars and holidays. No mention was made of their previous relationship or why Richard had made contact. Talking to Richard, he seemed to have no guile about him. It made such a pleasant change after the previous 36 hours where Charlotte had had to be on her guard the whole time even though all her hard work had eventually come to nothing. Charlotte was expecting a change of gear, a big reveal, any minute, but nonetheless that didn't stop her being gobsmacked when it did come. In a strange way it all seemed rather inevitable, just another part of the story, someone else needing her, complicating her life which was already quite complicated enough.

"Charlotte it's so nice to sit chatting to you. D'you remember all those weekends we used to spend together reading, watching junk TV, getting takeaways from..."
"The Raj – beautiful curries!"
"That's right we always used to go there. I've had a pretty bad time recently that's what made me get in touch. I'm going to be absolutely straight with you. Until Lauren died, that's my wife..."
"I'm so sorry Richard that's horrible!"
"Thanks, it was really sudden. When she died it made me think about my life – where I was and where I wanted to be and I thought of you. I've never really needed to look back. Lauren was everything I needed. We had a brilliant relationship on every level, but with her gone I got to thinking about you and me and I picked up on Facebook about Joe, that's why I messaged Laura. I know it's early and I know things for both of us are a bit raw, they certainly are for me anyway, but with no Lauren what I would like would be to have you in my life – permanently."
Charlotte nodded as Richard finished speaking: "Well, you seem to have made up your mind pretty quickly on this – no contact for three years and now, now you're wanting to spend the rest of your life with me!" Charlotte paused for breath and to try and make sense of what she had heard. "In one way I am really surprised. I want to come back to that, and in another I really like the idea of your plan or at least exploring it together, not dismissing it out of hand. From what I remembered before we met today we were a match made in heaven – I really loved you, felt queasy every time we met, got excited when

you phoned because you made the most amazing plans for us, just phoned me and I had a couple of hours to get ready for your latest adrenaline rush activity or weekend away. You see my problem is I cannot remember why you walked away, it's all very vague but..."

"I was scared Charlotte, plain and simple. I'm so sorry. I was frightened of the consequences of us being so serious about each other. I couldn't think of a way of slowing things down. I thought I'd lose you. So, I did the stupidest thing I have ever done in my life, I told you I didn't want to see you again, not that I thought we needed a break nor did I give you the real reasons for what I was doing. I hadn't actually got that job at the time we last met and it didn't materialise. And then within two months I met Lauren, fell completely and utterly in love, got married six months later and we were blissfully happy..."

Charlotte screwed up her nose hearing this and interrupted Richard: "Bit too much information there, I think!"

"Sorry but you see Lauren was really a MK II of you, obviously inferior in retrospect, but without her I really need you to make me complete again. I know this is a silly thing to say. I just want to start back up again, when you are ready, I fully get that, just like we were before only a bit older and wiser. Does that make sense?"

"Oh, my darling," Charlotte reached across the table and touched his face stroking him lightly. "This just sounds like another one of your great adventures. I can't think of a single reason why you wouldn't want to do that and think that, just like before I will be able to drop everything and join in. But things have changed, in fact, they've changed massively for me. Not only have I learnt a lot about myself and also about Joe. I've come into a lot of money and I realise that I really do want to do things differently in future – now none of these things necessarily mean we can't work through them, but there is one more thing. Before I tell you I need to know if Lauren and you had any children?"

"Not for want of trying, but no we haven't."

"Well, I've got myself into a situation – you know I told you I want to change the way I have been living? Well up until Joe died I was having an affair," Richard looked shocked hearing these words and started to speak. Charlotte placed a hand lightly over his mouth. "No don't, just let me finish, and I've just found out I'm pregnant and I have no idea which guy is the father. Classic eh?"

"Well, the getting pregnant bit could happen to anyone, having an affair, that doesn't fit with my fond memories of loyal, stable Charlotte. I never saw, or thought I ever saw, you look at another man all the time we were together. So, you must have really changed!"

"As I said I'm determined not to do anything like that again. My relationship with Joe was flawed, it invited me to find solace elsewhere. I wouldn't want to get into another relationship where I needed to."

"Are you sure we could manage a relationship which you would find totally fulfilling?"

"That's really what I'm intrigued to find out. Now that luck has dealt us a second chance."

The subject of Charlotte's pregnancy was not raised again in the following two hours. They spent most of the time happily reminiscing about the time they were together. It was as if, now Charlotte had revealed her secret, and Richard had explained, to the best of his ability, their breakup and subsequent events, that they had given themselves permission to wallow in their past with rose tinted glasses. One story led to another. Charlotte had not thought about Richard since the breakup but now all sorts of buried treasure was coming to the fore. "Do you remember..." "Thinking about that, what about..." "Oh the funniest thing that ever happened was when..." Charlotte had forgotten all about the funeral, baby Summersby and her decision not to allow herself to drop her guard. That decision was compromised very early on as the two held hands over the table, laughed together and bared their souls. Charlotte confessed in detail her relationship with Henry, Joe's foibles and her continuing to be sexually involved with both her partners. She felt so comfortable with Richard, any idea of her keeping her distance or not giving away too much of herself, without getting some reciprocation, was completely forgotten. At last, for the first time since Joe died, she was able to fully express herself. She felt quite differently about Richard compared to George. Even though she thought she had got on really well with him during their two days together Charlotte now felt she had been played by George and no longer felt any closeness to him after his feeble attempt to seduce her.

Richard was really enjoying her company. They had always been very relaxed together although they had never lived under the same roof.

Charlotte was struggling to understand how things had changed for Richard – from being so scared of any deeper commitment to leaping at a second chance after the death of Lauren. He had made no further mention of their permanent relationship since his earlier revelation. So much had been left to one side, particularly Charlotte's pregnancy, she felt that it would be better to try and redirect the conversation to more practical issues. She felt they had spent enough time establishing what they had had, what they needed to do now was to see how they saw the future - together.

"OK so you said before that..." Charlotte began rather hesitantly after returning from a visit to the toilet.
"Yes I know, rather blurted that out. Just wanted to put down a marker really. I'm really sorry for what happened before. Truly sorry for that and I want to..."
"Yeah I appreciate that but..."
"But you're pregnant. You've not really talked about that. Must've been a shock for you. Bit of a weird time to find out as well. How do you feel about it? From your point of view now. Do want to keep it?"
This was the first time since she found out that anyone had asked that question. Of course, only one other person knew, and he had only found out in the most peculiar circumstances and, Charlotte realised, she had not really considered this herself. Hearing her baby referred to as 'it' as in 'are you keeping it' made the baby sound like an alien. Suddenly Charlotte felt very protective of her foetus, her decision. She had started the conversation but very quickly it had turned into an emotionally charged exchange. As she had become so much more likely to do, with her emotions being ripped asunder so frequently, she began to cry. Softly at first into the sleeve of her cardigan. Richard proffered a tissue to enable Charlotte to try and stem the flow. She was unable to speak for a few minutes but was able to just about contain her grief so that no one else in the pub noticed sufficiently to feel the necessity to stare at her.
"I've not really thought much about the baby's future," she said after taking a deep breath. "I've always been in favour of a woman's right to choose, but it's different when it's your right to choose. When it's your possible child. I need to have that conversation with myself, absolutely. I was going to leave it until after the funeral to be honest."

"OK, so do you want any help to tease out the issues or shall we leave it? I'm happy either way. For what it's worth I'm happy whatever you decide. I'd be just as happy to explore a future together with you with or without a baby. You are my focus. I have to say that, and whether that includes a ready-made family is entirely your decision."

"You mean you wouldn't want to influence my decision in any way at all? I seem to recall that you were never shy of offering an opinion in the past."

"Yes but this is rather different. At the moment we are talking freely, we're not 'together'. A few weeks down the line we might hit the rocks and if we do if I would have had a disproportionate role in you deciding one way or another against your own gut feeling, and you'll blame yourself for allowing me to influence you and hate me for making you live with the consequences."

"I can see that and I don't know if I should tell you this or not..."

"Are you scared of letting your guard down too far? Scared of giving me an unfair advantage? Don't be, please. I only want to help."

"You see, I never loved Henry. My relationship with him was a means to an end. Satisfying my lust, pretty despicable really. If the baby was his, if I could find out beforehand, I don't think I'd be able to really want to mother them - it wouldn't feel right. If it was Joe's it would be different, very different. I'd be in a proper dither. They would be a bit of Joe that I was left with and I really don't know whether that would be a good thing or not. As you can see, my life was and still is in a right old mess. Blithely having sex with two people I did not care very deeply about in the sure and certain belief that no harm would come of it except that now it has. What a bloody mess! Where do I go from here?"

"Well, I'm sure it would be possible to do a DNA test to see if Henry was the father, with his agreement of course, but is that really the issue for you?" Richard was speaking very carefully and softly. He was looking straight into Charlotte's eyes and holding her hands in his as he spoke. "I really don't want to influence you, honestly. The issue as far I see it is – do you want to have a child, have you ever wanted to have children? Isn't that the first question you need to answer? That gives you..."

"Thanks. Thanks Richard, but I really don't want to talk anymore about this now," Richard tried to butt in but Charlotte pushed his hands away. "No, it's too complicated and I know you're trying to be helpful, I appreciate that but... I'll have to leave that for another day. Let's get this funeral over with first."

"You did bring it up and I..."

"I know, Richard, and you've given me lots to think about. Thanks."

Charlotte and Richard's meeting stuttered to a halt after Charlotte's emotional outburst and the subsequent attempt to analyse the choices moving forward. Charlotte was anxious not to reveal any more of her secrets and Richard seemed to be at a loss to know how to move things forward. Having had such a positive conversation they were left saying a rather awkward goodbye accompanied by a fairly unconvincing hug which Charlotte rather regretted. Charlotte promised to send Richard full details of the funeral and, in turn, Richard promised her that he would come.

"Look, we can talk afterwards."

"I'd like that."

"Dinner or a drink?"

"Yeah, we can sort something out. I'm still OK with exploring plan A, it's just that..."

"I know. I'll see you at the funeral."

"Good. Thanks."

Richard walked off, half turned to wave and then disappeared into the late evening crowds. Charlotte sat down on a convenient bench. She was beginning to feel that baby Summersby was getting in the way, was becoming too much of an issue for her to deal with logically at the same time as sorting everything else out in her life. She decided to leave any decision until she had a clear head and resolved not to mention the fact that she was pregnant to anyone else until she had made up her mind as to what she wanted to do.

Looking at her phone she realised that Laura had been phoning and texting for the last couple of hours. Though she really wanted to catch up she decided she needed to make her way home and head for a scented candle filled bathroom to soak away her troubles in a heady mixture of cloves tobacco and mint tea.

Chapter 8 : Impressions

With a rather miserable and confusing weekend behind her Charlotte returned to Lediard Avenue and began to reflect on her long lasting struggle relating to the opposite sex on equal terms. No matter how hard she tried, the men she had had dealings with over the years always seemed to gain control from the outset. In her younger years Charlotte suffered from low self-esteem and was convinced that she would never get a boyfriend because she was ugly, this in spite of the fact that she had lots of friends and was popular in her peer group. The upshot of her self-pity was that, to compensate for her self-perceived ugliness and lack of opportunities, she tried too hard. The minute a boy so much as talked to her she was in ecstasy scribbling his name in her school-books surrounded by hearts and arrows and agreeing to what she later realised was called 'light petting' almost as soon as they were alone, leading on in many cases to 'heavy petting' straight afterwards. She blushed to remember what that had entailed at the age of 16. In the days before Google, Charlotte and her friends had no access to the Internet to get advice on what they should and shouldn't be doing so used to discuss what happened when they were making out with boys. Most of Charlotte's friends were horrified at her antics and worried that she would let one of her admirers go 'too far' if she wasn't careful. They also noted, like some kind of secret police force, that Charlotte was getting a 'reputation' for being too 'easy' in conversations overheard over lunch or on the school bus. Getting a 'reputation' was something to be avoided at all costs for a girl because it meant none of the nice boys would be interested in anyone who had, by definition, 'been the rounds'.

Charlotte was largely oblivious to any of these criticisms as she was too involved in her latest short lived relationship. She found herself in a self-fulfilling prophecy of disillusionment. As soon as she threw herself at a new boy they became nervous not wanting to get 'too involved,' so as a result she was dumped, thus reinforcing her low self-esteem and leaving her moping on the settee at home. Her mother would be urging her to go out with her friends or, for some unknown reason, to get some fresh air as if that would ever be able to cure a totally broken heart.

As she remembered more of the details of earlier sexual activities Charlotte was quite shocked at the sorts of things she had got up to and realised, not for the first time, that many of those earlier insecurities had played out in her relationship with Joe. Joe fulfilled many of her needs, physically and emotionally, and yet she had still found time for Henry. Joe left her alone on a regular basis so she felt as if she had been given permission to look elsewhere for her amusement and fulfilment. Joe never asked what she'd been doing while he was away and Charlotte learnt, very early on, that there was no point in cross-examining Joe because he would always avoid the issue in his usual self-effacing way. To disarm her he would make a comment about how beautiful she was looking or change the subject to one of his favourites: food, eating out or cultural experiences they had shared accompanied by a warm hug.

Charlotte had hoped for some clarity to emerge from her short-listing over the weekend but instead she had gathered a further cloud of confusion around her. She was quite impressed with how she had dealt with George; she had made sure her head ruled her emotions and rather than succumb to his advances, which would have been much easier, she called him out for what he was, a predator whom she wanted nothing more to do with. However, her pride was also considerably diminished by the possible loss of a friend and potentially a partner, especially in view of the situation pertaining to Richard who, against all expectations, had laid himself completely bare by announcing he wanted to spend the rest of his life with her without any pre-warning.

Several days after these unexpected events Charlotte was still unable to decide what to do next, especially as most of her time had been filled with administrative affairs. She had had to wade through a long list of emails, missed phone calls and subsequent voice messages and even a couple more cards and letters. She prioritised attending to any variations in attendance at the wake because she was most anxious not to incur any unnecessary costs. Four cancellations equalled £50 which she did not want to afford - she had much better uses for Joe's money than wasting it on the overordering of vol au vents and cupcakes. Apart from that, there were more condolences from people she had never met and, even at this late stage, offers of help.

Charlotte was conscious that, at least at the start of proceedings, she would have a number of visitors as she had agreed to a foregathering at Lediard Avenue so that close friends and relatives, George, could either grab a ride in the funeral cars or form an albeit rather short procession behind. She was planning tea, coffee and nibbles but realised that in order to facilitate that she would need to do a considerable amount of cleaning and tidying.

The first stage of the process took longer than intended as Charlotte sorted through all the cards she had received and put as many as she could on display on any available horizontal surface. Sorting actually meant reading every card as well which took much longer as some of the thoughts from people she had never met stopped her in her tracks and, on more than one occasion, brought her to tears. Joe, her Joe, had elicited expressions of loss so heartfelt they could only have been from people who knew him personally and reflected favourably on Joe as a person she had never known. Happy-go-lucky, lad about town Joe was completely missing and in his place was a hard-working, fountain of all knowledge person who was always going the extra mile, inspiring, guiding and counselling people who, it appeared to Charlotte, would have achieved considerably less in their lives without the influence of her Joe.

Many of the cards came as a complete surprise to Charlotte mentioning aspects of Joe's character she had previously been unaware of especially the thoughtfulness that was mentioned so frequently.

"Special day? Not really, give us a clue?"

"It's my birthday Joe. It's 9pm and, as yet, there has been no sign of a card, some flowers or a present. Did you forget?"

"Well actually, no. I mean yes. I know this sounds really weak, but I've been extra busy lately and I've just not had a chance. I'll make it up to you. Promise."

Charlotte was clearly angry and not in the least placated by Joe's promise of better things to come. She was even less happy when moments later he squeezed past her in the kitchen, patted her bottom in a masterful way, and squeezed one of her bum cheeks.

"There love," he schmoozed. "I will make it up to you. Tomorrow. Meal, flowers, the lot. I'll text you."

Joe's lack of attention to detail in relation to her never ceased to amaze Charlotte. She had lost track of the number of times when she'd expected or he had promised 'something nice' and nothing had happened. He always managed to talk himself out of such situations but molesting her in the kitchen or bathroom or worse still when they were out together, did nothing other than annoy her. In fact, if she was ever in a situation where the conversation turned to attentiveness amongst partners she always took the opportunity to go to the toilet or offered to help with the washing-up, always something so she could avoid coming clean about Joe's 'shortcomings'.

Charlotte reasoned that if one or two tributes had been paid she could have taken that, but she felt she was being subjected to an organised campaign to rewrite the history of Joe and all this at a time when it would make no difference as he had unfortunately passed away. She hoped that things would become clearer on the day of the funeral, because as time went by they were getting more and more confused.

Cards arranged, flowers reorganised, Charlotte turned her attention to the bedroom, toilets and Joe's area, including the very revealing filing cabinets. There were still lots of papers and files strewn over the area and although Charlotte did not pay too much attention she felt that she should at least leaf through them quickly in order to try and ensure she hadn't missed any vital piece of information relating to her late partner. She was mindful that the last thing she wanted was any more surprises on the day which might cause further embarrassment – forewarned was always forearmed as far as she was concerned.

As she was assembling the last of the pieces of paper to put back into the filing cabinet Charlotte concluded that she had not found much of interest other than a rather obsessive stock of old utility and council tax bills, and bank statements going back over 20 years, and minutes and agendas of Labour Party meetings going back furthest of all. Seized by a curious indecision about what should happen to these records she decided to put them back where they came from without any further consideration. At the very least there was a considerable amount of shredding required that would definitely have to wait. The last folder she picked up contained one letter in a sealed envelope which bore no address. Curiosity got the better of Charlotte as she carefully opened the letter and began to read its contents:

2nd June 2015
Dearest Hannah [his second wife]
I realise that this letter will come as a bit of a surprise to you but no matter what has happened I did want to let you know that I did love you, truly I did. Our marriage was a bit of a rollercoaster, babe – after all we'd only known each other a couple of months before we

got hitched [that was, according to Hannah, because she'd managed to get pregnant]. We were an ideal match – you were so beautiful, babe ['so beautiful' so what happened in the eight years they were married – a real fall from grace] and I loved coming home from work or the football or the pub and you were always ready for me. [She was obviously a good actress because she had told Charlotte that he was insatiable, and although she hated it saw it as a price worth paying to enable her to enjoy their lavish lifestyle]. I always remember the way you kissed me and our little bedroom games which used to spice things up. To you making love was never a chore in contrast to most of the lads' wives. They reckoned they put up with it because it meant the bills got paid. Not you, my darling! [Joe's gullibility had never exhibited itself so clearly in the short time she had been with him – he always called the shots] you always laughed at my jokes and loved the games I kept playing – making out I was leaving and then buying you a flash meal or a new dress or some sexy lingerie [Charlotte could not remember Joe ever buying her presents although it probably was just as well as Hannah had told her that although she loved going out, because Joe's taste was so appalling it meant she was really embarrassed to wear them, and kept having to take things back so she could buy something she liked]. If I stayed out late with my mates I never missed bringing back a takeaway or some flowers to say sorry.

I know things didn't end well between us and for that I must apologise. We were a good couple while it lasted. Maybe if you fancy a drink sometime we could get together for old time's sake. I'd like that.

Yours ever

Joe

Charlotte looked at the date at the top of the letter and realised it had been written several months after she had moved in with Joe, much to her dismay. She blamed herself for prying and ripped the letter into small pieces before throwing it into the wastepaper bin. While Charlotte was never clear as to what Joe was up to on his trips away she was amazed he was making blatant attempts to hook up with an ex-wife so shortly after their relationship began. Charlotte closed the drawer of the filing cabinet, turned the key in the lock and wandered into the kitchen to make a pot of tea which she planned to drink in a warm scented bath.

Sometime later her reverie was interrupted by a very loud banging on her front door followed by the merry jangle of the wireless front doorbell. Anticipating that such an outspoken assault on the door could only announce the urgency of a parcel delivery she leaned out of the bath and yelled down the immediately adjacent stairs: "You can leave it on the steps or in the blue bin. Thanks!" She slid back into the bath rather awkwardly occasioning her to bang her toes on the taps leading her swearing rather loudly.

At this stage, a rather muted voice could be heard from downstairs: "Sorry, sorry Charlotte have I disturbed you. It's Mr Westwood, the celebrant, I was due at 2pm sorry I'm a little early..."

This time Charlotte swore more quietly and only to express her frustration rather than any experience of pain: "Oh shit, shit, shit."

With this she leapt out of the bath, grabbed the nearest towel-like object and whilst struggling to put it on hurried down the stairs.

Mr Westwood's patience as he waited for the door to be opened reaped a rather unwarranted reward as Charlotte Summersby flung open the door revealing herself clothed in a sheer negligée which hid nothing from his gaze. The unfortunate celebrant gasped with surprise and immediately turned his back on the equally shocked Charlotte.

"Miss Summersby, I'm sorry but..."

"Oh, holy bollocks," Charlotte made her best attempt at covering her private parts with both hands, whilst looking like the unfortunate Barbara Windsor in one of the Carry On films, and in so doing let go of the door which promptly slammed shut forcing her outside the vestibule of her house.

Without turning round and, in an extraordinary gesture of chivalry given the torrential rain, Mr Westwood removed his coat and gingerly passed it back to the still shielding Charlotte who, in addition to her parlous state, was now drenched, so that the previously inadequate negligée was plastered to her skin making her job of trying to remain even half-decent even more difficult.

"I think this might help," he suggested.

"Thank you. Very kind, but I'm very sorry I'm going to have to knock up one of my neighbours to see if they've got my key. You go and shelter in your car and I'll just pop up the road."

Safely ensconced in his car Mr Westwood watched incredulously as his scantily clad client disappeared up the road in search of a spare key.

"Well Miss Summersby…"

"No, please call me Charlotte and I'm so sorry for keeping you waiting and the kerfuffle."

After considerable delay involving Charlotte finally rousing her neighbour to get a key and then towelling herself down and getting dressed, the newly acquainted celebrant and the bereaved party were sitting clenching their cups of tea sitting in reasonable comfort in the newly cleaned front room. Mr Westwood, who was rather inconvenienced by soaking wet trousers and waterlogged shoes was putting a very brave face on it rather like Mr Piggott had previously, in order to seal the deal.

"As I was saying, I don't think this needs to take long but I do like to get to know the deceased before the funeral so even though I have never met them I can base my opening and closing remarks on an understanding of what, for want of another word, made the deceased tick if you take my meaning – what job he did, what football team he supported, whether there are many relatives or friends present, where they're from etc. Do you get the picture?"

Charlotte listened to Mr Westwood's preamble with an ever increasing sense of foreboding and déjà vu.

As with the young man from the newspaper she was acutely aware she really was not going to be very much help in creating any kind of picture for him to refer to, with any degree of accuracy, which would chime with the experiences of the gathered multitude. She decided in the face of such cursory knowledge she had better not try to fabricate a story and just come clean.

"Well, Mr Westwood," she hesitated so long Mr Westwood feared the worst, and yet nothing could have prepared him for what came next. "Well, you see I hardly knew Mr Brunt at all even though we've been together for about two years."

Mr Westwood was flabbergasted. What he wanted to say, and indeed what he very nearly did say, was: 'Jesus Christ, woman, you're organising the funeral of a man who you hardly knew, can't give me any background detail and we're going live, forgive the pun, in a couple of days. What the **** do you suggest we do?'

Instead after a momentary pause to collect himself he said: "Well, Charlotte, that's very unfortunate but I expect you actually know him far better than you think you do. So, let's have a little think. Shall we?"

Mr Westwood left 42 Lediard Ave coatless and massively under prepared for the job ahead. He had spent over two hours trying to coax information out of the deceased's partner, but no matter how hard he tried there was very little forthcoming especially concerning the finer details of Mr Brunt's life. He reckoned that in the 40 years he had been a celebrant he had never found himself in such a difficult situation because of lack of knowledge. He often found he didn't like what he had heard from family and friends but never that he heard nothing to like or dislike. He was going to have to wing it and try and pick up on sufficient information from the eulogy to at least personalise his closing remarks leaving his opening phrases to depend on meaningless platitudes. As far as he could make out Joe's brother George was going to say a few words, but because of what Charlotte had referred to as a 'recent difference of opinion' he wasn't allowed to contact him to get any background information. He almost turned back as he reached the end of Charlotte's road but decided it was pointless and that he was going to have to put the Brunt funeral down to experience, in all probability a particularly traumatic experience.

Coincidentally on the day that the Orders of Service arrived featuring a winningly smiley Joe on the front, Charlotte also received a text from George regarding his eulogy. She had agonised over the choice of photo; the order of service; and also the number of copies she needed for considerably longer than she spent considering George's text which she replied to a little tersely: That's what we agreed.

As the day of the funeral grew closer Charlotte felt increasingly nervous about how it would pan out. Although she knew she had been distinctly unhelpful to Mr Westwood, just how unimaginably unhelpful she would never know, she was sure that he would pull something together. She was less sure about George's contribution. When they had first spoken about the idea it seemed very logical and even straightforward, although events since had meant it could prove to be very embarrassing in view of their now virtually non-existent relationship.

She could only hope that he would do his duty as brother of the deceased and go along with the idea of playing down the less desirable aspects of his character. What she didn't want to happen was for his character to reflect badly on her at the end of the day. She thought that was unlikely, especially in view of the effusive praise contained in so much of the correspondence she had received. However, another niggling doubt for Charlotte was her cavalier invitation to anyone, and, indeed, everyone to 'say a few words' which she had included in emails and letters relating to the funeral. She had wanted to be inclusive at the beginning as she thought there might be people she did not know who would want and may even be entitled to say a few words. Knowing what she knew now, that was a clear mistake. However, help was at hand because, with the clock running down on the event, she had no takers but she remained anxious that someone might still blow the whole event off course.

As she sat with a handful of orders of service in her hands and a glass of non-alcoholic white wine on the table beside her the doorbell rang disturbing her daydreaming.

"Hi Charlotte, how y'doing?" It was the elusive Laura dressed to kill and bearing Prosecco and flowers. "Sorry I've not been in touch but I've been a bit tied up, if you know what I mean!"

"Oh really!" Charlotte pretended to be excited. "Well, you'll just have to tell me about it." Charlotte was pretty clear that Laura had found herself a new partner, however temporary, as that was usually the reason for her not being in touch.

Having sorted out a vase for the flowers and a glass for Laura the two friends settled onto the settee after clearing off the orders of service.

"Lovely picture Charlotte. That really does him proud. Great smile."

"Took ages to choose as well. You know when you've got so many photos on your phone and then you've got to crop them and everything. I was in the original, we'd gone out for a meal and the waiter took it. He had a lovely face."

"That's going to look really good next to the casket as well. You have got one blown up for that haven't you?"

"Of course. Robert..."

"Oh, it's Robert now is it. Has he used his fatal charms on you?"

"Oh, do one will you. Of course not! He just went through all the details with me to make sure everything was properly sorted."

"So enough about the funeral. How did your weekend go? Did it live up to expectations?"

"In a word no," Charlotte leaned across and took hold of her friend's hands and looked straight in her eyes. "Oh, my god it was a real bummer – George tried it on when he got really drunk and then when I met up with Richard he'd decided - don't forget I'd not seen him for

3 years, he finished with me and then got himself married – he'd decided all on his own that he wanted to spend the rest of his life with me before he'd even seen me! You couldn't have made it up. I was looking forward to a possible new start or at least some time away from all the organising where I could relax, and I get two blokes who pretty much want to carry on where Joe left off."

Inevitably as Charlotte relived the weekend she began crying.

"C'mon now lovey," Laura had gently pulled Charlotte towards her and was cradling her face in her hands. "Hey, you're your own woman now. It was too much for you, too soon. I can see you didn't want to rule either of them out or put them off but there's so much going on and they've obvs misjudged where you're up to," she paused as she pulled a tissue from her pocket. " It's OK, it's clean." She offered it to Charlotte so she could mop up her tears. "Did you enjoy any of it?"

Charlotte was dabbing her eyes as she replied, "That's the trouble, George and I had a great time on our tour of Scarborough. It seemed like I'd known him forever, we've got lots of the same interests as well..."

"Charlotte can I just ask you – now don't shout at me – did you get..."

"No, I bloody didn't I told you. I was determined not to do my usual thing and be an easy pushover. I stuck to my guns – that's why he came and knocked on my door. I'd already tried to get him to go to bed. I was very clear with him."

"What happened then?" asked Laura very gently. She could not resist asking, even though she really knew it was none of her business and she was almost expecting to be told to piss off.

"Well, after I'd said goodnight to him and he'd phoned me to see if I wanted a nightcap he turned up at my door in the hotel with a bottle of wine and a couple of glasses. He was bladdered but determined. Don't laugh but I think he said it would be good for me or it was what I needed and he was patting the bed. I went berserk, guests complained, the night manager turned up but I wasn't having him..."

"Well done you! What happened? Did they kick him out of the hotel? He deserved it."

"No nothing like that, they just made sure he went back to his own room. I just wanted him out of my hair and at least I achieved that."

"Can't believe you were so strong there, Charlotte. I'm so proud of you!"

"And then in the morning he'd arranged for a great big bunch of flowers to be delivered to the breakfast room at the hotel. I mean I was really worried about even going to have anything to eat in the first place. The waitress asked me if I had a message for the sender. I just told her to tell him to get stuffed!"

Laura laughed, " Charlotte, you're a changed woman. The number of times I've told you in the past to be stronger, particularly with Joe, and now, finally, you're coming good. Have you heard from him since? Wasn't he supposed to be doing a eulogy?"

"Well, he's got to do that really. To be fair he has checked whether I still want him to do it and I said yes. I mean it's going to be awkward but at least he'll bring a personal touch to the proceedings and I'll have to hope he does a good job."

Charlotte and Laura's conversation drifted away from the minutiae of Charlotte's previous weekend for a few minutes as they discussed what they were planning to wear and Laura gave a few very limited details of her latest flirtation. Partly in order to divert attention away from herself and partly because of her innate curiosity Laura brought the conversation back to the subject of Richard.

"Enough of me chattering about Ben, you've hardly said anything about Richard yet and I need to go soon before I have so much wine I won't be able to drive."

"Nosey bugger!"

"Look, I'm your friend and I'm here to offer you support, but I need to know more of what happened before I can."

"Well, until he dropped the bombshell things were great. I'd forgotten how strong a relationship we'd had before he walked off. He said it was to do with him being frightened to get too involved at the time and then he told me that now that his wife had died he wanted to spend the rest of his life with me. Have to say right then, in some mad way, that was an extremely appealing possibility but, as I've explained, I needed more time and I didn't want to get into another situation where a guy makes decisions for me. I've decided I've got to take more control anyway and I needed to be sure that he wasn't going to change his mind again. He really hurt me back then. I'd really blanked it out of my mind but we were so in love. I thought we were going to get married, seriously."

"So did I, but after you two split we never talked about him. I think it was your way of protecting yourself."

"Honestly, I think you're right. By just blanking him out, forgetting he ever entered my life made it possible for me to carry on. If I hadn't I really don't know what would have happened. I was so depressed and now he's back in my life..."

"You're going to be careful."

"Yes I am. Now, while you're here you can help me with two things – what I'm going to wear and which poem I'm going to read at the funeral. I've left both of them a bit late, I know, but if I'm going to have to go shopping then it'll have to be soon."

"Let's go and have a look at your wardrobe then, no point in spending money unless you have to. Come on let's get on with it. I need to get home. Ben will be there soon."

Charlotte ignored Laura's reference to her new squeeze - she needed her help, not a long monologue on how fit Ben was; what sort of car he owned; where he lived; and whether she should go to bed with him yet, that is if she hadn't succumbed already. Time enough to have a good wallow in all things romantic about Ben when the onerous task of choosing her funeral dress was over.

"That one, excellent choice, vibrant colours, bit swishy will be just right."

Charlotte had barely opened her summer wardrobe when Laura marched forward grabbed said 'excellent dress,' held it against her and pirouetted round the room.

"This is so the one Charlotte. Just love the orange and red, providing you've got the shoes to carry this off you are sorted." Charlotte was surprised by Laura's unequivocal enthusiasm. They usually had very different ideas about what suited Charlotte, whether it was the style, the length or the colour and appropriateness to the occasion. If Charlotte liked it chances were that Laura would be looking somewhere else in the shop for THE dress which would do the job. Charlotte was pleased on two counts: she had previously bought something that so suited her that she could wear it, with Laura's complete blessing, to Joe's funeral; and second, she would not have to go on an emergency shopping trip. She hated shopping even more so when she was under pressure to deliver.

Seconds later Laura emerged from a separate section of Charlotte's wardrobe clutching a pair of blue shoes, 6" heel, blue shoes. Charlotte was unable to speak.

"Now I know what you're thinking," Laura started. "But these will look fantastic. Saw an article in one of those fashion mags they always have in the hairdressers – blue and red are so in, especially this particular shade. Try them on, come on you'll see what I'm on about then," Charlotte was looking unmoved. "You will, honestly, you will!"

Before she had a chance to protest Laura was tugging her clothes off and holding out the red dress for her to slip on. Charlotte was happy with the dress, perfectly happy with the dress, what she did not want to wear were 'shouty shoes' and particularly 'shouty shoes' she had never worn before, couldn't remember why she bought them and shoes which she knew would make her the laughingstock of, what after all was supposed to be, a sombre occasion.

Deciding that she had to make a clear stand on the shoes issue Charlotte kicked them off as soon as she put them on. "No, I'm not going to wear them. Look stupid can't you see that. Sure, Rhianna or someone like that would look terrific but this is a small funeral, at a woodland burial place that DOES NOT lend itself to..."

"Oh, come on Charlotte don't be such a wimp. They'll make a statement..."

"Too bloody right, people will just think I've lost my mind. I'm not wearing them and that is final. OK?"

"OK I can see you're not happy with that choice. Come back to it – look for some others and then just see what you think when you're calmer."

"Don't patronise me, please. I'll find another pair, white or even red, classy not shouty!"

"Anyway, I've got to go. You said something about poems, what's the issue? I'm not an expert, there must be loads on the Internet. My Mum and Dad used to have a couple of collections of well-known poems, we could look through them if we lived nearer," Laura had talked herself into a cul-de-sac. "What sort of poems d'you want?"

"Well, I've been looking and there's lots of sad, reflective poems and not all of them are religious, which is good, but I don't know if that's what I want my contribution to be. Joe wasn't really like that was he? I mean, I've asked everyone to wear bright colours wittering on about sad images clashes a bit don't you think?"

Laura was staring at her hands unable to look at Charlotte. There was an uncomfortable silence.

"You still sulking about the shoes," Charlotte tried not to sound too aggressive but she needed a response. "Do you think we need to go all traditional, 'weep not for me' or ' dry your tears' all that sort of crap or something more hopeful, more uplifting?" Laura still wasn't engaging. "Laura you listening? Help me will you, please."

Laura breathed a huge sigh before, still staring at her hands, she started to speak: "Look, Charlotte, he's your guy, rather, he was your guy. All along you've done things your way, that was what the two of you decided or you thought Joe would have wanted it that way. Now you want me to like make a decision. No, I'm not sulking, don't look at me like that. OK, if you really want to know what I think, I think it should be a hopeful poem. When I was with Joe he was always the life and soul of the party. Don't forget we did a few of the late-night gigs when you peeled off early..."

"I didn't force you to you know," Charlotte didn't want to be reminded of Laura and Joe's never completely clarified 'activities'. "You always seemed pretty keen to spend time with Joe so don't get all critical."

"I wasn't, you pillock. I was just saying what happened. Me and Joe did quite a lot of drinking and dancing. It was fun and Joe was fun. That's why I think you should reflect that in the poem you're going to read."

"Yes you two were always very keen on staying out at the slightest excuse. I often wondered..."

Before Charlotte could finish her sentence her phone rang. Glancing at the screen. She looked at Laura, "I'd better take this if that's OK?"

"Yeah sure, I need to go anyway. I'll be here about 10 on Friday morning to help with all the arrangements. You don't need to worry..."

"OK, thanks Laura that'll be great."

She slid a finger across the screen of her Sony Xperia.

"Hi Alice, how are you?"

"Hi Charlotte, I'm sorry to bother you, I know there's probably never a good time to be interrupted at the moment. Have you got a couple of minutes?"

"Of course," Charlotte had learnt the benefits of patience since Joe's death and this was an excellent example of her putting her new-found skill into practice. Laura had left so there would be no eavesdropper and she could sort out whatever needed to be sorted out and move on to other things.

"W-e-l-l, I was really phoning about dress code," Charlotte, in an instant, was losing her newly found patience. WTF was she on about 'dress code,' she didn't have to wait long for an answer. "We know you said bright colours to be worn?"

"Yes that's right."

"W-e-l-l," Alice's extended 'well's' were becoming more and more annoying as she continued to not get to the point of her phone call. "Well, the thing is we, that is Hannah and I, we thought it was a really good idea but we didn't want to in any way clash with or upstage the widow, or not the widow actually but you know what I mean...."

"The partner of the deceased," Charlotte suggested helpfully.

"Yes, thank you Charlotte. Well, we've been talking and..."

Charlotte seized the initiative: "I'm wearing a bold orange and red print dress with blue shoes," she announced.

She could hear Alice gasp at the other end of the phone and when she started to speak, it sounded very spluttery: "Oh I see, well, that that sounds like a great combination I'm sure we can work with that. I hope you see my point, Charlotte, and that you didn't mind me asking?"

"Of course not, Alice. It wouldn't have occurred to me but if it was worrying you then it's best to get it sorted out, otherwise it only creates anxiety. Doesn't it!"

After Alice had gone Charlotte rushed into the kitchen and poured herself a small glass of a nicely chilled non-alcoholic Pinot Grigio, in deference to baby S, so she could sit, relax and sip whilst celebrating her sartorial victory over Alice and Hannah. Laura would be delighted to hear that her outrageous suggestion had won the day, but most importantly she had fired a broadside across the exes to say you won't be attracting as many looks as the 'partner of the deceased' and you won't upstage her no matter what you decide to wear on the day.

Chapter 9 : Approaching

"It's all a bit awkward really isn't it? I mean going to your ex's funeral. By the way, thank you so much for offering to drive. Makes it so much easier – going with someone and not having to do anything," Alice was enjoying being chauffeured in Hannah's delightfully comfortable BMW 428i SE Coupe.

Since Joe's death the two ex-wives had met up for afternoon tea, with Prosecco, and discovered that they had more in common with each other than they had probably ever had with Joe. As Hannah put it: "I know you're not supposed to speak ill of the dead but Joe was a bit of a bugger." pause "Well actually he was a full-blown bugger if I am being honest."

Their afternoon tea had consisted of two bottles of Prosecco, the usual sandwiches and cakes, a number of cocktails, and was only brought to a conclusion by the afternoon tea slot coming to an end and being replaced by the early-bird dinner service. They had become increasingly aware of the amount of clearing and cleaning that was going on around them and finally succumbed when a very pleasant young waitress approached them with a well-rehearsed opening gambit for use with overstaying, Prosecco infused, guests: "If we're all finished here would it be OK if I cleared up for you? Your bill will be along in a minute."

Not wanting, nor being able, to argue against this very reasonable statement of facts they agreed to relinquish their table.

As the wine had flowed they had both taken the opportunity to vouchsafe their experiences of Joe's peccadilloes. Both referred to his secretiveness, his attitude towards money and his sexual proclivities as constant causes of irritation and inevitably arguments.

"I never knew how we managed from week to week. My wages covered food and petrol for my car, my stuff really, and he insisted, without ever disclosing where it came from, that he would pay for everything else. He was an archivist at the time for the council. I think he might even have been chief archivist for all I knew, but I don't think that sort of job, looking after old documents and stuff, ever paid very well. Even so we always managed holidays and trips out."

"Oh yes, holidays! Always the same place – his favourite childhood haunt..."

Alice paused and then they both shouted in unison, as if pre-rehearsed:

"Salcombe!"

"Sunny Cove!"

"Gara Rock!"

"North Sands!"

Giggling they ticked off the local highlights which they had both shared with Joe every summer.

"I never thought it was that good, but there was never any question was there?"

"Oh no. I don't actually think it was a question of money either. I think he actually really enjoyed it. Must have taken him back to a time when he was really happy."

"If we get a chance we really ought to ask Charlotte whether she has been offered the Devonian experience. See if he'd got it out of his system with us."

"Not sure we'll get a chance. There'll be lots of people there – it might be inappropriate delving into stuff like that."

"Yeah, I know, we'll just have to slip it into the conversation. Shame we can't really find out if he'd changed at all – you know the money and everything."

"We sound like a right couple of bitches burrowing into his private life. Y'know, what do you really care? In a funny way I feel sorry for Charlotte and I'm really going to the funeral to support her. Been here, done that, move on."

"Think it's more closure for me. I've been on anti-depressants since we split up. I've had so much to deal with, so much I wanted to sort out. Hardly a day went by without me wanting to clarify something with him. When he left he ripped me apart. I didn't want to go out. Didn't want to see my friends. We were, or at least I thought we were, so happy yet, like you said, there are always doubts, but I just used to try and ignore them. Afterwards I just couldn't believe that I hadn't questioned more. Why did I let him rule my life? I haven't really got back to normal yet and he's been out of my life for years."

"So, I don't want to sound like your therapist but I really don't think you should blame yourself for any of this. Let me ask you a question: Joe never wanted children yet he said he had a brilliant childhood –

Salcombe, dam building, rock scrambling – so why didn't he want children? What did he tell you? Did you ever discuss it with him?"

"Of course we did. At one time I was desperate couldn't think about much else but he wouldn't have anything to do with it. He told me he thought he would be a crap father; he didn't trust himself to have anything to do with children."

"Did you ask him about his father, and their relationship?"

"No point. He wasn't for debating it, just shut up shop completely. He either left the room, went down to the pub or just changed the subject like he did with everything else he didn't want to talk about."

"Same here, although once when he had been drinking he did say that I'd have to wait until his job situation was more secure. Seemed to be saying he didn't think we could afford to have children. Couldn't get any more detail than that. So, the point I'm making is that there is no point in blaming yourself on that issue. He behaved in exactly the same way to me. You couldn't make any difference – look what happened to me – it's all to do with Joe. It was just one of his foibles, you just need to rise above it. I'm not saying that is easy but it's possible. Blame him, he's dead. It can't hurt him, but it might help you."

"That's really helpful, honestly, talking to you is brilliant!"

Lucidity and profundity lessened considerably as the wine flowed and both women began to reveal more of their experiences, mainly bad, a few good, with the deceased.

"I really enjoyed our afternoon tea – that was like a light bulb moment for me. I've felt so much better since. I've been re-evaluating our relationship since then and I see things in a totally different way. I had always thought I was a failure, never got a good job, never had many friends, he didn't really like the stuff I cooked, he was controlling me, playing me, destroying my self-confidence for his own purposes. Our relationship was all about him, that's all I can say. Instead of seeing our split as an opportunity I just carried on the same just thinking I couldn't do things because I never had, rather than just trying anyway and starting again. That's where I went wrong, not seeing the shackles had been removed."

"You never know, I mean I'm not a doctor, but you might be able to stop the pills with time. You need to go and see your GP and discuss the situation, see what they think. Are you still in the same job? Have you ever thought about any other jobs you could do? You know, transferable skills, things that lend themselves to all sorts of possible opportunities."

"Thanks anyway. I'm really so much more positive now having talked things through with you."

"That's good."

"I'm so glad we're going together. Any idea who else might be there? I expect his brother will be there won't he? Never really got to know any of Joe's family. I kept in touch with friends from uni and work and that really kept me going."

"Same here. He kept his private life very separate and at the time what with work and housework I never really thought about it. We did quite a lot of things on our own in the week but we always managed a meal or the cinema at weekends."

"Anyway, we'll just have to stick together when we get there and try and get a word with Charlotte at some stage. See how she's doing."

"I bet she'll be glad when the whole thing is over. Whenever you end up organising, no matter how many offers you get from people who want to help, it's all down to you in the end. Not easy at all.

"Very impressive!"

"Hadn't expected anything like this. Looks beautiful."

The ex-wives had arrived at the entrance to Green Acres Memorial Park and had paused to get their bearings and appreciate the beautifully manicured lawns and elegant topiary either side of the sweeping drive. As they took in the view they realised everywhere was very quiet, eerily quiet. Alice checked her printout of Charlotte's tasteful e-invitation – the celebration of Joe's life was to commence at 12.30pm. They were 45 minutes early. Having found themselves out in the countryside, miles from the nearest COSTA, or indeed any sort of coffee facility at all, they parked the car in a conspicuously empty car park and decided to occupy their spare time walking round the cemetery grounds, rather gaudily clad in their almost matching yellow getups, reading the many memorial plaques which commemorated the lives of the eco-warriors who were resting there

Assembling the team had been a bit like herding cats as far as John was concerned. He had picked up some basic information about Joe's death from social media and then he had made contact with Charlotte to get the full details. He then had to not only break the news to the rest of the gang but also to check whether they were willing and able to attend the funeral. As time was short he ended up emailing and phoning in pretty short order so he could make arrangements to get everyone to Green Acres at the same time. It was a great relief to pick them all up from Manchester Piccadilly station for the 20 minute drive to the funeral location. The rest of the group were all in high spirits as they had travelled on the same train for the last stretch of the journey and had been swapping anecdotes about Joe.

"What I could never figure out was what he did, for work like. I mean he's not been an archivist for years and yet he was still on the National Executive until recently."

"He was the treasurer as well for ages. Not sure why anyone would trust him with their money."

"Yeah I get that but he was such a nice guy wasn't he. Life and soul of the party. Lots of stories to tell. How do you ask him to step down. I bet no one would have had the nerve."

Everyone in the group was utterly confused by Joe. This was not the first time they had tried to figure out what he was up to. Having worked together for many years, in more recent times their only contact with each other had been one day every year watching or, according to the vagaries of the English weather, not watching cricket – either one day of a test match or a 50 over game.

"The best thing about Joe was he always, always insisted on bringing his own alcohol," Jacob was laughing as he started to describe the lengths that Joe would go to go to smuggle alcohol, usually red wine, past the ever vigilant, or not so vigilant, security personnel at the gates of cricket grounds across England.

"Remember when he finally cracked it..."

"Yeah, he figured out they couldn't stop him bringing water so he used to have a big metal water bottle full of red wine. But he must have had to hand over so much stuff before as he always tried to get away with it," explained John.

Ernest continued the story: "He was always late as well, often didn't arrive until nearly lunchtime, with various different excuses about work making it impossible for him to get there any earlier..."

"...And then he disappeared early to catch a train. He never really watched any of the cricket. Not really sure why he came at all," John sounded confused. "A true enigma I'd say."

"Absolutely," Jacob agreed. "That's one of the reasons I wanted to come today to see if I can find out more about him. Remember he used to talk a lot but never say much. He talked in riddles most of the time. I have to say quite often I just used to switch off."

"What's his wife's name? Be good to know that before we get there," asked Gerald

"Not his wife," John jumped in. "His partner, Charlotte. I seem to remember he'd been married before. Jeff, you used to spend more time talking to him, any ideas?"

"As far as I can recall he had two wives, Alice and Hannah. He was married to one of them for quite a while. He always spoke very highly of them both, not one to really bare his soul. He used to miss out a year every so often so it was always difficult to keep track. Always used to call his other half 'the lioness' so unless you appreciated when a change occurred you were none the wiser." Ernest shook his head as he spoke. "I hope I can find out more later on today, but I'm not holding my breath." As the stories continued they prepared themselves to be regaled by John recounting his remarkable train journey with Joe coming back from some far-flung cricket ground after imbibing far too much beer. Everyone remembered the story but they all pretended that they had never heard it before as of all the tales about Joe this was accepted as being the best.

"I can't remember where we'd been now. Nottingham or somewhere like that. It was one of those days when nothing was going well on the railways. Joe and I were really pissed and we were running out of ways to get home. Eventually we found this train that went through my station on the way to Joe's. But it wasn't due to stop at my station. So, we had this prolonged conversation about what we were going to do. Joe was convinced it wasn't going to be a problem even though it was about 1am and the train was absolutely racing along. We both went to find the train manager to explain the situation. I mean speaking lucidly was a big problem for both of us and I just thought he was going to tell us to sod off. Joe tried everything, even offered him a drink from his wine stash, and then I think just to get rid of us he said he'd have a word with the driver and see what they could do. Couple of minutes later he came back and said everything was arranged and then, dead on cue, the train screeched to a halt at my station. Of course, we were ecstatic and there were loads of hugs and high-fives and then I stumbled down on to the platform. It was pitch black. I was pissed and the exit on my side of the station was locked, at least when I finally found it I couldn't open it and then I had to cross over the track to the other platform to make my escape.

No easy task I can tell you, and all because Joe insisted on having one more for the road!"

Guffaws of laughter greeted the end of the story as they always did. Just on cue Jacob, who was the navigator, i.e. the person who was holding the smart phone which had the route, announced their destination would be on their left in a matter of a few hundred yards. It was 12.15pm and they were early. They could see a number of people, including two ladies who subsequently became known as the 'Canary Twins,' had already arrived and were standing around singly or in small groups waiting for something to happen.

"OK let's mingle," said John rather over enthusiastically for a funeral. It sounded as if he was about to go on a pulling mission rather than attend the solemn farewell of their good, if rather bemusing, friend.

George had been struggling all week since his catastrophic attempt to seduce Charlotte. He'd been reading an article on women flirting which had really caused the altercation. The writer had said, "The demeanour that most indicates to me that women are flirting with me involves a slight head tilt, eye contact and a little smile. Think coy nun," and that's what he had seen or had wanted to see. He had been convinced that he was pushing at an open door. All the signs had been there and yet he obviously misjudged the whole thing. It was the coy nun look at the swimming pool that had done for him. He was mortified as soon as it happened which was why he had, at great expense, organised the flowers. He had asked for a response in the hope that they might have gone some way towards apologising to Charlotte for his gross misconduct. He could tell the waitress was hugely embarrassed to be involved at all. She had smiled wanly and passed him a small piece of paper on which she had written in a polished hand, 'Get stuffed'. He screwed it up turned on his heels and left the hotel feeling utterly deflated.

His melancholic state led to the consumption of numerous bottles of beer, wine, and rhubarb flavoured gin in the succeeding days such that he had not had a shave, a decent meal or even a bath or a shower. In fact, he had managed to arrive at the day of the funeral, of his pretty much estranged brother, in a complete omnishambles. One thing he had somehow managed to do during his stupor was to confirm with the irascible Charlotte whether she still wanted him to do a eulogy for Joe. Having received a brief, if not curt, confirmation that this was still required what he had manifestly failed to do was to write said eulogy or even to think about what might go in it or made any notes that might in any way contribute to it being spoken at the appropriate time. Mercifully at the eleventh hour George had managed to pause his alcoholic frenzy so he had every hope that with the few hours remaining he would be able to go some way to make amends. He was keen to do so for two reasons, which he found impossible to put into any sort of order: because it would impress Charlotte if he could pull it off and he really wanted to do that – he had hoped that, until the fateful incident in the hotel, he had been making a good impression on Charlotte and was now pinning his diminishing hopes on a funeral eulogy, a desperate state of affairs; and for his brother – since his death he had felt a responsibility to step up for his brother as he was the last man standing. He not only wanted to, but he also needed to, in order to achieve closure on a fairly fraught relationship.

Shortly after making his first coffee and catching a glimpse of his raddled face in the hall mirror George Brunt realised that he had quite a mountain to climb before 12.30. He decided to prioritise his physical appearance and a rather unpleasant odour which seemed to be following him around.

After a long warm shower and a careful, comprehensive shave, not only had the smell disappeared, but he also felt he looked the part of the brother of the deceased. He had also had a bunch of ideas for his eulogy and decided to forego a written speech and would instead use some notes and rely on how he assessed the mourners as to which way he should go. Charlotte's notice of the funeral had asked the attendees to wear bright colours; this was to be a celebration of Joe's life. George's role in this, he decided, was to concentrate on Joe's good features and to ignore the rather more controversial aspects of their relationship concerning his appalling attitude towards the women in his life, at least the ones that George knew about. He had been a trenchant critic of the way in which Joe had dealt with Alice and Hannah both before and after he broke up with them. He would be the first to admit to being jealous of his brother's ability to attract women – they had had many an argument about what happened subsequently. Joe was always disparaging in his comments about the women in his life in a way that George found offensive. He had in fact made contact with either Alice or Hannah after their separation partly to commiserate but also to see if they might be interested in meeting up but to no avail. He concluded at the time that things were probably still too raw for them to be able to contemplate seeing or being with Joe's brother. Now he realised it was probably an early case of acting inappropriately, possibly for the best of motives, which seemed to be occurring on a depressingly frequent number of occasions.

As he continued to gather his thoughts he was increasingly annoyed that he could not remember which ex-wife he had communicated with. As he arrived at Green Acres he scanned the assembled multitude, consisting of perhaps 20 to 30 people, and immediately picked out Joe's exes dressed in striking yellow dresses standing apart from the general throng deep in conversation. At least he now knew which ex-wife he had been thinking about but he was no clearer about her name.

Since Richard left Charlotte after their lunchtime meeting he'd been rather baffled. Before they had met he decided that he wanted to convince Charlotte they had a real opportunity, with the unfortunate death of Joe, to build a future together. What he had not factored in, how could he, was the new situation Charlotte found herself in both relatively rich and pregnant. Richard had been rather hoping that Charlotte would be in a position where she would welcome his intervention as an unencumbered woman looking for a new opportunity with someone she not only knew from before but who was economically viable. He was perturbed by both the baby and the money she had come into. Richard was hoping that he would have been able to offer a financial lifeline, which would be attractive in itself. However, his immediate reaction to the other news was that he had absolutely no interest in raising anybody else's child, especially when he wasn't exactly sure who the anybody was. Even so his feelings for Charlotte were so strong that he reasoned over the ensuing days that it would actually be a price he was in fact prepared to pay. He tried to avoid influencing her decision whilst still hoping that what he would see as common sense would prevail and she would either not go through with the birth or place the child for adoption.

In the short time that they had spent together Richard was really pleased there still seemed to be a buzz to their conversation, they had laughed themselves silly at some of their memories. He just hoped that he hadn't pushed Charlotte too hard too soon. He was wary that they had found themselves in a similar position before even though their roles had been reversed in that case. He was looking at the long term, but felt in order to be in with a chance, he needed to make his intentions clear right from the beginning. He had no idea how to embrace the bright clothing protocol as he didn't want to look a fool or give the impression to Charlotte that he wasn't joining in with the spirit of the event. After a lot of agonizing, he went for a pale cream suit, a pale green shirt, and a jazzy tie which he hoped would tick all the boxes.

As he arrived at the impressive Green Acres Memorial Park he could see he blended in nicely as there was a good mixture of pastel shades for the men and rather more vivid splashes of colour for the women. It looked as if everyone had got the message and somehow that seemed to have translated into a more upbeat vibe than the sombre atmosphere that often pertains when all the mourners wear black. Not knowing anyone there he stood next to the nearest tree, partly for support as he needed to lean on something as he still wasn't feeling hundred percent or even 75% for that matter, and partly to hide himself from everyone else. He had no idea how Charlotte would behave towards him. When he discussed whether he was going to attend Charlotte seemed genuinely pleased he was going to make the effort but that was before. The question now is whether he was going to get a look in when there were so many other people around. He reasoned that by being there he was showing his support which he could refer to when he contacted her again. He didn't expect Charlotte to show any outward signs of affection, It was the wrong time and place and he had a lot of ground to make up. He was just very anxious that he was able to do everything right for Charlotte and for their possible future relationship. Peering out from behind his tree Richard could not see anyone who was looking in need of company. Single males were in short supply and the last thing he wanted to do was to be seen by Charlotte in deep conversation with another woman. He decided to hold his position until the crowd began moving towards the ceremony room.

Harriet wasn't at all sure about going to Joe's funeral – it meant taking a day's leave, she'd have to drive. There was a crowd going from the Crown and Anchor in a minibus but she didn't fancy that, and she hadn't got anything to wear. Furthermore, she was no good at funerals. She always cried, not just cried but usually sobbed her heart out. She knew it was ridiculous but somehow or other a particular event – the curtains closing in front of the coffin; or the vicar saying: 'Dearly beloved we meet today etc etc'; or a poem; or the eulogy, and she had both taps on full flow in seconds. In fact, at a second cousin's funeral only a couple of weeks previously she had had to leave the church altogether she was crying so loudly and that was as a result of merely seeing her photo in front of the coffin when she first entered the church. Straight in and straight out. Shocking.

Having gone through her entire wardrobe several times in the search for something that was respectful whilst not being too dull she finally settled for what she regarded as the classic funeral outfit shortish, short-sleeved black smocked dress with thick black tights which she had actually worn for her short lived appearance at the most recent funeral she had attended. Hair brushed, matching accessories chosen, she was good to go and determined to behave herself for the first time at a funeral in living memory.

After an uneventful drive, as she pulled into Green Acres she could hear the processional music playing, Jackson Browne's: For a Dancer, and she could also see, to her dismay, a crowd of brightly dressed women moving towards the ceremony room. Somehow or other she had missed the 'wear brightly coloured clothes' bit of the invite. She was dressed in black. She'd messed up. The taps were turning on.

James Betts was not known for his punctuality. In fact he was the butt of many jokes about his tardiness, the most frequent being that he would be late for his own funeral. Today and the funeral of Josiah Brunt, was going to be no exception to the long catalogue of latenesses which had accrued in the past few weeks alone: late for the train (three times), late for the dentist, late for school play (major calumny, missed only speech by youngest daughter), and finally late for a surprise dinner for his birthday (James would seek to blame the person who was giving him a lift to the venue but their immediate riposte was that he had not been ready at the appointed time).

He left work late; one of the main sponsors of the charity he ran called and asked him to give a special message to Joe's widow; he missed the train; and then when he did arrive the final straw was that the pre-booked taxi was conspicuous by its absence. As he arrived at Green Acres there was no one to be seen and the doors of the ceremony room were firmly closed. He had wanted to be early so that he could make Ms Summersby aware of his presence, however as she had assured everyone in the notice of the funeral that anyone who wanted to say a few words would be very welcome to do so he realised he only had to negotiate his way into the building to be sure of being able to play a part in the farewell to Mr Brunt.

Chapter 10: Funeral

It was 10:30am. At 11:15am a foregathering was due to commence at Charlotte's house. 42 Lediard Ave was due to host a gathering, albeit briefly, of very close relatives and friends of Josiah Brunt prior to forming a cavalcade behind the funeral cars bearing an exquisitely tasteful and highly environmentally friendly wicker casket containing the body of the deceased. All the plans had been made: close friends and relatives in the first car: Laura and Charlotte (George had, mercifully texted to say he would be making his own way there); other close friends who had been carefully selected from what was at the beginning a very short list and not including either of Joe's exes, they weren't relatives anyway, or Henry or Richard, although they had both been included in the numbers for the wake at the Crown and Anchor. Absolutely nothing had been left to chance: Abigail from the woodland venue had been in constant contact regarding the setup, flowers, orders of service, photo to be placed on an easel adjacent to the casket, preparedness of the speakers: Charlotte – poem; George – eulogy and then, the only worry for the whole day, a possible free for all as the celebrant was going to ask if any of the mourners wanted to say a few words. Surely, Charlotte reasoned, no one would be foolish enough to thrust themselves into the limelight at such an event, a funeral was not the best place to make a speech, at least not without some prior agreement or acknowledgement. Anyway Charlotte was pretty sure that no one would be barging in and yet, there was still a niggling doubt. Some of the cards alluded to issues and closenesses that gave her rather more than a momentary pause for thought. Charlotte had dismissed these possible insurgents on the basis of 'what happens happens', 'it is what it is' blah, blah, blah.

If the woodland venue had been in constant contact then words failed Charlotte for the unnecessary frequency with which Robert Piggott Esq had been phoning, texting, emailing and twittering about the arrangements. She was aware right from the start that R Piggott had had no previous experience of woodland burials, she was also aware that he was exceedingly uncomfortable with the whole idea of an eco-friendly concept of burial and how that might impinge on the service his staff would normally provide. Although she was totally up to speed with all Robert's peccadilloes she was unprepared for the veritable

blitzkrieg of questions emanating from this needy and, apparently, wholly unprofessional individual. Despite having gone through every aspect of the journey to the cemetery, the unloading and carrying of the casket into the ceremony room and events at the graveside, and the later transportation of guests to the Crown and Anchor, as recently as 5:37pm on the previous evening Robert had contacted Charlotte to check how many men would be required to effectively convey the casket on its various journeys. Charlotte, by this time, was so fed up with Mr Piggott that if she could have she would have cancelled the arrangement with R Piggott & Sons Funeral Directors. Speedily Googled for an alternative purveyor of assisting in the dispatch of deceased persons and, in fact, in the absence of this alternative had a crack at doing it herself. In the absence of any alternative Robert received a full volley of abrasive and derogatory words, a fusillade of infective sufficient in fact to halt a herd of stampeding buffalo in their tracks let alone put Mr Piggott in his place. "Look, you fuckwit. Have you ever organised a funeral before? Do you know anything about my requirements? You have run me ragged for days..." and so it continued until Mr Piggott managed to break in by shouting: "I get it Mrs Summersby. Don't you worry, everything will be great. See you on Friday, I'm sorry..."
Charlotte had slammed the phone down with such force that she had broken the plastic cradle so that her final words: "I really hope so you complete and utter wassock!" were lost of Mr Piggott. Even though Mr Piggott had not heard and the phone was beyond repair above all Charlotte felt she had made an important point.

Charlotte was, notwithstanding all that had happened previously, in a pickle or maybe even a piccalilli. Very tentatively she withdrew her head from the bowl of the toilet so conveniently located in the Brunt/Summersby ensuite facility. She performed this movement extremely tentatively because she had tried this idea of disengagement several times before to no avail. As she felt no immediate need to return to the bowl she glanced at the chaos around her. Despite her best efforts both her funeral dress and funeral shoes, the outfit which she had described in such vivid detail to Alice in order to avoid, horror of horrors, a clash with Joe's previous love interests, were now bedecked in an orangy brown slime that had emanated from her guts some minutes previously making it impossible for her to stun the other female mourners with her sartorial elegance. Not only did she have to stem the flow of sick she also needed to select another complete outfit, without the help of anyone else, a feat which she had rarely performed successfully in the past. She mistakenly looked at herself in the full-length mirror which had featured so frequently in her lovemaking activities with Joe and, as she guiltily remembered, also with Henry. In fact as she absorbed the awfulness of her bedraggled appearance she was reminded that mirrors had often played a part in her lovemaking activities for a plethora of different reasons. She also realised that as well as ruining her outfit she had also managed to get more than a few flecks of sick in her hair which she had carefully, and very unusually, put in curlers overnight. Her whole look was utterly compromised. She needed to start from scratch and that, visits to the toilet bowl allowing, meant a shower and a quick rummage through her wardrobe to find another dress and matching/clashing shoes.

Charlotte was fairly certain that she had recovered the situation: she had washed every trace of sick from her body, and, as a major bonus, found one of her contact lenses that had unfortunately fallen into a previous sick receptacle, her bedroom wastepaper basket. She had also found a clean, virtually new dress, that she had decided would be ideal, no brighter colour to celebrate Joe's life than yellow, canary yellow, according to the label. It matched quite perfectly another recent acquisition a pair of six-inch heeled red stiletto shoes and, even though Charlotte's hair was not quite up to scratch, she felt ready to face the day. All she had to do, all she had to do, was to make sure that she was not sick again even though as she had been going through the cleaning up process she had felt really nauseous such that keeping a clean sheet or dress for the whole day seemed highly unlikely.

"It's only me. How y'doing?"
Bright and cheery and beautifully attired Laura had arrived utilising a key Charlotte had given her after the last time she locked herself out of the house.
"You look great, Laura. Oh I'm so pleased to see you. Had a dreadful morning so far. You cannot imagine!"
"That dress looks fab – is that the one you were going to wear?"
"Well spotted, that's where things started to go wrong."

Charlotte had just finished updating Laura when the front doorbell chimed closely followed by a breezy flourish on the door-knocker. "I'll go!" Laura was on her way even before she had finished speaking: " Wonder who it'll be?" Of all the six or seven people it might have been it was in fact Mr R Piggott of Piggott & Son Funeral Directors who announced, as Laura opened the door: "No cause for alarm. I always like to be a bit early so everything goes to time. We've got a bit of a drive ahead of us so..." Charlotte could hear his sonorous tones in the lounge and called out: "OK Robert rather thought you'd be early. Do you want to come in or do you want to wait in the car?" Robert shouted back from his position firmly rooted outside the front door; "No we'll be fine. We've got 20 minutes yet before the get go so I'll come back later. I've got a bit of a surprise for you as well, to fit in with the environmental theme of the occasion. Whenever you are ready. Until then don't worry about us we've got provisions in the cars."

Eventually, irrespective of the best efforts of Robert, the cortege departed from 42 Lediard Ave ten minutes late eating considerable chunks out of his wiggle room for the journey to Green Acres Memorial Park. He tried to stay especially calm through the whole process sensing as he had, not only a high degree of tension between some of the guests, but also a certain animosity towards him for some unaccountable reason. The fact that he had managed to get the use of the firm's very first electric hearse had hardly caused a ripple of interest which had rather dampened Robert's enthusiasm. However he was clear he was acting in the best interests of all parties, after all he had been taught by the best – his father and his grandfather before him. Charlotte would, eventually, realise the considerable efforts he had gone to to meet her eco requirements. He had always been prepared to accommodate a degree of what had become known as 'personalisation' and he felt that as the buck stopped with him he had to decide how much of 'that' was acceptable. He had hoped that the initial 'problems' he had encountered were now a thing of the past, ignoring his most recent and somewhat traumatic telephone conversation with Charlotte, but it was clear from glances and sighs and real or imagined asides that his professional reputation was at stake and he needed to ensure, more than ever, that nothing at all went wrong.

Assembling the cortege had been problematic due to the narrowness of the street in which the process was taking place, so much so that in the end the best Robert could do, much to the annoyance of Charlotte, was to ensure the funeral cars were in sync leaving the other 4/5 cars, he was never quite sure how many were involved, to join in as and when. Regardless of the efforts some of the mourners had made to be part of the procession Robert made the call that they should flounder in the wake of the lead cars because the integrity of said cars was, as he saw it, of prime importance and his core responsibility.

Charlotte was not the only person who was observing Robert's herculean struggle with more than a little interest and concern. Charlotte's neighbour at number 63 had been twitching the curtain since first thing in a desperate bid to catch all the action. Charlotte was fairly certain that she would have been aware of her unstoppable retching some hours previously such had been the severity of her affliction, but realised that that was as nothing compared to Robert's antics strutting up and down the road, somewhat in the fashion of John Cleese's silly walks, as he first tried to ascertain who was planning to be in the cavalcade before trying to assemble them in some sort of order. That they left at all Charlotte regarded as some sort of minor miracle. She was, however, greatly relieved to find that Robert was driving the lead car containing the casket so that she and Laura could travel together in the second, where, in hushed whispers, they were able to discuss Robert's shortcomings and their feelings about the rest of the day and how they felt it would pan out without involving George. They both agreed that they just wanted to get to the wake unscathed and hoped that there would be nobody who wanted to give an impromptu eulogy.

By the time the funeral cars, followed by two of the intended cavalcade, drew into the car park at Green Acres they both felt much calmer. All thoughts of continuing Charlotte's close relationship with a toilet bowl had disappeared from her mind and she was ready for the ceremony. As she followed the wicker casket into the ceremony room she linked arms with Laura and was pleased to see the kaleidoscope of colour stretching either side of the aisle. Joe would have been so pleased. Neither of them had any time for stuffy do's and a colourful funeral, although unexpected when first discussed, was just so right for both of them.As Laura and Charlotte took their seats at the front of the room she watched closely as Robert personally ensured the wicker casket was arranged properly and then propped smiling Joe at the front. At last something he had done had gone to plan and Charlotte felt relaxed and ready to play her part, or at least as ready as she thought she would ever be. She exchanged smiles with Laura as they sat with their arms closely linked.

Charles Westwood had been waiting patiently at Green Acres for the arrival of the casket and the mourners, still mulling over the details of his conversation with Charlotte and not being utterly, or even at all, convinced that what he was going to say would really hit the mark. He had wanted to spend more time with Ms Summersby, especially in the buildup to the funeral, but he had been told politely, but firmly, that that was not what Charlotte wanted and so he had decided not to make any further problems for someone who, he realised, was extremely distressed following the untimely death of her partner. As the room filled up with brightly dressed mourners to the strains of 'For the Dancer' he noticed two people in particular: one young lady who had clearly misread or omitted to read the dress code for the event and a nervous looking young man who was almost the last to arrive. He assessed the mood of the gathering as ideal both from the point of view of Charlotte and for himself as a proper celebration was going to be so much easier to lead than a mournful event as dark as the clothing of the participants. On a signal from Robert, a hearty double thumbs up, which he presumed meant that everything was good to go Charles moved to take his place at the podium.
"Good afternoon everyone," he began enthusiastically.
There was enough of a murmured 'good afternoon' in response from the gathered throng for Charles to feel more relaxed and happy that his few words would not fall on deaf ears.
"It's great to see all your colourful outfits – you look like you should have been at Ascot or Henley Regatta." Appreciative muted laughter.
a"We are gathered together here in this beautiful setting to celebrate the life of someone very well known to you all, Josiah Thomas Brunt. I very much regret that I never met Joe. From what I've heard from talking to his partner, Charlotte, he was quite a guy: larger than life, great sense of humour and a love for life. Of course it's always very sad when someone with those characteristics is taken from us. Hopefully, a day like today will not only enable his partner and

231

relatives to get some closure but also for them to gain something from celebrating his life with other people who knew him from other walks of life. I'm sure we all enjoyed the music that was playing as everyone assembled and the casket was brought into the ceremony room. There will be more music later but first can I ask Charlotte Summersby, Joe's partner, to come forward. Charlotte is going to read a poem."

As Charlotte heard her name her stomach started churning and she began to feel hot and clammy. She pulled Laura towards her and then used her as a launching pad before she tottered to the podium cursing her choice of 6 inch heels for such an important gig.

Having managed the steps to the podium by way of grabbing hold of the reading desk to steady herself she looked up briefly in order to get her first proper glimpse of the crowd. She recognised quite a few from the Crown and around where they lived, however many more remained a mystery to be solved during the wake, if there was time. She took a deep breath, she felt more settled now. This was for Joe.

"Thank you. I'm going to read the poem 'Afterglow' by Helen Lowrie Marshall in memory of my Joe." As she spoke Charlotte realised there were two other women, at least two other women, in the room who would at sometime have thought of Joe as 'their's' but she wanted to put down a clear marker. She wanted to nail it for Joe.

She coughed nervously before she began reading:

I'd like the memory of me to be a happy one
I'd like to leave an afterglow of smiles when life is done
I'd like to leave an echo whispering softly down the ways
Happy times and laughing times and bright and sunny days
I'd like the tears of those who grieve to dry before the sun
Of happy memories that I leave, when life is done.

As Charlotte read the last words a murmour of warm approval emanated from the assembly. She waited for that to subside before speaking: "That poem, which I only found via Google a couple days ago, has given me great solace. For all his idiosyncratic ways, and boy there were lots of them, I'm firmly of the opinion that Joe would have wanted us all to remember him with a smile. That is how I intend to remember him."

As Charlotte returned to her seat she smiled at Laura as she realised that prior to his death so much about Joe had been unknown. This poem was a fitting epitaph in so many ways.

Laura and Charlotte held hands as the celebrant rose to, if he was sticking to the plan, introduce a piece of music and invite George to give his eulogy.

Charles resumed his position at the podium and paused before speaking:

"Thank you Charlotte, that was a lovely poem and not one I am familiar with. Now today at the special request of Charlotte I'm not going to say very much at all but I will end the ceremony with a few words," which he fervently hoped would be suggested by the eulogist himself and anyone else who felt moved to join in. "Now its time for another piece of music which was a favourite of Joe's and while it's playing can I suggest you reflect on Joe's life and the happy times each one of you spent with him over the years. This is Waterloo Sunset by the Kinks."

As the opening chords filled the room Charlotte started to giggle as she remembered Joe prancing about in his underpants singing the chorus raucously as he went through one of his playlists on his cherished Sonos sound system. Laura realised what was happening and gave her a stern look and a nudge while holding a finger over her mouth. The moment passed and Charlotte sat looking at her hands until the song finished.

Charles was back in position at the podium smiling warmly. "OK. I hope everyone enjoyed that. Now it gives me great pleasure to call upon George, Joe's younger brother, to say a few words. George."

George cut quite a figure as he marched towards the podium. His choice of pale cream suit, pale green shirt and a jazzy tie meant that he had nailed it in the fashion stakes. He looked, as far Charlotte could see, much more together than when she had seen him previously which was just as well as his speech was pivotal to the success of the ceremony as, hopefully, he was to be the only speaker.

"Hello everyone, good to see you all here today. I'm sure Joe would have loved to be here especially for the wake!" George paused and drew a slightly embarrassed reaction - a mixture of laughter and some deep inhaling of breath from the audience.

"As Mr Westwood has said I'm George John Brunt brother of Josiah for the last 58 years and what I'm going to try and do is pay tribute to my older brother, to tell you some stories about our lives together and apart but, and I'm sure you will be pleased about this, I haven't got a massive speech which I am going to read out I've just got two prompt cards which I am going to use as what I believe some people refer to as an aide-mémoire. So let's get going. Josiah was born in 1957 to Mr and Mrs Brunt in a little two up two down in Beswick. Dad was a carpenter and Mum did all sorts: looked after other people's kids, took in washing, cleaning in the evening anything so as to be able to make sure there was a meal on the table every night when her husband came home from the pub. Things were tight and they got tighter when Joe came along weighing in at 10 lbs 6 oz. He nearly killed my Mum coming into the world. We weren't the easiest growing up. We got into some right scrapes at school messing teachers about, bunking off and generally being a right nuisance. I think Mum and Dad must have lost count of the number of times he had to plead with the Headteacher not to expel us. It always worked they told really good stories about the difficulties they were facing and they always fell for it and let us stay on..."

Charlotte could sense that the detail of George's story was not going down too well. People were shuffling in their seats, even talking to each other – they had signed up for a celebration and what they were hearing was a mildly interesting social history which, at the rate he was going, would mean they had a good couple of hours to go in spite of George's earlier promises. How she wished she had at least talked through with him what he was intending to say. She thought he was going to be a safe pair of hands, especially as he might have been thinking of giving Joe a good send off as a way of rebuilding his relationship with her. Charlotte was getting more and more embarrassed and was about to try to intervene when the celebrant rose to his feet and walked quietly towards George. He must have sensed what was happening because he paused and looked round. Charles beckoned him away from the podium and as soon as he was standing by his side he walked forward and addressed the audience. "Well I think you'll all agree that George has painted a very interesting picture of his early life in a very deprived area of Manchester in the 60s and 70s but now I think we'll listen to another of Joe's favourite tracks while George and I have a little chat."

At no stage while he was speaking had Charlotte given any indication that George was doing anything wrong, in fact Charlotte was quite confused as to what was actually happening. She just wanted to call the whole thing off and go to the pub and apologise to everyone for wasting their time. She turned to Laura in despair as tears started rolling down her cheeks, but before she could speak the first chords of Bob Dylan's Positively 4th Street began to issue forth from the speakers and, in a moment of group catharsis, most of the audience started to sing along led by a woman whose voice bore an uncanny resemblance to Joan Baez. Their combined voices raised the rafters: "You've got a lot of nerve treating me the way you do etc etc..." and Charlotte still dabbing her tears realised that, copyright infringement notwithstanding, printing the words in the Order of Service had been a 'good idea'.

Not only did the assembled crowd continue to sing they also started to stand up and, in what must have been a first for a rendition of a Dylan song, started to sway and if they didn't know the words hum along.

As the song drew to a close everyone joined in clapping, some people even started cheering. Charlotte's mood changed from despair to exhilaration in the space of a few minutes. Never before had she felt so grateful to Bob.

As the crowd stopped clapping Charles and George moved away from the rear wall where they had been in intense conversation. Charles mounted the podium steps. He was beaming.

"What a wonderful rendition of what has always been my favourite Dylan song. Thank you for your patience and your participation! Now George and I have had a chance to have a chat and we've come up with a plan. George tells me seriously he was only planning to talk for 8/10 minutes max and on reflection he wishes he had written the whole thing out so he knew exactly what was involved. So here's the thing, what George really wants to do is to talk about his relationship with his brother and pay tribute to his memory he assures me this will not take too long."

Whether as a show of relief or just a further indication of how relaxed everyone was feeling a roar of laughter greeted these comments.

George rather sheepishly returned to the podium: "OK guys this really won't take long and can I just apologise for getting more than a little bit carried away at the beginning. My brother Joe was a great bloke — we had a rough start but we both did well at school, much better than expected, and he was my inspiration. After all he fought all my battles for me and passed on several of his girlfriends to me, so I felt I had no real alternative but to outdo him at my O and A-levels and I have to say, though he missed out, he was really chuffed when I got good enough grades to go to uni. Not that it did me much good but that's another story. Joe never told on me when I was drinking underage, always backed me up when I was in trouble for not doing my chores – he was my brother and my very best friend. I always remember he used to come and pick me up if I missed the last bus or let me use him as a taxi service. I remember he even helped me to get my first girlfriend by agreeing to team up with her best mate who can I just say was not really his type! We had the best of times together and, regretably, the worst of times. Joe Brunt we didn't talk to each other for the last five years of your life and I'm really sorry for that. I owe you big time bro and I promise that as best I can I'll make amends. Thank you."

Charlotte realised immediately that this last sentence was meant specifically for her especially when she saw George lift his eyes from his prompt card and look straight at her. She blushed visibly as he made that public pledge and at the same time sealed his fate as far as Charlotte was concerned. She did not want to be coerced into restarting her relationship with George just because he had made an overture to her in front of a large number of witnesses. In fact by not making his statement in private he had brought the stubborn streak out in Charlotte, so much so that in those few moments she decided that if the only way to make George realise there was no future for them was to give him back the inheritance money, then she would. As far as she was concerned this was another in a series of serious errors made by Mr Brunt Jr which made any further meaningful contact impossible. Having caused so much embarrassment with his eulogy she just hoped she would be able to avoid any contact with him at the wake which might involve her in an argument. He had already made his feelings very clear so would probably not take very kindly to what might become a public rebuke. Laura was whispering to her as George left the podium. She turned to give her her full attention.

"That was nice, wasn't it? What he said about making amends. Maybe..."

"That's me totally finished with George," Charlotte hissed fiercely to Laura. "How could you think what he said was 'nice'. He's still trying to manipulate me. Don't forget what he did in the hotel in Scarborough."

Charlotte was livid with George and now Laura for having been taken in so easily. However she realised that her hissing was attracting attention from other mourners so she stopped and just scowled at Laura who had finally got the picture.

As George went to sit down amongst the sea of bright, some would say lurid colours, he felt very uncomfortable and almost headed straight for the door. People were looking at him - sidelong glances, quick glimpses designed to exploit his situation. There was no sympathy in their eyes, just different levels of contempt for the guy who messed up his brother's eulogy and had to be rescued by a celebrant and Bob Dylan. He was mortified. It was a hide under the table type of moment. He'd been so sure he could carry it off but standing there the memories had just flooded back. Joe and he had it rough, no doubt about that, but they had also done well either because of or in spite of what happened. He just wished he had been able to pull off what he had wanted to say more succinctly and more ringingly rather than appearing to be a buffoon.

Sitting six rows behind George and slightly to the left was someone who had been feeling a different sort of discomfort for much longer than George had been suffering. Harriet had arrived in her classic funeral outfit only to realise immediately she had got it wrong. Sitting in between a lilac suited middle-aged man and what she imagined was a version of a hula hula dancer she had felt considerably more than awkward for the duration of the ceremony. She had also been subjected to 'the look' from all her neighbours which was meant to make her feel utterly foolish for turning up in black when EVERYONE else was adhering to the dress code. She knew exactly how George must be feeling and far from wanting to be critical she was waiting to reach out a sympathetic hand to offer him support. They had both got something wrong so at least they had that much in common. She just wondered whether George would actually remember her. She determined that she would make it her mission to find out as soon as she could.

As the last notes of Truly Madly Deeply echoed through the room Charlotte realised the celebrant was about to ask the assembled multitude if anyone else wanted to say a few words in memory of the deceased. So far Joe's funeral had featured the humiliation of Joe's brother for his sheer incompetence and then an uplifting rendition of a Bob Dylan song, of all things. What else could occur to top that? Charlotte was past caring, even if nothing else happened everyone would go away having something to remember Josiah Brunt by and there should also be plenty to talk about at the wake.

"There we had another of Joe's favourite tunes. Must say from my perspective he had very good taste in music. Now if you are following your order of service you will see the next section is entitled: Other contributions. Now Charlotte was very clear that although she did not know all of Joe's friends personally she did not want anyone to feel left out. Now I know no one has been in touch to say they wanted to take advantage of this slot but as they say it's never too..."

At this a short man with dark hair who was, in keeping with the event, wearing a sand coloured suit that he had failed to iron before setting off for Green Acres, bobbed up and started making his way to the podium. As he walked he reached down to pull his glasses from his jacket pocket thereby causing a substantial amount of confetti to be strewn along his path. Astonished by such an inappropriate event a number of the mourners began to laugh.

Arriving at the podium James Betts was able to see quite clearly the problem he had caused and in fact was still causing as the occasional piece of confetti fluttered from his pocket whilst others adorned his jacket and trousers.

"Not a good start, I'm afraid. I'll have a word with the manager at the end and then I'll clear everything up. Can't remember when that wedding was... Anyway I'd like to start by apologising to Charlotte for not giving her advance warning of my contribution. To be fair I've been very busy lately and only finally decided I was actually going to come yesterday. Sorry Charlotte and I hope what I have to say will be of interest to you and to everyone else.

My name is James Betts I am the CEO of All Kids Matter, a mental health charity for children. I first met Joe some years ago when he came to us in order to complete 50 hours of community work after he was convicted of an offence which I don't really want go into here. Joe was a huge hit with the kids, he just had a natural way of talking to them and they idolised him. He played football with them, went on trips with them and, when I come to think of it, he actually made our organisation what it is today."

Charlotte could scarcely believe what she was hearing – Joe youth worker, a role model for young people – he had never said a word about his involvement or for that matter about his criminal conviction. Whilst she was obviously completely in the dark about her partner's 'other life' a group of people sitting close to the door knew all about his activities and applauded at several stages of James's speech.

"On his second visit to the project Joe admitted to me he had had what he now realised were serious mental health issues when he was a child. He reckoned he was very depressed by the conditions in his house, his father's drinking and his mother working all hours to keep him and his brother fed. He had had no one to talk to about his problems and he was determined to make sure that the kids who used the project would be able to get the help they needed. After he'd finished his statutory hours with us he became one of our principal fundraisers as well as a Patron. He even managed to get his employers, an internationally recognised logistics firm, to adopt the centre and arrange collections, sponsored walks and the like. In all, over the three plus years he was involved, in fact he was on his way back from a visit to us when he died, he had been instrumental in raising at least £500,000. In all seriousness without Joe the organisation would not be here now and for that I thank him from the bottom of my heart"

At this a group of about 15 people rose as one shouting, cheering and clapping. In reaction to this display and also as a response to what they had just been hearing about one by one then in groups the whole assembly rose to their feet whooping and clapping. The ovation lasted for several minutes until James raised his hands and motioned them all to resume their seats.

"Joe was an extraordinarily generous man with both his time and his money. Thank you for showing your appreciation, I'm sure Charlotte will value that at what must be a terrible time for her. Well I've taken up enough of your time so I will hand over to anyone else who wants to pay tribute to Joe's memory."

Before anyone could react to this invitation Charles stepped forward: "I think before we move on can I just thank James for telling us about Joe's vitally important work. I'm reaching out to Charlotte now just to check this out but I just wondered if we could arrange for a collection to be taken at the end of this celebration for All Kids Matter. Is that OK Charlotte?"

Charlotte didn't hear Charles's question she was still trying to come to terms with the new Joe. Joe the philanthropist who, in view of his many statements on the 'youth of today', she would never have believed could have benefited so many people in such unusual ways.

In the continued silence Laura turned to her friend to make sure she knew she was required to respond. Charlotte was staring blankly at the floor in front of her.

"Charlotte are you OK?" Laura shook her, a little harshly in the circumstances. "Did you hear what Charles has asked you?"

"What, what did you say?" It was as if Charlotte was coming out of a trance. She looked confused. "Can you believe that, my Joe doing all that for young kids. I never knew. Oh Christ there is so much I'm finding out and its only because Joe died otherwise I'd never have known what he'd been up to."

Laura put her hand over her mouth to silence her mumblings: "The celebrant person wants to know, in light of what James just said, whether we can arrange a collection for Joe's charity. Is that OK with you?"

"Yeah, yeah course. Anything to help. One of the things I forgot to organise yeah of course."

"Thank you Charlotte. Hopefully the manager can arrange collection plates to be placed near the exits." Charlotte could see Abigail's deputy nodding her head at the back of the hall. "Yes I've just had confirmation of that, thanks so much, now can I just ask everyone who is able if they can put some money in on the way out. OK now I'm sorry if I've kept anyone waiting I think we're ready for any further contributions if there are any?"

Without any further hesitation a tall lady at the back of the hall put her hand up on hearing these words and rose to her feet. The celebrant looked directly at her and smiled encouragingly: "Yes, was there something?"

"Yes, well actually there is if that's OK," the tall lady looked very stressed, the words were tumbling out of her mouth. She was shaking.

Beckoning her forward Charles said very calmly: "Please come forward so we can all hear."

As she approached the podium carrying her handbag and coat she started speaking again: "I knew Josiah Brunt, very well. In fact, I was Josiah Brunt's lover for many years."

As she spoke and people realised what she was actually saying there were shocked gasps from all round the ceremony room. From hero to villain in an instant.

Charlotte was in turmoil. She had just heard Joe lauded to the rafters now this rather peculiar looking woman, definitely not Joe's type, was telling all and sundry that he was a philanderer of some years' experience. She had heard enough and using Laura's shoulder for support stood up in order to remonstrate with the interloper. She regretted her decision as soon as she was vertical as the room started spinning wildly and she slumped to the floor mid-stride and came to rest at the base of the podium.

The interloper looked at Charlotte's comatose figure and screamed, flung her coat onto the floor and burst into tears. In obvious distress she stepped down from the podium and marched out of the hall and the woodland cemetery never to be seen again.

When Charlotte came to some minutes later she was slumped in a chair in the manager's office with George leaning over her whispering words of comfort as only he could. She had no idea how she got there but what she did know was that she did not want George anywhere near her. She pushed him away and tried, unsuccessfully, to get to her feet.

"What's going on? What happened?"

"You passed..." George started to explain.

"Don't want you to explain. Where's Laura? She should be here. Where is she?"

Laura who had been standing just inside the door eased George gently out of the way and slowly walked towards Charlotte's prostrate body.

"It's OK lovey, I'm here. Sorry. You passed out. Some woman stood up and said awful things about Joe then rushed off. I thought you were going to deck her but she managed to get out of the room before you could and then you passed out. They wanted to call an ambulance but I managed to stop them."

"What's happened to the funeral? Has everybody gone home?" Charlotte was still trying to get out of the chair as she was speaking. Eventually Laura took pity on her and helped her to her feet.

"Everyone's still here, except the interloper. She's long gone. Just keep drinking some of this water for a few minutes then we can go back in. Charles, the celebrant, is just going to wrap things up, I think, then we can move on. As far as I can remember you were going to have a word with everyone in the garden. I think we'll get everyone to form an orderly queue. I'll make sure you've got a chair and," she lowered her voice, "I'll be there between you and George to avoid any more friction."

By the time Charlotte and Laura rejoined the mourners one or two had already drifted off. Charles, who was obviously anxious to bring things to a speedy conclusion, reclaimed the podium as soon as they were seated.

"Well yes. Before we go any further, I'm pleased to say Charlotte is much recovered. I hope you're feeling a lot better now?" Charlotte returned his gaze and nodded as enthusiastically as events would allow. "This has been a, what can I say, interesting funeral so far, to say the least. I'm sure you'll all be very relieved to hear that there are no further contributions so I think we should move on." Charles bowed his head slightly before he continued: "This service has been a celebration of Josiah Brunt's life and we have heard how rich and worthwhile a life it was. Joe will clearly be missed by many people but I'm sure the good he has done will be remembered long into the future. I often ask people at funerals to think of life as a coin and to see that the flip side of grief is love. I'd like you all to think about that. So just as we welcome a child into our lives we must also say goodbye to those who leave us. This celebration of Joe's life is complete. It's time to say farewell to him. This may be difficult but it is important. I hope the memories we've talked about here may give you all some comfort and can I just take this opportunity to remind you of the collection being taken for All Kids Matter, and also the wake being held at the Crown and Anchor. I'm sure Charlotte would love to see as many of you as can make it there."

"Well I'm a bit disappointed, telling the truth, Charlotte..." The queue of people who had filed past Charlotte and Laura had, in the main, been very solicitous or at least monosyllabic. However the lady now towering above Charlotte dressed from top to toe in canary yellow was an exception to the rule. "... after all I thought we had an agreement, you know, regarding what we were wearing, you know, to, well in all truth, avoid this embarrassing situation. I mean I feel..." Charlotte was not feeling well. If she had not found or rather had not been found a chair to slump into she would have been lying in a darkened room by this stage. Her shredded nerves had already coped with more than enough during the previous two weeks.

She replied through gritted teeth in a hoarse whisper: "To be honest I couldn't care less, Alice. I had a disastrous start to my day and as you will no doubt have seen it hasn't got much better since and now you're getting arsey about the dress I chose in desperation just as everyone was arriving at the house. Go and do one will you. I've not got time for getting a shedload of criticism from you. Thanks!"

Whilst Alice may not have been expecting an abject apology from Charlotte she certainly had not dreamt she would be subjected to quite such a verbal dressing down especially, not at such a sensitive time and in front of so many people.

She stumbled backwards and nearly tripped over a curb stone but for the timely intervention of Hannah.

"Well," she spluttered, "I can see you're under a lot of stress dear. Maybe I'll catch you later."

"Maybe you won't!" spat an incensed Charlotte at her retreating figure. She turned to Laura for support . "Bitch. I was super surprised she came and then to make a fuss like that. Unbelievable."

Laura, who was more than a little taken aback by this exchange, took a deep breath before replying: "Absolutely, can't believe some people. Really!" was all she could manage.

Someone else shuffling along in the queue brought this unfortunate episode to an end.

"Hi!"

A freshfaced man was now standing over Charlotte smiling warmly.

"Hi Charlotte. We are all old friends of Joe's from his archivist days. Really sorry that he passed away. We wanted to come and pay our respects. Joe was quite a bloke by the sounds of it. I mean," he looked round to his colleagues for support, "all his charitable works and we," they all shook their heads, "knew nothing about it. Amazing really!"

On a scale of 1 to 10 Charlotte reckoned she was considerably more amazed that earlier in his life Joe had been an archivist than the archivists were about his charitable works. Acutely aware that the burial still had to take place before the wake could properly commence Charlotte did not want to explore this 'fascinating' facet of Joe's life at this stage. Furthermore she was absolutely exhausted and very thirsty. Her response needed to be couched in those terms but of course the archivists weren't afforded that luxury.

"Well that's very interesting. To be honest I never knew anything about Joe's archivist tendencies – bit of a surprise actually! Do you want to catch up later when we'll have more time. You're coming back to the pub?"

"Absolutely, wouldn't miss it."

"Well that's sorted. Catch you later."

"OK we will."

As the group drifted off Charlotte nudged Laura whose attention had begun to wander: "What on earth was that about?" The number of rather fit men in Laura's age group who had decided to pay their respects had rather diverted her attention from her key role of supporting Charlotte.

"Sorry lovey, what were they saying? I was just..."

"I don't need any excuses, thanks. Those guys said they used to work with Joe. They're archivists. Archivists, shit all I knew about Joe's work was something to do with being logical..."

"No Charlotte not logical – logistics you know, transport solutions."

"Never could be bothered with any of that stuff. It paid the bills, that's all I really cared about but those guys – they've intrigued me. Need to track them down later. Where's that James gone, that one from the charity?"

"He's over there with that group of people who came in the minibus."

"Oh good, I'm glad he's not gone I need to have a word with him before he disappears."

The queue of people had subsided and Charlotte could see Robert Piggott signalling to her. He was obviously impatient to complete the 'next phase' of the funeral as he would doubtless refer to it. Charlotte waved to James and beckoned him to come over to where she was sitting. As he approached she began to feel much stronger and she rose to greet him.

"James, well, where do I start. I knew absolutely nothing about what Joe was up to in relation to All Kids Matter. Nothing at all!"

"Well, that's interesting. I really wasn't sure about Joe and who knew what he was doing. His employers did an amazing amount for us."

"What, the Council? I mean he was an archivist for a long time."

"No XXL Logistics. They're an international company and they really did everything they could to support Joe's work, gave him time off, supported all the fundraising he did and everything."

"That's amazing!"

"It's true to say that, as I said before, without Joe's help we wouldn't be in the position we are today. We probably would have had to close down. Running any charity takes a lot of money – people don't seem to realise but XXL Logistics definitely did."

"Well, I'm really glad you came and told everybody what an incredible job Joe was doing. I probably shouldn't say this to you but I'm sure you wouldn't repeat it, would you?"

"Of course not, Joe was our patron and a very good personal friend. I would never do anything to harm his memory, he was far too important to our organisation's survival to do that."

"Well I, I suppose it's not that terrible, actually, because of the way things have turned out but well it's personal and I feel a bit foolish now having broached the subject."

"Well let's leave it then. Just let's leave it there. I think that would be best honestly. Look, all the others from the charity have got to go back down now. I'm coming to the pub if someone can give me directions and I think the gentleman in black over there is getting a bit desperate. He's been waving at you..."

"Oh yes I know, that's Robert, he's done a good job today but he does get rather anxious. A small group of us are going to bury Joe and then we'll be straight off to the pub. You can come with us if you like. I think it would be really good if you could." With that Charlotte moved towards James and embraced him affectionately.

James stepped away after a few moments: "Thank you so much for the invite, I'd love to join the group. That would be really special. Thank you!"

As Joe's wicker casket was carefully lowered into the beautifully prepared grave Charlotte could barely concentrate as she was trying to work out what she needed to accomplish at the wake. On reflection she felt she probably needed to apologise to Alice for her rant, although she had no intention of bringing up the subject of colour co-ordination. She also needed to find out more from James about Joe's charitable involvement. She was intrigued as to how he had got involved with something that was so out of character for him: why kids and why so far away and, major why, why had he not mentioned anything about such a worthwhile involvement and there was, of course, the archival conundrum.

"Joe, Joe – look I know you've been away and you're busy but I could really do with your help here. Joe, are you listening?"

Joe was reading and he certainly wasn't listening. Charlotte was feeling very unloved as she often did after Joe had been on one of his 'trips'. Usually, she left him to it but tonight she really needed to get his attention and ultimately, some co-operation.

"Look Joe listen to me!" no reaction "I'll chuck that wretched book in the bog if you don't... Joe please!" As she could see Joe was still not bothering to drag himself away from his book Charlotte marched towards him, ripped the offending item from his hands and threw it into the middle of the room. As she did so she realised that Joe had his ear plugs in which explained why he had previously been ignoring her.

"Hey, what's going on Charlotte? What d'you do that for? I'm just chilling here. What's the drama..."

"Sorry, sorry Joe. You just weren't responding. I was trying to talk to you. Didn't realise you'd got your plugs in." She gathered up the book from where it had fallen and placed it gently back in his lap.

"Look, I need to talk to you. You've just been sitting all evening – you see we've got a couple of problems – no, didn't say that - issues." Joe would never acknowledge something as a problem it was always a challenge or an issue which meant it could be easily sorted. Charlotte nearly committed the cardinal sin but had quickly got herself back on track.

"There's something wrong with my car. It's the exhaust I think, it's rattling and the back gate blew off in the storm the other night. I mean you don't need to do anything now I just want to get them onto your to-do list. Is that OK?"

"Yeah, no problem. I'll have a look at the weekend."

"Thanks. Did you have a good time while you were away? Everything go to plan?"

Charlotte had absolutely no idea what Joe did when he was away for two or three days at a time but she still liked to ask, hoping that she might, at some stage, be able to gain an insight into his activities. She had reconciled herself to the knowledge that he was, in all probability, playing away but, without proof, she was left supplementing herself with the somewhat guilty pleasure of Henry's attentions.

"Yeah, went OK thanks. I'll have to bring you up to speed one day but it's all a bit fluid at the moment. Be better when something concrete is in place."

Charlotte had no idea what Joe was talking about. All she knew was that he had used most of the same words before in answer to similar questions. For some reason that left her feeling comfortable with the situation and went some way towards assuaging her guilt

"OK whenever you're ready will be fine. Sounds fascinating whatever it is. Look forward to when you can give me the lowdown," Charlotte always tried to include an ego boost when commenting about Joe's project in the hope that it might encourage him to come clean. It never worked, but Charlotte could see no alternative other than to keep trying to nibble away by keeping up her one-sided dialogue. In fact, she realised to her horror that much of her communication consisted of a one-sided dialogue with her erstwhile companion - a situation which she felt needed to be resolved at some stage.

Charlotte was also determined to get to the bottom of the archivist phenomenon and grudgingly admitted to herself that she needed to speak to George and Richard if there was time. She had also been aware, she thought, of the presence of Henry in the flock at the outset but felt he might have excused himself before the line-up.

"Ms Summersby." Charlotte's musings had meant that she had lost track of the process of interring Joe. Mr Piggott, in his most gentle manner had taken hold of her elbow in order to attract her attention. "Charlotte you're being invited to throw some earth onto the casket," his voice fell to a whisper. "Often people make a wish or say goodbye to the deceased while they are doing it."

As Charlotte looked round she could see George, James and Laura were poised, damp earth in hands waiting for her to lead the way. She knelt quickly, scooped up some earth and let it trickle through her fingers onto the casket. Her head was full of all the people she needed to speak to, with no room for romantic thoughts or idealistic promises. As the last piece of earth fell through her fingers she turned away and taking Laura's hand she walked slowly to the cars parked nearby.

By the time the burial group reached the Crown and Anchor the party was in full swing. Even though Charlotte had decided against a free bar everyone seemed to be entering into the spirit of the occasion with the mood being set by the many and varied colours being worn by the mourners.

Charlotte decided to say her piece and then try and catch everyone she needed to talk to before she would have a drink which would uncharacteristically be a J2O rather than her more usual flavoured gin.

Charlotte made a rather feeble attempt to get some attention by banging a glass with a spoon but to no effect until George started clapping his hands loudly and shouting: "Quiet please, everyone. Your attention please. Thank you, thank you!" As the noise of chatter began to die down George reduced his volume as well and then without any bidding made a formal announcement.

"Ladies and gentlemen Ms Charlotte Summersby would like to say a few words to you." How George had known what Charlotte planned to do she had no idea, but his bravado achieved the desired result although she was rather worried that his role as MC might give people the idea that they were an item.

"Thank you, George, for that introduction and thank you, every one of you, for coming today. First of all, can I apologise for the interloper and for what happened as a result of her contribution. I have no idea who she was and I hope I never see her again but I can confirm I'm feeling much better now." Murmurs of agreement greeted Charlotte comments. "You all look absolutely stunning, Joe would have been so pleased. Before I came here today I wasn't expecting to find out anything new about Joe and especially not that he had been playing a vital role in supporting the charity that James told us about earlier on," Charlotte paused as she tried to catch her breath, her eyes filled with tears as she continued with some difficulty. "Joe was a real character, I wish I'd known before just how important his involvement was to All Kids Matter. I intend to find out more about the charity and how I can help them in the future and would urge you all to empty your pockets, if you haven't already, into the collection plate at the door in Joe's memory. I've already spoken to many of you. I've read your cards, texts, Facebook posts and letters – thank you so much for all your kind words, your memories, and your best wishes. We have the run of this room till 6pm so hopefully there will be lots of time for me to get to know at least some of you a little better."

As Charlotte finished George rushed to her side nearly spilling his glass of lager.

"A toast ladies and gentlemen. Please raise your glasses, the toast is Josiah Thomas Brunt – a life well lived!"

As the chorus of noise accompanying the toasting began to recede a rather well dressed man in a multi-coloured suit, a deep tan and a panama hat approached Charlotte.

"Hi Charlotte!" He beamed. "So good to meet you at last. I've heard so much about you from Joe. Never stopped talking about you, matter-of-fact."

Charlotte stepped back as the cliché ridden smooth operator invaded her private space. She had taken an instant dislike to him and was unsure as to how to react.

"That's great Mr?" was the best she could manage.

"Sorry Charlotte darling. Sorry. My name is Andrew Henderson and I'm the regional manager for XXL Logistics. I've come, with James, to pay respects to Joe on behalf the company. He was such an amazing guy I mean he wasn't just ace at his job he was also involved in so much else you must have been so proud of him."

Once again Charlotte was lost for words especially since she had only recently, very very recently in fact, found out about Joe's 'other life'. Everything was too complicated – she really only wanted to sit down but Mr Henderson was very persistent and seemed to want to engage with her such that she felt she had to engage back.

"Yeah, he was a great bloke doing all that stuff for AKM but you guys at XXL really helped as well." As she spoke she hoped she wasn't overdoing her enthusiasm but she wasn't sure what else to say.

After what seemed like a lifetime Andrew made his excuses and left Charlotte to digest what she had heard about Joe and XXL Logistics and all their money raising activities. However, what really stuck in Charlotte's mind amongst the plethora of stats about how much been raised, how many kids had been helped, how great Joe was etc was the fact that Mr Henderson had dropped into the rather one-sided conversation, details of Joe's pension that she would be entitled to which, apparently, included his pension from his archivist days. All in all, another pleasant surprise which meant that on a week to week basis Charlotte would have a lot more help to pay her bills.

Charlotte decided as her first job she should make peace with Alice, not least because she was so easy to identify among the crowd. As she made her way slowly across the room gently easing people out of the way her plans were scuppered within a few yards of her starting point.

"Charlotte, I'm so sorry. I'm really embarrassed, about earlier, you know. I really wanted to do a better job than that for Joe and for you, especially for you. You know that don't you?"

George was really the last person Charlotte wanted to deal with. Both before and after his awful eulogy Charlotte had had a very bad day at the office and rather than analyse what went wrong with one of the chief culprits she really wanted to spend her time finding out more about Joe's previously unknown activities.

"Yeah George, thanks for the apology – these things happen you know. Best laid plans and all that..."

"Yeah I know I was just wondering..."

"George I don't think there's much point just wondering. No point at all to be fair. It just didn't work out for us or for your speech. You must admit that so I think I need to be clear. OK?"

"Well, yes but," George was stuttering and making very little sense. "I'm sure I can do things better in the future. I think you'll still need me, moving forwards..."

Charlotte heard those words and a red mist descended: "George!" she hissed, "I'm through with you. I can't make it any clearer now please leave me alone. I've got a lot of people I need to see."

With that Charlotte continued her slow passage through the throng towards her canary yellow clad adversary.

Charlotte had already spotted poor Harriet, who was the only person not following the dress code, earlier in the day and was surprised to see that she was still there. As she was making her way through the throng she became aware of a heated argument starting up concerning the very same person.

"How rude! Do you have no principles at all young lady. The invite said..."

"I really don't care what the invite said. I missed it, OK! I'm here aren't I! That's the important thing – being here for Joe. "

"Well," the offended lady wasn't backing down, "Well at least you could show some respect. At least you..."

The disgruntled lady was unable to finish her sentence as George, doing his best imitation of a knight in shining armour, got involved.

"Excuse me, Madam," he began politely but rapidly lost it. "How dare you cause a fuss, abusing this young lady. She's done nothing wrong. What right have you got to get involved anyway?" with that he grabbed Harriet's arm and ushered her away.

Ms Unhappy snorted: "Well I never," before storming out of the pub nearly knocking Charlotte over as she went.

"So, you see I had a terrible start to the day. Couldn't have been worse to be fair, so that's really why I bit your head off..."

"It's OK I can't imagine what you have been going through with all this to organise and then finding out about his charity work on the day of his funeral. I never would have thought he had it in him to be honest. I mean..."

"Yes I know amazing. That's where I'm off to now to see James and find out a bit more. Anyway, I'll catch you later – thanks for your support."

"It's OK don't know what I'd have done..." Alice's voice grew fainter as Charlotte moved away from her. She had spotted James who seemed to have struck up a conversation with the archivists. They had found themselves a corner table and judging by the way they all stopped talking as she approached them Charlotte deduced they been talking about Joe.

"Hi there, wanted to have a word with all of you but can I start off by being a bit rude and just borrow James for a bit. I'll be back afterwards, lads, so don't go away. Thanks."

After they found a quiet space away from the bar Charlotte continued: "James, as you know, what you said at the funeral today came as a complete surprise, but I really want to know more about what Joe was involved in and I wondered if, in the future, I might be able to help. Would that be possible?"

"I don't see any reason why not, but it depends on what you want to do I suppose, because you live quite a long way away from our base."

"Well I've never done any fundraising but I'm willing to give it a try. I could help on the admin side. I've got lots of experience on Facebook and Twitter so I could try raising your profile, that sort of thing."

"Well, Joe was really good at hands-on stuff with the kids really, I'm not sure how we're going to replace him or the money he brought in. His death is going to lead to us making changes on a number of levels really."

"OK, well, have you got a card or something? When things settle down a bit for me I'll get in contact and come down to London so you can show me round and we can see how things go from there. It's a bit awkward today because there are so many people here, haven't got as much time as I would have liked."

"No, that's fine. I mean it's brilliant that you arranged the collection – I think that's done really well – when you're ready we can talk further."

"OK good. Well thanks again for making the effort to give Joe a good send off."

"I know it's a cliché but it really was the least I could do. It's been good meeting you, Charlotte, I look forward to meeting again, hopefully. Shall we say in the next two to three months?"

"Yeah, good, I'll be in touch."

James had obviously finished whatever he was saying to the archivists as he headed off in a different direction, leaving the field open to Charlotte. In a repetition of what had happened previously as she neared the group they stop talking rather abruptly.

"Hello again guys. Are you rushing off? Because I'd like to chat."

"No problem Charlotte. Is it OK if I call you Charlotte?"

"Of course, don't want you to stand on ceremony..."

"This is Gerald, Jacob and Ernest. My name is John." As each of the group were introduced they proffered their hands and gave a cheery: "Hi."

"Well, the point is, up until today, I think I've already said this, I had no idea about Joe's career as an archivist. I had no idea about lots of things, as you will have heard, but maybe you can help with the archiving – is that what it's called?"

"Well, we can, as much as we know, but to be perfectly honest Charlotte we came here hoping to find out a bit more about Joe ourselves. Not to put too fine a point on it he's, sorry was, a bit of an enigma to us."

"How do you mean?"

"Joe was a really nice bloke; I think that's why he wanted to stay involved actually."

"I'm really not sure when he stopped working for Newborough Council, it must have been some years ago but he was still on the NEC of the Archivists Association. He was treasurer for ages as well. None of us are really involved anymore but whenever we met up he would always bring us up to date."

"So what did he do for Newborough Council? Sounds very dry if you don't mind me saying so."

"It's one of those areas where you either like it or loathe it," Gerald chimed in. "Ten years ago, it was more to do with preservation of records and cataloguing collections and managing information. Latterly it has become much more about the digital age. You have to be more focused on customers' needs so that archivists have had to get much more involved in digitalisation of records and computer-aided search systems. Joe was really good at promoting his work through exhibitions, presentations and talks and liaising with donors etc. He really wasn't a detail man, he loved being out and about and clocking up the mileage claims."

As Gerald spoke his colleagues were laughing amongst themselves and reacting to what he was saying.

"Basically, he was a really nice bloke who never took anything too seriously," said Jacob.

"Not at all," Ernest chipped in.

"I can't really see him getting all excited about old records. Although to my surprise when I started going through his stuff at home it was really well organised. Everything was filed away in filing cabinets, colour coded and in alphabetical order!"

"We often wondered how he managed as an archivist as he was so easy-going, always ready for a pint or a glass of red wine."

"Or both!"

"But obviously it was in his DNA!"

Talking about Joe's chaotic, drink-based lifestyle caused considerable laughter amongst the group whilst at the same time making Charlotte feel rather awkward. For the first time she had heard Joe praised to the rafters for his crucial role in helping a charity not only keep going but also flourish, and now some of his erstwhile friends were traducing his reputation and making out he was some kind of drunken time waster.

Charlotte felt she needed to defend Joe: "Hey guys he can't have been all bad!"

"No, no I'm not saying that," John leapt in having realised that maybe some of their comments had gone too far. "Now we realise from what we heard today that he was really engaged in some very useful work and good for him." Cue supportive noises from the rest of the group.

"It was just his laconic style that really gave the impression of a happy-go-lucky guy who never took anything seriously. That's just the way he appeared Charlotte. Although sounds as if your experience of his home filing system is anything to go by he would have been good at his day job as well. It was a demeanour that he cultivated while actually, certainly more recently, acting so totally differently. I'm sure you must be really proud of him."

"I am. Truly I am. I just wish I'd known before. Things would have been so different between us but you don't need to know about that really." Charlotte was conscious that her emotions were still all over the place, especially having to deal with the funeral and all of the revelations about the 'other Joe', but she knew she didn't want to get too involved with people who she would in all probability never see again.

"I know what you mean," added John who thought Charlotte was getting rather tearful and was keen to finish the conversation. "Well I think we know more about Joe now, all good stuff eh guys? We've got a bit of a journey to get back home so I think we'll be making tracks if that's OK with you Charlotte," John tried to inject a note of empathy for the way Charlotte was feeling as he spoke whilst he himself did not want to get too involved either. "Thanks so much for your hospitality Charlotte, really glad we were able to make it. Great bloke Joe, we'll miss him."

"So will I," replied Charlotte as tears began filling her eyes. "So will I. Nice to meet you all. Lots of happy memories there."

"Yeah, all the very best to you for the future as well Charlotte."

The four men started to get ready to leave at this point and after lots of hugs and air kissing they left, leaving Charlotte feeling rather despondent and confused. No one seemed to have the whole picture regarding Joe and his true character – how could he on the one hand be a complete jack the lad and on the other a saint-like person devoted to fundraising for a children's charity.

Her baby had made its presence felt several times during the day causing her to consider, fleetingly, life with them and without Joe. Whatever his previous character he was ultimately leaving her literally holding a baby which he had known nothing about. Knowing now that there was a totally different side to him she started wondering whether, if he had known, he would not have driven so recklessly. Putting 'what ifs' behind her she decided to try and track Richard down for a few words. She was pretty sure he had kept his promise to attend but he had not managed to appear even though she thought she had glimpsed him briefly in the line-up. The room was less crowded by this time and once she started looking properly she was able to pick him out in his particularly fetching outfit lurking in a corner sipping a pint of lager.

"Hi Charlotte," Richard greeted her warmly as she got closer. "Mad day? What with George and the wronged woman and you passing out. You OK now? Seemed to be quite enough people trying to look after you so I left them to it."

"I feel fine now although I've not really processed all the information about 'new Joe' yet. Just so much I never knew..."

"Yeah that stuff about the children's charity – amazing."

"Yes I know, hopefully I'm going to go down and see James and have a chat. I mean I'll never be in the same league as Joe but there must be things that I could do to help. We'll see."

"I'm sure they'll be very grateful for any help."

"Well, I've got a couple of ideas."

"Good, good." There was a pause before Richard spoke again. "Look I've been thinking about our previous conversation and, well, on reflection, to be fair, I behaved like a twat. I'm really surprised you didn't tell me to piss off. Seriously, I was well out of order, especially with, you know with Joe's dying and me going all stupid. I nearly didn't come today because I was so embarrassed. Stupid..."

Charlotte had not planned what she was going to say to Richard. In fact, she had barely had any time to reflect on his declaration let alone make any decision, so surprised had she been by his determination to change the course of her life. His abject apology came equally suddenly. One thing she did know was that she wanted time and space, to do things her way and not to be dictated to by someone else. Richard seemed calm as well as contrite, but a funeral wake was not really the place for her to discuss her future plans.

"I really don't know what to say Richard, you keep doing this to me – proper man of surprises. I mean things haven't really changed much for me since we last talked." Thinking on her feet was not something Charlotte was very good at, particularly when she was feeling stressed, but she knew she wanted to keep things simple. The less Richard knew about everything else that was going on the better.

"Well I'm really not sure, I'm being totally honest here, I'm not sure what is best for me. I'm still really in shock from what has happened, Joe dying and then finding out that I never properly knew the bugger. And then there's you promising undying love and commitment and now you're apologising. We need to have more time really. I'm so glad you've apologised, that's good, so now what about we leave it for a couple weeks, I've still got lots of stuff going on, then we can have a catch up meal and then..."

"I'd like that. I've been thinking about you non-stop since we met..."

Richard was getting too anxious for Charlotte now. She was losing patience and he was speaking too loudly; people could hear. It was all too inappropriate.

"Look Richard calm down. You're making a show – don't want that. OK?"

"Yes, OK sorry I just wanted..."

"I know and you have. OK? I'll ring you when my head is clearer and we can talk. We can sort this but you are going to have to go more slowly so we can see what is right for both of us." Raising her voice from her previous hushed whisper she said, rather over cheerfully, "OK Richard, look forward to seeing you soon."

Richard nodded in meek agreement.

As Charlotte wandered away from Richard she did a quick run through of all the other people she had wanted to 'touch base with' just to make sure she had not left anyone out. Looking around the room she realised that numbers had thinned out considerably. George looked as if he was having a fruitful discussion with Harriet as they had more or less jammed themselves in a small alcove, whilst the newly named Canary Twins seemed to be having an intense conversation with some of the archivist boys who had previously told Charlotte they were leaving! James, however, cut a somewhat solitary figure. She knew very few of the others so after a nod and a smile in the general direction of James she decided to pop outside for some fresh air as she was almost certain that Laura would be hovering near the door having a much-needed fag.

"Hi there! You had enough now?" was Laura's mid-puff greeting.

"It's been a long day. A really long day. I need a drink, but I can't really have one and I don't really want to stay here. D'you know what I mean?"

"Absolutely. There's lots of memories in there after all. Sometimes it's just better to leave while the party is still going rather than be the last saddo standing. Where shall we go?"

"Let's go to the Boar's Head. Have you been drinking up to now?"

"A bit."

"Is that a little bit or a lot in bits"

"Oh don't try and get me all confused – I've had three or four large glasses of wine. People just kept on..."

"Yeah I know. It always happens to you people, men, wanting to get you drunk. Eh? So we'll need a cab then, with a bit of luck, we can walk back from the Bull's Head."

"Or we could go for a curry. Just to round things off nicely."

"Good idea. I'll phone for a cab." On balance Charlotte decided that all things considered, and especially the future life chances of baby Summersby, much as she wanted a drink, lots of drink, a quick drink and a curry would be a much safer bet.

Having phoned for a cab Charlotte went back into the function room and waved goodbye to everyone who was left. Several people had brought bunches of flowers and, even though she wasn't sure how they would manage to get them home from the Boar's Head, she gathered them up and as people began to realise she was going and edged towards her she said: "Folks I've got go now. It's been a long day. Thanks so much for coming. Your support has been amazing, absolutely amazing. Bye!"

A chorus of "Best of luck!" "Hope it all works out for you!" "We'll miss him" etc followed her out of the door.

Mercifully, she had got her timing exactly right and Laura was holding open the door of the cab so they could make a quick getaway.

The Bull's Head was quiet for a Friday at 5pm and Laura and Charlotte were able to occupy a spot next to the Inglenook fireplace.

Taking advantage of the fact that she knew the barmaid she got her to stash the flowers behind the bar so she and Rachael were able to sit down unencumbered.

"Oh my God! I'm glad that's over. George was so embarrassing, I mean what a tosser! And that woman!"

"Well don't worry too much, Charlotte, I was talking to a few people who've had more experiences of funerals than me, and that, I can tell you, was nothing compared to what they were talking about! People, I mean dead people, falling out of coffins, funeral cars breaking down and people not arriving like the deceased's family and that's not the half of it. Honestly!"

Charlotte had slumped in her seat and was slipping further and further under the table as tiredness took hold and she became more animated about the disaster which had just unfolded at Green Acres Memorial Park.

"That wretched woman who was she? What right did she have to say those things? Never seen her before in my life and she just..."

"Charlotte, calm down, please!" Laura was utilising her most empathetic soothing voice as she tried to calm her friend down. "Hopefully, we'll never know. She might've come to the wrong funeral. I mean we heard a lot of things today we didn't know before..."

Charlotte was beginning to pull herself back into a sitting position and seemed to be preparing to launch a fierce defence of her partner. Laura motioned her to keep quiet.

"I'm not saying he had anything to do with her. Unless...no never mind about that, forget it. Forget the shitbag. What amazed me and what I think we should be celebrating was all that stuff that James was saying. I mean that was amazing, wasn't it. Your Joe a philanerthingy"

"A philanthropist!"

"That's right. One of them like the Victorians who spent their wealth on doing good – building schools and hospitals and stuff. And we knew nothing about it. Bloody dark horse him!."

"I mean I feel really guilty now because I always thought he was playing away. That's why I got involved with Henry, as my way of getting back at him."

"Really?"

"Really. I mean, you know me, I probably needed both of them to keep me happy if truth be told."

"You always were a greedy bitch though."

The two friends chuckled at this and then began, very inappropriately, to regale each other with tales of their sexual exploits. They had shared many of them before but nevertheless each revelation was greeted with shrieks of laughter such that they began to draw attention to themselves as the Friday evening drinking session got going.

Charlotte was first to realise things were getting a bit out of control and that her promise to limit her alcoholic intake had long since been forgotten. She tried to get Laura to quieten down with little success.

"Laura love look I think..."

"No never mind about that," Laura was slurring her words now, but was determined to carry on. "Now listen, listen did I tell you about that time when..."

Laura's voice was clearly audible to a number of drinkers now. Charlotte pushed her hand over her face to stop her elaborating on what Charlotte remembered was a particularly lurid story. "No, stop now. We've had..." Laura tried to tear her hand away as she tried to splutter out her story. "It was those lads, you remember."

"Laura, come on we're going NOW," and with that she managed not only to stand up without incident but also to haul Laura to her feet and propel her towards the door. Sheer determination on Charlotte's part meant they arrived back at her house without anyone falling over or being sick and with all the flowers which she felt was a remarkable achievement.

After having put a very drunk and still talkative Laura to bed Charlotte made herself a pot of tea before curling up on the settee. The last two weeks had been a whirlwind and now, after an incredible day, at last, she could relax certain in the knowledge that she had done more than her duty by Joe. She owed him nothing now. In fact, even before burying him she realised she had been planning her future and reminiscing about her past life because she realised that even with everything she now knew, Joe had not really been the love of her life. She certainly hoped for better in the future, she felt she deserved that at least. As she played the events of the day back in her mind the lasting memory she settled for was the warm feeling she'd got from hearing James's astonishing revelations about Joe and the All Kids Matter charity. As she mused on whether she would ever have found out about Joe's charitable works if he had not died prematurely she remembered the letter which the solicitor had given her on the day of the reading of Joe's Will. Glancing up she saw it neatly nestling among the sympathy cards on the mantelpiece.

She took it down and carefully opened the envelope.

Chapter 11: Letter

Dearest Charlotte,

I cannot believe that I'm writing this letter. It is the most difficult letter I've ever written and I'm writing it because I have finally made my decision. You probably won't have noticed but for the last few months I've spent every spare moment trying to sort things out without success. I wish I could have talked to you but I know that would not have worked, even more so when I found out about Henry, that was really when I knew there was no future for us and, logically, for me.

I cannot describe how I'm feeling now, like nobody loves me and the stuff at the charity's falling apart. I can't stop it and when the shit really hits the fan my name will be mud. Trying to do everything myself was, I realise now when it's too late, a big mistake. It worked beautifully after I found All Kids Matter when I had to do 50 hours of community service after I was found guilty of a crime which I didn't commit, I promise. Anyway, I got time off to help AKM and even got the firm to make it their charity so we got donations from all over the place. However, I must have overdone it or someone complained, there's some right arseholes around, anyway a new CEO came in and told me I'd got to pack it all in. Couldn't believe it I mean, to be honest, it's given meaning to my life these past couple of years.

I've really enjoyed our time together, don't get me wrong, but I don't ever seem to get women sorted out. I love them like but I'm not really the sort of person who can make do with just one person. Have you met Alice and Hannah? I bet you have by now, they always followed me on Facebook so I'm sure they'll have muscled in on things. Well, truth be told, I was always at it even when I was married, couldn't keep my hands to myself, they never knew. That was the one thing I was good at, keeping all the balls in the air at the same time!

The more I'm writing, the more I think I ought to explain, but I'm not sure whether it will help you or not but I'm going to anyway. I'm shaking like a leaf as I'm typing I'm just so nervous and feel so guilty but honestly this is the only way.

I know you will be OK, you've got your job and there's money in the Will to help you get somewhere. The more I've thought about things the more I thought you're probably better off without me anyway. I'm sure you don't think so now but you'll see it my way. You're strong. You'll make it.

Charlotte stopped reading, her eyes were full of tears, she couldn't see clearly enough to read any more and she was beginning to get a headache which she put down in part to the strain of the day and in part to the amount of wine she had regrettably imbibed. Either way she decided she needed a break so she rifled through Laura's shoulder bag until she found a pack of cigarettes.

Standing in the porch smoking her first cigarette for aeons she realised immediately why she had given up in the first place. The cigarette tasted disgusting but sucking on it and inhaling deeply so that her head spun brought some relief from the angst induced by Joe's letter. She wanted to stay in the porch forever so she could avoid finding out the details of the plan. Nothing was going to bring Joe back. She was at a loss to understand and, far worse, didn't really want to understand why he had ripped her whole world apart. A series of 'If only's' started to come to mind, the main one of which related to Henry and the part he had played in Joe's demise. She also still had no idea why Joe had ever committed a crime which warranted a Community Service Order and what was happening with the CEO of XXL Logistics. She had met Mr Henderson only a few hours previously and he had had nothing but praise for Joe's humanitarian endeavours.

Two cigarettes and lots of sighs and sobs later Charlotte returned to the settee and resumed her somewhat macabre night-time activity of reading Joe's letter from beyond the grave.

I needed to square everything off: you've got £100k, I gave the other £100k to George, really for old time's sake I suppose, don't tell him this but I never really liked him. I suppose actually its more about guilt and I've paid that off. For the charity, and I hope to God this works, I've set up a life policy in trust to them for £200k payable on my death. When I first set it up it was for the long term but now, and I can hear you saying you could've helped and lots of other shit, it's the only way I can keep them going. I've checked and as long as they can't prove I committed suicide they'll have to pay. You'll have to wait for that to be sorted out before claiming for them or passing the policy on, whatever you decide. I read an article recently that said loads of road traffic incidents are classed as accidents which are actually suicides. I hope they're going to make the same mistake for me

One last thing about Rebecca and Henry, more about Rebecca really. By this time you may or may not have come across her, be very careful, she is poison. I really mean that. I had hoped you would never find out who she was but in this situation I need to make sure you are prepared. I know I should have dumped her, she was always really bad news but she had always promised that if I dumped her she would make sure you knew so I would lose you both. I didn't dare to take her on. I'm so sorry. I'm so bloody sorry about everything really, it's been a mess which you will have to clear up just to see the back of me. Of course, I'll never know why you needed a Henry. From his Facebook page he didn't seem to be much competition but then perhaps that shows how little I really knew you! Honestly, I couldn't see another way out. I'm really sorry but it is what it is. Isn't that what everybody's saying!

I really hope you have a good life without me, you've got good friends, you're strong.

Goodnight my love.

J

Charlotte threw the neatly typed pages of Joe's letter onto the floor and screamed. In fact, she screamed so loudly she woke Laura up who promptly ran into the room with a somewhat incongruous looking loofah shouting: "Get off her! Leave her alone!" in her best blood curdling roar.

Chapter 12 Afterwards

A soft breeze was blowing off the sea, gently skittering the blackout blind of a small pastel coloured bedroom. Wind chimes jingled in the distance. The sound of a washing machine on its spin cycle permeated the house. In the narrow terraced street residents of all ages were about their business, carrying shopping from the Co-Op on the corner or speeding along on bicycles. The world was at peace. Early autumn and the trees were beginning to reveal their orangey brown glory. With each gust of wind more leaves tumbled to the ground and skipped along the pavements.

Charlotte was preparing a vegetable soup in her kitchen. She had just gathered carrots, spinach and tomatoes from her vegetable patch, and was supplementing them with the best organic produce from her local greengrocers. She liked to make sure that everything she ate was healthy and nutritious. As a confirmed vegetarian unable to take the final step to becoming vegan, she was pleased to be living without anyone in her life who might want to make her compromise her new idealistic standards. Just as many ex-smokers would say they could easily start again, still miss the weed every day. For Charlotte the idea of a bacon barm doused in brown sauce of questionable origin was an ever present temptation. So far she had staunchly ignored the craving even after having savoured for only a moment or two the blissful memory of the taste and immense satisfaction involved in eating one.

Charlotte's new life of working with a job share partner meant that while she was still able to continue her career as an Arrears Assessment Executive she was also able to spend lots of quality time at home with Mary Josephine Summersby, and she had not regretted a moment. After the initial doubts had subsided, following her decision to base her life around her baby, the pregnancy had gone quite smoothly. Whilst the idea of Laura being her birthing partner had initially been greeted with derision, she had soon warmed to her role and played a major part in the smooth running of the delivery even to the extent of embracing a birthing pool, something which she would never have countenanced previously. For Laura if she was going to have a baby, which she had not really considered, the perfect solution would have been a general anaesthetic until her joyous experience with Charlotte. Subsequently she had really thrown herself into the role of indispensable Auntie Laura. Not only had this meant spending lots of time holding, bathing and amusing Mary it also extended to relocating back to Scarborough, vetting any involvement with previously unknown males: casual pick-ups were banned and Laura was never happy if Charlotte had a conversation with a male personage on a bus. Men were falling over themselves to help Charlotte with her buggy in the supermarket queue when they were keen, too keen in Laura's considered view, to let Charlotte and buggy jump in front of them. Neither of the friends could understand quite why a lovely looking woman and buggy were such an attraction to men. Nevertheless, Laura was sure nothing should come of such interactions on her watch. A man for Charlotte was something for the future, the long-term future, as far as Laura was concerned, and Charlotte was happy to acquiesce as Laura had played such an important part in stabilising her life after Joe's death. This had included the period leading up to and after the birth of Mary, who had rapidly become the centre of the universe for them both.

Apart from the vital emotional support Laura offered, in uncharacteristic fashion she had also provided very important practical support as well. Determined to resolve the issue of paternity as far as Mary was concerned Laura did all the research required and actually paid for the DNA test which proved unequivocally, or as unequivocally as these things can be, that Joe was Mary's dad. Charlotte had always believed this was the case and had decided that Mary's middle name should be Josephine to celebrate that fact. Charlotte had struggled from the start with Joe's lies, the fact that he'd actually been involved with yet another woman, the redoubtable Rebecca, and that she had hardly really known him after being together for two years. However, on balance at the time of naming her gorgeous baby, who in any case bore more than a passing resemblance to her late partner, she felt it was only right that his name should in some way be incorporated in hers. Subsequently she had questioned that decision but at the time that was what she wanted to do. She was going to bring her daughter up to admire the father she had never had a chance to know. She knew he would have been very proud of his progeny. Tickled pink!

*   *   *

"Are you sure you're going to be able to come?"

"'Course I will. You want me to be there don't you?"

"But you've had lots of time off lately. You sure they won't mind?"

"It'll be fine, honestly."

Charlotte had been very anxious about the inquest ever since she had read Joe's letter. Although she had had some contact with James from AKM subsequent to the funeral it had mainly been about the money raised from the collection, almost £4000, and how to get that to the charity and what it would do with the money. James wanted to make sure it wasn't frittered away prior to the inquest but he had not made a definitive decision. Charlotte had postponed her trip to the charity until she knew exactly what the situation was relating to Joe's insurance policy.

"I've been Googling what happens and it sounds pretty straightforward. It's inquisitorial not adversarial so, according to the Council's website, they just want to establish the facts of the matter. They've asked me to submit a written statement relating to events leading up to Joe's death. As far as I knew, at the time, there was nothing untoward going on. So I've glossed over a few things, just talked about how he often spent weekends away, as far as I knew for work etc etc. I've tried to make it sound plausible. I mean I can't tell them about the letter, I don't want them to smell a rat at any stage. Anyway, he hadn't shown any signs of being stressed or unhappy to me so..."

"It's tricky isn't it. I mean what he was doing was very altruistic, the firm even gave him time off. The fact you didn't know was weird but does that really have any bearing? He was just a bit weird altogether actually."

Laura and Charlotte were most impressed by the whole process. Somebody had obviously gone to a considerable amount of trouble to establish the facts. Statements were read out from Charlotte as well as Joe's employers and James from AKM. There was also a lengthy contribution from the collision investigator who had obviously spent a lot of time trying to work out how the crash occurred. His professional opinion was that there was no evidence that Joe had applied the brakes. Everyone present was asked if they had any questions at each stage but Charlotte was quite unprepared for such an eventuality and decided not to get involved for fear of confusing things.

At the conclusion of the evidence the coroner ruled that Joe had died an accidental death. Having made her announcement the coroner left the room and Charlotte squeezed Laura's hand hardly able to believe that not only was the case over, but that now Joe's life insurance policy would pay out. She felt very guilty as she looked round at all the officials and realised the seriousness of what she had been a party to, but she was very clear it was for a good cause and, in any event, no one had asked her about the existence of such a policy. She just hoped her good luck would hold.

When they were safely away from the court the two conspirators hugged each other and Charlotte and Laura shared a couple of Proseccos to 'celebrate' their success.

Charlotte was in a state of shock when she returned to her home after the inquest. She went to collect Mary from her nursery and drove to the coast and sat on a bench holding her and talking to her, telling her that she was so pleased to have her in her life.

"Mummy's been a bit silly today. She might have got us into a bit of trouble with the police because Daddy asked her to tell a lie. I wish I hadn't though, as I might have lost you." Charlotte squeezed Mary so tight that she started to cry. Charlotte relaxed her grip and held Mary high in the air. "Silly old Mummy but I hope it's going to be all right. Everything is going to be all right, I hope."

Safely at home and with Mary asleep Charlotte opened the envelope containing the life insurance policy. Prior to that moment she had not thought about checking any details about pay-out etc nor, surprisingly for her, had she Googled the obvious question. As she read through the pages of the schedule it became abundantly clear that Joe had not done his homework very well. It was obvious that Legal and General paid out after a policy had been in effect for over 12 months even if the person committed suicide, so Joe had unnecessarily put her through hell and because he had not read the small print.

*   *   *

"Hi James!"

"Hi Charlotte, so good of you to come all this way to see us."

"Well, it's been on my to do list for ages and now I've got some really good news for you. I expect you'll be needing some."

"How do you mean?"

"Well as you know from the funeral I knew nothing about Joe's involvement with AKM before your contribution. I was absolutely stunned that Joe, my Joe, been so involved in the charity. Just not in his character."

Over the next 20 minutes Charlotte gave James the full lowdown about Joe's letter, life insurance policy and the coroner's inquest giving him all the details of how she was able to confirm that the charity was going to benefit to the tune of £200,000. As she spoke James was nodding enthusiastically and generally responding very favourably.

She finished the story with a flourish: "Well, you see, James, thanks to Joe's policy you won't have to close down after all, thank goodness."

James looked at Charlotte with an ironic smile playing on his lips. He took his glasses off, perched them on his head and rubbed his hands over his face before he spoke: "I don't want you to take this the wrong way, Charlotte. I'm really grateful for this donation. I'm sure the trustees will be delighted. I really do wish Joe hadn't played his cards so close to his chest. Why didn't he talk to people instead of just taking it all upon himself as if he was the only one who could make a difference. Why did he keep you in the dark? Why did he assume that no one else cared? No one else could help. I'm going to be blunt with you Ms Summersby if Joe had been more open with us he would still have been here now."

Charlotte couldn't believe her ears. She started to speak while still processing what James had said: "What, what are you saying? Joe needn't have died. You don't want this money. All this has been in vain." With her eyes full of tears and hardly able to catch her breath she continued. "So Joe... what Joe was doing...was a waste...you didn't need him. He's dead because of your wretched charity. Can you not have a little..."

"Charlotte, Charlotte please," James leapt to his feet and put his arms around Charlotte. "Please just listen, listen." As James held her close Charlotte relaxed and stopped crying wiping her eyes with the sleeve of her coat.

"Excuse me, have you got any tissues? Bet I look a right mess!"

James fetched some tissues from a box on his desk and offered them to Charlotte.

"Look, Charlotte, I'm not saying what Joe has done is in any way bad. Personally and financially, he's been a great help, honestly, it's just that we now have a lot of other corporate and individual sponsors.

Without XXL Logistics and, of course Joe, there would have been a massive hole to fill but we have the resilience built into our business plan to deal with things like that. We have to. People change, strategic goals change. We need to cater for every eventuality if we are going to be able to continue to keep the trust going. I don't want to belittle what Joe achieved, and you remember at the funeral I said Joe's demise would give us some problems. Well, that situation was very short-lived. Both XXL Logistics and a partner organisation of theirs stepped up to the mark within a few weeks and pledged even more support than previously."

"Yeah, sorry, what you said just seemed to be so unfair as if Joe's work had been wasted..."

"I'm not saying that at all. Sometimes for the best of reasons people make really bad decisions because they haven't got the right information. That's what I meant. I'm really devastated for you, for Joe – there are other ways to have dealt with the situation, we could have worked together. It would have been OK. If only Joe could have seen that. So sad, so really really sad."

The rest of Charlotte's visit was spent gaining some appreciation of just how involved Joe had been in the work of the Trust. There were videos of some of the projects he'd been involved in and she was able to speak to some of the young people Joe had inspired. She was really moved by the whole experience as she was able to sense just why the Trust had meant so much to him. However, all her admiration was tinged with sadness as she realised, from her point of view, that a lot of what he had done was about satisfying his ego. It was about Joe and how important he was as he, apparently single-handedly, funded the work that was going on.

"Well, thank you for your time today James," Charlotte was preparing to leave and was anxious for there to be no misunderstandings between them: "I've got a really good picture of what you do and how Joe fitted in. Thank you for letting him find himself. I can see it must have been massively important to him. Neither of us is going to be able to understand him now. We just have to move on. I'm really glad though that you got your £200,000, you deserve that, and perhaps for that we can excuse Joe what he did, perhaps?"

"It was a massive sacrifice though, your lives together, everything else he could have achieved, a real pity that, but thanks Joe. I know he meant well and all the very best to you and the baby as well. You've got a mountain to climb now."

"Thanks for that. I'll be in touch again. I want to make sure everything is OK."

"I'm sure it will be. Thanks for coming."

As Charlotte walked away James ran after her shouting: "Charlotte there's something I forgot." She stopped and waited for him to catch her up. "Look I don't know what you think but we, that is the Board and me, would like you to become one of our Patrons in memory of Joe as much as anything else. Don't want to rush you, but will you think about it, please?"

"Of course I will. I'll get back to you about it OK."

"OK."

Charlotte's move back to Scarborough had had several beneficial effects apart from the bracing air and a better work/life balance. It also meant that she had left behind a lot of unhappy memories and relationships. She had not bothered to let any of her former adversaries know her change of address, nor had she kept in touch with Henry as he had become very much surplus to requirements.

The only person she did regret cutting herself off from was Richard. Initially she had thought with Scarborough not being such a massive place they might bump into each other and so left matters to chance. However, with Mary taking over most of her spare time and not having many opportunities to savour the nightlife a chance meeting had not occurred. In any case she was convinced if Richard wanted to get in touch he would. That he left it until just after the second anniversary of Joe's death was rather a surprise. She had pretty much given up hope of hearing from him again. She rather suspected Laura having had a hand in facilitating the contact but she was still pleased that he had, albeit somewhat belatedly, decided to get in touch. After a brief exchange of messages, a date was arranged for them to meet up which Charlotte had planned to be when Mary was at nursery.

"How y'doing Charlotte. Good to see you!"

Richard's warm greeting took Charlotte by surprise as she opened the door. She was expecting a more restrained approach and was even more surprised when he unceremoniously pulled her towards him for an unnecessarily sloppy kiss.

Having learnt from previous experiences how to deal with Richard she gently pushed him away: "OK Richard stay calm. It's good to see you too. Come in."

"It's been ages. You look absolutely great," Richard was still in overly effusive mode which rather worried Charlotte. She knew Richard was not very good at reading signals so she decided to take control of the situation.

"Now Richard sit there. Don't move. I'll get some drinks. Tea or coffee?"

"Tea please. Thanks."

Several cups of tea and a couple of hours of conversation, which had consisted of Richard listening and Charlotte talking, had again convinced Charlotte, even though she thought Laura was hoping something concrete might come from this liaison, that Richard was not a keeper. In fact she was even more certain that he could not actually be trusted to act properly in the future.

After an overlong pause Richard asked his first question of the afternoon: "What happened about that charity that Joe was involved in. From what I could make of it you really didn't know anything about it. Did you?"

Richard had already disqualified himself from any opportunity to rekindle a relationship with Charlotte at her front door and even though she had found the afternoon's conversation quite entertaining and a good opportunity for her to let off steam, she really wasn't very sure why Richard should be so interested in her ex-partner's activities. Beyond that she did not want to retell the details of Joe's involvement with the AKM trust so she decided to bring proceedings to a close.

"Well actually it's a long story, quite personal actually and, oh goodness me, is that the time! I need to dash to the nursery now so I think we'll have to call a halt. If that's OK." Before Richard had a chance to reply Charlotte continued: "It's been good to catch up, Richard, thanks for coming over."

Unusually for him, Richard read the situation perfectly and got up from his chair: "Sorry to have kept you waiting so long. It's been great talking. Let's keep in touch."

As Charlotte opened the front door to usher him out and keep him at arms-length she replied: "Yes we must." Without any real conviction in her voice.

"I've got a bone to pick with you missus."

"What d'you mean coming on all serious," Laura was looking a little confused.

"Richard messaged me and he came round today. Was that one of your ideas?"

"Well to be fair it was. He's been pestering..."

"Oh, for God's sake if he's been 'pestering' why didn't you tell him to sod off? Anyway, he's not changed one little bit, unfortunately."

"Well, I'm sorry. That wasn't the impression I got at all. Sorry."

"It's OK no need to apologise. I've got a clean slate now. Just have to see where life takes me from here, won't I?"